AN EYE FOR AN EYE

AN EYE FOR AN EYE

THE MALLET MURDERS

DENNY DARKE

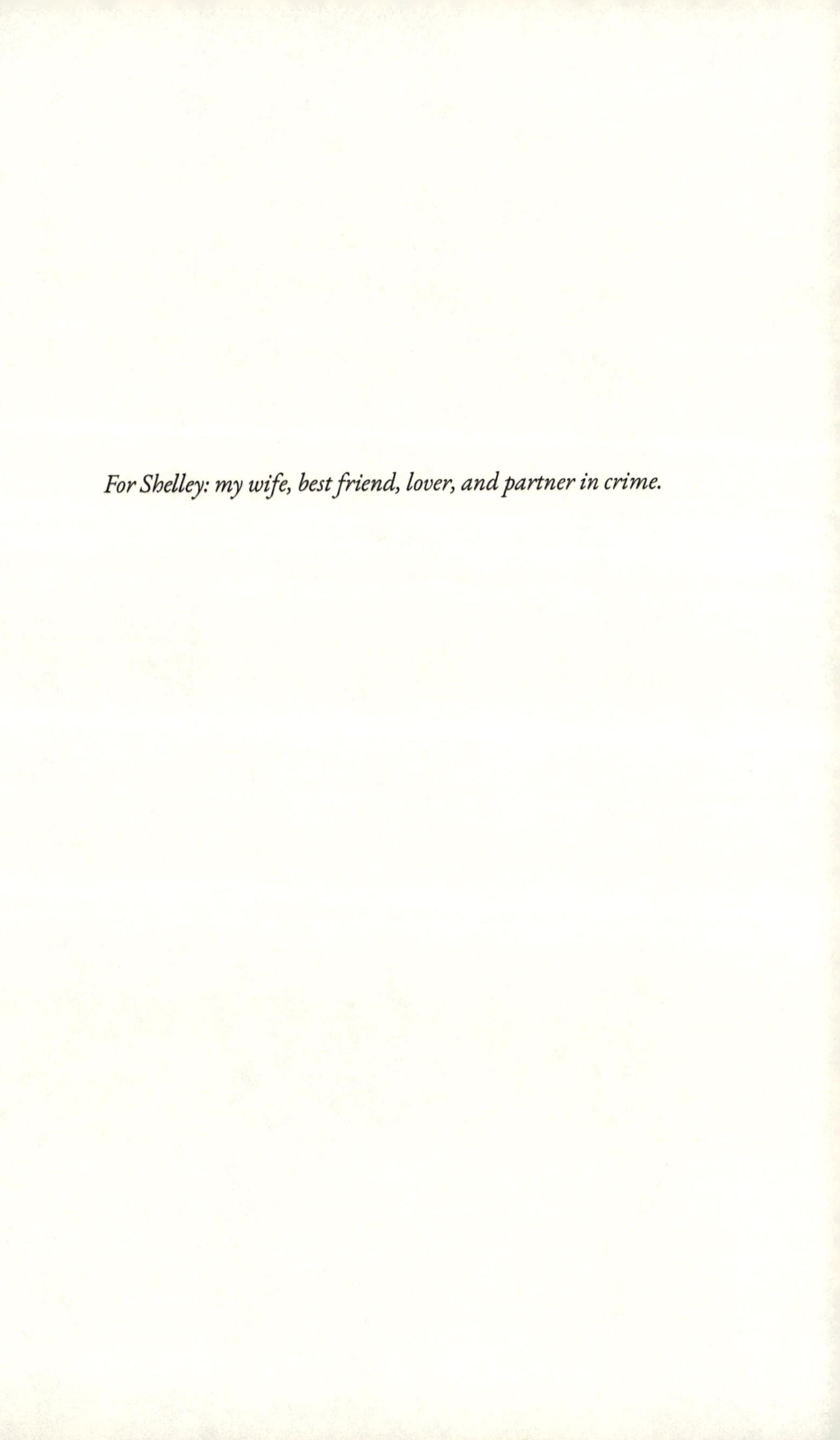

For Shelley: my wife, best friend, lover, and partner in crime.

CHAPTER 1
THE INVADER

He has remarkable skills in examining cubby holes and opening drawers, revealing secrets that have long been forgotten. He isn't interested in money, jewellery, or collecting trophies—he will leave his calling card in due course. One thing alone dominates his mind. So, he moves silently as he expertly navigates the squeaky wooden floorboards and those laid with tacky-to-step-on linoleum. As he disables hidden cameras and snips through landline wires, he experiences a deep sense of detachment, awakening his resourcefulness— expecting the unexpected. The exhilaration of anticipation swells when he senses others can feel his dark, unwanted presence. Fashioning a super-charged atmosphere in any dimly lit room, he delights in the pungent smell of fear. However, true relief and satisfaction lie in setting free what was once confined and caged. He is the intruder, invader and, more importantly, he is the liberator.

His well-worn leather work boots were covered with extra-large disposable booties purchased from an online vendor. The protectors were useful, of course, but looked ludicrous—they were also annoying, as they stuck to the doctor's blood that was seeping out from her head wound. He stood over the victim, leaning his head in a crooked way at the lifeless body.

No doubt, she had died from catastrophic head trauma; blood splatter was everywhere, or so it seemed. The intruder admired his work—quick, painless, and satisfying. His large, oval-faced mallet was in his right hand, now lowered and pointing towards the wooden floorboards. It dripped with blood. At least he didn't have to use a melee of blows, as he had done with his first victim; he didn't mean to dispatch her. Wrong time, wrong place. The adrenaline buzz had been divine. He needed to take all his angst and aggression out on these outsiders, but he knew he had to rein it in the next time it occurred. He noticed the first victim had left a half-open can of Clover Leaf tuna on her quartz countertop, and he smirked. He would use this as one of his calling cards.

He loved the darkness. He felt comfortable not being seen, not being the centre of attention, not being singled out as "odd," "weird," or "different" by strangers who didn't know him. He savoured the thrill of entering her home, creeping carefully on the darkened hardwood floors. Hardwood—restored flooring in particular—had a special place in his heart. He knew her routine and was versed in the plan of the home. Minimalist tastes, creams, and taupes. A picture of a child on the fireplace. She would awaken at four o'clock, and he'd hear her alarm from his hiding place in an alcove in her kitchen.

THE LIGHT CAME on in the upstairs hallway that dimly lit the staircase. It was a nice staircase, wooden and vaguely curling from the first to the ground floor. She went down the stairs, thinking only about the coffee she needed to make before showering. A latte and square of Cadbury's chocolate. Maybe two squares.

She shuffled into the dimly lit kitchen, careful not to turn on the lights as they were way too bright for her eye in the morning. Damn, migraines. These wretched things had lessened since menopause, but sharp hospital lights and constant ER stress couldn't be helped. With a playful grin, she rubbed her tummy, a gesture that always brought a chuckle to her lips, especially when she thought about her frequent bouts of constipation. The chocolate, with its decadent sweetness, would bring some relief, just as the triple shot latte, with its intense kick, would provide a much-needed caffeine boost.

"*Astrid, du musst dich entscheiden.* You have to decide. Migraines or being bunged up?" She touched her chin in mock contemplation. "It's choc and coffee all day, baby." She giggled. "Failing that, we still have Mr. Metamucil to work its magic."

Astrid wore a white Kate Spade cotton bathrobe that she had purchased from The Bay. She smiled. Thank God for the Nespresso maker gifted to her by a friendly colleague. She knew she had put on a few pounds and was much heavier than she would have liked.

"Damn him," she muttered. The divorce from her Middle Eastern proctologist husband had been a messy one. She should have listened to her friends and family. No matter how negatively she thought about her failed marriage, she couldn't help but smile that together, they had created a handsome, intelligent, and gorgeous little boy. The only way out from the abusive and toxic relationship was to agree to his terms and leave Jordan without her son. A heavy load to bear. She would see him only twice a year, which felt like a painfully small amount of time. However, she was confident he would want to be with his mother as he grew older. From the safety of Canada, she would be in a strong financial position to fight for him.

The doctor turned on the Nespresso, inserted the first of three pods into the unit, and pressed a couple of times to produce enough espresso to get her started for the morning. She poured the skimmed milk into the frother and muttered away to herself how much of a blessing the coffee maker was. By the time her third pod had finished producing its sweet, sumptuous aroma, her frothy milk was ready.

She sleepily muttered, "Yum, yum. At least I'm alive, here in Canada and not as-good-as-dead living with my deadbeat ex." Nodding, she said to herself, "One day, I'll come and get you, my lovely boy." She poured the milk into her favourite bone china mug and added the coffee to the espresso cup. "Oh, I wish I could make a fancy design like the Starbucks barristers do. I would make a heart for you."

"DON'T MOVE, doctor. Not until I tell you to."

Her body jerked with surprise, eyes opened wide and rooted to the spot.

The intruder's voice was deep and calm. He jabbed something in her back. Astrid breathed in sharply, placing a hand over her mouth.

"I'll blow your spine to smithereens. You wouldn't want that, would you?"

Her voice quivering, she lowered it to a whimper as she stammered, "N-n-no."

With a nudge from the intruder, she cautiously made her way into the living room. From behind he could see her jaw clenching—the tension evident on her hidden face.

"Please, I have money in a purse on the sofa. I have a few jewels. Please—" she begged, her voice trembling "—there's no need to hurt me."

He grunted as she shuffled forwards, step by step, into the lounge, stopping when she reached the middle of the room. A knee-high coffee table blocked her path.

His voice was gruff. "Stop. Wait there. Do what I say, and I won't touch your body. I'm after one thing, and one thing alone."

The doctor gasped for air. "Please take whatever you want. I'm a doctor at the hospital. I p-p-promise I won't call the police or report what's happened."

He tilted his neck to the side. "Promise?"

"Yes, I do. I swear on everything that's sacred or holy."

"Pinky promise?"

"Pinky promise? What's a pinky promise?" she said, scrunching her face.

The intruder fixed his eyes on the back of her head, captivated by the cascade of her long, wavy, dark brown hair. He craned his neck to his shoulder as if considering options and possibilities. "A sacred vow between you and me."

"Okay. Okay. Pinky promise. I swear on a stack of pinky promises."

The voice from the darkness said, "Wiggle your pinky finger." He stepped back from her, a couple of feet to her left.

"Oh, I see. Okay," she gulped loudly. "No worries, my word is my bond."

"Mine, too."

She wiggled her small finger that was by her side.

"I can't see you doing anything."

Before Astrid raised her hand up in the air to show the world her sacred promise, he swung the wooden mallet into the back of her head with full force. She fell like a tree at a woodchopper's competition, flat on her face. Her knees buckled on the small coffee table, making her fall even more spectacular as she landed on her forehead with a thump.

"Whoopsie. Sorry, not sorry." The ten-pound mallet had caved in the back of Dr. Hussain's head. "See, I didn't touch your body when it was alive."

He really did want just *one* thing. Well, maybe two. He glanced across at the front door at the green painter's tape he'd placed around the small rectangular flap, stopping any entry or exit. He lifted up his blood-splattered face shield and called, "Here, kitty, kitty. Here, cat. Come here, kitty, kitty."

The executioner bent over an empty cat box and retrieved a small packet of Friskies, and shook the packet several times. He stepped past the prostrate doctor; the slick, viscous blood beneath his disposable booties made a sucking sound with each step. He spoke into the air, "Here, cat! Here, kitty, kitty."

Laying the bloody mallet on the floor beside its victim, he made his way to the bottom of the stairwell, leaving bloody foot smears behind him. Making strange tutting and squeaking noises, he kept calling the cat. He walked slowly and deftly up two stairs and, this time, rustled the bag of Friskies, shaking the contents as he climbed further up.

"Cat. Cat," he called out, puckering his lips as he continued to kiss and clack. "Here puss, puss. Good boy," accompanied enticing tutting sounds.

A faint, soft meow sound spoke back to him. A pair of ears became visible and even though the light was not the brightest, a shimmery blue-grey coloured cat with large greenish eyes peeked around the top of the staircase. The pussycat softly chirped, looked inquisitive, and tentatively showed more of himself to the intruder. He laced a few treats onto his hand. "Come on, boy. Come and take them." The cat was now fully visible from head to tail. In the gloom, his short-haired coat shimmered, showcasing his beauty. In a deliberate and graceful manner, the cat carefully descended the stairs, seeming to detect the distinct smell of the fishy morsels that the odd-looking man had sprinkled on the stairwell. When the man was within two stairs of the lithe, muscular feline, as quick as a flash, a latex-gloved hand grabbed the startled creature by its scruff in a Vulcan-neck pinch.

"Gotcha. Now calm down, puddy cat." He held the wide-eyed creature, which was in a frozen state, in front of him. The man's cold, grey eyes stared into the pair of green peepers. "I'm your master now," he grinned. He knew how to handle and disable cats with one squeeze of the loose skin on top of their neck. Cocking his head to the side, he briefly held the cat up to his face, kissed him, and retreated backwards down the stairs to the bloody living room.

"Fine critter, you are," he said, holding the paralysed cat out in front of him.

The remaining pack of treats was dropped onto the top of the box, and he used the free hand to pull the cat basket toward him. He opened the door and gently placed the startled cat into the container. A blue-grey blur darted to the far end of the box and trembled.

The intruder gazed at the dead doctor's body one more time, admiring his work. He wasn't quite finished. He unzipped his onesie, reached inside to the large fanny pack he wore on the front of his bare skin, unzipped it, and removed a pair of secateurs and a Ziplock baggy. The intruder slammed down the raised face shield, took hold of the dead doctor's right hand, and with a crunch and a snap, he cut off a finger between its proximal and middle phalanx—its penultimate joint. He repeated this for the two other fingers, taking the three digits in his hand and placing them in the baggy, tucking the fingertips into a pocket.

Smiling like a cat that's got the cream, he wiped the secateurs on Dr. Hussain's blood-stained, now not-so-white cotton bathrobe, returned them to his fanny pack, and zipped up the onesie. Something caught his eye in the gloomy light. It was but a few feet away from the doctor's crushed head.

"Wait there, cat!" he said, placing the box on the wooden floorboards, ignoring the many shrills and meows. He took a couple of strides toward a small, glistening object, bent down, and picked it up. A wave of excitement washed over him as he held it in his gloved hand.

"My damned lucky day, cat. Mother is looking down on us, for sure." He gazed at an eyeball that eerily stared back at him. A bright, emerald green iris appeared to follow him as he cupped it in his hand, moving it from side to side, reminiscent of the Action Man figure with "Eagle Eyes" he used to play with as a boy. He bent over and held the glass prosthesis with finger and thumb, so the iris pointed into the cat box. He muttered, "Look puddy cat, your doctor momma is watching you—so you gotta be good for old Saul."

A loud meow echoed through the living room. He smirked, unzipped the onesie, and placed the eyeball into the fanny pack, joining the three fingers and the bloody pair of clippers. Letting out a huge sigh he said, "Today is going to be the best day of our lives!"

CHAPTER 2
THE MEMO

THE INTERNAL MEMO caused Detective Sergeant Daryl LeBlanc-Smith to stress out. He had been summoned to the chief's office with the following morning email:

> Sgt. LeBlanc-Smith, please attend my office tomorrow at 10 a.m. PROMPT. Ensure you bring your service firearm and warrant badge with you. Yours truly, Chief Jamie Hislop.

Yours truly? He is one of the biggest advocates of informality in the detachment. Why the firearm? Warrant Card? Daryl began to fret. *What have I done wrong?*

It wasn't April 1st, the day that Jamie often sent newer team members to verify a death or identify a corpse. His own hazing had involved running after an assailant, who'd brutally murdered a victim in their own home. Hislop had put out the call; Daryl was in the immediate area and was first to respond. Daryl radioed in his location. Quite overweight then, he had a hell of a time keeping up with the killer. Hislop chastised him for not checking that the victim was dead or alive and ordered him to return to the crime scene. The out-of-breath detective arrived at the victim's home to find out that she had been butchered in her own bed.

"Feel for a pulse, man!" Hislop snapped out orders on the police radio.

"Okay, sir, but there's a lot of blood."

"Quickly, LeBlanc-Smith. You may be able to stabilize her."

"Sir, she is as white as a sheet."

"So is a bloody polar bear. Quickly."

Daryl threw caution to the wind and placed his fingers on the victim's neck.

"ARGGHH," shouted the corpse.

"ARGGHH," screamed the detective as the victim rose from the dead. It had been recorded on camera—his teammates burst into the room, laughing, and welcoming him to the Serious Crimes Unit.

That was then, and the chief continued to be playful with his team. He was a great boss, and Daryl loved working with him.

Like a worm in his brain, the more he thought, the more he worried.

I have an exemplary service record and have been recommended for further promotion by the chief. It was true that his dedication to all things policing had, ultimately, led to the breakdown of his marriage to Alice. He was now separated from coast to coast by the world's second-largest landmass. Alice had taken their two kids to her home province of Nova Scotia—mainly for support. Daryl simply wasn't at home enough, despite the myriad of promises he had made. Alice, Chuck, and Jean-Paul's departure had left a massive hole in his heart. Skype calls were not the same as one-on-one time with his boys. He didn't blame Alice for pulling the separation trigger, as he didn't know when to draw the line; his work-life balance sucked.

He tossed and turned all night long. Naturally a worrier, he constantly thought the worst-case scenario would occur because it always seemed to happen to him. Like that time at the cinema, post-COVID, when the person behind him coughed up a considerable-sized loogie, and it landed in his popcorn—initially unnoticed by him as he watched *Spiderman Eight* with the boys. Upon realising the salty taste was not just the popcorn, he threw up over the person sitting in front of him, and the movie was ruined for everyone. Daryl was banned for life and then developed COVID-19, infectious mononucleosis and mumps (his mother had been an anti-vaxer). To top it all off, as his immune system had been severely compromised, he manifested a lousy case of orchitis, and his testicles swelled to the size of two watermelons. Of course, Chief Hislop and the team thought it was hilarious and called him "Buster Gonad" for a season.

It could only happen to me, he'd shake his head and lament.

As the team's skipper, he was well-liked and respected. The squad's main gripe was that he took forever to make a decision that needed to be made promptly. Daryl was thorough; his favourite phrase was, "Let's look at the crime and assailant from the multiple hypothesis perspective."

"But boss—it's an open and shut case."

"Explain your theory, detective."

"Husband cheated on wife. The wife confronts her husband. The husband tells the wife that he's leaving her for his brother-in-law. The wife picks up a carving knife from the knife rack on the kitchen counter. Husband laughs and berates wife—telling her that her brother is a much better lover than her. Wife waves the carving knife in his face. The husband scoffs and tells her to put it away—walks towards his wife and calls her a slutty whore. The wife warns her husband that she will cut off his testicles if he gets any closer. The husband mocks her and reaches for the knife. Wife plunges the knife into his neck; he falls to the kitchen floor. She leans over and pulls the blade from his neck, then proceeds to behead the man. Her final words to him were, 'Eat shit and die, Mofo.' Open and shut, sir."

"But what if the husband slipped, the knife went into his neck, and as he fell, he kept moving his head to the right and to the left, in a sawing motion, then auto decapitates his own head?"

"Skipper, the suspect-not-a-suspect, confessed to everything during the interview."

"What if her secret lover darted out from the walk-in pantry, drove the blade into his neck, and then cut his head off his shoulders?"

"It was all on her nanny camera, Skip. No secret lover. No 'suicide by carving knife.'"

"Very well, detective, I will sign off on that. You must look at all possible hypotheses—that's why a Mountie always gets his man."

Sergeant LeBlanc-Smith, also known as "Pounds," as his initials looked like an imperial unit, LBS, also possessed a keen sense of dark humour unless he was around his equals or senior officers—constantly worrying about being chastised for saying something that was either culturally inappropriate or politically incorrect.

DARYL ARRIVED at the detachment early, as was his habit. He made sure his suit was pressed so he was immaculately presented. He eyed himself in the washroom mirror, and although nervous about the meeting, he muttered, "Damn it Daryl, you look hot to trot." Signing into the police federal computer, as was his custom each shift, he liked to see what other crimes were committed in other British Columbia towns and provinces. He noticed that there was a brutal slaying of a doctor in Nova Scotia. He immediately worried for his family. However, a possible serial killer was at large in the southern part of the province; Alice and the boys were closer to the northern part of Nova Scotia. This new crime occurred in a municipal police service and not under the watch of the RCMP. Maybe, by some quirk of fate, the chief had recommended him for temporary assignment there for family reasons. No, the snow, black flies, mosquitos and being in hurricane alley did not sit well with him.

Chief Hislop snapped open his door. It was 10 a.m.

"Daryl, please come in." The chief wore a very fake smile.

Crap, he didn't call me "Pounds."

Ushered in through hand signals, Daryl was told to take a seat; he obliged, and Hislop walked behind his desk, pulled out his own chair, sat and faced Daryl with a grim expression. Folding his hands so as not to fidget, the chief stared at what looked like a personnel file and several other loose-leaf papers.

"Your wife went out east with your boys?"

"Ex-wife," corrected Daryl.

His boss offered a sympathetic nod, "Working here—with Alice, living halfway across the land—can't be easy?"

"No, sir," Daryl sighed.

"Any chance of reconciliation?"

"I'm always hopeful, sir." Daryl looked at his waistline and patted it with both hands. "I've been working out and watching my calories, Ian."

"Chief Hislop," snapped his boss.

His head jerked back. "Sorry, sir. I've called you Chief Hislop before, and you rebuked me."

"That was then, and this is now."

"Yes, sir. The job always comes first, sir. I'm passionate about my work."

Chief Hislop shook his head, "Not good, Daryl. Work-life balance is taught to us all. After my fifth marriage, it finally sunk in."

"Yes, sir."

"Would you like to be closer to the boys?"

Daryl sighed. "Yes, sir, of course, sir." Although moving would be a bummer, he may be able to get his marriage back on track—and it may only be a temporary assignment.

"Great. Do you want the good news or the bad news first?"

"Good news, sir."

"You will be able to see your boys more regularly, and your marriage may be patched up."

"Yes, sir. Good news, indeed. The bad news?"

"Well, Pounds, you're in deep shit."

Daryl's eyes widened, "Sir?"

"Someone in HQ in Vagina—"

"Regina, sir."

"Yes, yes, Regina. Some admin freak was auditing records, and they pulled out your personnel file."

Daryl looked perplexed; his mind raced.

"They found . . . they found anomalies."

"Anomalies? What *anomalies*, sir?"

Hislop took one deep breath. "Your application form. Eighteen years ago, you made certain *declarations*."

Daryl's brow furrowed, and his eleven lines became super-prominent. His mind raced, and he tried to process what his chief had just stated. *I'm a by-the-book kind of guy. Anomalies? No freaking way. There must be some kind of mistake.*

The team laughed at him for being a stickler for policy and procedure. However, he was happy to glide into the "grey" area occasionally. But, his application form? No way.

"Pounds, it's in black and white." He pushed the thick service file towards him.

Daryl reached out, took the file, but had no idea what he was looking for, so he looked up at his chief and scratched his wiry salt and pepper bearded cheek.

"Daryl, we all know how you love and embrace your French heritage and culture."

Daryl stuck out his broad chest and nodded proudly. "*Viva La France!*"

"I've even heard you say, '*Bonjour*,' '*Au Revoir*,' '*Merci*' and '*Solar Prestige a gammon*,' when you've, unsuccessfully, ordered frog legs at the local KFC."

Daryl stared at his boss. He had no idea where the conversation was going to land.

"You know much about Napoleonic history; your favourite movie is *Moulin Rouge*, and you know a line or two from *La Marseillaise*."

"*Aux armes, citoyens!*" he cried out. Hislop drew back in his chair. "To arms, citizens!" he translated.

"Quite, quite." Hislop leaned forward and stared his subordinate in the eyes. "However, the admin bods at Vagin—Regina—whatever the heck it's called, think your Frenchness is a croc of shit."

Daryl's lips curled. "A croc of shit? What does it have to do with them?"

"You ticked the box on the form that stated that a) you were in a minority group, b) you claimed you were bilingual, and c) your father was French." Hislop grabbed a tagged paper from the file. "It states here: 'Papa was a politician from Montreal who was assassinated by the Mob, as he bravely wouldn't take a bribe.'"

"Yes, sir. That's what my mother told me. That's why I have a double-barreled name."

"The admin folk dug out your birth certificate."

"That's excellent news, sir, as Mother said it went up in smoke with Papa."

"Sounds like a nasty family situation, for sure. Well, they've found your live birth documentation. You claimed to be 'LeBlanc-Smith' on your application form."

"Yes, sir. I am LeBlanc-Smith. I provided all other documentation that was asked of me, including a sworn affidavit from Mother."

Hislop swallowed hard. "The admin team obtained a Power of Attorney from a judge, and as your mother was not cooperating, obtained your birth document. No easy way to say this. You were born: Jethro Daryl Jebidiah Smith."

"What?" Daryl's jaw dropped open as he learned that his father, who he had always believed to be a Leblanc, was actually a Mennonite potato farmer from Wisconsin.

"Admin contacted your mother and offered her a plea deal. She made a statement under oath admitting perjury. They have the confession."

Daryl cradled his head in his hands, fingers digging into his scalp as he shook it violently, a frustrated groan escaping his lips.

"She confessed?"

"Yep. Confessed to shagging the Mennonite farmer on a spiritual retreat to Wisconsin, where the Bhagwan Umpresh had set up base camp, before being driven out of the States back to India. Disappointed that she had missed the Bhagwan, she seduced a guy with black robes and a cowboy hat, who happened to be a Mennonite, and you were conceived."

"No way."

"Yes way! In order to avoid being ostracized by her French Catholic community in New Brunswick, your mother crafted a grandiose fabrication to keep her secret hidden. Apparently, they hold a strong dislike for Mennonites and consider them to be devilish. Your mother is currently serving a six-month sentence in a jail near Fredericton, which is why you haven't received any recent communication from her."

Daryl sat in the chair, stunned. "Okay. Then, how is this *my* fault? This is shocking to me. A revelation. I never knew."

"I know. I know. Rules are rules. The admin staff sit in a circle and jerk off when they find a case like this."

"B-b-but—"

Hislop held up his hand to stop his subordinate from speaking. "That's why I propose *a solution*. You face disciplinary action, a service discharge, considerable disgrace, and a loss of pension and benefits."

"A solution?" Daryl said, hopefully.

"You have three choices."

Daryl listened, his heart thumping out of his chest.

"One: resign with a good reference—maybe the local mall would hire you. Minimum wage, but a job is a job. Two: be reassigned to RCMP headquarters in Regina to work with the admin team that outed you. If so, you'd need to be 'reprogrammed,' study shorthand, type at speed, use Excel spreadsheets, and gossip like a fishwife."

"Option three?"

"Reassignment to Nova Scotia—"

"I'll take it."

"Wait. Let me finish. You'll keep the same pay grade and pension—"

"Sir, I'll take it."

Ignoring the interruptions, Hislop said, "You'll have a service weapon and a uniform will be provided."

Daryl swallowed hard. "God, I hate being in uniform."

"Yes, yes, but you'll still be a cop."

Daryl raised his eyebrows. "What kind of cop, sir?"

Chief Hislop stifled a laugh, he cleared his throat. "A fish cop."

"A fish, what?"

"Cop. A Department of Fisheries Officer—a fish cop."

Hislop went on to explain that as luck would have it, because of the past election and the Conservative Blue Wave that swept across the country, the DFO had to make significant cuts that had a far-reaching impact. As the rich enjoyed tax cuts, critical areas such as social work, mental health, and fisheries suffered from significant service reductions. Hislop highlighted that the successful candidate could engage in close collaboration with the municipal police, working together on a joint task force. The police urgently required a Fisheries Officer to tackle the rising cases of lobster thefts and unlawful fishing practices.

"I know zero about fish," muttered Daryl.

"I was on the phone yesterday with their chief, a man named Kennedy. He sounded a prat but was keen to take you on as one of his team members. You'll hand in your service weapon and get a newly issued one there. Plenty of new kit, too.

"Don't tell me, a gill net, lobster trap, and a harpoon gun?"

"You can always choose the first couple of options. Who knows, your crocheting may come on leaps and bounds with the Vagina admin team." Daryl didn't have the fight to correct his boss for the nth time. "Keep your badge until they sort you out with a new one from the DFO."

Daryl sighed a deep, deep sigh.

"You'll love it. Open air. Riding a Zodiac on the choppy seas. Boarding boats, arresting smugglers . . . and you'll be closer to your loved ones. A slam dunk offer. Better than sitting in a jerk-off circle with a load of short-sighted morons—while living in that godforsaken place in Susqasquatch."

"Saskatchewan, sir. Can't I go there as a detective? A serial killer may be on the loose."

"You'll be a great *fish* detective, Pounds."

"Can't I come back here, sir?"

"I will see what I can do. Your Air Canada plane leaves YVR to Halifax in a few days. We will pass the hat around for expenses, as the Feds are tight with their budgets and are baulking at $50 a day for meal allowance." Chief Hislop stood up and stretched out his hand to Daryl. "You were a bloody good detective, Pounds. You'll be missed." Daryl reciprocated the gesture and shook his chief's hand.

"Close the door when you leave. We'll go out for a drink or two tomorrow, your last day. Happy fishing, DFO Smith."

CHAPTER 3
TWENTY-TWO MINUTES

CHIEF INSPECTOR KENNEDY stood at the open door of Dr. Hussain's home. He was a tall, lean man with a mix of thick blond-grey curly hair, deep-set eyes, an aquiline nose, and a moustache he'd tried to grow for decades. Guys felt he looked uncannily similar to the actor from the *Elf* movie; ladies found him cute looking, not due to his Hollywood doppelgänger; rather, he looked like the spitting image of a labradoodle. Forensics were busy dusting for prints, taking pictures of the doctor's body, blood spatter, and undefined red footprints that started near the cadaver. The staircase was marked with bloody tracks that went most of the way up and down, then circled around the doctor, finally leaving a trail towards the door and along the path.

"Thankfully, we'd taken photos before you put your big, size twelves over the assailant's boot prints," said Sarah Mills, the Scene of Crime Officer (SOCO), snarkily. This was the second time she'd been "borrowed" by Chief Kennedy's team from the RCMP.

"You forensic bods have been here long enough. Your acerbity is not welcome. As senior officer, I can walk over whatever crime scene I bloody well like."

Sarah returned a hard smile.

"I've watched them damned crime shows, like *The First 48*. A&E's film crew need to come to *my* town to see how *real cops* solve crime. I would call it 'The First 22.' If my team hasn't compiled a list of suspects within the first *twenty-two minutes* of exploring the crime scene, then the investigation is essentially complete. We call the condition cold case central. Let me tell you this, nobody wants to catch a train at that icy junction."

A hazmat-suited detective nodded and said, "Who needs forty-eight hours when we just need twenty-two minutes. Genius, sir."

"Thank you, Barnes."

Detective Sergeant Alfonso Barnes approached the chief, ignoring the bloody boot prints he walked on. "Blunt force trauma, once again, boss."

"This has become problematic, sergeant."

"Yes, sir," he said, his words laced with a note of dull obedience."It's the second time in a couple of years."

"Barnes, tourist season is just around the corner—the mayor and the town are buzzing with excitement and preparations for a bumper financial harvest."

"Sir?"

"We absolutely don't need this kind of thing right now. When is that damn Fisheries Officer due to arrive?"

"Anytime soon, sir. He was picked up by Constable Noble. I've heard that he's the typical west coast type. Big ego, but lacks a sense of humour."

"Judging by the sounds his superiors in B.C. are making, it appears he's trying to pass off as a Frenchie, but he's not convincing anyone."

Barnes turned his head and gazed at the carnage that lay before him. "Do you plan on staying at the crime scene, sir?"

"No, I have a damned meeting with the mayor, who's going nuts over the price of lobster. It's nose-diving due to illegal fishing and sales. Bloody fisheries need to figure this out—it may cost her and me re-election bids next year. These damned murders are giving us a headache. Why couldn't they get themselves bludgeoned in Digby County?"

"I'm sure they'd rather not have gotten murdered at all," Sarah Mills muttered loudly to herself, as she took yet another photo of blood spatter on the lounge wall.

Kennedy stared at the insolent female officer. Breaking the tension, Sergeant Barnes looked floorward at the doctor's corpse. "She's only been working at the hospital for a few months, was well-liked, and treated me once in the ER."

"Treated you for what?" Sarah's voice echoed from behind the camera, "Syphilis of the brain?"

"Close. Gonorrhea."

Chief Kennedy scrunched up his face.

Oblivious of his boss' displeasure, the detective sergeant asked, "Sir, why did the murder happen here?"

Kennedy's eyes widened with a "WTF" expression. He shook his head and gestured with open palms, clearly remonstrating that it was the senior detective's job to solve the crime.

Sarah patted the detective on the shoulder. "That's what you get the big bucks for, to figure this stuff out."

Kennedy rolled his eyes, huffed, and asked, "Is anything missing? Did someone open the safe? Has the perp stolen her jewellery? Officer, does the scene suggest that someone has unlawfully entered the doctor's home? Tick tock goes the clock, Sergeant Barnes." Kennedy tapped his watch, reminding his subordinate of the twenty-two-minute rule.

"No, sir. Not that we can be sure—"

Chief Kennedy continued to ask curious questions. "Any jihad connections?"

Barnes rubbed his chin. The SOCO blinked rapidly in disbelief.

"Jihad, sir?"

"With its Middle Eastern origins, Hussain is a name that embodies the diverse and vibrant cultures of the region—including terrorism. Additionally, didn't the doctor choose to end her marriage with her Jordanian spouse to begin a new chapter in her life? Was the motive behind the crime an honour killing, a brutal act meant to preserve a distorted sense of reputation? Or, a terrorist cell gone terribly wrong?" He tapped his watch. "Two motives in less than eight seconds."

With a quick roll of her eyes, Sarah made her disapproval clear. Barnes held his hand to his chin, deep in thought, and said, "Never thought of that, sir."

"Look, Barnes, we need to sort out these lobster crimes, the deer poaching, the liquor smuggling—the kind of stuff that will affect re-election."

"Serial killer on the loose not a worry then?" asked the disbelieving SOCO.

"Woman, just do your job, and let me do mine. Of course, these murders are worrisome."

Sarah's jaw went slack. "Woman?"

"However," Kennedy looked directly at Sergeant Barnes, "the price of lobster has plummeted—harming our fishing communities. We're all dependent upon lobster sales. The damned rum and hooch smuggling is also causing us heat as alcoholism is rife. Anything else to tell me before I go?"

The SOCO coughed. "The good doctor is missing an eyeball," she said matter-of-factly.

"A what?" snapped Kennedy.

"An eyeball. Her left one." Sarah Mills continued snapping pictures, this time of the doctor's face. "The pretty doctor had a fake eye. A good one at that. It's missing."

"Did she keep it in a glass jar beside her bed like Fanny Muise's teeth?" asked Chief Kennedy.

"Sir, Fanny actually keeps her teeth in a fishbowl," added Barnes, helpfully.

Sarah chimed in, "No. The huge bonk on the back of the head must have dislodged the eyeball, and it flew out of the socket. It probably shot out of her like a cannonball, such was the force at the back of her head."

Barnes added, "It must have been a decent one, sir—most of us had seen her around town and didn't know she had a fake pork pie."

Kennedy's nose wrinkled. "Pork pie?"

"Eye, sir. Heard some cop saying it on *Line of Duty*. Cockney rhyming slang, sir. Pork pie is eye."

"Well then, where is the bloody pork pie?" hollered Kennedy, looking increasingly agitated. "Good policing is not rocket science. There's an eye missing. It's got to be somewhere in the damned house."

"It's not here, sir."

"You find the eyeball . . . you find the killer."

"That's brilliant, sir."

"I know." The chief opened his own set of eyes wide. "Maybe the killer came to the home, disturbed the doctor, and he plucked out her eyeball. Yes, it starts to make sense. It could be her crazy ex-patient from Frankfurt who finally took his revenge. It was in the news."

The SOCO rested her camera and looked up at Kennedy. "Maybe your theory about Dr. Hussain's jilted, crazed ex was spot-on. Dr. Hussain split from her husband and took the fake eye with her. Her husband, wanting half of everything for the divorce settlement, sent over an assassin to bring back the eye. It's a bit like the dispute over the Elgin Marbles."

"Are you serious, Officer Mills?"

"No. You are looking for a man, 6' to 6'5"—right-handed, who bludgeoned the back of her head with a large blunt, possibly wooden instrument. The force was such that her prosthesis popped out of her socket and onto the floor," she pointed at the assailant's isolated footprints, "then her killer picked it up. Oh, and the doctor's expensive cat is also missing." Kennedy looked at his watch, his mind clearly on someone or somewhere else.

The SOCO continued, "The assailant used painter's tape to seal up the cat flap, and once the cat had been secured, he peeled it off. We found traces of green sticky fibres. Oh, and there was a half-eaten can of tuna on the coffee table and three of her fingers were cut off. So, no Jihad, no angry German patient, and no jealous husband claiming back his half of the eyeball."

"All I know is we don't need a killer on the loose in my municipality."

Barnes asked, "What do we tell the press, sir?"

"Don't tell anyone about the eyeball. I don't want the press releasing stories that a serial killer is on the loose.

"The Cyclops Assassin?" suggested Sarah unhelpfully.

"No, no. Tell the press it was a *suspicious* death."

"That we are keeping a close EYE on the situation," sniggered the SOCO. "Maybe leak the name to the media: the Pussycat Killer?"

Chief Kennedy gave Sarah Mills the stink eye. If he could pull out his service weapon and shoot her in the head, he would have been tempted to do so. He abhorred indiscipline and snark. Another police unit employed her, so he couldn't take any action against the rude woman, not even tasing her. At least, not yet. "We need to keep this local, Barnes. We don't want the Feds snooping around. Our budget couldn't handle it. The mayor is likely to fire us all and ask the RCMP to police the area once again."

"Yes, sir."

"Twenty-two minutes, sergeant. I want a report on my desk before the morrow with suspects and possible motives."

"No pressure," cackled Sarah.

"Yes, sir. On your desk by the morrow, sir."

Kennedy left the scene, looking at his watch, shaking his head as he made for his unmarked vehicle. He would be late for a meeting with the mayor, who would surely tear a strip off him for not doing his job correctly. "Damn lobster thefts. Damn poachers. Damn SOCO. Damn, missing eyeballs and cats. Damn, damn, bugger damn."

CHAPTER 4
THE SPERM SPRAYER

THE LANDING at Pearson International Airport was smooth; the two-and-a-half-hour flight to Halifax was uneventful. What was memorable for Daryl was the four-and-a-half-hour ordeal endured on the Air Canada flight connecting Vancouver to Toronto.

The bumpety bump of the aircraft hitting the frequent weather fronts en route was something he usually despised. However, this time, he would have embraced their presence. The cacophony of a crying child behind him was accompanied by the unpleasant presence of a grown man's dirty-socked feet on his armrest. He spun around, his eyes locked onto the man as he shot him a firm glare. He was determined to ask Mr. Putrid Feet to take his smelly socks off his armrest. The mind was willing, but the body was weak. Instead, Daryl greeted him warmly with a smile.

"Hey!" The large man grinned, making eye contact.

Before Daryl could politely ask him not to use his aisle seat armrest, the large guy gave him a thumbs up and introduced himself. The name Howard Dorcas echoed through the cabin, causing heads to turn and eyes to lock onto the source of the sound. "Howie," he introduced himself, extending his hand for a friendly shake. "I've been working in Camp Fort McMurray, and now I'm going to visit some kids I sired in Mississauga."

Before Daryl could get a word in, Howie took the opportunity to tell him all about his life. Removing his feet from Daryl's chair, he leaned in to continue their chat. "I have nineteen children, and I've never been married. My gals tell me I have 'super-swimmers,' as I had only had sex with them the one time. God's truth. A couple of social workers from Child Protection Services tell me that I'm known as the 'Sperm Sprayer.' Kinda true. Anyway, I work up North as I owe so much child support. Thankfully, some of the gals I impregnated live far away in countries like Italy, Belize, and Ecuador. Stroke of luck. I send 'em all birthday cards. I know the names of each of 'em. Cost me a small fortune."

"Sweet," was all Daryl could respond. His neck started hurting from the 150-degree angle his head had to turn to keep eye contact. Finally, he broke away from the man's conversation, turned and faced forward. With a sense of contentment, Daryl appreciated that he had chosen an aisle seat and had the bonus of an empty seat adjacent to him. Due to his size, Daryl opted for extra legroom, allowing him to reach the washrooms without disturbing his neighbour.

He was startled by a gentle tap on his shoulder. Looking up, he strained his already sore neck to see Howie looming over him.

"Hey buddy!" A big smile spread across the stranger's face. "If that seat ain't taken, can I perch next to you? Time flies when I've got a pal by my side."

"Well. No-no—"

"No one sitting there. Awesome smoresome."

Howie grunted and groaned his way past a now standing-up Daryl.

Why me? Just . . . why me? It could only happen to me.

The large, tall man now sat next to his new-found bestie. Daryl reached for his headphones to pretend to listen to music from his phone.

"Hey, Merrill, I have Air Pods too. Mind if I listen along with ya?"

Daryl didn't mind being called the wrong name. In fact, noticing that Howie didn't like to use his seat belt, he dearly wished that the Boeing 737 Max's door plug would blow off—sucking the bothersome passenger out of the plane.

"This COVID shit pisses me off, man. All the sheepies and libtards wore their masks and disinfected their hands every three seconds. Glad you ain't one of them, brother!" Howie clearly had issues with boundaries as Daryl could smell the Lays Barbecue Beef flavour chips on his breath. His face was inches from Daryl's, and although Daryl tried to move his aching neck as far away from Howie's lips as possible, he reluctantly decided to not make a fuss and share his playlist with his new acquaintance.

"Merrill, that music sucks! Let me put some real old country muzak on —it will surely man you up."

Daryl inwardly groaned. The mere thought of country music made him cringe, but Southern blues rock was on a whole other level of detestable for him. Howie, having already subjected him to Dolly Parton, Tim McGraw, and Garth Brooks, proceeded to play Lynyrd Skynyrd's lengthy "Free Bird" on a loop, five times in a row.

"Man," he yelled at Daryl, "lighten up, Mel. Sing along with me."

Daryl became desperate, took out his air pods, and shook his head. "Shucks, the battery is on red."

"I have a charger, dude."

Daryl quickly declined the offer. He would rather saw off his arm with a plastic fork than listen to another verse of "Free Bird."

As the distressed child sitting behind Daryl whined to his parents about feeling unwell, Daryl felt something warm and wet splatter onto his thick, brown hair.

"Holy shit. I'm glad I moved seats. You've got a gallon of kid-sick on your head, dude—I wish I could have made a TikTok of that."

The mother apologised to Daryl, offering him a wet wipe. The child bawled. Daryl took his own wipes from his fanny pack and started to sponge the vomit from his hair. He unbuckled his seat to retire to the aircraft's rear washroom.

"Sit down, sir," yelled the steward. "The seat belt signs are on red."

"Oh, dude. Now I have to sit next to you. You stink!"

You can always move back to your seat, dumbass. "Your bad luck, I guess."

Howie held his nose with his fingers.

This smells better than your rank feet.

Daryl tried to regain his composure using a dozen or so wet wipes. *Why me? Universe . . . why me? Haven't the last six months been bad enough? Can't I catch a break? What about the past three days? Once I'm all settled in, I promise to go to church. Lord Jesus, I will try to believe in you, despite the bullshit televangelists and the abuse in the Roman Catholic Church. Religion? The President of the Free World and our own right-wing Prime Minister, amidst ludicrous election promises to their evangelical base, are also busy making millions in deals and cultivating a friendship with Russia and North Korea. The hypocrisies of it all. Despite my skepticism, I'll look for a church and desperately try to better myself. Dear God, I only ask for the cards to fall kindlier for Daryl, your would-be servant.*

"Do you do coke?"

"What? No," said Daryl, stunned at the question.

"You look like a cokehead to me."

"I've *never* used cocaine."

"Yeah, right. I see how you sniff like a mo-fo."

It's your feet! They smell worse than a three-day old corpse.

With a mischievous sparkle in his eye, Howie said, "Man, let me tell you," his voice filled with excitement, "I *love* the stuff. Trouble is, it's so dull at camp that I spend most of my pay on it."

Swallowing rapidly, Daryl was thinking about flashing, accidentally on purpose, his warrant card/not warrant card to his druggie pal.

"I also do a lot of speed, Jellies, GHB, Vitamin K, Sunshine, Mexican Tar, Moon Rocks, Skunk, Molly, Rocket Fuel, Black Mamba . . . and when I get really desperate, I indulge in a few Shrooms and Spice."

"That's a lot of—"

"I know, man. I feel bad for my kids. But what can I do? Life at camp is so boring that you gotta do what you gotta do to stay sane."

Daryl choked.

"Heavy equipment operator, me. Great money but a shitty life."

How can I subtly tell this guy to stop using every drug under the sun, pay his child support, get a vasectomy and don't work at the camp?

"Truth is, Merrill, I'm thinking of packing it in. I've taken six months of compassionate leave to travel around Canada. I'll drop in to see one of my brats—maybe have some nookie nooks with the mother and look for other job opportunities."

Vasectomy. Have a vasectomy, man. Please, dear God.

Howie frowned. "You're a quiet one. What do you do for a living?"

Shit. I'll tell him the truth. "Fisheries Officer. I work for the DFO."

Howie's eyes widened, revealing severely dilated pupils. "Holy crap! You can't be serious. A fish cop. I would not have sat next to you if you had told me earlier. I would have spat on the back of your head. I would have paid for that brat to throw up over your head, again."

Daryl sighed.

"Then again, ain't fair to judge. A man's gotta earn a living, even doing what you do. I have one or two buddies that are sex-traffickers. Hell, my cousin is a road-kill collector." Howie paused, raised his eyebrows, nodded and smiled. "I bet you have some hilarious tales to tell?"

Before Daryl could make up a few stories from his imagination, Howie couldn't help himself.

"Like when you gave a ticket to a cancer-stricken senior citizen whose salmon fishing license was overdue. Like the time you shot a sea-run trout fisherman who didn't want to accept a ticket for having a barbless hook. Or maybe when you fired your taser at a pike as it became hostile and attacked you." Howie was guffawing at his own jokes, continuing to press his face into the side of Daryl's. This time, spittle was landing on Daryl's ears.

I will never, ever complain about someone's stinky feet being on my armrest.

Howie was right, in a way. Time flew by. The captain announced the landing at Toronto Pearson Airport, and his ordeal would soon end. At one point, he feigned sleep, but Howie kept talking to him, occasionally digging him in the ribs.

As Daryl pressed the upright seat button as instructed, he heard, "Man, where are you heading? I can't think they need fish cops in Toronto, eh? Where are you travelling to?"

As far away from you as possible. Daryl smiled, "Nova Scotia."

"Sweet. I knocked up some hot, pocket-sized fisherman's wife from Pictou, Nova Scotia a few years ago. I met her at a trailer park when she was vacationing on Vancouver Island. Her husband was Chinook and Coho fishing on some native land. I was poaching some deer and met her. Ended up banging her against an Old Growth tree—it was quite a spiritual experience; I can tell you. Knocked her up, and she claimed it was her old man's."

Daryl's jaw was now wide open.

"Told ya. Sperm Sprayer, they call me. Her old man thought it was a miracle—divine intervention, as he hadn't banged her in months. I always leave my calling card." Howie reached into his jean jacket and gave Daryl a business card:

Howard Dorcas, Heavy Machine Operator. 'A listening ear in your times of need.' Bringer of sunshine and good cheer throughout B.C., Alberta, and the rest of the world.

"Let me have yours."

"It's a new position, and I don't have any yet," he explained. "But just to clarify, my name is Daryl, not Merrill."

"Surely, you must have *an address* to go to."

"Yes," he lied, "The Rodney, in Yeovilton." He flipped open his wallet and displayed his RCMP detective badge. "I'm on secondment there. Working undercover for the DFO. Drug and Liquor smuggling. Cartel stuff."

Howie went white as a tray of cocaine.

Daryl waved Howie's card before his nose. "Don't worry, Howie. I'll keep this card as a memento. It's been an interesting flight."

"Well, old Howie knew you weren't dumb enough to be no fish cop. You look like a man with more than half a brain. Good for you, fella."

With that, Howie held out his hand to bid the passenger goodbye and all the best. Passengers were disembarking, and Daryl had several carry-on bags to retrieve from the overhead lockers.

Instinctively, Daryl stuck out his hand. He remembered the Sperm Sprayer's nickname. *Shit, what if I get pregnant?* They shook hands, and Daryl retrieved his luggage and scurried along the thin gangway.

CHAPTER 5
WHAT'S NEW PUSSYCAT?

HAVING ARRIVED from the doctor's home, Saul Maçon began removing his blue, blood-spattered disposable hazmat romper suit, face mask, latex gloves, fanny pack and booties. He stood in his undies by a large, rusting, fire-scorched oil barrel and placed the soiled items one by one into the giant drum. Saul pulled a box of matches and lighter fluid from a nearby drawer. Pouring the inflammable substance on the barrel's contents, he struck a match and PFHOOM—all went up in flames; dark, acrid smoke bellowed into the air. It took twenty seconds, and it was all over. Saul threw in a few more oily rags and walked away to be closer to his barn, twenty feet from his house. He opened the palm of his hand and looked at Dr. Hussain's eyeball and her three fingertips.

"Good quality glass, you are." He placed it on a wooden chest adjacent to a large orange cylindrical container. "I know you want to watch.," he laughed. After removing the robust orange polyethene lid, he gently dropped the digits one by one into hydrofluoric acid, carefully resealing the tote. "All gone."

Saul retrieved the eye, kissed it, and replaced the eyeball on top of the chest so that the eye could see what he was about to do next. He turned on the faucet of the outside shower unit. Cold water rained down from the shower head. Saul loved the cold water—imagining he was a Navy Seal and having to embrace "the suck." Scrubbing his upper half with coal tar soap, he removed his underwear and threw his gnarly-looking whitish pants to the ground. He hated buying new underwear and had kept his white cotton Y-front collection for the past decade. "You'll need a-bleaching," he said to the underwear as he scrubbed away, humming an old Acadian tune.

"Dr. Hussain, look away if you're shy," he said, chuckling, as he cleaned his foamy nether regions from the night's macabre activities.

He felt satisfied. Another privileged outsider had been removed—another cat saved—and a magnificent eyeball had been found.

"What were the chances," he kept telling himself. Now thoroughly scrubbed from head to toe, he rinsed himself again and turned off the shower faucet. With hands raised high in the air, he stood facing the lake, his naked body on display for everyone. A bunch of cats peered out from behind the window in the dining room, meowing and scratching at the double-glazed glass with their paws.

"I'll be there in no time, my beloved chil'ren. Be patient. Your father has a couple of errands to take care of before I can come in and give you's your breakfast."

Dressed in an ancient brown robe, he walked over to the wooden chest. Gently, he plucked the eyeball from its resting place and carefully tucked it into his robe's pocket. The eyeball was a gift from the heavens—justification from God, or his mother, that he was doing a higher power's bidding. Before her spirit left her eighty-two-year-old body, she opened one eye, craned her neck to look directly at her eldest son, and said, "I'll always have my eye on you, son." It was her last breath.

Six hundred and eighteen Colonel Road was given to him by his mother. Saul cared for her most of his adult life; she could be a punitive, controlling, and jealous woman. Philomena Maçon was old money and a proud Acadian to boot: she only spoke Franglish, a French, English and Creole patois. Although harsh, she ensured her children had full bellies, and her beef and barley soup was something to die for.

After enduring relentless bullying from the kids of wealthy newcomers and outsiders, Saul made the choice to drop out of school after seventh grade. He found acceptance among the locals due to his family's prominence in the community. However, he stood out conspicuously amidst the crowd. Others found him gruff in his demeanor, often brusque or unfriendly. With his tall stature and sinewy body, Saul seldom initiated a conversation. One glance at his weathered, sun-damaged skin, thinning strawberry blond hair, and piercing icy grey eyes showed that he was not to be trifled with. His vocabulary wasn't the greatest, but he spoke very passable English. The man worked for several professional people with large yards and acreages. He loved his Husqvarna ride-on lawn mower and happily split numerous cordages of wood for the outsiders. Some he tolerated; most he couldn't stand.

CHAPTER 6
SQUAD CAR

THE BAGGAGE WAS COLLECTED without a hitch, and Daryl thought his promise to God to attend church might be working. No lost luggage. No delays once arriving in Toronto. No more Howie the Inseminator. He'd even emptied his bowels—a rare event when travelling. Blue skies and crisp fresh air were expected in Halifax's spring weather. Flying over Amherst, he thought of Alice and the boys. How he missed them—but they were all so much closer now. He'd try to find rented accommodation as soon as possible. He hated hotel stays—they encouraged him to binge-watch cable TV and eat crap foods. A new start in Yeovilton County—wherever the hell it was. He couldn't bring himself to google the area as he knew it would make him depressed. Still, house prices were much lower on the East Coast, and once settled, he'd buy a plot of land and build his own home by the lake or buy somewhere for a quarter of the price of a property in British Columbia. He'd still have a good salary and earn lots of overtime due to the manpower shortage. He gave imaginary Alice a wave from his window seat, determined to never sit in an aisle seat again.

"Fisheries? What the flip?" he muttered to himself. What did he know about fish? He liked shrimp cooked on the barbecue and cod and chips from the British fish and chip shop near the detachment, but that was about it. He had been too disheartened to find out about the role of a fisheries worker.

Daryl chuckled thinking about the great send-off his team gave him. They clearly liked their "Skipper" despite his idiosyncrasies. Fresh fish were in every desk drawer; two giant inflatables were hung over his desk—a starfish and an enormous dolphin. They had passed around the hat on hearing of his sudden departure. The team purchased a vintage Billy Bass fish mounted on a wooden plaque engraved with, "To Pounds, the best fish cop this side of the Atlantic." On the rear of the plaque, his comrades had written personal messages like:

"Give Salmon 'Satanic Verses' Rushdie a high five from us," said Chief Hislop.

"What's the difference between a fish and a piano? You can tune a piano, but you can't TUNE-A fish!"

"Do you know how to keep a fish from smelling? Cut off its nose!"

His favourite was, "Poundsy, The Best Boss in the World"

Rumours about why he was leaving the Serious Crimes Unit had spread like wildfire.

"He's been caught shagging the boss' wife."

"No, Daryl wouldn't do that. He got caught exposing himself. His wee willy winky was so small—the size of a shrimp—that the boss thought he was better suited to being a Fisheries Officer."

Chief Hislop ended the gossip and told the team that it was a combination of factors, including him slipping up on his application form and wanting to try and salvage his marriage.

"Sounds fishy," scoffed a civilian employee and was met with raucous laughter.

Despite his sniggering, there was an unmistakable sadness in his eyes. For years, he had boasted about his rich French lineage, proudly sharing stories of his ancestors. To mark Saint-Jean-Baptiste Day in June, he proudly displayed tricolor flags in blue, white, and red, along with the Quebecois' Fleurdelisé, both inside his man cave and outside his house. He subscribed to Duolingo to learn French, and although his skills improved, he could only manage basic grocery orders at the local Seven-Eleven, leaving the workers confused. Now, he was just plain old Daryl Smith. He lamented, *Fish this; fish that. I never thought I'd miss being called Pounds.*

Upon exiting the airport baggage area, he was met by a uniformed police officer holding a giant whiteboard with the words "DARYL—FISH COP, YEOVILTON COUNTY."

Daryl approached the cop, set down his luggage, extended his hand, and said, "I'm Daryl."

The cop reciprocated. Charlie Noble introduced himself as a senior constable of the Yeovilton County Police Force, South Shore, Nova Scotia. The police officer was well turned out in his dark blue uniform and bright fluorescent all-weather jacket with "Police" on both front and rear. With his charming face and strong square jaw, Noble appeared as if he'd stepped right off the cover of Montblanc Legend, his image reflecting the fragrance's smooth, clean-cut appeal.

The bastard is too good-looking.

"I knew it was you. You have that fishy look about you."

"Very funny. Yes, I'm the new fish cop."

Yep, I might as well get the jibes in first. As my now-imprisoned mother used to tell me. "Daryl, those that laugh the last laugh the longest." Not sure I agree, dear mother.

"Glad you have a sense of humour, Daryl. You'll need it."

Constable Noble took one of Daryl's suitcases, wheeled it out of the airport, and moved it towards a squad car parked in the no-parking zone. Noble opened up the rear door and shoved the suitcase onto a seat. "Lob the other one, the other side, will you? I'll put your girlie bags in the trunk."

Daryl looked inside the vehicle and blinked rapidly. "Please don't tell me I'm travelling in the rear of the vehicle, like a crim? If so, I'll take a cab."

Noble waved away his new colleague. "Silly ass. You're in the front of my chariot."

Daryl was a big fellow—a gentle giant of a man. At 6'5," he had a robust frame. He'd battled with his weight over the years. Unsociable hours, his enjoyment of craft beer, and a terrible fast-food diet had added quite a few bulges to his tummy. Although his ex-co-workers called him "Pounds," after the "lbs" initials to his name, he suspected that the nickname was used passive-aggressively, at times, as a dig about his size. He always felt conscious when he and Alice went out together, as she was built like a person who had to run around the shower to get wet. She was lean, muscular, and as fit as a fiddle. He was "Poundsy." He had variable success working off the excess weight with regular gym attendance and a savage dirty ketogenic diet. Still, his poor work-life balance caught up with him every time. After the split-up with Alice, he had worked super hard to turn his life around and was now back to the lean, mean French fighting machine he used to be.

Tired from travelling, and exhausted by listening to the Howie guy, Daryl remained quiet at the journey's onset.

"Can I play a few tunes on the way?" asked Noble.

"As long as it's not country or Lynyrd Skynyrd."

Noble laughed and pressed the play button. Katy Perry's "I Kissed a Girl" blared out on subwoofers inserted into the squad car.

Awesome—love this!

When the chorus was reached, Noble sang, "Daryl—Kissed a *fish* and liked it, halibut, and cod roe were fantastic!"

"Funny, not funny."

Noble turned down the music, and his handsome face became serious. "I'm sorry, Daryl. The squad couldn't figure out why you changed career paths."

Daryl needed to be in the mood to explain. "Well, I did."

Noble shared that he lived with a local lady he met online. He'd taken her two kids from a previous relationship under his wing and they tried to buy a house together but were ripped off by a local builder. Daryl listened but said little about his own situation.

"Okay, Mr. Chatterbox. I'd love to fill you in with the latest drama from the fisheries and oceans world. I'm not well-versed on recent lobster busts or the unlawful selling of mackerel and barnacles along the south shore." He giggled, turned towards his passenger, and noticed Daryl still wasn't smiling. He awkwardly cleared his throat. "Lots of poaching is going on. Illegal lobster fishing has caused the market prices to plummet, causing a big stink with the mayor—which has repercussions with your new boss, Chief Kennedy. He wants an immediate crackdown on smuggling hooch in and out of Neck Point."

Daryl grimaced. "Isn't that the Coast Guard's responsibility?"

"Nope. It's DFO territory since the New Blue Wave made their cutbacks. You have a speedy little Zodiac at your disposal. You can also use our profiler to go out on busts with—she is a terrific Zodiac rider who will help you not get lost."

"Hooch smuggling?"

"Yep. Thanks to prohibition it's rife in these parts. Didn't you hear about what's happening in the rest of the country in your hippy, granola-crunching province?"

"It may be granola-crunching to you, but at least we can still drink booze, and we aren't pressured into going to church."

Noble was up for a bit of inter-provincial banter. "Your government still hand out free cocaine and fentanyl?"

"That's bullcrap, Constable. It's given to help junkies not kill themselves."

"Senior Constable, actually. How's that working out for the druggies?"

"Early days yet. The trouble is most of Canada's addicts and alcoholics are migrating west."

"See, it's working. The Blue Wave is clamping down on crime. All the shit in society is moving away from our Atlantic hood."

Harsh. Addiction and homelessness are a societal problem. People don't choose to have dependencies and low income.

"As a do-gooder, you'd be better off choosing social work as a career than Fisheries."

"No firearm for social workers, although they deserve them."

"You'll be lucky if your DFO-issued firearm functions. I believe the DFO provides you with a First World War revolver. The good news is you'll receive a harpoon gun, bear spray, mosquito repellent, and a gill net," chortled Noble. "Enjoy."

Daryl faked a tired smile.

"Oh, and a taser. However, due to the power outages during Christmas and spring season, the mayor has forbidden us from charging them up."

Daryl sighed, wanting to change the subject about his new position. "Any factoids about the South Shore that I should get excited about?"

"We have one movie theatre there. A Sobeys and a Mark's Warehouse. The most famous store is Cabela's. I'd stay away from there. As a fish cop, you'll be the most hated person on the planet."

Noble shared that unemployment was rife. Everyone had a side hustle to supplement their benefit cheques. Fishing is the main industry and many local folks were at odds with the Indigenous communities due to their fishing rights and treaties. He added that racism was also brutal.

"It's the opposite in B.C.—a very inclusive demographic. Lots of collaboration with native groups."

"Not here, pal. I feel for the MikMaw. However, some of us 'settlers' find their 'rights' hard to swallow."

"Well, these people were here long before we landed and spread our fatal diseases and took away their culture."

The cop guffawed. "Oh, the people of Yeovilton will surely take to you."

Once again, the ex-detective changed tack. "Crime. What's happening locally?"

Noble continued to remain laser focused on the highway. "Dan Saulnier's car was broken into a couple of weeks ago. Harold Boudreau was bumped into by a youth, and he fell and broke a dozen eggs he was holding. Maizy Campbell had four lobsters stolen from the back of her truck. Noise complaints by Aimee McDougall—her neighbours like to party. Fanny Cruz lost her teeth again."

"That's it?"

"There's some kind of serial killer on the loose."

"That's more like it. How many have been murdered?"

"Two."

"Any leads?"

"My partner, Sergeant Barnes, is the lead investigator. Well, I say lead … he's the *only* detective on the team. The chief has been on his back to solve the crimes. He's pressured by the mayor to use police resources to focus on illegal lobster fishing. Bad for the economy."

"And murders aren't?"

There was a silence for a couple of minutes. Daryl couldn't give a damn about lobsters, missing teeth, and noisy neighbours. He wanted Noble to spill the tea on the killings and proceeded to pepper him with questions.

The trip should have taken three hours. The presence of the squad car caused traffic ahead of it to slow down to a painful crawl. The highway from Halifax to the South Shore was two lanes and a single carriageway. Very few cars passed by in the opposite direction. Barnes flicked on his strobing lights and siren to overtake a convoy of trucks, travelling as slow as Brian the Snail from *The Magic Roundabout*.

Daryl looked surprised.

"Don't worry," he informed his passenger, "we do this when the chief wants us to get him a McDonalds or something from Taco Bell."

Daryl wasn't worried. He was lost in thought about the slayings. Two of them. No sign of break and entry. Pets taken; fingers removed from the latest victim. Blunt force trauma from behind. The victims were relative newcomers to the county. No prints or DNA were left at the scene. No suspects apart from murmurings about jihadists and vengeful Germans. On the surface, the chief sounded like an imbecile—caring more about petty crime and infractions than a juicy homicide or two. *Why oh why didn't I come here as a detective?* Daryl let out a humongous sigh that wasn't lost on the other occupant of the vehicle. *No, it makes total sense to make me solve pickerel and trout crime rather than the murder of human beings.*

As the sun set, they passed the Yeovilton county line. The trip had made Daryl feel isolated and discombobulated. It felt like he was entering a time warp. A popular tourist town in the 1930s, it had brightly coloured, detached houses covered in wood slate and tiles. He liked their homes. Many flew the Acadian flag—French blue, white, and red tricolor with a large papal-coloured yellow star in the top left-hand corner. For a moment, a shiver went through him; tears welled up in his eyes. He loved the French flag and promised to learn more about the Acadian heritage and the Indigenous peoples living there. Traffic lights hung in the air, from lamppost to lamppost. They passed several small stores, a small strip mall, the humongous Cabela's, and Sobeys. Noble indicated left and pulled into the triple-storied Best Western Hotel.

"Here we are, my good sir. Our profiler and jack-of-all-trades, Yvonne Sparks, booked you under the name of Mr. Kipper. Are you okay with your bags? I'm late for the chief's mandatory book club. I don't want to piss him off."

"I'll be fine. Thank you for the ride and the company."

"You're welcome, Daryl. Remember, the cop shop is a ten to fifteen-minute walk along the highway, past the mall, across two sets of traffic lights, and it's on your immediate right. The chief wants you there at nine o'clock, on the button. You'll have a quick intro to your new team; Yvonne will fit you out in some old Fisheries uniforms that we inherited from the last few workers. Just make do until they fit you out with a new one. Failing that, dress up in camouflage and say you're going on a stakeout. The boss will love your keenness."

Daryl smirked. He hated first days, and he'd struggle sleeping tonight—that was for sure. A concierge and porter appeared at the sliding doorway and took Daryl's luggage. He waved at the squad car that had put on its blue, red, and white flashing lights in a hurry to pass the red traffic lights and get to his important book club meeting.

Having checked in as Smith, and not Kipper, he entered the elevator. When the doors closed, he looked into the large mirror and said, "A mandatory book club? Please, God, don't make me have to join one. Attending a church will be challenging enough, never mind discussing Dostoevsky's *Crime and Punishment* in my downtime."

CHAPTER 7
THE RUM RUNNER

GABE MAÇON WAS A WELL-LIKED figure in the community. He was a skilled musician known for playing Jimmy Page riffs on his cherished Les Paul guitar and was often seen as a lovable yet happy drunk. Not being one to listen to any kind of national or provincial news, never mind CNN or Fox, Gabe heard through the Yeovilton grapevine that not only had the Tories won the general election by a landslide, but the New Blue Wave had hit Nova Scotia-like a tsunami, heralding in a staunchly conservative and evangelical government to all the maritime communities. Premier Angus McDougall was all for Making Maritimers Awesome Again. British Columbia and Quebec were the only provinces that held back the Blue Wave and remained staunchly New Democratic Party and Bloc Québécois.

Nova Scotia's government had quickly banned booze and pork and took on a more biblical worldview. Church membership had swollen due to tax breaks being offered for attendance and tithing; working visas had been handed out to many Christian missionaries to plant new churches and convert the heathen population.

It was a Brave New World, and Gabe Maçon loved every minute. Despite finding church attendance a pain in the ass and being an unashamed alcoholic who loved nothing more than a bacon sandwich, he was making a small fortune running an illegal distillery and drinking establishment called The Rum Runner. Liquor officers didn't exist in these parts, and law enforcement were some of his most loyal customers. The only awkward git was the Chief of Police, who encouraged reading, temperance, chastity, and church attendance.

Gabe attended the newest and now largest congregation in the county, The White Hart Lane Fellowship, located downtown. The "church" had grown exponentially these past few months. It relocated to a vast auditorium once rented to the Wesleyan church. WHL Fellowship hosted a new English pastor and his hot-as-hell wife. Gabe was encouraged to attend by his brother, Blaze, who clearly was besotted with the pastoral couple, as were most of the male population of Yeovilton. Gabe attended and used the opportunity to take orders for his three most popular brands of Moonshine: Traditional Olde Smokey (on the Water) Hooch, Rappie Rum, and Gabe's Blind Drunk Destroyer. Gabe was exporting his booze to New Brunswick, Newfoundland, and across the Atlantic to Maine, Massachusetts, and New Hampshire, as these were now dry states. Things were going so well for Gabe that he was considering moving vast quantities of his booze further west into Ontario, Manitoba, Saskatchewan, and Alberta.

Now sending his two children to an exclusive private French immersion school with $40,000-a-term fees, he was one of the most generous givers at the new fellowship. Despite Gabe not knowing much about spirituality, Pastor Harry considered appointing him to the church leadership board due to his bulging wallet and charitable giving. When asked to pray over the congregation, Gabe spoke in Acadian patois, informing the worshippers when the next batch of hooch was ready for collection. Pastor Harry was astounded at how Gabe had connected with his church members. The congregation appeared to have replaced traditional sounds of "amen," and "preach it bro," during his sermons, with the more Acadian-sounding, "hooch, hooch." Pastor Harry turned a blind eye to his members embracing a form of cultural appropriation because they shouted it out with such gusto.

Through the Brits' selfless "flirty-fish" evangelism, the pastor and his wife, Raylene, were advancing the "Queendom of the Goddess," whatever that was. Gabe Maçon didn't care; he was rock solid in his faith—radical entrepreneurship—and money fell upon him like manna from heaven.

Gabe raised his glass in a packed Rum Runner and made a toast, "Here's to Premier McDougall."

"Premier McDougall!" roared the masses.

"Four More Years!" cried out Gabe.

"Four More Years," repeated his inebriated customers.

"White Hart Lane Fellowship."

"White Hart Lane!" they cried.

"And to Raylene's tits!"

"Raylene's tits!" they cried, downing another glass of hooch.

Gabe left his chair, stepped onto the stage, grabbed his Les Paul, and started the tuning ritual.

"Let's party!" he yelled, as The Rum Runner came alive to the sound of Led Zeppelin's "Whole Lotta Love."

CHAPTER 8
THE NEW GUY

DARYL HATED FIRST DAYS. At school, he was the tallest kid in his grade. He hadn't expected vitriol from fellow five-year-olds. However, two "ruffians" and would-be career criminals welcomed him with a glob of chewing gum on his chair seat. They named him "Beanstalk Boy," and Daryl was too tall to slink into the background. At Secondary school, newer, meaner boys nicknamed him "The Tower of Babel," not solely due to his height but also because he'd tend to babble and stutter when he was super-stressed or embarrassed. So, early puberty wasn't a joyous affair for him; early facial hair sprouted under his nose and cheeks, his face erupting with angry acne patches. Wannabe tough kids pushed him around, and for a year or so, one particularly hefty fellow and super-Francophobe named Dorian Axemaster made his life an utter misery. Proud of his French heritage and surname, Dorian's incessant French jokes drove Daryl nuts.

"Hey Daryl, how many Frenchmen did it take to defend France from foreign aggression during World War Two? You don't know? Nobody knows, as it's never been done!"

"Hey Daryl, what do you call two million Frenchmen with their hands raised? The French Army."

"Hey Daryl, how many gears on a French tank? Six. One forward and five in reverse."

"Hey Daryl, did you hear about the French kamikaze pilot? He's now on his forty-third mission."

"Hey Daryl, double knock, knock?"

"Who's there, Dorian?"

"French."

"French who?"

"French Fries and his buddy, French cross-dresser."

He laughed along, of course, but the jokes had run thin. Quick-witted himself, he made many jokes but always doubted if the other students "got" his joke or sarcasm and ended up explaining the joke to his small audience—which itself was hilarious to those listening to him. Yes, his first days tended to manifest PTSD, and his debut appearance at Police HQ and his new colleagues at the Joint Task Force (JTF) proved to be no different.

"Here he is! *Monsieur Poisson*," welcomed Constable Noble.

"It's old Fish Face," said another guy dressed in a smart two-piece suit.

Noble held out his hand and welcomed Daryl to the JTF. In a dreadful French accent, he held up a magnifying glass that made one of his eyes the size of a baby's head. "*Ecu-tay. Sil-Vous-Play*. Is this the famous Hercule Poirot of Agatha Christie fame?"

The suited guy said, "Fish Face, shake hands." Daryl held out his hand. A giant, pink lobster, with opening and closing pincers appeared from the man's sleeve. Daryl withdrew his palm like a man given a cobra to hold. Laughter erupted from his new team.

"Detective Sergeant Barnes." The suited guy smiled. "You must be Daryl LeBlanc-Smith, no doubt."

"Just plain old Daryl Smith."

Barnes turned to the other room members and exclaimed, "He's a proud Frenchie. The Acadian hooch smugglers are going to love him."

"So are the poor fish license-avoiders," said the canteen lady, shaking her head in disgust.

Daryl lifted his arm in a Queen Elizabeth II-like gesture, smiled, and waved hello.

"Attention! Troop!" Barnes stood erect and saluted.

Noble stared at Daryl, opened his eyes wide, frowned, and yelled, "Officer in the house! Men, Daryl, atten—shun!"

"And ladies," snapped an attractive dark-skinned lady dressed in a smart, navy blue suit.

"Thank you, Sparks," groaned Sergeant Barnes.

Constable Noble bellowed, "All present and correct, sir!"

Chief Inspector Michael Pretorius Kennedy stood tall and proud at the doorway. Returning his men's salute, his eyes moved from left to right, making brief contact with each person present.

"Stand easy, men."

"And women," Yvonne Sparks added.

Daryl had arrived on time. It had been an uncomfortable experience as his initial greeting had been awkward. Constable Noble reluctantly pulled himself away from playing *Tetris* on his desktop and ushered Daryl to a desk in the open-plan office.

"I see that we have our new recruit?"

Daryl was aware the chief was referring to himself.

"Yes."

"Yes, sir," snapped Noble, clicking his heels.

"Stand easy." The chief stared intently at Constable Noble. "Noble, great job on your mini-synopsis of *Angela's Ashes* last night. Your analysis of Frank McCourt's theme was excellent. You stated, 'Poverty and perseverance serve as a living record of the stoic and indefatigable sense of his values, maintaining a solid sense of humour despite the suffering and misery he endured as Angela's child.' That is truly worthy of an A-plus grade."

Daryl looked like he had woken up in the middle of a literary class.

Constable Noble blushed.

"However," the chief scowled as he stared at his detective, "Sergeant Barnes' input, which can be best summarized as, 'I despise books with excessive British slang and a lack of punctuation,' was not very helpful."

"Irish slang," chimed in Sparks, with a twinkle in her eye.

"Quite, quite. British, Irish—same shit, different bucket."

"The Irish, Welsh, Scottish and English may beg to differ," muttered Yvonne, under her breath.

"You weren't there! What's your excuse this time?"

Yvonne rolled her eyes, as if having been asked the same question repeatedly over time. "I was tucking my children into bed after completing my eight-hour shift. Before that, I picked them up from soccer practice, dropped in on Marge McKinnon after her cancer surgery, made sure we had enough groceries in the home, had shower sex with my husb—"

"Yes, yes. Though not mandatory, Mrs. Sparks, book club participation is *expected*."

Yvonne smiled, shook her head, and mouthed "whatever" to the chief.

Chief Kennedy turned his head towards Daryl. "Sloppy salute. We'll have to work on that. Fisheries bods can be an undisciplined bunch. We soon lick them into shape here, LeBlanc-Smith."

"Just plain Smith, sir."

Daryl learned that until the feds dug into their pockets and sent a senior DFO commander to the county, Chief Kennedy would be his commanding officer. Daryl asked when he was scheduled to attend the sixteen-week fisheries training in Ontario. Kennedy curtly informed him he had failed to attain high enough grades to be available for selection. Confused as he had not taken any assessment or exam, Kennedy told him that he had been *secretly* assessed by Senior Constable Noble during the trip from the airport. The chief pulled out a rumpled document from behind his back.

Clearing his throat, he read, "Pros: He is tall. Cons: Sulky and quiet. Secretive. Pro-indigenous. Pro-left-wing politics. Sketchy AF. Possible substance abuser and rule-breaker. Wannabe social worker and extremely woke with zero sense of humour."

Daryl laughed. "Oh, because I wasn't interested in hearing about the pastor's wife's perky cleavage?"

Kennedy continued with the long list of cons, "Possible sexual dysphoria—"

Daryl's face scrunched up. "What?"

"Permission to speak, sir?"

"Go ahead, Detective Sergeant Barnes."

"As the task force's most senior detective—"

"Only detective," chuckled Yvonne.

"It is my belief that Mr. Smith's low marks could be a result of his struggle with intersexual, queer, or pansexual feelings."

"Possibly sapiosexual, gynesexual, or skoliosexual urges," came a voice from the canteen area.

"Excellent, Mrs. Gagnon."

"Possible lesbian?" quipped Noble.

Chief Kennedy smirked. "Men, and the random canteen lady, you all did well in the Diversity and Inclusion seminar. Good job."

Daryl sighed.

"You could always leave the poor man alone," snapped Yvonne.

Daryl turned to her, smiled, and mouthed, "Thank you." He felt like he had walked into a scene from *The Office*, with the manager, Michael Scott, welcoming him on his first day.

"Now, LeBlanc, don't be offended. Just a bit of first-day banter. There's lots of important work to do here. We have a small but good team."

"Sir, are you serious about the training?"

"Yes, yes. Noble scored you a C minus. You needed to attain at least a B to qualify for this year's Fisheries Academy."

Daryl smacked his head with the palm of his hand in mock disgust.

"Smith, you'll get another chance next year." It was time for formal introductions. Chief Kennedy pointed at each team member in turn. "Sergeant 'Iceman' Barnes—our crack detective. Constable Noble—your assessor and chauffeur from the airport. Melony Gagnon—our canteen lady, who may be in her seventies, but is studying for her psychiatric certificate at the local college."

Mrs. Gagnon blushed, smiled, and waved. "And last but not least, Yvonne Sparks, our Quantico graduated profiler and ad-hoc officer, an essential gasket in the efficient running of the engine."

Daryl nodded to each in turn. Smiling at Sparks, he said, "A profiler. That's awesome!"

"Yvonne's feet are in three camps. She profiles human, arthropod, and crustacean suspects. She led the last DFO to solve the *Barnacle Bill* murders on the craggy rocks of Mahone Bay," chortled Noble.

"Give it a rest," spat Yvonne, clearly irritated at the idiotic remarks that Tweedle Dee and Tweedle Dum were coming out with.

"Quite, quite. Yvonne provides support as a Zodiac helmsman, and has excellent boat craft skills. DFO used to have a 44-foot patrol vessel. Canadian made."

"Used to have?" queried Daryl.

"Yes, it was stolen. We have reason to believe that the smugglers took it, kept it, and now use it for their rum-running exercises. Vital for our local economy—so we turn a blind eye. Anyway, we have our Zodiac. You will also be issued a DFO firearm, a speargun, a gill net, soft body armour, and a Mae West life jacket."

"What type of firearm, sir?"

"I believe the Department of Fisheries and Oceans issues its personnel with a Smith & Wesson 5946. 9 mm. Stainless steel. Ten and fifteen round magazines. Ambidextrous safety levers."

That's a tad 1990s. Oh well, a gun is a gun.

"Unfortunately, the last DSO officer dropped it in a saltwater pool, and by the time it was retrieved, it had rusted badly. A newer version is on order for you."

Daryl shook his head.

"Meanwhile, we have managed to get our hands on a very reliable and rugged firearm. It won't let you down—a Webley Mk V revolver. The crème de la crème. Served my great grandfather well in the trenches, and I have a couple of boxes of .38 cartridges."

A First World War antique. OMG.

"Incidentally, Indiana Jones used one," said Kennedy, matter-of-factly.

Barnes and Noble sniggered.

Daryl could not get over the fact he was a Fisheries Officer with zero knowledge about Fisheries. The training course would have given him a foundation, but now he had to do the job blindfolded.

Chief Kennedy's mouth opened and closed. The newbie Fisheries Officer heard he had access to a mobile hideaway in the middle of a place called Quincy Woods. He had to keep watch for smugglers, rustlers, and poachers. Daryl also had access to a paddle board for stealth operations. Yvonne would issue him his kit, and he could keep his RCMP badge until the DFO replacement turned up.

"One last thing."

"Yes, sir."

"Are you a reader?"

"Not really, sir."

"Well, you are now. We have a keen reading group here. I hand-selected Barnes and Noble for that purpose. No officers called 'Amazon' in the RCMP—that's a terrible shame. Anyway, it's mandatory. Tuesday evenings at 8 p.m., even if you are on a stakeout. You can use your iPhone for the

Zoom meetings or satellite phone dial-up. I'll send you your reading homework in due course."

"But sir—"

"*Mandatory*, Smith. You don't want that C Minus dropping to a D Minus, do you? You'll never get out of here! Yvonne, make sure you show Smithy here the ropes."

Daryl's frown was virtually permanent. Chief Kennedy continued to brief his subordinates, mentioning one or two of the latest police reports, ranging from indecent exposure at the elementary school to the theft of a Mars Bar from the Circle-K garage in Plymouth. There were two new reports of noisy neighbours.

Daryl plucked up the courage. "Sir?"

Kennedy stared at his watch and tapped the face. "Time is money, Smith. Last question."

"The murders, sir. Read it on the RCMP bulletin before coming here. Blunt force trauma. Like the banker two years ago. Any update?"

"Barnes? Update?"

"Sir. Sarah said there was very little forensic evidence. Another perfect crime. Still a mystery about the eyeball."

"Eyeball? What eyeball?" asked Daryl.

"Look, I will be late for my appointment with the mayor. Get up to speed yourself—Yvonne will fill you in. Or, take Barnes out for lunch, give him a kiss on the cheek and he'll spill the tea. Otherwise, think lobster, lobster, lobster."

Daryl weighed up the kissing option. Sergeant Barnes snarled at him.

"Squad, attend-shun," yelled out Noble.

This time, Daryl automatically stood up.

"Stand easy, men." Kennedy turned and walked out of the briefing room towards the detachment exit.

"And women," snarked Yvonne defiantly.

CHAPTER 9
THE BROTHERS GRIMM

Saul stepped through the rear door and into the crowded bar. Nodding to one or two regulars, he kept his head down shyly. He felt as uncomfortable as a man who had accidentally walked into Walmart wearing nothing but underwear. Saul wasn't a drinker but was happy that his brother was making a success of his mother's bequest—unlike the profligate young Blaze.

The Maçon brothers were well known in Yeovilton County. Saul had a reputation for being a tad odd. It wasn't an unusual trait, as many people from the Lake Quincy area had more in common with the "Squeal little piggy" baddies from the *Deliverance* movie than the Yeovilton townsfolk. Quincians spoke patois, and several families from the area didn't speak at all. Outsiders had assumed that it had to do with too many inter-familial marriages. Brother was secretly betrothed to a cousin, and sisters hooked up with their uncles. Lake Quincy was one of those areas that you wouldn't set foot in if you weren't brought there by a local.

Saul made his way to the front of the Rum Runner. The brothers acknowledged each other with friendly nods, silently acknowledging their shared camaraderie.

Gabe asked, "Have you come to listen to my music, dear brother?"

"No. I'm here for business. I've got a new breeder for you's. A good-lookin' tom—ready to mate with a classy molly—for the right price, of course."

Gabe patted his brother on the shoulder. "When will your boy be ready?"

"A month or two, maybe more."

"And, Old Tom?"

"He's doing well, brudder."

"Unfortunate you had to take him to that darned vet. I don't trust him, bruv. There's something of the night about him."

"If his mouth starts a-flapping, he's not going to be long for this earth. He was paid handsomely and Old Tom is doing well. In fact, *our* boy will be good as new—you mark my words."

"I love Old Tom, truly. But the mollies are getting scared of him."

"Old Tom will be ready. Saul always delivers."

"This Yankee molly will be here in the not-too-distant future. I've received the down payment. I can't believe how much money this lady is investing in this match."

"Old Tom will be ready." Saul rubbed his hands together. "This will be our biggest payday yet."

"Send me details of the new tom. Usual specs. Does he have a name?"

"Boris. A short-haired Russian Blue—a stunner. Sparkling green eyes and a coat to die for. These cats are mighty clever. They play fetch and you can train them all kinda things. Worth a small fortune."

Gabe wore a grin from ear to ear. "I'll send pictures when he's ready. He's gonna be homesick for a bit. Old Tom took to me real good. This Ruskie will do the same. Meanwhile, let's give Old Tom a couple more tries."

"Okay, we can't afford for him to scare the bejesus out of either the molly or her owner."

"Trust your brudder. Old Tom will be the looker he once was. One thing's for sure: he can sure breed some beautiful kitties."

"True, that."

Gabe punched the air, yelled, "Yes!" and gave Saul a high five. The brothers loved making money.

With a last handshake, Saul turned his back on his brother and walked through the crowded saloon. He held up the back of his hand to acknowledge Gabe, made his way out of the Rum Runner, and headed to his truck.

52

CHAPTER 10
SPILLING THE TEA

Yvonne Sparks was the most likeable and least annoying of Daryl's new teammates. In her forties, she was dark skinned, wore a Sigourney Weaver crew cut shaved in a Grace Jones kind of way. Bright, sparkling brown eyes —she presented with a confident and calm demeanour.

"Here's your firearm, a Webley Mk V, and don't lose it. It's the only working firearm the DFO has provided its staff. We have a Smith & Wesson Model 5906, but it's not operational. The last Fisheries dude used to take it out with him as it 'looked' cool and functional."

Daryl's jaw dropped as he stared at the First World War officers' sidearm.

"The other working piece is a double-barreled DILLINGER 1847 piece —that Chief Kennedy brought in when he reviewed the book, DILLINGER and CAT BALLOU."

Daryl shook his head. "No worries, I've not lost a firearm yet. The weapon will come in useful if I find myself in a trench in the Ypres Forest in Belgium or if I'm playing a hooker in a '60s cowboy movie."

Ignoring the jibe, Sparks continued, "So, please don't misplace it as it causes a ton of paperwork for us both. Detectives here often 'lose' their sidearm because they tend to be morons," Yvonne glanced over in Sergeant Barnes' direction, "like some people in this detachment."

Daryl smirked.

Daryl learned that although Fisheries and the Police worked as a "team," they were very different beasts to work for. RCMP had federal funding; the municipal cops had less and were financed by the mayor—then there was the DFO. Since the New Blue Wave, business and personal taxes, red tape, and essential services had experienced cuts, and more cuts. Yvonne believed there would be more chance of obtaining funds if Daryl set up a religious bookstore in the province. Daryl's poker face did not betray his inner anger.

"I don't understand why you left your RCMP job in British Columbia to become a Fisheries Officer in Nova Scotia?"

"I've always wanted to be a fish out of water," Daryl replied with a smirk.

"Technically, your position is varied and interesting if . . . Chief Kennedy wasn't your immediate and only supervisor."

Daryl nodded, tight-lipped.

"You'll do stakeouts in Quincy Woods. There's a large and beautiful lake nearby. Smugglers often use small boats to ferry contraband from one side to the other."

Daryl's eyebrows raised, "Contraband?"

"Hooch, lobster, fish, weed, pelts."

"Why do I need the Zodiac?"

"To do circuits around Smuggler's Cove. Purely superficial, as the mayor wouldn't want you to mess with the hooch trade. It's all in the job spec."

"I haven't seen it."

"I believe Chief Kennedy is writing it as we speak."

Daryl let out an involuntary groan. "This is a *joint* task force, right?"

"Sure is, technically."

"Then, what about crime? Will Chief Kennedy let me get involved when need be?"

"To answer your question: I'm a highly qualified profiler. Spent a few years at Quantico. Here, I make the tea, work in the armory, and run courses like Diversity and Inclusion, Dealing with and Reporting Bullying, and Creating a Safe, Religious Workplace. The latter is mandatory government training."

Daryl closed his eyes, breathed deeply, and opened them again. "Do I get some kind of small boat training?"

"Yes, we have a local guy who'll test you. Unfortunately, it's an online test."

He shook his head. "Terrific."

"Chill. I'll show you the ropes. The only people that are going to write you up for not being licensed are your colleagues and yourself."

"The way my colleagues recently 'assessed' me, I don't have great confidence that they won't jail me for a violation."

"Kennedy wouldn't allow it. He won't admit it, but he needs you, Daryl. Yes, he presents like a man who has an IQ of a sea urchin but he was thrilled to find another—"

"Pair of hands."

"No, another *book club* member." Yvonne and Daryl both laughed.

"So, where did *you* get your watercraft skills from?"

"My pappy taught us all to be water proficient—in case we must flee again."

"Flee?"

Yvonne sniggered. "Man, you need a history lesson. The Sparks family *fled* from Virginia. After the War of Independence, many Black Loyalists found a new home in Nova Scotia. Escaped slaves sought refuge with British authorities, who granted them freedom. In 1783, the Brits brought a large group to Nova Scotia."

Yvonne shared that she has a partner, two girls and two boys. Her husband ran the popular local store, "Sparkling Stationary." Daryl would go there for books, pens, notepads, and iPhone stuff, as the DFO provided employees with very little. Yvonne shared that Daryl's pay would be the same as before and that there was more bang for his buck on the South Shore than in British Columbia. Fisheries Officers collaborated with the local vets; one was helpful, Susan Van Aarden, and the other, Timothée Caniton, was "an arrogant and snarky bastard." Yvonne mentioned that he performed lots of sketchy practices on animals and treated wounds or injuries to gang members, smugglers, and Acadians who didn't have a doctor.

"Do you want me to give you a tour around the county?" she asked Daryl.

Daryl looked to the sky and mouthed a thank you.

Yvonne smiled and curtseyed. "At your service, Mr. Fish Cop."

Daryl and Yvonne hopped into the DFO Tacoma, an aged yet reliable truck, and the tour commenced. Yvonne took the wheel while Daryl eagerly absorbed every word she uttered. Yvonne brought attention to a camouflaged mobile home called "The Den" in the Quincy Woods area, which was owned by the DFO and in a run-down state. While the cell service was unreliable, he could access a satellite phone for emergencies or book club meetings. Despite needing some TLC, the mobile home remained sturdy and weather-resistant. Daryl would have to make the trip to The Den on another occasion.

"When you're in the woods, ensure your backpack has a first aid kit and camo bug spray. Buy your own mozzie spray and face net from Cabela's."

"Camo bug spray?"

"BOGO. Buy one, get one free. It sprays out a dark purple and brown paint laden with DEET and dioxin to repel the bugs and bless you with long-term illness. During the Vietnam War, they used the stuff as an anti-foliage agent in the Mekong valley."

Daryl jerked his head back. "What?"

"The U.S. Air Force disposed of two million gallons of Agent Orange, White, and Purple and the DFO bought up a shit load of the stuff as it was such a screaming deal. Spray it on your skin, and your face will look like you've been celebrating Mexico's Day of the Dead."

"*El Día de los Muertos?*"

"Yup, if you use it on your skin, it eats through, and you'll end up like a sugar skull. Take it with you; it is as good as pepper spray."

Daryl shook his head. "Man, this is a crappy gig."

"Woman, actually. Be careful, or I'll report you for sexist language."

"Curious question. What happens if you do that?"

"I report it to the chief. He copies it and submits it to the mayor. She takes it and shreds it. They probably bonk each other afterwards."

Daryl's eyes bugged out. "Are you serious? The chief and—"

"Yes. It's the biggest secret since Clinton and Lewinsky. By the way, ticketing folk for illegal fishing and using non-compliant equipment is a no-no. Ditto for smuggling hooch or contraband."

"What's the point of my job?"

"Daryl, everyone around these parts does it. You don't want to be as popular as a used condom thrown at the Pope in the Vatican. You are a *visual* deterrent. Listen, focus on the things that harm the community. Poaching pisses off people, as does drug trafficking. If you catch folk using illegal lobster traps, confiscate a case or two and ticket them for a misdemeanor. It will curry favour with the locals and show the mayor you're working hard in the field."

Daryl gulped and shook his head, "So, the mayor and Chief Kennedy?"

"Kennedy will nag you with what pisses off the mayor, Bronwyn Quipp. She's a formidable character and wields way too much power. Yes, they are an item—rumour has it that she's a bit kinky—"

"Shut up!"

"You didn't hear that from me. Word is that she self-publishes erotica. *Fifty-One Shades* is heavier and kinkier than the well-known book with a similar name. She writes under the name of *Mistress Piggy*."

"You're kidding?"

Nope. She's a stunning woman, full of curves and charm, whose alter ego is a rather hefty dominatrix. She makes our chief read at least one erotic book a day and tests him on them during their evening 'meetings.' Poor man, I think he's a reluctant participant. Kennedy loves his books and uses 'the book club' as an excuse to escape from the world of whips, nipple clamps, and chastity belts."

"Wowsa. You *attend* this club?"

"Sometimes, depending upon how busy I am. Kennedy is a dick, but a harmless one. He means well; he's just a terrible police officer. Attending keeps him sweet, and he throws me scraps of real work as a reward."

Yvonne continued her guided tour. She said in the summer, Yeovilton was a picturesque fishing town that Americans loved to visit. A high-speed catamaran travelled to Boston via Portland. The town boasted an impressive collection of vibrant Victorian houses painted in a delightful array of blues, yellows, and reds. Three lively wharfs dominated the waterfront, attracting crowds and stealing the show during summer and fall events. A couple of kilometres from the town centre, a large, old, red and white lighthouse was perched on tall, rugged rocks. It provided a picturesque view overlooking Yeovilton Harbour.

Along with its other issues, the town had the unfortunate distinction of having the second-highest teen pregnancy rate in the Maritimes. This phenomenon had been attributed to the county being part of the Atlantic

Bible Belt. Although predominantly influenced by evangelical and Roman Catholic beliefs, the area is also known for its tolerance of alternative religious philosophies. This includes a small sect led by Bhagwan Ramadamadingdong and his Shree Mud-Muk devotees, who are recognized for their bright yellow onesies and the male followers who wear long, yellow beards.

Daryl pointed at a safron-robed shopper carrying a large number of plastic Sobeys bags packed to the brim with groceries. "Hey, Yvonne. That dude with the yellow beard and romper suit, what's going on with him?"

"He is part of a sect with a large plot of land north of Quincy Lake. Occasionally, they appear in town when there's a saffron delivery. They have a strict diet and only eat yellow fruit and veggies."

Daryl chuckled.

"The other . . ." Yvonne paused to find the correct words, "sect—"

"You mean, cult?"

Yvonne cleared her throat, "Yes, cult—is the new 'church-not-a-church' located downtown. They worship—wait for it—the Goddess Aphrodite."

Daryl laughed out loud. "The British folks who run the biggest church in town?"

"The Skanks. Harry and Raylene. They're a nice couple with seven children, all girls. If you ask me, the eldest three are little brats—wild alley cats. Get up to all sorts of shenanigans. The 'church' has grown exponentially. Incredible."

Yvonne shared that Barnes and Noble and nearly a thousand other folk attended.

"Why is it so popular? Goddess Aphrodite? It seems totally whacko."

"One word. Raylene. Enough said."

Yvonne pulled into a large car lot next to the Tuff Mudder, a popular seafood and refreshment hangout. The smell of grilled seafood wafted through the air. Inside an appealing glass exterior, Daryl observed sizable aluminum/steel containers.

Yvonne bragged, "Although they can't sell beer, they still make the best fishcakes in the world. They're very popular with locals and have live music twice weekly. It's almost as popular as the Rum Runner, up in Quincy Lake."

"The moonshine joint?"

"Quick learner. By the way, you don't want to go anywhere near the Rum Runner. Police and DFO are persona non-grata. You can order your hooch from various people in the town or at the church, but give it time, as the locals won't trust you one iota. Losing that source of booze would be catastrophic for all the alcoholics in the county. The proprietor, Gabe, has a philanthropic heart and gives to many needy people."

"Two wrongs don't make a right."

"I'm just giving you some advice. Stay away, my fish cop friend."

"Yes, ma'am."

CHAPTER 11
FLIRTY FISHING

T HE S KANK FAMILY hopped aboard the Good Ship Yeovilton nine months before Daryl's arrival. At the elections, Nova Scotia's Blue Wave Tory landslide opened the door to several new policies, including: favourable visa requirements for spiritual missionaries to "convert the heathen." Ultimately, the vision was to take Nova Scotians to a new, religious utopia. Prohibition and tax incentives for church membership all helped the Skanks make the decision to relocate across the "Pond." Turning down offers of "alternative" churches at Bethnal Green, the Isle of Dogs, and one next to the Asda Superstore in Stepney—they bravely chose unknown shores of Yeovilton County to plant the good seed of the gospel of the Goddess Aphrodite. A bizarre advert placed on Craigslist did the trick. Raylene mistakenly used her previous email address, *FoxyRoxy69*, which she had used during her time as an escort before meeting Harry Skank. Inundated with offers to pick the family up from the airport, Raylene and Harry soon found themselves surrounded by friendly and welcoming Nova Scotians, eager to share their spiritual journeys.

Eighteen large suitcases accompanied them on an Air Canada flight across the Atlantic. He called his daughters, The Seven Sisters, after the tube station closest to his beloved Tottenham Hotspur Football club. Three of the girls were from Raylene's previous relationships. Siobhan, Desiree, and Savanna were baptized into the Aphrodite faith and renamed Blanche

Flower (the eldest), Alison Gilzean, and Stevie Perryman. Four girls were from his loins: Martina Chivers, Christine Waddle, Glenda Hoddle and the newest arrival, Patsie Jennings.

Controversial from the get-go, Raylene and Harry Skank were the talk of the town. Their "flirty fishing" evangelism strategy paid dividends. It became the envy and angst of the church minister fraternal in Yeovilton County.

"They shouldn't use sex to attract people to their church."

"She's nothing more than a harlot."

"Jezebel and Ahab, the both of them."

When the most senior pastor in the community made salubrious comments during devotionals, the ministers felt that mere discussion of the couple's peccadilloes should be forbidden as Raylene was clearly beguiling even the most reverend of them all. Father Murphy was the culprit; the other ministers held crucifixes and crossed towards the hapless priest. "Guys, all I said was I thought her pouty, perfectly formed lips dripped of honey, and her flawlessly molded breasts were as perky as gazelle's horns."

Despite the hostility, rejection, and shunning from the traditional religious community, the Church of Aphrodite grew exponentially. Realizing the growing hostilities, Harry took a leaf out of L. Ron Hubbard's Church of Scientology's book, reimagined the organization, and it became the more mainstream-sounding White Hart Lane Fellowship. A clear case of the whacko becoming the norm.

CHAPTER 12
THE YEAR OF THE CAT

Saul Maçon had to add another cat to his expanding feline clan. Old Tom was an imposing figure with a powerful, muscular physique, dense grey-blue coat, and lightning-fast reflexes. Generally, the rare French Chartreux breed was characterized by their loving nature, bright intelligence, affectionate disposition, and playful personality. Old Tom, much like his master, possessed the same aloofness, intelligence, observance, aggression, and loyalty. Dogs quickly learned to steer clear of Old Tom, as he would chase them away without hesitation.

Old Tom's yelps echoed through the forest after he lost an eye while chasing a porcupine up a tree. The cat scampered after the creature, and as he lunged forward, his head brushed against the porcupine's rear, causing a flurry of quills to be released in self-defence. Three hollow, barbed spines penetrated Old Tom's stunning amber-coloured left eyeball, causing extensive harm and ultimately leading to the loss of the eye.

Not only was Saul heartbroken at the sight of his precious Chartreux, but he also felt crestfallen and frustrated after all the effort he had made to include him in his family. Upon seeing the damage caused by the porcupine to his beloved possession, he couldn't help but confront the sad, wounded creature. His words were laced with betrayal and regret. "I killed for you, and this is how you repay me?" Reflecting on his first murder, Saul regretted the act of taking another person's life—not due to guilt or shame—but more because unwanted attention had been brought to the county.

Another hard truth was that he and his brother, or "brudder" as Saul called him, had made a ton of money breeding Old Tom with female cats, or "mollies." Before accepting a senior managerial position at the Royal Bank in Yeovilton, Old Tom's French owner had paid vast amounts of euros for him. Although loving the company of cats, the intent of the catnapping was a financial one. The tomcat's seed was in such high demand that people were willing to pay exorbitant prices to get their hands on it.

After the incident with the porcupine, Saul and Gabe had the task of finding particular cat breeds with which Old Tom could mate. No easy feat, bearing in mind his new "look." Saul went to great lengths to persuade his discerning cat to sport an eyepatch and emulate a *Pirates of the Caribbean* character. Once Saul was out of sight, the cat wasted no time darting around the house, sending the other household cats into a frenzy. It was as if Old Tom had adopted a swashbuckling persona and relished terrorizing Saul's feline family. Now, with his sinister, one-eyed gaze, Old Tom had a penchant for scaring off the wealthy molly owners, who feared that his missing eye resulted from illness or bad genetics. Drastic times called for drastic measures, and a new tomcat had to be acquired. As the murder of the banker was now a cold-case file, thanks to the stupidity of the local cops and the absurdity of the mayor, the time was ripe for an addition to Saul's family.

This time Saul went to great lengths to arrange the next catnapping, ensuring nothing was overlooked. He would not only be a liberator; he would act to exterminate certain vermin that did not deserve to draw breath. Dr. Hussain would be the target. As was tradition, Saul would talk through his plans with his purring companions. He confessed to them that although he initially regretted his first act of murder in order to take Old Tom, he admitted it left him feeling strangely empowered. He looked a Ragdoll and a Main Coon in their eyes and told them he wanted to be straight up with them—he took pleasure in killing the French banker, especially someone who had little regard for her cat. She had planned to spay the creature. To Saul, it was like Horst Schumann sterilizing Jewish patients at Auschwitz. The more he thought about the banker's slaying, the more he was thrilled to have done it.

In reality, Saul's ill-fated attempt to just snatch Old Tom took a turn for the worse when she crept in front of him in the murky light, holding a slipper in her hand for self-defence. It was an unintended act of violence, a killing that was not supposed to happen. Yet, the experience was undeniably exhilarating. As he returned from the crime scene, the sound of Willie Nelson's "Right or Wrong" played repeatedly in his mind. With a mischievous grin, he sang along to the song. Yes, it felt so wrong to slay the woman, but it also felt so right. He began to see himself as a liberator with unwavering conviction, bringing justice to oppressed felines. The cat was going to be spayed. "What kind of person would do such a thing to you?" he asked the terrified Chartreux contained in the cat box. He didn't consider asking the same question to the tomcats he had neutered himself.

That was then, and this was now. His newly acquired cat was a sight to behold: a stunning Russian Blue with sleek, silver-blue fur. Being well-versed in cat breeds, Saul recognized that this cat would serve as an excellent breeder for him and Gabe. The expensive purebred would take some time to adjust to Saul and his furry clan. Russian Blues were known for their initial shyness, unwavering loyalty, and tendency to form strong attachments to a single member of their human family. Although the cat had not seen his beloved owner's brutal murder, he was a helpless observer as Saul callously pruned her fingers and toyed with her eyeball. Saul speculated that trauma could impact future bonding and attachment to him, albeit to a limited extent. However, if Old Tom moved on from his trauma, why couldn't the doctor's moggie?

Saul understood the doctor's cat was a valuable and highly desired breed. Blaze, Saul's brother, captured a picture of the doctor's pet using a Polaroid camera while working at their house. Taking the cat was a necessity due to Old Tom's predicament. Other factors came into play. Saul was still indignant that the Russian Blue's owner left him alone in the house, missing out on the warmth and affection this intelligent and owner-friendly breed craved. What sealed the deal was the disturbing news Dr. Hussain had told the handsome carpenter who'd been renovating her home. Dr. Hussain was considering taking Boris to Timothée Caniton's veterinary clinic to have him declawed. When asked why she wanted to remove her cat's claws, she confided in the inquisitive worker that it was a necessity because of her unsocial hours at the hospital and Boris' destructive behaviour when left alone for extended periods. The doctor wanted to prevent her cat from damaging the luxurious furniture in her beautifully renovated home.

Blaze also informed his brother that the doctor pressed herself against him, walking her fingers from nipple to nipple on his chest, unbuttoning his shirt and rolling his chest hairs with her fingertips. Blaze recounted how the doctor, with a broad smile, leaned into him and whispered in his ear, sharing that her house was home to a powerful cougar named Dr. Astrid, the true queen of the household. Blaze, with a mischievous grin, told his big brother she wanted to be "the only cat in the household with nails." Saul just about blew a gasket.

Unbeknownst to Saul, Blaze embellished the incident to the nth degree, as he liked to see his elder brother's vein throb in his forehead. Recalling his tête-à-tête with his little brother, he shared the story and his displeasure with his captive audience. "Stupid cow. I should have cut off her slutty fingers with my secateurs when she was *alive* to see how she liked it." Eyes wide open, Boris meekly meowed at his new master. "Nah, you're right. It would've been too loud and a waste of duct tape to cover her mouth."

OLD TOM HELD a high position in the family hierarchy as Saul's stud. There was no way that his new breeder tomcat could be called, "Cat," like the other couple of dozen. No, he would have to have a name commensurate with his standing in the family.

The German doctor's choice of name for her tomcat, Fritz, disgusted him. To honour the Blue Russian's heritage, he renamed the tomcat "Boris" after Boris Yeltsin, the infamous Russian president. Yeltsin once warned Queen Elizabeth II about having a bayonet "stuck up her ass" if she wasn't careful. He loved the sassy attitude of the Russian statesman.

Of course, it would be hard for Old Tom to share his master with another player—but he'd have to suck it up. Saul decided to separate the two tomcats for a season to avoid any fighting. With the cat box in his hands, he could feel Boris' gentle purring vibrations as he entered the barn. Once there, he wasted no time and reached into the container, his hand closing around the warm and squirming body of his new stud. Holding Boris to his chest, he roughly pressed the cat's face against it so he could hear his new master's heartbeat. "My heart is now your heart," he said, lifting him up and looking his cat in his startled eyes. With Boris still trembling in his hands, he imitated a Russian accent and said, "I'll feed you later. You've been through some trauma—so let's settle you down."

He opened the container, repositioned his hands, grabbed Boris by the scruff, and gently placed him into a much larger, fur-lined box. He assured his new acquisition that he could use the new play area once he had settled in. While Saul rubbed sanitizer on his crinkly hands, Boris was notified that he would be introduced to Old Tom, his new buddy. They would have to cooperate as they were both responsible for "earning their keep" for the two brothers. Huddled in the back of his cat box, the petrified tomcat trembled, his ears drooping, as he let out a quiet meow of distress.

With a smile, Saul revealed Dr. Hussain's fake green eyeball from his robe, hoping it would comfort Boris. "Rest assured, your mom's green eye will always watch over you. If all works out well, we'll soon have you making babies with plenty of hot mollies."

Saul walked away, slammed the barn door, and made his way to the front entrance of his house. The sound of countless meows filled the room as he stepped inside. His numerous feline companions flocked to him, except for a distinctively coloured grey-blue cat that maintained its perch on the kitchen counter, locking its master in a penetrating gaze with its solitary eye. He commanded the cat to get down, his tone firm and authoritative. Despite the threat, Old Tom stood his ground, his amber-yellow eye locked on his opponent. "Damn, cat. Don't mess me around—or I'll replace you as number one. Just a reminder, I have Boris now, so if you continue with insolence, it won't end well for you."

Old Tom, displaying an eerie understanding of his owner's irritation, quickly jumped off the counter and disappeared into the bathroom.

CHAPTER 13
MORE TEA VICAR?

Daryl and Yvonne were on the road again. This would be one of the last opportunities for Yeovilton's new Fisheries Officer to ride shotgun with Sparks and familiarize himself with the area and some of the more colourful members of the community. Bobby Bobbitt was mentioned. Yvonne believed that he was "one of the good guys." Bobbitt was in the septic tank business. This was a vital service as over 70 percent of homes were disconnected from the town's sewage system. Bobbitt's home was in the northern part of the county, near Quincy Lake. "If you get lost, wind down your windows and follow your nose."

Daryl opened his palms and shrugged. "Follow your nose?"

Yvonne giggled. "He dumps raw sewage in a huge landfill on his land. Locals refer to it as *Lac Caca*. It's okay, he has a license."

Daryl wasn't sure if the profiler was pulling his leg or not.

"Bobby Bobbitt is sound as a pound and knows all the local gossip. He's not a snitch but is as law abiding and honest as the day he was born. Bobby's one weakness is fresh lobster."

Daryl's eyes opened wide. "Don't tell me . . . knock-off."

"You would be well-advised to turn a blind eye. He is the one guy who would help you out if he thinks you're a decent bloke."

Yvonne's driving was excellent—she managed to avoid the plethora of potholes on the roads left by the harsh East Coast winter. Yvonne chatted away about her life, her hopes, and her dreams. Daryl noticed her accent did not sound like she was a local; it was more like a Massachusetts drawl and pleasant to the ear. She turned into Colonel Road.

"This highway takes you to Quincy Lake, where your wee hideaway is. I'd go there sometime soon. Check it out and see what state the place is in. Give it a clean and buy some provisions. A great excuse to escape Chief Kennedy, Tweedle Dee, and Tweedle Dum."

Daryl nodded.

Yvonne slowed the Tacoma down again, pointing to her right and pulling over five feet from a driveway. "You can't see it from here, but if you follow the driveway, you'll reach Saul Maçon's lakefront place. Before you go creeping, he has cameras in the front of the building but not in the yard area. Like his brother, Gabe, the Rum Runner guy, he's super private. He owns acres of land, which was handed down by his mother after she passed. There are three brothers in all. Blaze, the younger one, is the local Casanova; he's a builder. It's common knowledge he has a liking for recreational substances, if you know what I mean?"

He shrugged his shoulders again. "Yvonne, I really don't care—the joys of not being a cop anymore."

Yvonne put a foot on the gas paddle and carried on her journey. Once again, she slowed down after half a mile and indicated to her right. Yvonne pointed at a large, blue house at the end of a curved driveway with spectacular lake views. "The most expensive in the county," she added. "This is the new pastor's manse. The Skanks came here from the UK and bought the property with cash."

"Sweet. It's huge!"

"Has to be—two adults and seven kids live there."

"Noble shared a little about the pastor's wife. I had to shut him up and change the subject."

"Raylene." Yvonne grinned, showing off her pearly white teeth. "There are lots of rumours. I don't particularly like gossip, but this is a small town. I'm a profiler who gathers intelligence about the locals."

"And?"

"Well, the church has grown and grown from a handful of people to nearly a thousand—pissing off the other local churches as so many of their members have switched fellowships."

"Wow! A revival."

Yvonne smirked. "Or, something a little less spiritual, perhaps."

"Like?"

"Raylene is charismatic, *and* this is only the rumour—"

Daryl stared at the side of her face. "Go on."

"She gives a mean blow job."

"W-w-what?"

"Rumour, Daryl. Rumour."

"What about her husband? Doesn't he know about her 'extra-curricular' activities?"

"Harry Skank. He turns a blind eye. Apparently, her behaviour is called 'flirty fishing.' It's a way of attracting new converts."

Daryl laughed. "What's Raylene's history? Spill the tea."

"She was an escort. I also discovered some old YouTube videos—an accomplished pole dancer. I'm sure she leaves her past discoverable; maybe it's part of her 'flirty fishing' strategy."

Daryl laughed. "I promised my ex I'd attend church in Nova Scotia."

"Apparently, it all cracks off on Sundays at 10 a.m."

"I might just check her—I mean, the church—out." Daryl blushed and hoped his colleague wouldn't report him to the mayor's kinky ethics committee.

Yvonne didn't bat an eyelid. She shared that Harry Skank was soccer-obsessed, and his three stepdaughters were little minxes. All seven were angels in their parents' eyes, but to most other folk, they were little buggers.

"Blanche, Harry's stepdaughter from Raylene's first relationship, has a potty mouth that would rival drunken sailors visiting a brothel."

Yvonne pulled away and turned onto Quincy Drive. The cedar trees were so tall that it was dark and gloomy despite the blue sky and sunshine. Yvonne came to a halt at a fork in the road.

Pointing to her left, she said, "If you take that road up there, you'll get to Bobby Bobbitt's home and Lake Pooh Pooh. As I said: follow your nose. There is a *crapload* of super-sketchy people that live up there. Just don't break down. There's hardly any cell service; if a local sees you in the area, they will likely put a bag over your head, hang you up in the barn, bugger you senseless, and cut you up with a chainsaw."

The words burst out of him like a jolt of electricity. "What?" he exclaimed, clearly taken aback. "Seriously?"

"Just kidding."

Daryl breathed a sigh of relief. *If anyone is going to break down in this area, it will definitely be me.* "Thank goodness I have a non-functional gun, a gill net, a whistle and a taser that doesn't hold a charge to protect me."

"Don't forget you have a top-of-the-range paddle board and notepad," Yvonne jested, taking a right at the fork, and heading towards Quincy Lake. After another twenty-minute drive, Yvonne slowed the truck and nodded towards the left. A fancy sign, "The Rum Runner Tavern," was hanging from the branch of a tree.

"FYI, if you follow the dirt road a quarter of a mile, you'll see several CCTV cameras. There are anti-vehicle barbs that pop out from nowhere onto the road. If you think Gabe is not serious about security, there's a camouflaged machine gun nest and large signs that say, 'Trespassers will be Shot' and 'We Behead Stickybeaks.'"

"What the heck?"

"So, the bottom line is . . . your colleagues at the detachment don't bother him, and he doesn't bother our team. It's just a case of live and let live, Daryl."

CHAPTER 14
OPERATION CHURCH

Daryl Smith had given his word to God that he would attend a Sunday service, and everyone was buzzing about one particular meeting place in town.

"It's so rad!"

"I can't get enough!"

"I run to each meeting; I leave feeling like a million dollars."

"Always a happy ending."

These comments influenced his decision to not attend the local Wesleyan, Baptist, Anglican, or Catholic Churches. The name "White Hart Lane Fellowship" had a comforting and friendly ring. Following his conversations with Yvonne about the Skank family, he thought, "What's the big deal?" and decided to give their church a chance, and see what all the hullabaloo was about. The sight of hundreds flocking to the large, modern building in the town centre was quite remarkable.

Walking to the church on Sunday morning, he passed several ladies carrying banners and placards, their voices raised in passionate chants against the "British Satanic Cult," and "The Abomination that Leads to Desolation." One elderly lady, who appeared to be over ninety years old, raised a megaphone to her mouth and shouted, "The Priestess is a promiscuous slut! She only wants to suck your c—" whereby a younger gentleman, in his sixties, grabbed her loud hailer, put it up to his lips and yelled, "Cash."

The news of the new church spread like wildfire, with many locals lured in by its charm. The church saw an influx of visitors from various towns and villages in the southern part of Nova Scotia. He quickly realized that White Hart church was anything but mainstream, with its unconventional practices and beliefs.

The service was taking place in a spacious building that was once the property of the Wesleyan church, but the Skanks made an irresistible cash offer to the church board. Faced with a vexed congregation without a church building, the Wesleyan leadership resigned. As part of the New Wesleyan Fellowship's church mission, they took shifts to demonstrate against the newcomers who had not only taken their place of worship from them but had removed almost all of the males who had faithfully worshipped there for decades. The White Hart church overflowed with devoted worshippers, and amidst them, Daryl tried his best at concealing himself.

The initial "church" experience was a sensory overload of sights, sounds, and emotions. Daryl found solace in the building being filled to capacity, offering him the chance to effortlessly vanish amidst the throng of people. He dreaded the anxiety that came with new beginnings and unfamiliar experiences. Deep down, he couldn't shake the belief that something would inevitably go awry. True to form, Daryl's self-serving prophecies would once again be proven right.

He occupied the centre seat in the crowded auditorium, right in the middle aisle. He wouldn't normally choose these seats because sitting at the end would make it easier for him to leave if he felt uncomfortable. Not a single sign in sight mentioned Jesus or displayed a cross. The words "Goddess," "Passion," "Lust," and "Intimacy" blazed out from an array of lights.

He chuckled. *Goddess? Lust? This feels a tad weird.*

A ten-piece band played soft rock instrumental music; dry ice filled the stage area. A middle-aged male, dressed in all black and looking like the lead singer from Depeche Mode, appeared through the smoky set on stage. The music abruptly ceased, leaving an eerie silence. From the front, the goth guy's booming cockney voice echoed through the air.

Daryl disregarded the request to stand up if it was the visitor's first time at the fellowship. Awkwardly, he fumbled through his jacket pocket, searching for something that wasn't there. When he heard, "Don't be shy; raise your hand if you're new to our family," he shifted his gaze to the floor.

He let out a long exhale of relief when the same voice boomed out, "This is the *final* opportunity to raise your hand . . . the ushers will hand out free swag for anyone brave enough to tell us you're new to the fellowship . . . I can see you're just waiting to get your hands on that goody bag."

No way, Jose. As much as I'm addicted to receiving swag at events, not this time, matey. Keep your arms down and remain seated.

Sadly, he couldn't escape the profound awkwardness that was about to occur. Congregants were told to hold hands with the person beside them and raise the hand of any unfamiliar faces. Several rows in front of Daryl, there was an elderly lady who had been watching him closely. Her eyes bore into the back of his brain, making him feel uneasy and self-conscious. It was as if his very existence relied on avoiding eye contact, so he fixed his gaze on the ground. Daryl could've sworn that her head swivelled behind her like a tawny owl seeking prey. Beads of sweat started to form on his forehead. He felt like Goose in *Top Gun*, his heart sinking as his F-14 had just lost power in both engines. He peeked, hoping that she had finally stopped staring at him.

Shit. She's waving at me. Goose's fighter went into a deadly flat spin. *Maverick, get me the hell out of here! Go away, woman. Leave me be.*

The lady's arms flailed like a windmill, creating a gust of wind that ruffled his hair. Daryl felt the weight of everyone's stares as he sat rooted to his chair, with people on his left, right and directly in front, all shifting their gaze towards him. He shut his eyes tightly, pretending to be absorbed in an intense moment of prayer. *Oh God, make her disappear.*

The wind grew less intense. He half-opened one eye and peeked. *Take it easy, Daryl. Don't assume the worst. Inhale and exhale.*

Someone gripped his shoulder. Daryl jumped into the air.

"Gotcha!" The crazed grandma stooped and wrapped her bony arms around his head.

In that split second, his heart seemed to freeze in his chest. He couldn't help but feel relieved that he didn't have a full bladder. He was speechless, wanting to fall into the aisle into the fetal position.

Disregarding any objections, she firmly seized Daryl's left hand, summoning the strength of King Kong, and effortlessly pulled him out of his chair, raising his hand high into the air. Looking up at his face, she introduced herself as Mary. Turning to the stage, she flailed her arms frantically towards the goth guy. "Pastor, Pastor," she yelled, "we have a shy one here!"

Daryl tried his best to pull his arm away from Mary's grasp like a man trying to avoid a puff adder strike. The silver-haired banshee was determined —she wasn't letting him out of her grasp. "Pastor, Pastor, his sin is resisting me."

Daryl's face scrunched up. "Sin?"

Nine hundred eyes stared at the unfolding scene, shown on several large screens dotted around the sanctuary. The goth guy at the front of the building with the microphone in his hand yelled out, "Devil, release her in the Goddess' name."

It looked to all and sundry that the man with the mic had the power over both Daryl and or the devil. Daryl gave in through sheer embarrassment. Mary jumped up and down, muttering words in a different language that Daryl did not understand. At first, he thought the woman was speaking in tongues. However, he later found out she was swearing in Acadian patois.

The man with the microphone cried out, "Sister Mary, bring the young man forward."

"OMG, please don't," he pleaded with the old gal, his blood pressure going through the roof.

Mary dragged Daryl through the row of seats, gripping him tightly as they made their way to the front of the building. "Hurry up, little lamb," she panted. Daryl wished for the ground to open up and devour him. It was his absolute worst nightmare. Upon reaching the stage, Mary joined the music team, choir, and the man in black holding the microphone.

Daryl felt the guy's brawny arms envelop him, embracing him in a tight bear hug. The man's face was so close to his that Daryl thought he was going to kiss him.

"Are you a first-timer?"

"Yes." *And a last-timer.*

The person with the microphone asked him his name, whether he was new to the area, his marital status, and whether he had accepted the Goddess into his life.

Daryl cursed the day that he came to church.

"Yes, sir. No, sir."

"No need to call me sir. My name is Harry. Pastor Harry," he said, gesturing towards the congregation with an open hand, "and these are my beloved sheep."

The auditorium erupted with cheers, and baa-baaing filled the air.

Daryl nodded, feigned a smile, and quietly said baa-baa in response.

"What is your impression of the church thus far?"

"Um, it's . . . interesting."

"Just . . . interesting?" Harry turned towards a mass of people. "Brothers and sisters, Daryl here finds us . . . interesting." Many people laughed. Pastor Harry made a sad face, sticking out his bottom lip. He followed this with a series of contorted expressions, drawing riotous laughter.

The mic went back and forth between them. "Why did the Goddess bring you here to our meeting?"

"It's a long story. I was passing by and thought I'd check it out."

Harry Skank turned to the congregation and repeated, "He's got a *long* story. We have all the time in the world, don't we Church?"

"Hallelujah," cried out the entire congregation.

"Preach it, Brother Harry," yelled Mary.

"All the time in the world," he repeated, looking at his Rolex watch and exaggerating a yawn.

"I really don't—I would rather not—I'm feeling uncomfortable—"

"Brothers and sisters, I feel deep within my heart that Brother Daryl is undergoing spiritual warfare."

Boos and hisses rang out from the crowd.

"Prince of darkness, we bind you in the Goddess' name," the pastor yelled.

A cacophony of chants filled the building, "Goddess! Goddess!"

Daryl would rather have soiled an adult diaper in the local mall than endured this craziness. He became ghostly white.

"Do you have friends and family that live with you, brother?"

Daryl shook his head, fearing what else he would be asked.

Pastor Harry turned to the congregation. "He has no friends. In the UK, we would call him 'Norman, No-Mates.' But *we* are his *new* family. Do I get an amen?"

The congregation roared a ferocious AMEN!

Mary, the silver haired matriarch, took the mic from Pastor Harry. "Pastor, this boy is a lost soul."

"A lost soul," yelled the crowd.

"My family will make him welcome. I'm inviting him to lunch with us after the service."

Whoops and cheers rang out.

No, I do not want to go. Daryl stood on the stage with another fake grin, pulled the mic towards himself and said, "I'm sorry, I can't. I'm . . . er . . . working."

Harry addressed the crowd. "Our brother says he's too busy to go to Sister Mary's house for lunch. What do you all think?"

Shouts of "You should go," "Miserable bastard," "Ungrateful swine," and many booing sounds rang out at once.

Daryl squinted at the bright stage lights. A person stood up from their chair and walked to the front of the church. They waved at Pastor Harry to get his attention. The microphone was passed down to the silhouetted figure. Daryl strained to see who the person was.

"Alfonso," cried out the pastor, clearly recognizing the man.

"Pastor, I know this man. Brace yourself, for I have a word of revelation from the divine one that will leave you in awe. This man is definitely not working this afternoon."

Gasps and murmurs from the congregation.

"He is Yeovilton County's new Fisheries Officer."

Sergeant Barnes. You traitor.

Boos and hisses filled the air. A half-full can of Pepsi bounced onto the stage.

Tough crowd!

"Pastor, he is also struggling deep within himself. He is very lonely. He has gayness seeping out of his soul."

Daryl shook his head and blinked rapidly. *Gayness? WTF.*

"He needs our fellowship and kindness," shrieked a middle-aged woman waving a flag the size of South Dakota. "He needs love," yelled another.

Harry retook Barnes' microphone and cupped his hand to his ear. "I hear the Goddess whisper something to me." He stood on tiptoes, reached up, and placed his hand upon Daryl's head. "You must go to Sister Mary's and eat her humble pie. The Goddess extends an olive branch."

What's with the goddess stuff?

Cheers and applause from the crowd.

"Pastor and Mrs. Pastor are included in the invitation, along with anyone needing a delicious meal." Mary was working the crowd. "Who here can vouch for my pie making skills?"

In an instant, countless hands reached for the sky. With a confident gesture, Mary directed Daryl's attention to the excited crowd, a silent plea in her eyes. "Look how much people adore my rappie pie. Can you really say no?"

Daryl gulped. He knew he was fighting a lost cause. He didn't want to hurt the old lady's feelings, despite preferring to grab a ghost pepper spicy chicken with bacon burger from Wendy's.

"Sure," he said. "I'll come."

Pastor Harry addressed his flock. "Let's give Daryl a handclap and tell him that we love him." Raucous cheering greeted Daryl as Mary led him by the hand to return to his seat. Daryl gave Barnes a scowl as he passed by the third aisle. Barnes returned a beaming smile, made a tipped-hat gesture to him, and laughed.

So now it was written in stone, Daryl was going to eat some kind of pie with these crazy people, and he could do little about it.

CHAPTER 15
DOCTOR, DOCTOR

Dr. Hussain's popped-out eyeball was the biggest piece of luck for Saul. Dispatching her was like a "BOGO" deal—Bosh One, Get One free. Not only did he rescue a precious cat, but he also found the evil doctor's eyeball. Saul examined the bottle-green prosthetic eye and googled as much information as possible using a VPN and encryption device. Clearly, her fake eyeball had been made of glass rather than hard acrylic plastic—a sign that it had been made with German precision, as the Germans were one of the few nations still producing and manufacturing prosthetic eyeballs that way.

Saul told his feline family that he had an "eye" for a story and was "looking" to find out the story behind the eye. He surfed the net with his fingers, holding the eyeball near the screen in one hand and the keyboard mouse in the other. Several cats were slouched around his feet and lay prostrate on the dining room table, appearing to watch their master do his thing.

"Eye spy with my green eye, something beginning with F."

He turned the eyeball to look at himself and muttered, "I don't know, Saul?"

"F is for fry. Look and see."

The eyeball stared at the MacBook screen.

Saul had found the story in *Der Spiegel* explaining why Dr. Hussain received her prosthesis. With the help of a translation app, he discovered her obituary and a link to a two-page article regarding the loss of her eyeball. He read aloud so his purring audience would be privy to the information.

Dr. Hussain, formerly known as Astrid Maria Schmidt, was born in the bustling city of Frankfurt am Main, Germany. Saying goodbye to her earthly abode, this remarkable individual, with her precocious demeanour and captivating green eye/s, leaves behind her esteemed father, Herman "Mesher" Schmidt, an esteemed ophthalmologist. Mesher Schmidt's brilliance in his field opened a door for intelligent young Astrid to breeze through medical school and take up residency in emergency medicine.

Astrid wedded Fakir Hussain, a prosperous businessman from Lebanon, and together, they had a son named Jamil, also known as Jamie. The couple were legally married but were living apart at her death. The high-profile breakup occurred due to allegations of domestic violence and the alleged financial connections between the Hussain family and the Abdullah Azzam Brigade, Hezbollah, and Hamas. Full custody was awarded to Fakir based on the laws of Sharia and the Ottoman Empire. Seeking refuge from the tumultuous events of her past, Dr. Astrid opted to start a new chapter in Canada. Astrid Hussain (formerly Schmidt) was discovered brutally killed in her residence in Yeovilton, Nova Scotia. She was 36 years of age.

"Pardon any mistakes in my translation, kitties. It's weird that there's no obituary for her in our local newspaper. I guess the authorities here don't want any bad press." Saul extended his hand for a fist bump with one of his American Shorthairs, and she responded with a loud meow while raising her paw. He adjusted the eyeball to view the screen and continued to read his discoveries out loud.

Doctor Maimed by a French Fry. Infuriated Patient X sues Hospital. Civil Court Finds In-favour of Patient X. Undisclosed settlement awarded to the victim.

Saul learned that a deranged patient in the emergency ward of *Das Bürger* Hospital blinded the "OG" owner of the prosthesis in one eye. While performing her rounds, an incensed patient in the emergency ward stabbed her in her left orbit with an overcooked French fry.

The patient expressed their dissatisfaction with the hospital food, calling it inedible. Paying no mind to the patient's grumbles, the doctor diligently checked him for anemia, specifically examining under his eyelid for telltale signs of iron deficiency. To get her attention, the patient tried to push her away and gestured towards the overdone liver, ham shank, and fries that had been microwaved to death by the hospital's kitchen.

To assess the patient's condition, Dr. Hussain firmly held down the eyelid, scrutinizing for the characteristic pinky-red shade that indicated a healthy state, free from anemia. With the agility of a striking cobra, the unhappy patient seized the charred potato spike and stabbed her in the eye with its sharp, crispy end.

Although initially charged with assault with a deadly weapon, the patient ultimately prevailed in a civil case against the hospital for serving inedible meals to its patients, highlighting grave mistakes made by the German police. Eight months after the stabbing, the plaintiff presented the ham shank and liver as evidence without requiring preservation due to their jerky-like consistency. Patient X introduced a dartboard in the courtroom and skillfully threw the objects at it, achieving a double sixteen and bull's eye, demonstrating their exceptional toughness and inedible qualities. The defending attorney wasted no time in rebuttal, mentioning that the food items were actually called *"Tomahawk-Leber und Schweinshaxe"* or "Tomahawk liver and pork cuts." This gave the patient a heads-up to the food's throwing and impaling qualities, much to the disbelief of the jury.

In the final *coup de gras*, the judge was approached by the plaintiff with a peculiar proposal: to throw the hospital's so-called edible "meat" at the hospital catering manager, Herr Grindlewald, who would act as William Tell, standing next to the jury with a Golden Delicious apple on his head.

The judge, Frau Axtwürdig, an esteemed Olympic bronze medalist in tomahawk throwing, was asked to see if the liver, fries, and ham shank were as accurate as her competition blades. The plaintiff argued that hospital patients should not be expected to eat something so inedible that it could be used in a sporting event or a zombie apocalypse scenario when weapons were scarce.

> *Der Spiegel* reported that, like the French Army during WWII, the defence capitulated without a further fight and agreed to pay millions of Euros in damages. The judge was so impressed with the liver and ham shank exhibit that she asked to take them home with her after the trial.

Saul's jaw remained open throughout the reading. The fake eye looked back and forth from the screen to Saul to the cats and back again as if it was as stunned by the story as Saul was. He read on:

> Due to Astrid's father's connections in ophthalmology, the best prosthetic was created for his daughter's eye. It was a work of beauty as none that came into contact with Astrid could tell she had a fake eyeball unless she looked left or right and her eyeball didn't follow. She learned to always turn her head in either direction to avoid looking like she had lost her mind.

Eight or so cats climbed onto the kitchen table, where his laptop was situated, meowing, and purring as Saul muttered his contempt towards Dr. Hussain and the German Catering Industry.

"Overcooked French Fries are awful. Burnt liver is worse. Acadian fries and sheep liver are the best in the world, my dear kitties."

He wondered if he should have yanked out a couple of the Doctor's crowned teeth to help the police focus upon an even more bizarre motive for her slaying—namely, a homicide fuelled by a need to take artificial body parts rather than simply an eyeball. The local media reported the slaying on page nine of the *Yeovilton Bulletin*—no mention was made of the missing glass eye.

"Here, cat," he called out to an attractive beige and white Turkish Angora. The cat leapt upon his knee. Stroking her long, soft fur, he said, "Maybe they didn't realize she had a fake eyeball, my lovely! After all, the cops here really are that stupid."

CHAPTER 16
HOWIE OF GREEN GABLES

Howie enjoyed his flight from YVR to Toronto, admiring the breathtaking aerial views of the city. Spending time with Daryl was like being in a ray of sunshine. Howie loved a good listener, and it seemed he had found someone he could count on in a crisis. "The guy should become a clinical counsellor; his Rogerian counselling skills were exceptional," he shared with a server he met for the first time at the drive through Tim Hortons on Glen Erin Drive.

Tired of toiling away in an isolated camp and squandering his earnings on illicit substances, he realized it was time to turn his life around. Money wasn't everything, especially when most of it was snorted away, leaving him empty-handed. Seeing his little girl, he felt a rush of warmth spread through his chest. Sure, Megan, his ex, had moved on with her life, and rightly so, but had made it clear if Howie were to be involved in Chloe's life, she would ensure it happened, as long as he stayed sober during their interactions.

Howie had booked three months off work to tour around and try not to spread his seed. It was getting really disheartening with all these paternity lawsuits. Hell, maybe it was time to invest in a prophylactic or two.

Memories of the tall, affable fisheries dude from the aeroplane kept resurfacing in his mind. Daryl's quiet demeanour didn't stop his words from resonating with logic and reason. Sometimes, a person had to follow their heart, and Howie's blood pump urged him to head east towards Nova

Scotia. "I'm gonna fly to Halifax and discover what the universe has in store for little ol' Howie," he declared to a convenience store manager called Mr. Kim on Queen St. East.

As always, little Chloe had lifted his spirits. Saying goodbye to her was difficult, given her stunning blonde curls, striking blue eyes, and contagious smile. Megan's guy didn't seem too bad, but hearing him ask over and over when the dumbass from the oil fields would stop talking, give them a break, and eff off back to Alberta, Howie knew it was time for him to leave. The bittersweet moment of kissing his little angel goodbye was quickly replaced with the exhilaration of reuniting with his pal, Daryl.

Once he searched on Google, he quickly reserved a car and identified several interesting places to visit. Nova Scotia was a hub for lighthouses, and Howie Dorcas had a deep affection for these structures. Hotel reservations had to be made in person, so he couldn't plan to stay at either of the two hotels in the area. Thankfully, there were a plethora of guest houses, so he wouldn't end up out on a limb. Howie meticulously planned a schedule that included travel distances, estimated durations, and occasional coffee breaks.

He had never visited Newfoundland or Nova Scotia before, and he was thrilled to hear that the locals were known to be the friendliest people in Canada. After reconnecting with Daryl, he planned to spend a few weeks with him before travelling to Truro, Nova Scotia; Moncton, New Brunswick; and potentially visiting Anne of Green Gables on Prince Edward Island. Having heard about Anne at school, he assumed the little orphan girl had blossomed into a grown woman. While Howie couldn't find little Annie's hometown of Bolingbroke in Nova Scotia, he thought reaching out to her and exploring Green Gables would be fun. Hell, yes, maybe he could help on the farm for a week or two. Better still, he may be able to spread some of his famous seed and sire some Dorcas-Gableses.

"First things first, Howie, my man. Daryl, I'm coming to see you, buddy. I have some great news to tell you. Then we can hang and spill the tea until the cows on Anne's pastures come home."

CHAPTER 17
THE RAPPIE PIE INCIDENT

MARY TOMAHAWK's dining table overflowed with guests. He knew the Skank tribe, with Raylene and Harry sitting directly across from him. The boisterous Skank children, with their loud laughter and playful shoving, were seated at the far end of the table. To Daryl's left sat Blaze Maçon, the smell of resin and wood smoke clinging to his clothes, and to his right, an Icelandic lady called Björk, her hair like spun gold. An elderly lady, Fanny, sat beside Raylene, her hands clasped in her lap, a quiet dignity about her. However, the old woman's dentures made a disturbing clacking sound against her gums as she moved them around, and Daryl tried hard not to stare.

John, Mary's husband, walked into the dining area, sporting bright red lobster-shaped oven mitts. He held an enormous casserole dish and placed it in the middle of the dining table. Like the calm before the storm, there was silence for the first time since Daryl had entered Mary's home. With a flourish, John exclaimed, "Ta-da!" as if pulling a rabbit from a hat.

The oldest Skank girl pointed to the casserole dish, scrunched her face, and asked, "What is that?"

Raylene glared at her daughter. "Blanche, pointing is rude."

"It's a pie," said John.

"Mum, it looks like shit."

Daryl tried very hard not to laugh. Yes, it was rude and insensitive, but her observation was spot-on.

"W-w-what kind of pie?" asked Blanche, with her mouth upturned.

"Rappie pie," exclaimed Mary. "A genuine Arcadian rappie pie."

Blaze smacked his lips. "Mary has won awards for the best rappie pie in Canada."

Mary blushed, waved her hands at the happy carpenter, and sat at the head of the table.

Daryl stared at the steaming, bubbling, white, and yellow mass before him. Blaze rubbed his hands together.

"Dad. I ain't eating that—I want chicken nuggets," yelled Blanche.

"You can't make us eat that," said one of the Skank twins.

"Why can't we have fries," said the other twin.

Together, they cried out, "We want Burger King!"

Daryl muttered to himself, "Amen."

Harry frowned and gave his children a death stare with his deep-set brown eyes. He reached over to the casserole pot and ladled a large glob of bubbling yellow and white pie into it, then deposited it on his own plate.

To Daryl's surprise, Raylene gagged, took a deep breath, and asked Mary if there was something else she and her girls could eat.

"Pastor Raylene, you've lived long enough in these parts," snapped Mary. "It's time you tried some real, genuine Acadian cuisine."

Daryl swore the pie was moving by some mysterious kinetic energy. Its texture looked as horrendous as anything he'd ever seen—and he'd witnessed some gruesome crime scenes in his past.

The host, John, leaned across the table with a broad smile, grabbed the serving spoon, filled it to the brim with steaming pie, and slopped it onto Daryl's plate with a splash. There was no escape—he'd have to taste it. With disdain, the Skank girls pushed away the Acadian delight and focused on picking at their bread rolls. Following the host's lead, each guest served themselves a modest portion of the fragrant main course. Blaze was the exception, serving himself a triple portion.

Each guest's plate overflowed with rappie pie. Fixing her gaze on Raylene Skank, Mary declared firmly, "Dig in, Goddess! It's time for you to relish our delicious food. I know you'll ask for seconds once you finish your plate!"

Björk said, "Eat up, Mrs. Skank. We Icelanders eat a similarly foul-smelling dish called Surströmming. It is considered by some people to be the stinkiest food in the world. It makes us very frisky. Sometimes, we rub it on our bodies before sex."

Raylene made a huge gulping sound. She appeared to be struggling more than her children. "Just take one big mouthful and swallow. The aftertaste is something else," Blaze, who was halfway through his meal, said with a wink.

The children laughed. There was no way they were going to eat Mary's offering. Instead, they looked at their mother and started to chant, "Mummy, eat! Mummy, eat!" and "Eat the snot. Eat the snot."

Soon, the whole table was chanting "Mummy, eat!" including Daryl, who found it hilarious because Raylene's face had gone from a green hue to a dead skin colour.

"Eat, snot. Eat snot," chanted Björk, not having a clue what snot was.

Raylene took her eyes off the smouldering, moving mass of viscous chow for a few seconds, held up her hands to stop the chanting, swallowed hard, took a small spoonful of pie, and placed it in her mouth. Everybody stared at Raylene.

"See," said Blaze. "I told you it was the best!"

All eyes were fixed on Raylene Skank as the table fell deathly silent. Just as she gulped down her mouthful, Daryl was about to take his first bite of pie.

"Eww," yelled out one of the twins, who turned to the other and grimaced.

Daryl followed suit. He tried to taste it by subtly taking in a breath to mix air with the glob of food. It wasn't that it tasted terrible, but the texture was nothing like Daryl had ever experienced. The mishmash of gooey potatoes, clams and pork fat sent severe warning signs to his amygdala, coupled with Raylene's retching sounds triggered a response he could no longer control.

URGH! GAKK! Retched Raylene.

From deep within his bowels, Daryl found himself joining her: HUUUURGGEHH. HUUUURGGEHH.

URGH! GAKK, responded the distraught woman.

HUUUURGGEHH. HUUUURGGEHH echoed Daryl.

Raylene did the unimaginable and vomited onto the table.

The girls next to John started to dry heave. Daryl could eat most things; however, he had a fragile stomach when it came to folk retching and vomiting. Raylene caught some of the puke in her hands, turned her head and threw up over Harry's shoulder. Harry, in shock, started to gag. Raylene wiped the remnants of rappie pie and vomit from her mouth using a napkin. Without warning, like a fire hydrant expelling water under pressure, she threw up directly across the table and onto Daryl's plate.

Daryl, in turn, threw up over Blaze. Fanny Cruz held her hands over her mouth. Her aged, leathery skin turned mortuary grey; she pushed back her seat and scampered to the guest's washroom. Gut-wrenching sounds were heard from the closed washroom door. Fanny appeared a minute or so later —wiping her face with a bath towel, she sobbed, "My teesh went down nuh toilet." Her husband, Danny, leapt from the dining room table, wiping throw-up from his black hoodie and sprang to Fanny's aid.

The Skank girls giggled and simulated vomiting like it was really funny. Raylene was incredibly unwell, so much so that her face was pressed firmly against the tabletop. Daryl was experiencing relentless bouts of retching and burping. Meanwhile, John valiantly took on the task of cleaning up the mess.

As a French historian, Daryl thought Mary's dining room was a cross between the Battle of Verdun and the "Mr. Creosote" sketch from *The Meaning of Life*. Mary stared catatonically at the table. Blaze wiped Daryl's rappie pie from his face and arm with a napkin—he hadn't batted an eyelid and kept eating the pie. He cleared his plate, burped, rubbed his tummy, and complimented Mary on her spectacular dish.

Daryl stood up, excused himself and left Mary's home. He knew he had to wait for a ride back to the hotel as he had left his car there. Having heard stories of the Quincy Lake folk, he was reluctant to start walking home or hitch a ride, even though he was covered from head to belly in Mary's regurgitated rappie pie.

"What a day," he muttered. "This could only happen to me." Daryl started to laugh, smelt himself, and laughed even louder.

"Something funny, Mr. Fish Cop?" Blaze was by his side.

"Sorry, you just couldn't make this kind of shit up."

Blaze smiled. "I'm heading home. Do you want to catch a lift with me?"

Daryl couldn't face returning to the home to apologize to Mary and John. The chances were he'd never see them at church again. Daryl thanked the man, who appeared to have the constitution of a feral dog and jumped into the passenger seat of Blaze's truck.

The half-hour journey passed quickly as he shared some personal anecdotes. Blaze seemed harmless enough, albeit a little soft in the head. Daryl learned that he was a talented carpenter and generous, as he offered a discounted rate on home renovations for friends, family, and fish cops. Despite Blaze's dislike for religion, he found the church enjoyable and had a soft spot for Raylene and Harry.

When they reached the Best Western Hotel, Blaze asked Daryl if he wanted to indulge in snow-snorting. It was like déjà vu with the Howie guy, sitting next to him on the flight to Toronto. Politely declining the invitation to purchase an eighth of a gram of cocaine, Daryl wished him success in his home renovation business. Blaze dropped him off at the hotel with a mischievous grin as he mock-saluted the Fisheries Officer. The red Tacoma screeched its tires and raced off, leaving a cloud of burnt rubber in its wake.

CHAPTER 18
BLACKMAIL

AFTER THE "QUILL IN THE EYE" incident, Old Tom was in considerable pain. Saul decided to risk taking his beloved cat to the vet as he knew that Dr. Timothée performed outlawed surgeries on cats and dogs, including declawing, tail docking and ear clipping—all performed at outrageous fees. Timothée Caniton would be aware that Saul's cat would be the same one "missing" from the murdered banker's home back in the day. Dr. Timothée accepted a large wad of cash for the procedure.

The vet removed the quills and the damaged eyeball from Old Tom. The operation went without a hitch and the vet commented that it was nice doing business with the gnarly-looking Maritimer. Saul took his trusty mallet, "Thor," to the after-hours appointment, just in case it was needed.

Old Tom's empty eye socket had healed up nicely—he wore a permanent "wink" when looked at. His master fitted him with an eye patch when he was introduced to mollies for breeding. Even before the accident, Old Tom looked like the kind of tomcat you wouldn't want to mess with. Now, the eye patch made him resemble the feline version of the notorious Long John Silver character from *Treasure Island*.

When Saul took his expensive Chartreux to Gabe's for breeding, the molly and the molly's owners were hesitant about allowing their kitty to be accosted by a ruffian tomcat, such was the snobbery existing in the breeding world. Removing the eyepatch made Old Tom even shiftier.

Finally, Gabe had to say something to his brother about the situation with Old Tom.

"Saul, your damned cat keeps winking at everyone."

"You're drunk again, brudder. Get a life."

Gabe pointed at Old Tom, who had journeyed with his master in the truck's passenger seat to the Rum Runner.

"Bro, look at him. He *used* to be handsome. Clients would come across on the fast ferry from Bar Harbour to Yeovilton, just for their mollies to get a bit of Old Tom's super swimmers. Now they take one look at old 'Patch Adams,' there, or 'Henry Winker'—"

"Henry Winkler, The Fonz. There's an 'L' in Winkler," replied Saul defensively, not catching on to Gabe's humour.

"Henry Winker or Cyclops, whatever—they take their molly and run a mile. We are losing money."

Saul went red in the face, and the veins in his forehead pulsated. "Brudder, enough! Old Tom was attacked by a porcupine. Wasn't his fault."

"Porcupines don't attack anyone, dear brother. Old Tom was too stupid to realise that sticking his face into a sea of quills wasn't a good idea."

Saul shook his head. He felt for his favourite cat. Old Tom purred and raised his behind as his master stroked his blue-grey fur. Saddened by Gabe's attitude towards his favourite cat, Saul took possession of his new tomcat, Boris.

As luck had it, he also "found" Dr. Hussain's fake eye and knew what he had to do—make Old Tom handsome again. The choice was to approach Timothée Caniton and ask him to put the eyeball into Tom's empty socket, or leave Old Tom as is, and rely on Boris to start earning his crust. Reluctantly, Saul called the vet. Dr. Timothée had provisionally agreed to perform the surgery, for yet another wad of cash—half now and half post-surgery. This time, the stakes were higher as it would raise questions regarding the origins of the human prosthetic eyeball. The added awkwardness for Saul was that he had found out his cousin, Frankie, had dated Timothée Caniton for a short season. It was all hush-hush as the vet had yet to come out, and he didn't want his practice targeted by the hardline evangelicals in the area.

With a week to go before the surgery, Saul received a call that sealed the deal. Dr. Timothée contacted him late one evening when he was clearly intoxicated. He informed Saul that he needed a lot more cash for his silence. He shared with Saul that he intended to live abroad as he had met a guy called Mario on a dating app who was from Milan. Timothée needed a retirement fund, and Gabe and Saul's enterprise was the very thing that helped him live his best life. He also demanded a greater piece of the pie: 50 percent of all income from wealthy molly owners.

He could also provide additional veterinary services at a premium price in return for his silence. The vet talked way too much during the call, mentioning that he dumped Saul's cousin because Frankie was allergic to cats and dogs and wanted Timothée to find another occupation, move in with him, and live happily ever after as two husbands, despite the government's oppressive anti-same-sex policies. He told Saul he chose to dump Frankie, the looney-tune, and go back onto dating apps to find the man of his dreams, preferably one in another more open-minded country. A stunned Saul listened to Timothée's demands and his dating history.

"Listen, Maçon, I know what you are and what you guys do with the pesky breeder cats. I want a piece of the pie, and I want it now."

"Really?" asked Saul.

"I hold myself to high standards and have a refined palate." Timothée giggled, remarking, "This place is way too outdated for a man of my tastes," before a sudden bout of hiccups interrupted him.

"How much do you want on top of what I've already given you?"

"Fifty thousand, for starters."

"I'll need to talk to my brudder. It's a business decision. I'll get back to you."

"Sure, homie. But do it quickly as I may change my mind and start singing like a canary."

Timothée poured himself another large glass of chardonnay and raised his glass to a white rabbit called George, who was being treated for gastrointestinal stasis. "Georgie boy! You and I are going to be rich!"

George scrunched up his nose and continued to nibble on a piece of lettuce.

CHAPTER 19
A SEPTIC SITUATION

BOBBY BOBBITT HAD BEEN in the septic tank business since he was knee-high to a grasshopper. His No Shit Sherlock septic tank business thrived in an area where the municipal sewer system only served a fraction of Yeovilton's homes. A towering 6'5" of solid muscle and a heart as big as the town itself, Bobby was popular with both the locals and the newcomers. His thick, dark, wavy hair and deeply tanned skin, combined with his customary ear-to-ear smile, were a welcome sight for whoever he came in contact with.

He appeared to work twenty-four seven and always responded to emergencies despite how inconvenient the callouts were; Bobbitt's family were equally amicable. Outsiders chuckled at the name of his septic tank enterprise; they weren't sure how it passed Nova Scotia's registry of companies, but it did.

On one New Year's Eve, Bobby received a call from eighty-four year-old widower Fanny (Nee Crosby) Cruz; she was in total meltdown mode.

"Bobby, I've had an accident—an utter nightmare. The worst thing to ever have happened in my life . . . apart from the death of my husband twenty-three years ago."

"Oh dear." Bobby grinned.

"On the most important night of the year."

"Important . . . 'cause of the New Year's Eve Ball?" asked Bobby knowingly.

"Yep, so please come over. I'm sick with worry."

"I'm getting my own family ready for the ball. Are you sure it can't wait until tomorrow?"

"No, Bobby. I'll die if . . . if . . . if . . . you can't come over."

Bobby sighed. "What's happened?"

"My dentures—they went down the toilet again."

"Can't you pick them out of the bowl yourself?"

"No," snapped Fanny. "I thought flushing them would help them travel into the cistern—then I'd fish them out."

"OMG, Fanny. The cistern feeds the bowl to wash away the—"

"Shit."

"Yes, the wee and poop."

"Oh, I forgot, Bobby. Remember, I'm eighty-four years. Like the parable of the lost sheep: my gnashers are lost and need to be found."

Bobby laughed. While many would have sighed or found an excuse not to attend Fanny's house again, Bobby's generous spirit compelled him to lend a helping hand on her special evening. There was simply no way he would let her down. Bobby also knew Fanny's secret—her habit of purging herself by putting her fingers down her throat before going out on a date or to a meal—so that she would look slimmer in her mind's eye. This would be the sixth call-out in two years.

"Fanny, you're built like a stick insect. Why do you do this to yourself?"

"Young man, I don't need a lecture. I need my gnashers."

Bobby chuckled.

"You see, there's this man I have my eye on, Daniel something. He is so hot—how can I possibly kiss him without my gnashers in?"

Bobby apologized to his family again and told them he would meet them all at the ball later on as he had an emergency. Fanny lived nearby, on an adjacent plot of land to Gabe Maçon and his Rum Runner bar—where the New Year's Eve ball was being held. Everyone who was anyone would be there at the event, as it was the only place in the province that was known to sell booze.

Bobby donned his boiler suit and sped over to Fanny's home. He parked his bright orange septic tank truck with a distinctive Sherlock Holmes pipe logo, unwound a large tube, and went to Fanny's yard without bothering to touch base with the old lady before rescuing her teeth. He dragged the heavy, cream-coloured tube to the area where her septic tank cover was concealed amongst the frosty covered ground.

Bobbitt had regularly cleared out her tank so the job wouldn't take too long. Once the lid was removed, he grabbed a fishing net attached to a pole and plunged it into the dark, smelly abyss. With a bit of luck, he would find the missing teeth in the net and wouldn't have to suck up the sewage from the tank to retrieve them. His arm stretched into the tank and dragged the fishing net back and forth. No luck. He then placed the net deeper, putting his face as close to the septic entrance as possible. He pulled out the net and briefly examined it for her teeth. No teeth. He tried once again. Something solid had been trapped in the net. Bingo! He lifted it up, and Fanny's gnashers smiled back at him. Bobby picked them out of the poopy mess, shook off the crud with his disposable-gloved hand, and walked back to his truck, happy that she did not require the large suction gear. He stored away the pipes back on the rear of his truck. With Fanny's gnashers in hand, he walked swiftly to her front door, knocked, and entered the kitchen.

"Did you find them?"

Bobby produced her teeth, which were in the palm of his large right hand. Fanny was elated, and she jumped up and down with glee on the spot.

"Oh, Bobby, you are my knight in shining armour. Thank you."

Fanny took her teeth, walked a few paces to the sink, and turned on the faucet. Holding her prized possession under the tap, she rinsed off the gunge. Finally, she held them up for Bobby to see. "Look, they're good as new. I can get my midnight snog from that Daniel Cruz." Popping her teeth back into her mouth, she smiled and asked Bobby if he'd like to kiss Daniel's future bride as payment. Bobby laughed, shook his head, held up his hands apologetically, and turned to the door.

"How much do I owe you?" Fanny yelled as Bobby walked away.

"Have it on me, Fanny. Happy New Year."

Bobby loved to tell the story of Fanny's gnashers to all, especially those who were squeamish, something that Bobby certainly was not. Incidentally, Fanny did get a kiss from the unsuspecting Daniel. "It was a good long pash," she told her friends. A week later, Daniel proposed to her, despite being almost half her age; Fanny and Daniel became Fanny and Danny Cruz. Bobby loved that he had been instrumental in bringing the happy couple together.

It came as no surprise to Bobby that Fanny had lost her dentures once again—this time at Mary and John Tomahawk's place. He walked into the front lounge and saw the rappie pie apocalypse in the dining room. The scene of carnage was so shocking that it almost traumatized Bobby Bobbitt.

"So, your guests didn't like your pie, Mary?" Bobby said with a grin.

The Icelandic lady, John, and Mary, were trying to mop the mess on the floor.

"They ain't no Acadians . . . them Skanks," Mary said.

"Well, I'll always love your rappie pie, Mary—next time, invite the Mrs. and me over, and we will eat together."

"Fanny's teeth are stuck in the toilet. We can feel them with our hands. They're jammed around the U-bend of the toilet. We don't want to push them all the way down into the tank."

Bobby took his tool bag into the offending toilet.

"I realized," the sullen-faced octogenarian said, "I love Mary's rappie pie; it was the pastor's wife's fault. She puked over the fish cop guy across the table, and he threw up on young Blaze. The sound of them retching set me off. I ran lickety-split to the washroom, but I ejaculated my teeth."

"Ejected?"

"Yes, ejaculated my teeth into the toilet bowl."

"I'm sure there's a better word you could use, Fanny?" sniggered Bobby.

"Well, my teeth came out and with all of the sick—"

"Enough, Fanny. You're making everyone gag once again."

Bobby removed the toilet bowl and put his hand deep into the pipe. "Thankfully, you have another blockage at the end of the U-bend," he grunted and groaned, huffed, and puffed. He then yelled out that he'd found them. Bobby pulled out his arm and held the teeth up like a prize. "Fanny, before I give them back to you, these teeth need sterilizing. You can't just run them under the tap to clean them."

Mary produced a bucket of soapy water and plunged Fanny's teeth into the liquid. Bobby then walked across the room and gave Fanny a huge bearhug with his large frame, enveloping her lean body in his massive arms.

"I love your hugs, Bobby. It's a shame we are both married. You may have stood a chance with me back in the day before I met Daniel." Fanny looked across at her husband. "No offence; he's such a beefcake."

Bobby pulled himself away, fearing that Fanny's lizard-like tongue might appear behind her pinkish gums. "It's all good." Bobby disappeared to resume his Sunday time with his family.

CHAPTER 20
THE CAT CREPT IN

Saul selected one of his Ragdoll cats and administered a strong sedative. With Timothée's extortionate demands, battle lines had been drawn in the sand. Saul could not trust Timothée to keep his big, fat, greedy mouth closed. It was time to pay the vet an impromptu visit. An eye fell from heaven into his hands, and it was time to make his favourite cat handsome again. The ridicule and rejection were too much for Saul, so it was now or never.

Saul travelled from his home on Colonel Road to Timothée's practice to talk some sense into him with the help of Thor, his trusty wooden mallet. His small Ragdoll was in an extra-large carrier, shared with the mallet and a crowbar. He reassured Ragdoll that everything would be fine and they were on a mission to make Old Tom handsome again. Saul was on a time crunch, and he decided to visit Dr. Timothée at the last minute. As luck had it, Timothée's veterinary nurse had left for home, and the vet's driveway appeared deserted, save for the unmistakable presence of his beloved pink VW Bug, which he often cruised around town in. Saul parked his truck, giving a playful wink to Thor, lying beside the peacefully sleeping Ragdoll cat under a blanket, before hurrying up to the vet's door.

With a sense of urgency, he ignored the "Closed" sign and banged on the tempered glass window, the noise reverberating in the silence. Behind the frosted glass, Timothée Caniton materialized, his silhouette barely visible.

"Sorry, we are shut."

"I have a cat in distress."

"Find him a hobby. I don't take walk-ins unless it's an emergency."

Saul looked down at the cat box and began to sob as he looked at the mallet peeking out of the blanket inside the mesh bars. "It's urgent, he's dying."

The vet wouldn't open the door. "What's wrong with your pet? Is it a cat?"

Saul continued to sob, he was prepared to break into a wail when he heard, "Wait there, I'll get the keys," Timothée said in frustration.

"Hurry, Tiddles is in great pain."

The sound of keys jingling reached Saul's ears, followed by the ratcheting sound of several locks being undone. After pulling back the top and bottom bolts, the door was opened. He couldn't tear his eyes away from the peculiar figure dressed in a vibrant blue hazmat suit. "Saul Maçon! What the—"

"Quickly, quickly," he urged the vet.

Dr. Timothée sighed, his brow furrowed in confusion and motioned towards the inside of his practice.

"Come on in and head straight to my office. Go down the corridor to the right and take the first door on your left to my examination room," he said tersely.

Saul followed his instructions, walking briskly with the heavy cat box.

"Yes, go through the door, and let me see the damned cat," he muttered to himself, but loud enough for Saul to hear.

The veterinarian closed the front door after him and proceeded to his office, following Saul carrying the cat box.

"Now, take the cat carrier to the table and show me the wee thing." Dr. Timothée grabbed a pair of examination gloves from a receptacle on the wall and placed them onto his hands. "Well . . . let me see the critter."

"Tiddles."

"Let me see Tiddles. Tell me what's wrong."

Saul placed the cat box on the floor and reached for the wooden mallet.

"Come on, man, I haven't got all day."

"Tiddles does not want you to see him like this. You's turn around, and I'll put Tiddles on the table."

The vet scrunched up his face. Reaching out both hands to Saul, he said, "Give him to me."

"You's has to turn around. Tiddles ain't happy. You's got to turn around."

The vet rubbed the back of his neck, "Why, for heaven's sake?"

"He's shy."

"Look, Saul. It's late. I finished working two hours ago. I'm tired. I'm happy to help an animal in distress, but you have to give him to me," he said, glancing at his surgery's loud, ticking wall clock.

Saul's nostrils flared. "Turn around. DO IT!"

Dr. Timothée was shocked at the man's aggression. He rolled his eyes, shook his shoulders, and spun around to face his "Beware of Rabies" poster on the notice board. "I do hope Tiddles is overcoming his shyness," he said sarcastically.

"Good. Thor says 'ello."

"Thor? I thought you said his name was Tidd—"

With all his might, Saul swung the ten-pound mallet at the back of Timothée's head.

CRACK.

The vet fell onto the surgery floor with a thump. Blood seeped from his caved-in head. "Dat will teach you to try messing with my brudder and me. Oh, yes, serves you right for dumping my cousin—broke his heart, you did."

With his upper body resting on the examination table, the vet's legs were crumpled beneath him; his arms remained still at his side. Taking hold of his ankles, Saul pulled him facedown to the floor, and dragged the body into the waiting room—leaving a thick trail of blood in its path.

Saul bent down, unzipped his onesie, and retrieved a pair of secateurs and a Ziplock bag from his fanny pack. He held Timothée's right hand and positioned the clippers at the tip of the vet's finger joint. Taking a deep breath, he squeezed tightly, severing the joint. "This is for the declawing . . ." CRUNCH. Continuing his actions, he took the next finger . . . CRUNCH. "That was for the tail and ear dockings. And this, my greedy little blackmailer . . ." CRUNCH, "is for you extorting my brudder and me."

The two digits were left beside where his hand lay. Saul took Timothée's bloody index fingertip and placed it in the baggie, then put it and the sharp clippers back into the fanny pouch. He zipped up his onesie. He had much to do to accomplish his mission.

As Saul reached into the cat box to retrieve the crowbar, he took extra care not to disturb the sedated cat. He used the tool with skillful precision to pry open the vet's secure cabinet. Based on Blaze's verbal description and written plans, he was confident no security cameras were watching his every move. Being safety-minded, the vet had taken extra precautions by triple-locking his doors and using a massive padlock on the medicine cabinet. Saul carefully selected antibiotic meds and placed them into the cat box, one by one.

He grabbed handfuls of surgical equipment and laid them next to his newly acquired veterinary drugs—containers of ketamine, morphine, fentanyl, sodium pentobarbital, diazepam, Dilaudid, and Demerol. "It feels like Christmas, Dr. Timothée; you're so generous."

Saul's eyes narrowed as he spotted Timothée's sleek MacBook on the consultation table. He mercilessly pounded it into fragments with his heavy wooden mallet without hesitation. "That feels good, it does."

Behind the vet's desk, Saul marveled at the vast book collection, organized meticulously in tidy rows. Grabbing a few of them, he went to the front door with a handful of bulky textbooks and gingerly placed them on a chair in the reception room. He carefully grasped Thor, his mighty hammer, and positioned it against the entrance door. His focus then shifted to the lifeless corpse, its head smashed and three fingertips severed.

He bent down, wiped the index fingertip on the vet's green scrubs, and snatched Timothée's phone from his rear jean pocket. As he signed in with his fingertip print, he eagerly scanned the vet's private phone for any new messages, emails, or activity on his dating apps. Calls made to Saul's burner phone didn't bother him because he intended to dispose of Timothée's phone later, aware that only a few individuals knew of its existence. The vet used his primary iPhone for friends, family, and business use. The vet demonstrated his cunning to conceal his illegal wrongdoings by ensuring he left no breadcrumbs or clues. Saul realized that the vet was masquerading as a catfish, hiding his true self as he navigated through the dating apps. He smirked, his eyes gleaming with mischief, and carefully tucked the phone into the baggy. He still had some unfinished business with the finger. Like dipping a fountain pen, he used it to touch the blood pooled next to his head.

The vet's finger wrote "SWIPE RITE," "DIE CHEAT," and "PETA WOZ HERE" onto the floor beside the hapless corpse. "The cops are incredibly stupid and will see your murder as a result of a hook-up gone wrong," he chuckled. "Shouldn't have dated an animal rights activist, eh, you dumbass." The gory fingertip joined the bloody clippers in his pack.

Saul walked to another part of the clinic where several animals were in observation cages. He opened the doors for each pet, including George the bunny. "*Profitez de votre liberté*," he muttered and watched as each animal tasted freedom. A labradoodle made a beeline for the vet's body and tentatively pushed one of the fingers with his nose, which became crimson.

Saul opened the front door, stepped into the eerie blackness, clutched the cat box containing the sleeping kitty, crowbar, and mallet, and walked to his truck. Saul placed his box of goodies on the passenger seat. He returned to grab the large, heavy books, ensuring he left a half-eaten can of tuna on the receptionist's counter. On his return to his truck, he placed the books in the passenger footwell. Revisiting the crime scene for the last time, he shooed away the bunny and the labradoodle from the vet's body, grabbed one of the digits and dipped it into the thick pool of blood. He left the office, turned off the lights, and stopped at the vet's pink Bug. He wrote "YOU SUCK" on the car's windshield, hurled the finger through the office entrance, and yelled, "Field goal!" Saul laughed, hurried to the door, and slammed it shut.

Finally, standing by his truck, he glanced towards the driveway, took off the booties and gloves, and placed them in his bloody hazmat suit pocket. Without removing the soiled one, he stepped into a fresh onesie and climbed into the vehicle.

"I'm coming, Old Tom. Papa is on his way home now."

CHAPTER 21
ELECTRO MAN

The Poskett family had lived on the Poskett Ranch for many generations. To name it a ranch was a family joke. A hundred years or so ago, Grandma Emilia Poskett, a matriarch with thighs the size of a small narwhal, commissioned her husband, Sidney, to create a sign to hang over the entrance to their five-acre property. Sidney carefully and meticulously crafted the maplewood sign that proudly announced "The Poskett Branch" and was to add to it underneath, "Light amongst the Darkness."

As Sidney hung up the ornately carved wooden sign, a lightning bolt struck the top part that poor Sidney Poskett was holding and blasted through the "B." Sidney was not up to withstanding 300 million volts. The force almost cut the old boy in half, vaporizing him apart from a few bones and, miraculously, one bar of Pot of Gold chocolate in the rear of his charred Wrangler jean pocket. Pot of Gold, a Canadian staple—the equivalent of Chernobyl radiated Hershey's—but way "waxier" in taste, proved that it was not only indigestible, but it was also darn right indestructible.

Grandma Emilia refused to have her Sidney buried the traditional way and created a sarcophagus made of galvanized tin, where she lay the remainder of his relics. Every Easter, the Poskett family celebrated Sidney's martyrdom. Family tradition believed Sidney's death was a divine act of terrorism by the devil himself. The Poskett "Ranch" soon became a tourist attraction—not due to Sydney's martyrdom, but the Poskett family's annual Festival of Light celebration which heralded the Easter Bunny.

Many people in Nova Scotia struggle to believe in the resurrection of Jesus. However, the Easter Bunny was not something that was make-believe, and the Poskett clan attributed Easter Bunny Day to the occasion that Sidney Poskett was struck by lightning and shat his pants, or so assumed the medical coroner, who also had a side gig selling cough syrup called "Huck 'Em Up"—a robust concoction of berries, rosehips and cocaine leaves that guaranteed healing for every ailment known to mankind. The Huck 'Em Up remedy cured coughs, colds, lung cancer, rabies, and premature ejaculation.

On inspection of Sidney's carbonized body, the coroner saw some lumpy brown things lying next to Sidney's remains and assumed he had, indeed, pooped himself, as many executed fellows did when subjected to the gallows. However, the coroner's scientific nature got the better of him. He picked up a few brown lumps, popped them into his mouth, grinned and exclaimed, "If that is Sidney's shit—it be the best tastin' shit I've *ever* savoured!" The Poskett clan gasped, and the coroner proclaimed, "That ain't no shit. I believe it's a nut cluster from a box of Pot of Gold!" Everyone cheered, and from that day forth, across all of Canada, millions of boxes of Pot of Gold have been distributed at Christmas, Easter, and Easter Bunny Day.

Now the Posketts had experienced a genuine "act of God," they announced in the local *Yeovilton Herald* that they would put on an annual light display that outshone all other light displays. And so, the legend began.

One hundred years later, the front yard of the Poskett Ranch boasted a towering two-hundred-foot Easter Bunny created by Malcolm Poskett. According to tradition, Malcolm, or Mel for short (as he was known by his friends), would connect his colossal bunny to the National Grid and Old Sidney's Sarcophagus. When the bunny switch was activated, an extraordinary transformation occurred—the towering 200-foot rabbit effigy awakened, emanating a mesmerizing symphony of over 100,000 lights, strobes, and music that blended harmoniously with the pulsating light created. This all led to a power outage of epic proportions.

As the power outage hit the entire municipality, the hum of electricity was replaced with an eerie silence between 7 p.m. and 9 p.m. However, Bunny's lights shone so brightly that they illuminated backyards, roads, and sidewalks within a 10km radius. The regular power outages became commonplace much to the community's chagrin. Mel, who often struggled with forgetfulness, would frequently overlook the time, causing the lighting up to be neither as smooth as a German train schedule nor as accurate as a Swiss clock.

Mel's popularity declined as the residents' hydro bills increased two hundredfold during the Easter Bunny Light Up season. His relationship with his neighbours deteriorated even more when he made it clear that he would use force, including against officials from Nova Scotia Power, to protect his land and the family's sacred sarcophagus. Many people in town invested in generators, but the excessive electricity consumption raised concerns during Bronwyn Quipp's Town Council meetings.

Unconfirmed rumours circulated, claiming that Mayor Quipp indulged in a rather unconventional practice of firing tasers at the Chief of Police's behind during their intimate encounters. Not being able to charge up the taser for continued use disappointed her. However, as the Poskett family had given her a sizeable donation before re-election, she tried to turn a blind eye. Everyone on the council was terrified of her. Only anonymous sources dared to ask her more challenging questions.

Mel was well-known for another reason. When he was not lighting up the town with his Festival of Lights display, he was renowned as a part-time school bus driver who terrified each child that he picked up enroute to their elementary school. He informed each child that he'd rigged up each seat of his big, yellow school bus with an electric shock device and would activate it if miscreants had alighted his bus. Not a word was spoken out of fear of receiving a Mel Shock. That was until the arrival of the Skank family to the area.

In a predictable turn of events, the older Skank girls were banned from Mel's school bus. Mel had given the girls a firm reprimand, leaving no doubt in any of their minds that misdemeanors were punishable by minor electrocution. One of the Skank girls referred to Mel as "Electro Man."

Three of the sisters nodded in silence, a sliver of understanding reflected in their eyes. Blanche and Stevie folded their arms defiantly, their body language conveying their disagreement as he continued with his one-minute diatribe.

Referring to Mel's bushy white beard, the eldest, most "spirited" sister yelled, "Piss off, Father Christmas."

"Yeah. Go sit on a cucumber, dick face!" yelled Stevie.

Mel turned bright puce, his mouth opening wide like a freshly caught fish displayed in a market. He stood in the centre aisle of the bus with arms folded, blocking the Skank girls' entry onto his bus.

"Get out my way, you old fart," said Blanche, trying to push past him

Mel stood his ground and pointed towards the doors, "Get off my bus! Now!"

"Oh, calm down, you old bastard. You'll have a heart attack."

"Yeah, shit-for-brains. Do your thing and drive us to school. Mum and Dad said we had to go on this shit-heap of a bus."

Stevie Skank stuck her nose into the air. "Mum and Dad are the new pastors in town. We live in the biggest and most expensive house in this shithole of a place. So, do your job."

Mel shoved the girls down the steps of the bus, shook his head, which was as red as Rudolf's nose, looked at his watch, and closed the doors. He sat in his driver's seat, turned on the ignition, and pulled away into the road. Mel grabbed the intercom and reassured the other children that rudeness and profanities would not be tolerate. They would never be travelling on his bus again.

"Wanker. Fart catcher!" shouted Blanche as she gave the bus driver the finger as it trundled into the distance.

True to his word, the two older Skank girls never travelled on Mel's bus again. Raylene had agreed to take them back and forth to school daily, much to their father's chagrin. Pastor Harry had received a report about his stepdaughters' behaviour. With a stern face, he talked to the two girls in his study. Raylene was also present and, for support, had her hands on her daughters' shoulders.

"What happened with Mel on the bus?" he growled.

"Electro Man touched my minnie and said, 'I'd like to show you my big, fat snake.'"

"Yeah! He pulled his pants down, licked his lips, and we saw his snake."

"He also grabbed my tits," added Blanche.

"Breasts," corrected Harry.

"Whatever, Dad," sneered Blanche, who continued the lie. "I said to the old fart, if you touch me, you perv. My dad will kick you in the head. I said he used to be a hooligan before he went soft and did the whole religious shit—"

"Religious stuff," corrected her mother.

Harry rolled his eyes and sighed.

"Well, I swear to God that's what happened," said the sisters defiantly and in unison.

The two girls were dismissed. Raylene grabbed Harry's index finger and placed it in her mouth. Her two pouty lips enveloped Harry's finger as she moved back and forth, sucking his digit.

"Harry, forgive the children. Take me right now," she pleaded.

"Okay—but—"

"The girls mean no harm, Harry. They're trying to make meaning of their new environment. Let it go, my husband."

Harry shook his head, unconvinced of his wife's defence of her eldest children.

CHAPTER 22
THE CRÈME DE LA CRÈME

Arriving home at dusk, Saul felt a mix of exhilaration and exhaustion from the events that unfolded at the vet's clinic. Gently laying his snoozy Ragdoll on bedding in the barn, Saul went outside and hastily removed his blue suit, tossing it into the large oil drum. In minutes, the flames danced and illuminated the surrounding darkness. He dumped Thor on the concrete floor and threw the cat box into the burning barrel. He gripped the murder weapon tightly, its weight anchoring him as he stepped into the shower. The cold water cascaded over him and the mallet, cleansing the stains of the night from his skin and soul. The water, initially tinged with red, transformed into a clearer shade as it spun around the large drain. Standing by the barrel, he could feel its comforting warmth seeping into his bones, warding off shivers. Later that morning, he planned to meticulously clean and prepare Thor, using coarse sandpaper and his trusted sander to restore its original smoothness. The first task was to feed the cats—twenty-seven of them. To make things simple, Saul called each of them "Cat." He had three Siamese, four Maine Coon cats, a black as coal Bombay, a strange-looking Devon Rex, a pompous-looking Himalayan, four plain old Shorthaired cats, two super aloof Sphinxes, two Ragdoll blue-eyed beauties, two white Persians, two adorable Scottish Folds, one leopard marked Bengal, and two freakishly odd-looking Oriental Shorthaired cats. Finally, he had his one-eyed Old Tom, the Chartreux, and now, a new family member, Dr.

Hussain's Boris. Altogether, there were twenty-seven. Both male and female cats were spayed, except for Old Tom and Boris.

Saul's intelligence level was off the charts even without a formal education. He eagerly absorbed knowledge about veterinary medicine from online sources and a collection of second-hand journals and books from experienced veterinarians. Disposing of the odious Dr. Timothée had become a necessity. He knew too much and had the gall to want not a piece of the pie but the biggest slice—half of everything he and Gabe had worked so hard to build. Eventually, a handsome reward would be announced on Crime Stoppers, increasing the chances of the unscrupulous vet sacrificing them both. While at the clinic, he devised a plan to gather an abundance of medications and books and leave enough false evidence at the crime scene to confuse the police, mimicking the methods used in the previous two killings. Now that he was completely clean and had disposed of all evidence, he was eager to sit down with his famished family and explain what had happened and why he had been away all night.

Saul was aware that organizations like PETA were adopting increasingly radical methods to combat animal abuse. Timothée's list of heartless and illegal activities included dog and cat declawing, tail dockings, and ear cropping—a direct violation of Bill Z-444, the New Blue Wave's progressive animal cruelty legislation. Among the valuable possessions he had acquired was Timothée's secret portfolio, a compilation of well-to-do clients based in North America.

He gently lifted his one-eyed cat, and settled him on his knee. As he stroked the cat's shimmering coat, he felt its softness under his fingertips. Four other cats gracefully leapt onto the sofa, purring contently as they rubbed against their master. Old Tom ignored them as other family members slumped at his slippered feet. It was as if the cats were on the edge of their seats, eagerly waiting for their leader to spill the tea, and he did.

"The little shit deserved to die." Saul nodded, staring catatonically into space. "Enjoy playing the piano in Rainbow Heaven with your missin' fingers," he scoffed.

Old Tom purred as his neck continued to be stroked.

"I'm gonna make you's handsome again, Old Tom. You's always Ol' Saul's fav-rite. Don't go stressin' about young Boris. He's not like you are. You's always my number one."

Old Tom meowed gently as if he agreed with his master's proclamation. After all, Tom was his breeder cat—the beautiful, rare French moggie. "You's the *crème de la crème*."

It was true. Old Tom was in high demand, with owners travelling long distances to secure his services and ensure the best mating for their molly. His bright yellow-amber eyes shone with intensity, capturing everyone's attention. Old Tom's impressive strength and muscular build made him a prized individual at just five years old. In an unexpected turn of events, the porcupine incident took place. It would be the beginning of the end for the greedy vet, as karma finally caught up to him, and the end of the beginning for his half-blind tomcat, as a new chapter of freedom and happiness awaited.

CHAPTER 23
NO SHIT SHERLOCK

LOST IN THOUGHT, Daryl drove his Department of Fisheries truck, barely noticing the passing scenery. Heading towards Plymouth, east of Yeovilton, he navigated the bumpy highway, dodging potholes and cracks caused by the unforgiving winter weather. Despite being as old as Queen Victoria's Royal Carriage, the Tacoma held up well, cruising smoothly. From afar, he spotted a bright orange tanker parked beside a Ford truck, their contrasting colours standing out against the landscape. Two individuals were gazing into the rear of the truck. Getting closer, he noticed the truck was loaded up with blue crates tightly bound with orange nylon rope. Both individuals shifted their gaze to the oncoming Fisheries vehicle. A skinny man pushed a crate into the hands of another man, who wore huge gloves, and then hurriedly made his way towards his parked vehicle. He opened the door and leapt into the driver's seat. Daryl parked his Tacoma behind the orange tanker. He noticed a faded, hand painted logo on the vehicle's rear, "I'll Take Your Crap."

"Oh, it's Bobbitt's septic rig," he muttered.

The man holding onto the blue crate was enormous, both in height and build. He was wearing an all-in-one set of dungaree overalls without a T-shirt, with his heavily tanned skin showing off arms shaped like billy clubs. *I wouldn't want to get on the wrong side of you, Mr. Goliath.*

Despite looking like he should be on set in a gladiator movie, the man's dark, bushy moustache beamed a smile, baring a white set of gnashers. He put the crate on the tarmac. Meanwhile, the Ford truck sped away at great speed in the blink of an eye.

Daryl took his keys, grabbed his peaked cap, and stepped out of his truck. He pulled up his loosely fitted trousers and walked towards Spartacus.

"Howdy, there!" the big guy smiled.

"Did I drive up at the wrong time?" Daryl smirked.

"Just buying some supper for the family."

Daryl lowered his eyes to the blue crate, got on his haunches, and pulled back part of the lid. A mass of bright red clawed creatures was moving, all with huge pincers tied with green rubber bands.

"Yup, sustainably harvested from the cold, pristine Atlantic Ocean," said the big fellow.

Daryl flipped back the cover and stood up.

The man removed his right-hand glove. "Bobby Bobbitt, owner and operator of Yeovilton County's best septic tank company." Daryl nodded, walked to the side of the orange truck, and looked at a side portrait silhouette of Sherlock Holmes smoking a large, old-fashioned pipe. The smoke formed curvy text. "No Shit Sherlock," Daryl said, sniggering.

"Yep. Pretty darn catchy, eh?"

"Best I've seen in a long while."

Daryl held out his hand to shake and immediately thought better of it, considering the grubbiness of Bobbitt's fingers. Bobby's hand enveloped Daryl's, and his grip was firm but respectful.

"DFO Smith."

"The new guy at Mary's rappie pie dinner. In the flesh. What an honour," he said sarcastically.

"Yep, the same one," *Word sure travels fast around these parts.* "I'm told that you're a nice guy. Well respected in these parts."

Bobbitt smiled a large grin.

Daryl's eyes glanced at the blue crate. "Why don't you buy these at the local fish market or at Sobeys?"

"I'm too busy to get there, Officer Smith." His voice became shaky. "Are you going to give old Bobbitt a ticket?"

"No. I'll give you a pass this time."

Bobbitt bent down and picked up one of the bright red arthropods. "Want one? They cook up real good with butter."

Daryl's face flushed, and he shook his head. "Maybe you could help this new guy out instead?" Daryl mentioned the recent murders and asked the big fellow for his thoughts. Bobbitt's grin left his face. He took off his small peaked baseball cap to expose a mass of raven-coloured, curly hair. He scratched the top of his head and shared that the murders had been the talk of the town.

"Your cop buddies are next to useless; many of us are making sure that we've locked our doors and have our shotguns close at hand."

Not my buddies. "You have any ideas, even if they're wild ones?"

"The murdered folk appear to be out-of-towners. Posh houses, decent people. I welcome new folk moving here; it brings moolah into the community. They bring skills that are desperately needed. Doctors, dentists—"

"Vets."

"Yes, them too."

Shaking his head, Daryl cupped his elbow with one of his hands and tapped his lips with the other. "Why a vet? Did he upset anyone?"

"I didn't have much to do with the fellow. A Frenchie. Broke up with one of our locals, and you'd go to him if you wanted certain services for your pet?"

"Certain services?"

"Yup. Tail docking, ear cropping, debarking, and pet owners would pay a premium for his services. That said, he was good at his job."

"Interesting. On the subject of pets, I'd like to get some company for myself. A nice pet. A dog, maybe. No, a cat or some kittens. Does anyone here sell attractive, healthy kittens?"

"Gabe from Quincy, he's your man. A cat-breeder. High end if money isn't an object."

"I might pay him a visit."

"You'll not be welcome at his place. Hates all things uniform. Especially a lobster cop."

"Fisheries Officer," corrected Daryl.

"I live nearby and see him quite regularly. Want me to ask him? If you don't mind me asking, what are you willing to pay?"

"I'm not bothered about the price for the right companion."

"I guess you have your own place," Bobbitt said. "If you're out in the sticks, having the septic tanks cleared out is always good practice. Remember to give me a call."

"Of course. I'm staying at the hotel downtown. I do want to find my own place soon. An older home that I can afford. Get some renos. Who's the best at an affordable price around these parts?"

"Gotta be Blaze Maçon. Funny little guy, but he does good work. Lock up your wives and daughters, though."

Bobbitt smiled, placed his cap back on his head, and tipped the peak with his grubby fingers. Daryl once again looked at the newer logo on the side of the orange tanker, "No shit, Sherlock."

"You like my logo?"

"I love it!"

"I did a job for some Hollywood people making the sequel to *Love in the Lighthouse* with the actress Kate Wingnut."

Daryl nodded. He had yet to hear of either the movie or the actor.

"They filmed a set by our lighthouse. Trailers and mobile food trucks for the cast and staff. Kate had a luxury gaff." Bobbitt looked up to search his memory. "Yes, *The Lighthouse Keeper's Daughter*, you know the movie?"

"Yes, I think I do," he lied. Daryl was itching to carry on his day, but Bobbitt wasn't finished with his tale.

"Anyways, I got a call from some Hollywood executive, and they had an emergency. They needed me to attend asap. They offered triple-time rates. Kate's mobile cabin had a toilet blockage. Something about her being constipated and having taken some Metamucil or stool softener. Well, it all came out at once."

Daryl rubbed the back of his neck. "TMI."

Bobbitt waved a hand at Daryl. "The truth is the truth. The toilet was super-blocked, and the central pipe leading to all the other cabins was blocked. It had become a log jam, excuse the pun."

Daryl shook his head and giggled.

"I dropped everything and came over. The director sounded desperate, and it would be good call-out money. Kate introduced herself. Very classy lady. Hot as a firecracker, if you know what I mean. She was very embarrassed."

"Shit happens, I guess." Daryl laughed at his own pun.

"Sure does," Bobbitt grinned. "I crawled under the trailer to inspect the plumbing. It was a rookie mistake."

Daryl tilted his head to one side, now invested in Bobbitt's story. "Why?"

"I was under there, armed with my trusty wrench and flashlight. I gently unscrewed the U-bend to see if it moved. Then, I'd go back to my rig and attach the correct pump fitting."

"Right."

"Then WHOOSH! The U-bend section flew off under the pressure of Kate's poop, and the slight release of pressure caused paper and a ton of her scat to spurt into my face."

"Oh my gosh," he gasped in disbelief.

"Yes, sir! 'Tis the Truth. I nearly drowned in Kate Wingnut's shit. The crew pulled me out; no one offered mouth-to-mouth. Some dude, Leonardo De Jotta, the leading man in the movie, hosed me down, thank the Lord."

"The heartless buggers."

"My company, at the time, was 'Bobbitt's Septic Service.' Leonardo Jotta is famous for playing Sherlock Holmes in the *Ripper Mystery* movie."

"Right."

"He came over to me and bravely held out his hand to help pull my soaking body to my feet. I mentioned that it wasn't one of my finest moments, and he laughed and said in his clipped, British accent, 'No shit Sherlock.' We both laughed, and my company was reborn."

"What an awesome story," spluttered Daryl.

Bobby Bobbitt thanked Daryl, relief evident in his voice, for not reporting him. "Don't let me catch you again!" he warned, his voice filled with authority. With a mock salute, Bobbitt effortlessly lifted the crate of lobsters and carefully placed them on the passenger seat of his truck. Daryl returned to his vehicle and swiftly retrieved the Lysol. He vigorously sanitized both hands before heading to Plymouth to survey the surroundings.

The weight of the latest murders pressed heavily on his mind, leaving no room for any other thoughts. Yvonne had a discussion with Sarah, the

SOCO, who described the scene as a gruesome bloodbath, evoking memories of the infamous "Helter Skelter" murders in LA during the '60s. Next to the victim, words were written in blood, a chilling sight that sent shivers down her spine. Chief Kennedy's distress was evident, but he stubbornly refused assistance from the ex-detective sergeant. Instructing Daryl to go to Plymouth, he emphasized the importance of issuing tickets and ensuring the DFO presence was felt.

CHAPTER 24

THE ICEMAN

T HE VETERINARY NURSE discovered the gruesome scene at Dr. Timothée's clinic. Chief Kennedy, Sergeant Barnes, and other officers were at the crime scene within half an hour. Sarah from SOCO was on her way from Halifax.

"This is the third one, Barnes."

"Sir."

"Twenty-two-minute rule. Your thoughts, detective?"

"There's an obvious suspect, sir. Frankie Maçon-Muise. Jilted ex-lover. Frankie claims to be the gayest man in Yeovilton County."

"Probably the only one." Kennedy shuddered.

"Apart from Timothée."

"Damn it, why is everyone in the closet down here?"

"New Blue Wave, sir."

"Why Frankie?"

"He wrote vicious slurs next to his ex-lover's body . . . and on his pink Bug."

"Fingers and eyeball missing?"

"Just the three fingers on his right hand, sir. Both eyes in situ."

"Why three fingers, sergeant?"

"It might be a gay thing, sir. It's a top, bottom, or versatile thing, sir. One, two, three."

"Good, good. Bring Frankie in for questioning."

"Or it may be the number of dates Frankie had with the vet. Peter was the guy that the vet chucked Frankie for."

"Peter?"

"Look, sir, written on the Bug."

"The word is P-E-T-A."

"The serial killer is dyslexic?"

"Now you're clutching at straws, man. The sick and recovering animals were released from their cages. Bloody paw prints all over the place. Smells like animal liberation, if you ask me."

"Frankie may have tried to frame them. Until SOCO arrives, even though it might be a long shot due to the paw prints, we can't count out one of the animals may be the perp."

"Looks like he was bashed on the back of his head, like the other two victims. Unless the rabbit, guinea pig, labradoodle or kitten is over six feet in height when on its hind legs, we can count that hypothesis out."

"Sir, it means this Frankie dude killed them all."

"Exactly. Arrest him, get the confession, and we'll clear up the three killings. Job done, the mayor will be thrilled, and we can get back to our normal police work and our book club meetings."

"New book next week, sir?"

"A corker, Sergeant. A classic. It has an animal theme, so we can, at a stretch, link the book with our work here at the vet's clinic."

"Can't wait, sir."

Chief Kennedy looked at his watch, tapped the face a few times and told his subordinate that he had to debrief Mayor Quipp. He drove off into the early morning sunshine like a bat out of hell, not daring to keep the mayor waiting a minute more than necessary.

SOCO ARRIVED at the crime scene. Sarah was taken aback by the carnage. A dead body, smashed-in head, a pounded-to-pulp laptop, a broken-in meds cabinet, two fingers detached from the vet's hand, a half-chewed finger found hanging from a labradoodle's mouth, and a once-white rabbit called George was soaked in Timothée's blood and perched on top of the dead man's back.

Sergeant Alfonso Barnes was convinced that the culprit was Frankie and that the slaying was a crime of passion. This murder was right up his alley as he claimed to have a nose for sniffing out all things gay, much to his colleagues' chagrin.

Yvonne talked with Daryl before being sent to Plymouth on important Fisheries and Oceans violation duties. She had shared with him that she was increasingly convinced that Barnes was in the closet. His homophobia was so great that, psychologically, he fit the repressed profile perfectly.

"I wish he'd just come out and be at peace with himself rather than accuse everyone else of being gay. It's so childish."

"He accused me of being one in front of the chief and nearly a thousand people at the church. I don't mind, but this area has a reputation for being less than liberal in its views."

"Well, he's in his element. He's arrested a young man and is hell-bent on getting a confession from him."

"But that's nuts. If this was a crime of passion, what about the other two killings with a similar modus operandi?"

Yvonne shook her head. "Twenty-two-minute rule."

SERGEANT BARNES HAD TRACKED down Frankie Maçon-Muise. He had been in Halifax for the last couple of evenings. He returned home to find the interprovincial SWAT team intercepting him in his driveway. Although Frankie appeared to have a solid alibi, Barnes interrogated him for 5-hours without a break. Ultimately, the petrified and shocked suspect agreed to a polygraph test, where he was asked questions like:

- Are you gay, bi, or andro?
- What is your tag name on Grindr?
- Do you watch *Queer Eye for the Straight Guy* on T.V.?
- Are you a top or a bottom?
- Avocado or omelet for breakfast?

In fact, Sergeant Barnes appeared to be more obsessed with Frankie's sexuality and dietary habits than the murders, showing him images of naked men, grape-eating Romans, and a sheep wearing a leather bondage outfit.

Surprised by the ridiculous and inappropriate questions, Frank still managed to pass the polygraph with flying colours, much to Sergeant Barnes' chagrin.

Finally, Chief Kennedy intervened and released Frankie, stating that he was no longer a suspect. Firstly, to avoid a lawsuit from a human rights group, and secondly, Frankie was at a fisherman's convention in Halifax, followed by a '70s dress-up disco at the YMCA. Close-circuit cameras, fellow fishermen, and a doppelgänger of legendary singer Barry White, whom he copped-off with at the disco, corroborated his alibi.

With no other suspects for the brutal slaying of the vet, the mayor had a word in Chief Kennedy's ear, and the murder of Timothée Caniton became yet another cold case file. Sergeant Kennedy's legendary nickname of "The Iceman" came about due to the number of cold case files now on his detective's caseload.

Meanwhile, Saul Maçon could not believe his luck. The local cops were stupider than Jupiter, and he could, if he so wished, carry on murdering people with impunity. However, he had promised the cats and himself that he would go on a hiatus, as he had bigger fish to fry and tomcats to breed. It was time to restore Old Tom to his former glory.

CHAPTER 25
EYE OF THE TIGER

He held the eyeball with his left finger and thumb and called for Old Tom to join him. Initially, the cat appeared hesitant to obey his master's voice as Saul had been yelling at him for drinking water from the toilet bowl. Due to his impaired balance, Old Tom often found himself plunging headfirst into the toilet water. The cat panicked and desperately tried to free itself from the toilet to avoid drowning. His piercing cries and mournful wails sent the other cats in the household scurrying for cover. On several occasions, Saul had come to his rescue, and he had endured his master's scolding each time.

"Darned cat. How often have I reminded you to drink from the water troughs on the ground, not the toilet? What happens if you fall in while I'm away? Cut it out!"

Old Tom finally responded to his master's calls by jumping onto the kitchen table and joining him. Saul wanted to compare the fake eyeball to his cat's real one. Saul used his right hand, finger, and thumb as a makeshift measuring tool to gauge the sizes of his real and the glass eye and their respective orbits.

"Yup, it's bigger, old friend, but I think we can make it work." The tomcat let out a gentle purr. "With some buffing and smoothing, we can have you looking as good as new."

Saul had tritanomaly, a form of colour blindness that made it hard to differentiate between blue, green, yellow, and red due to the recessive gene inherited from his grandmother. In reality, the bright green prosthetic iris was a stark contrast to Old Tom's eye, which had a more subtle shade of amber and yellow.

"Perfect! Actually, it's PURRRRFECT!" Chuckling at his joke, he added, "It's almost as if the doctor gave you her eyeball posthumously."

Old Tom landed on the floor with a nimble jump and swiftly navigated through the sea of subordinate cats. He let out a menacing hiss, asserting his dominance and clearing a path to the feeding trough. Saul watched the other cats move aside for the alpha cat as he made his way to his food. He softly hummed the iconic theme song of the old *Top Cat* television show. "Yes, old friend, you'll soon be restored to your former glory."

Saul had meticulously set up a DIY surgery station in the barn, complete with a modified table for his DIY spaying procedure. He had studied the books he'd pilfered from the dumbass vet. He had to carefully operate on his beloved kitty, making sure to administer the precise dosage of anaesthesia. With only the *Cat Spaying Made Simple* book, a Christmas gift from Gabe as a reference, he was grateful for the vet's textbooks.

With little time to spare, he had hastily carried out the slaying of the vet. There was little option for him once he'd received the blackmail threats. He'd toyed with murdering him after Dr. Timothée had operated on Old Tom, but his angst was such that he couldn't wait a minute longer. "It's all about principle," he said to the cats. "Sure, your brudder would've looked better with some fancy vet work. But I care for him more than life. I may not have much surgical experience, but I make up for it with love."

Saul used large refrigerated grapes to practice his suture-dexterity skills. Occasionally, he'd use orange peel and potato skins. Reading his recently acquired *Atlas of Veterinary Ophthalmology*, he followed the instructions on the page to the letter. He played a veterinary school video and practised his suture craft on each grape.

"It will be easier with real muscle and tissue," he told three feline spectators.

Saul left Old Tom in the barn in his favourite crate, ensuring he'd administered the correct amount of pre-op sedation to the moggie. It was time. He said adios to his family and went to his make-do operating theatre in the barn. His laptop was hooked to a vast screen, and the books were nearby. Saul donned scrubs he'd previously ordered on Amazon, washed his hands, and took the surgical items from the autoclave that he'd used in the past.

Old Tom flopped limply in Saul's hands as he was transferred to the makeshift operating table. Saul carefully anaesthetized him with a concoction of dexmedetomidine, ketamine, and hydromorphone, as per the directions written in a paper dealing with pets that could not be knocked out the correct way, via gaseous infusion. Apart from spayings, he had pulled out porcupine quills from other cats that had lodged in their bodies, sometimes the facial area, but never before had he worked on an eyeball.

Saul talked to his out-of-it tomcat, "Silly, old bugger. Why do you have to do this to me? Them porcupines are nasty critters. Sorry, my old friend. You better pray to God that I get this right." Tears streamed down his face, but his hands remained steady. He held the sterilized doctor's eyeball into a bright lamp. Yes, it was a similar size to the eye socket. His head went back and forth deciding if the eye would be okay. It would be a snug fit, for sure; he had buffed the eyeball as much as he could, and it was still as smooth as silk. The doctor's bottle green-coloured iris and pupil were similar in size to Old Tom's one good eye. The shape of the iris was different. "Nobody will be able to tell the difference."

He carefully snipped and clipped the fur around the eye. Saul carefully followed a couple of informative videos on "intrascleral prosthesis" and "feline intraorbital implant surgery" and made an incision across the skin that had grown over Old Tom's eye socket. Saul pulled down what would be the new lower eyelid and slid the eyeball into the empty socket with a soft plop.

Saul stepped back and admired Mr. Tom's new eye. He was thankful Dr. Hussain's glass eye was high-quality German engineering. "Old Tom, it's a flawless ocular masterpiece—very few countries produce this kind of eye— you're a lucky cat, you are!" He was sweating profusely, and the bright lights from the array of lamps did little to reduce the surrounding heat.

Now came the difficult step. He patted the surrounding tissue with gauze and applied a hemostatic agent to reduce the oozing. With a deep sigh, he sutured up the skin so that the eye would not only be open to display the prosthesis but would stay firmly in place. "I'm sure glad Momma taught me how to use a needle and thread." He stroked Old Tom's blue-grey fur. "There you go: good as new."

Saul was chuffed he'd used the pilfered veterinary surgical books and was doubly happy he never had to deal with the greedy vet again in his life. He had been meticulous in administering the correct amount of anaesthesia to his favourite feline, and he had ample supplies of post-op pain meds to give him. "Come on, old friend. Time to wake up." His final act before the woozy cat roused was to tie a small Elizabethan collar around his neck. Saul continued to gently rub the moggie's tummy. Old Tom started to stir. Saul tenderly carried him to a freshly made bed in a large pen adjacent to Boris, who had witnessed the strange goings on from his own area of captivity. "I'll be back in the morning to give you more painkillers. Sleep, my precious, sleep."

CHAPTER 26
SNAPPY TOGETHER

IT WAS Daryl's first session in the field. Yvonne had given him a tour around the area—where to go—where not to go. Daryl had been online trying to learn a few federal and provincial regulations and policies regarding illegal fishing, lobstering, and some essential poaching legislation. He decided that a few stern warnings would suffice if he caught someone in the act. The Rum Runner's comments from Blaze had freaked him out somewhat, and he would do his best to avoid all things liquor until he established himself within the community.

His DFO base camp was a rusty trailer nestled half a mile into the forest near Quincy Lake. The thirty-five-year-old mobile den was in disrepair. Its exterior was coated in grime and adorned with moss, leaves, and vegetation. Looking at his new working environment, he couldn't help but sigh deeply, overwhelmed by the unfamiliarity of it all. With a mix of surprise and curiosity, he removed the rusty padlock and cautiously opened the door, unsure of what lay behind it. The air was thick with a putrid odour; a mix of must and dampness made him gag. Although not quite as overpowering as the rappie pie smell at Mary's place, it was still incredibly rank. The throwing-up incident at Mary's had left an indelible mark on his memory, forever replaying in his mind. He questioned whether he would experience PTSD in the future. Regrettably, this particular situation was far from ideal. Pinching his nose with his fingers, he stepped into the trailer and opened each window, welcoming the scent of spring into his new workspace.

"My God, when was the last time this place was used?"

He checked the cupboards and found a few expired tins of soup, some canned fruit, and a container of evaporated milk. Daryl grabbed his notepad and quickly jotted down a shopping list. He was relieved to find a sleeping bag neatly folded at the end of the built-in double bed and a few worn cushions for extra coziness.

"If I'm going to stay in this place for part of my job, I'm determined to make it homey."

There were definitely some positives. Escaping the Looney Tunes of a chief was a relief, and not having to deal with Tweedledee and Tweedledumbass was an added bonus. He noticed that the cell service was spotty, with only one or two bars. However, he saw this as a blessing in disguise, as it meant he could skip the mandatory book club meeting and have a valid excuse for not fully participating in the ridiculous gathering. He could make crackling noises intermittently, blaming it on Quincy Lake's notorious cell phone and internet dead zone.

He'd received an email on his laptop:

From Chief Kennedy. Urgent. Tuesday—8 p.m.—sharp. Pre-reading assignment: Chapter 1 PDF and Questions attached.

Daryl clicked on and opened the attachments.

National Velvet by Enid Bagnold.

Daryl rolled his eyes. "A children's book," he smirked. "Perfect. A classic story that never loses its magic!" he said, his voice dripping with sarcasm.

"I vaguely remember flipping through a few pages of this as a kid. I have a memory of Elizabeth Taylor and Mickey Rooney being the main actors in the film. Perhaps I can cheat by streaming the old movie. Way more enjoyable than slogging through countless chapters about a rambunctious horse. Oh God, please spare me from the mandatory book club. I just want to enjoy my own time. Could things possibly get any worse?"

Daryl, once again, felt sorry for himself as he continued to peruse:

Read the first chapter and answer the following questions:

1. *What age group would find this book suitable?*
2. *Where does the narrative occur?*
3. *If you were Velvet's ride—what would you like to jump?*

"Jump? What a stupid question. Durr. The horse would like to *not* jump fences. No, it would rather join the cow and jump over the moon." Daryl sighed and reluctantly read the next part of the email that Chief Kennedy had sent to the team:

Chapter One. I love kinky nooky. The smell of fresh rubber and leather. The squeals. The moaning and groaning. The sweating. The swearing. I love bondage.

Daryl's mouth fell open, his eyes bugged out, and he gasped. "What the flip?" He continued to read, hands starting to tremble.

My number one thing was they need to be my slave. I might give them a chance if they worship me, but if they don't obey—

Daryl snorted and barked out laughter. "Chief Kennedy. You, absolute knob." He rechecked the title. It was *not National Velvet*. It was titled *Velvet Nation: A Kinky Girl's Journey into Politics*," by "Mistress Piggy." Daryl coughed and started to laugh, holding his hand to his mouth in shock. "The idiot sent out the wrong PDF—the wrong freaking book!"

Normally, Daryl would do anything to avoid attending the chief's book club, even endure a root canal without anaesthesia. Now, he couldn't wait, his excitement bubbling up inside him. With a mischievous gleam in his eye, he devised a perfect plan to embarrass the chief.

"I'll deliberately be ten minutes late. By the time I join the meeting, the chief would have realized the error that he's made and apologized profusely, then quickly move on to the *National Velvet* book." With a sense of purpose, Daryl wrote an email containing his carefully considered responses to Kennedy's book club questions. He understood the email would be distributed to the entire group, fostering engaging conversations. He'd purposefully join the Zoom meeting late and ad-lib. Meanwhile, he'd send back answers to the chief's questions pertaining to *Velvet Nation's* opening chapter. Daryl giggled while he wrote out his answers:

1. *What age group would find this book suitable?* Although children are very liberated and worldly-wise these days, the ideal demographic would be 18 Plus.
2. *Where does the narrative occur?* From the vivid description, the chapter is written in a stable when Velvet encounters the submissive stable hand and racehorse owner.
3. *If you were Velvet's ride—what would you like to jump?* As long as Velvet met the legal age of consent, I would prefer to jump *her* rather than any of the horses, the stable hand, or the owner.

With a mouse click, he pressed "return to all" then exited the program. He felt a sense of relief wash over him. With three more hours until book club, his excitement was palpable as he eagerly anticipated the upcoming gathering. He locked the trailer and headed to his truck to retrieve some essentials.

He slipped the DFO ticket and citation book into his top pocket with the non-functioning taser and non-working firearm safely stowed on his belt. After grabbing his backpack, he shut the door of the DFO truck with a bang and headed into the woods. Armed with an old-school map and a basic compass, Daryl Smith ventured north towards the lake, which lay just one click away from the van. He took a deep breath, feeling rejuvenated by the invigorating spring air. The tall cedars created a natural canopy, with patches of blue skies and bright sunshine peeking through. His own breath was visible, suspended in the air.

Daryl didn't love woodlands or forests, claiming he suffered trauma from watching Burt Reynolds and the Banjo playing simpleton in the *Deliverance* movie. He nervously tapped his bright yellow taser and sidearm. "I'm not going to squeal like a piggy for you, Mr. Banjo boy!"

Aware that sunset would be in a couple of hours, he wanted to see the lake and truthfully say he had been on location there. Once back at the trailer, he could make himself a warm brew online and "enjoy" the book club. Then he'd return to his hotel and a nice hot shower, looking forward to a good night's rest. First thing in the morning, he'd shop to buy water, soup, coffee, camping gas, disposable bags and spend another day in his new environment. Peachy!

The light faded away with each step deeper into the woods, leaving an unsettling and foreboding atmosphere behind. The delightful melodies of birds interrupted the stillness of the surroundings, creating a peaceful but weird ambience. "Flip. I really don't want to encounter any unpredictable or shady characters, that's for sure." He checked himself. "Stop it, Daryl! There's a fat chance of bumping into any lobster smugglers up here. Calm yourself down."

Following the map, he made his way towards the lake, which appeared to be straight ahead after going up an incline and down a slight hill. There was a strange sensation of wetness on his neck. He wasn't hot, and there was no sweat on his brow. As he touched the back of his neck, a mysterious, wet feeling sent shivers down his spine, perplexing him. He paused, removed his leather glove, and ran his fingers over his neck, wiping off the dampness. Bringing his hand forward so that he could see what the wetness was.

"What the heck?"

Daryl's hand was a vibrant shade of crimson. He wiped his hand on his green jacket. It looked like blood. Carefully removing his other glove, he used his clean hand to feel the smooth skin on the back of his neck. It felt wet. Once again, he examined his hand and noticed it had turned red. The colour was crimson, like blood. "Yikes, this is definitely blood." Daryl started to freak out. His hand was covered in blood, the deep red contrasting against his pale skin. Daryl was bleeding and did not know why. Casting a quick glance behind him, he couldn't help but notice the ominous presence of a dark cloud hovering directly above him. Large black bugs were swarming all around.

"Oh crap, blackflies!" He started running towards the lake. It began as a leisurely jog, but his pace soon escalated to a brisk trot, and then a full-scale sprint like a swarm of killer hornets was following him. Daryl muttered a string of curses as he realized his mistake of not bringing any bug spray.

Yvonne warned me about the bugs and insisted that I bring bug repellent, the kind that's not good for the environment and savage on the skin because it's full of toxic chemicals.

The black swarm chased after him, and now, sweating like a man trapped in a sauna, he finally reached the lake. The lake was still and would have looked beautiful and tranquil in any other circumstance. Daryl reached the lake's shoreline. Shingle crushed under his size-thirteen boots. He reached down, scooped cold lake water in his hand and washed his neck. He was still bleeding. He opened his backpack to see what he could find. There was a small first aid kit with some hydrogen peroxide, witch hazel, antiseptic salve, and other small bottles. He threw the peroxide onto his hand and furiously patted the back of his neck, hoping to discourage the blood-sucking insects. Sitting on the shingle, he opened tubes of Savlon and TCP cream, mixed them on his large hand, and patted the mixture on the back of his neck. He remembered he had camo spray containing DEET, the type used in Vietnam. He sprayed it onto his face and the back of his neck.

I'd rather die of Agent Orange poisoning than be found in Quincy Lake, sucked dry of my blood by those pesky things.

Miraculously, the black flies backed off, and Daryl felt relief. He then let out an ironic chuckle. "It could only happen to me! The blackflies must've thought, *Yum, Yum. I smell the blood of a British Columbian!*" With an even bigger sigh, he got up, sprung to his feet, pulled up his collar to the max and decided that his day's adventure was over, so he checked the map. He needed to go due south on the compass and get back to base camp before he got himself lost in the woods, as only Daryl would do—then Chief Kennedy would send out a search party—not because he was concerned about Daryl's well-being, but because he'd missed the mandatory book club meeting.

The DFO walked briskly through the woods, not caring who he might bump into. Finally, he saw the dirty white camper alongside his truck in the distance and then sighed in relief.

HISS

"What's that?" Daryl hated snakes. "Hang on," he said to himself. "This is Nova Scotia. Snakes? Springtime? Surely not."

HISS

He glanced around, trying to locate the source of the peculiar sound, before shifting his gaze toward his feet. He was filled with dread at the thought of coming face to face with a Nova Scotia cobra or an Acadian reticulated python. It would be Daryl's luck that a deadly creature had somehow made its way from the Florida Keys and was now poised to take his life.

HISS HISS

There it was! Blended into the dirt path, a dark brown-shelled creature with a serrated back.

"Aww! A tortoise." Daryl laughed. "Hey, little fella!" Daryl bent down and reached out his hand to pet the cute creature. His hand was one inch away from the sweet little tortoise and—

SNAP

SNAP "Argh!"

The tortoise took a massive bite from Daryl's sausage-like fingers. Daryl instinctively removed his hand lickety-split and cried out in pain. "You little bastard!" Daryl had met his first snapping turtle. The offending critter plodded slowly away in the opposite direction. The turtle's powerful jaws took a small chunk out of Daryl's pinky finger, now bleeding and throbbing. "You can't be serious?" He looked at the heavens and said to the universe, "It could only happen to me!" He again grabbed his pack, pulled out the small plastic bottle of witch hazel, and poured it on his finger.

CHAPTER 27
CURIOSITY KILLED THE CAT

SAUL LOVED the peaceful solitude of his home, where the rustling of leaves, meowing of cats, and chirping of birds filled the air. As he dozed off in his mother's rocking chair, a horde of girls trespassed onto his land, shattering the tranquillity. The girls were the offspring of his new neighbours, who bought eight acres of land with 200 yards of lakefront. They ventured onto his private property and explored the large barn next to the white house. The girls stumbled upon a double metal trap door in the back of the barn. With curiosity getting the better of them, they opened it and leaned in to get a glimpse of the basement. When they switched on their flashlight, the dim beam revealed a disturbing sight—a macabre pile of bones stacked one on top of another. The eldest girl's eyes widened as she recognized the skull of a cow and broken deer antlers scattered on the ground. Before the girls could take another step in their adventure, Saul's unexpected presence startled them from behind the window. In an attempt to get their attention and shoo them away, he tapped at it. In unison, the girls spun around to face the source of the unexpected noise, their expressions mirroring a mixture of surprise and intrigue. Piercing screams erupted from the youngest ones.

With the flashlight in hand, the eldest one laughed and boldly shouted at the intimidating figure. Saul was certain that she uttered a profanity and defiantly raised her middle finger, silently mouthing, "Up yours, psycho freak!" Saul darted to the door and intended to grab the miscreant by the ear. Swift and elusive, they vanished into the woods, leaving a trail of laughter and expletives. Eventually, Saul discovered that his new neighbours were a British family who had been brought in to be the pastors of the new church in town.

He addressed his feline family following the trespassing.

"Them pesky girls came onto our land. It's not them girl's fault that they're so rude. It's their parents. Cats, I've never touched a kid, but if the brats' parents end up pissin' me off, Old Saul Maçon will deal with them." The cats meowed in agreement. Word had spread throughout the community about the eldest Skank daughters and their treatment of Mel on the school bus. "They accused Old Mel of diddling them, and he nearly got into a heap of trouble." Saul furrowed his brow and shook his head. "However, any more insolence from them darn oldest ones, and I'll take matters into my own hands. We can't have them sniffin' around these parts."

Saul hastily constructed a barrier with the intention of resembling the wall on the Mexican/USA border stretching from lake to Colonel Road. To do this properly, it would have taken him an eternity and an overwhelming amount of lumber—he had neither the time nor the inclination. Nevertheless, he constructed a fence stretching half a mile along much of the property's boundary. Several signs were erected, threatening trespassers with not only prosecution but also a gruesome fate of being skinned alive. He also communicated through his brother, Blaze, who had a surprisingly amicable rapport with the Brits, asking them to keep their children from trespassing.

Saul had two brothers—both were left property by their mother. Blaze was the youngest, most spoilt, and rebellious. Gabe raked in the money with his illicit moonshine still and Rum Runner bar. He was also Saul's partner in crime when they bred cats. Gabe had a small breeding annex sandwiched between his bar and home. Blaze was a lobster fisherman in the winter season and a carpenter by trade during his non-fishing days. Blaze liked his cocaine, and that, in itself, was an expensive habit to keep up. A lady's man, Blaze, found it a challenge to keep his pecker in his pants.

"Your momma would be ashamed of you," Saul would tell him.

"A man's gotta do what a man's gotta do. I'm just like Old Tom. Always ready to shag a molly, especially when she offers herself up to me. I can't help being blessed with a face and physique like this," he'd say, touching his face, chest, and groin seductively as if he were about to mount a stripper pole.

"One day, you'll cross the wrong woman's husband and you'll be in for it—only a matter of time."

Blaze shrugged his shoulders. "Until that day—I'll sow my wild oats and snort my coke, old man!"

Saul would walk away, shaking his head and cursing his brother for his profligate ways.

CHAPTER 28
A MEETING WITH A GRUFFALO

Ms. Ruffalo loved her job as a career counsellor at the local high school. A positive and happy mother of three, she looked forward to each encounter with her students, all apart from one. She squirmed in her chair, feeling the discomfort settle in as she anticipated the student's arrival. Fidgeting with her drop earrings, Ruffalo's gaze fixated on the large wall clock, bracing herself for the inevitable confrontation with the student. The two subjects he was moderately useful at were sarcasm and passive aggression. The teacher pulled his file towards her and flicked through her strength-based notes.

PLUS: He likes to read, primarily classic books like *Gulliver's Travels* and Frank Richards' *Billy Bunter* series. He enjoys Middle Eastern politics and would like to star in a porn movie.

PLUS: His use of pejorative adjectives to describe fellow classmates and teachers is second to none.

CHALLENGES: Too many to mention.

POSSIBLE CAREER CHOICE: Career criminal or police officer.

Ms. Ruffalo deleted the former with the eraser end of her pencil. *If we get audited, then my pension will be gone.*

The door flew open. In walked Alfonso Barnes, slamming the door behind him.

"Take a—"

Barnes sat behind the teacher's desk, munching gum with an open mouth like a cow chewing cud in a farmer's field.

Glancing up at the clock, she knew it would be the longest hour of her life. "So, Alfonso. Let's cut to the chase. Any ideas what you want to do with your life?"

Standing just under six feet tall, with brown curly hair, a pockmarked complexion, and deep-set hazel eyes, Alfonso threw himself into every hobby and activity imaginable. After a few days he was bored senseless. With the attention span of a wild turkey, Barnes simply found it a challenge to focus and he was known to cut corners to achieve his desired goal. He was quick to accuse his classmates of being "queer" or "gay," yet unbeknownst to anyone, he was in the closet. Alfonso deflected his sexuality upon classmates who were either shy, afraid of him, or both.

His favourite sayings were, "You're so gay," and "In the Middle East, you'd be stoned to death."

Ms. Ruffalo has her suspicions, like most people on the receiving end of Alfonso's acerbic tongue.

"Alfonso, please can you focus for me. What are your career aspirations? You only have a few months left before graduation. I'm here to help you find a job, choose a career path, or point you in the right direction for college."

"I ain't going to do nothing that's gay," he responded predictably.

Ruffalo scratched her head, trying desperately to ignore the homophobic remarks. This was his game, and she wouldn't take the bait. Thumbing through his school file, she had highlighted one or two courses that he'd taken. "You took drama last year—Mr. Sketcher said that you should consider theatre, as you showed promise."

"He's a flamer. He tried to touch me up in the props room."

"What? Alfonso, that's—"

"I'm just kidding. However, it's obvious that all drama students are flamers."

Shuffling in her seat and ignoring his inappropriate remark as best as possible, she countered. "You're taking biology this year. What about a career in nursing or—"

He violently shook his head, "No, thanks. All male nurses are homos. It's a fact."

"What about attending college? University? Technical school? I can help you with applications."

He scoffed, then said, "To do what? Join the Jihad Jane leftie pro-Palestinians on campus, protesting about the State of Israel. Maybe join them sniffing poppers and singing Village People and Gloria Gaynor songs?"

"So, you do care about the plight of the Jewish people?" Ruffalo scribbled some words onto a paper taken from the student's file.

"Piss off. I hate them. But not as much as the Palestinians."

"Language, Alfonso. Please tone it down."

Alfonso leant forward across the desk, smiled, and playfully punched Ms. Ruffalo on the arm. "No, I'm just shitting ya."

The counsellor tapped her fingers on the desk and clenched her jaw. "Alfonso, I looked through your files. You do like reading, and you like watching movies."

He shrugged, frowned, and sat back in his chair. "Woah. I ain't going to no movie theatre with you. You ain't my type. I ain't changing my name to Gruffalo, either. So, if we get married, you'd have to be either Barnes or Gruffalo-Barnes."

Taking a very deep breath, she replied, "It's Ruffalo. Bernice Ruffalo." She picked up a bunch of papers and waved them at Alfonso. "Look, it says so on your career form that you submitted. 'I like reading books and watching films.'"

"I guess I do like some books," he said, pinching the gum in his finger and thumb and pulling it out far enough to stare at it.

"Finally," she muttered to herself, cleared her throat, and asked, "Like what? What books do you like?"

"Pornography," he replied, grinning like a Cheshire cat.

She couldn't resist herself. "Gay pornography?" A playful smile crossed her lips.

Alfonso bared his teeth, "What?"

"Did you like *Brokeback Mountain*?" she smirked, leaned over the table, and punched him lightly on the arm. "Just kidding," she said, winking and letting out a little giggle.

Turning red as a beetroot, he said, "T-t-there are t-t-two jobs I'd like to do—if I could." Finally, her student was pulling a serious face. Ruffalo wondered if it had anything to do with the *Brokeback Mountain* comment. She leaned back and asked, surprised, "There are?"

"Yes. Now you mention it. I'd like to be a critic—either a book or a movie reviewer."

Her head tilted, and eyebrows raised. "Really," she said. "Seriously?"

"Yes. It would be a piece of cake. These critic dudes are stupid AF and have zero qualifications whatsoever—apart from being critical or being able to blow smoke up someone else's ass for a wad of cash."

"Go on."

"Now with AI, you don't even have to be that literate. I could do that job even if I was terrible at English." Alfonso appeared to be on a roll. "All I'd have to do is type it into an AI program, and it comes out with a load of flowery drivel."

"I think there's a bit more to it than that."

"Or I'd like to become a literary agent."

"Really?"

"Yep—I'd get ten per cent for doing absolutely nothing. What a job. Imagine being Prince Harry or Taylor Swift's agent? Badda-bing, badda-boom." He made hand gestures like he was throwing away dollar bills. "Cha-ching, Cha-ching. Easy money. These agents are the worst kind of parasite, and they are lazy shits. They do nothing but collect their ten percent."

"How do you know this?"

"I wrote two influential books: *My Important Life* and *Straight Men Do It Doggy Style*. Yeah, a couple of brilliant memoirs. I sent out a load of letters to various agents, but most of them didn't even respond. The ones that did suggested I send them a formal *query* letter. So, I responded that I wanted representation because I liked it up the ass."

Ruffalo nearly fell off her chair. "What?"

"I don't, of course, but these soul-suckers wanted me to '*query it up*,' so I did. I also attached a couple of dick pics—and didn't hear anything back. What a joke."

"Alfonso, when the agents asked for a *query* letter, it's nothing to do with sexuality."

"Whatever. They don't read anything and throw everyone's work into 'the slush pile.' They reject any newbie authors who don't have ten million social media followers, aren't stuck-up sports or movie celebrities, and aren't their buddies in the publishing or journalism realm. Even you could do that job and never have to do diddly shit for the rest of your life."

Ms. Ruffalo laughed, as much of what Barnes was saying was true.

"Finally, if I had to choose a proper career—I'd like to be a cop. A homicide detective."

Ms. Ruffalo clapped her hands. "Yes, yes. A police officer?"

"Yep. Cops are mostly thick as shit. I like the nice blue uniform, for starters. I'll progress through the ranks as I have an IQ of over 78, and then I'll wear a smart Ermenegildo 'up yours' Zegna fitted detective's suit."

"A police officer's salary isn't—"

"A Glock in my holster—and the best part about the job is I can be as racist and homophobic as I like . . . AND get paid for it!"

"Alfonso. Stop. Your worldview and your language—"

"Sorry, Miss Buffalo."

"Ruffalo, Ms. Ruffalo."

"Whatever."

She composed herself once again. "A police officer? Your worldview, stereotypes, attitude, and language are . . . a perfect fit for such a career." The counsellor glanced at the wall clock, cleared her throat, and said, "I'll note down your choices. I'll put them in order for you based on your probability of achieving your aim."

"Fine."

"One: police officer. Two: a book critic. Three: a literary agent."

"My grades aren't good enough to be a cop. The other two occupations are a better fit as it's easy for me to be a judgemental and useless prick."

"Yes, yes. However, you can be that too as a police officer. I'll look into the qualifications required to join the municipal police rather than the RCMP. You may not need a high IQ; you just have to pass the basic fitness test."

"Sounds good, Miss Gruffalo."

And so, it came to pass. Cadet Barnes graduated from The Maritime Law Enforcement Academy with a solid C-minus grade, spending two years as a probationary constable with the Tatamagouche police force as the shoplifting liaison officer. Out of the blue, Barnes received a call from Chief Inspector Kennedy in Yeovilton on the south shore, asking if he would be interested in joining his book club. If so, he could transfer to Kennedy's elite task force as a detective. The chief had noticed that Barnes had posted a decent review on *Goodreads*, so he used the police database to track down Constable Alfonso Barnes.

Once at Yeovilton, he discovered that he liked Tuesday more than any other day due to the Book Club meetings. As a detective, Barnes underperformed and was swiftly promoted to Detective Sergeant. He was glad he managed to deflect his own insecurities regarding his sexuality onto the new fish cop. His buddy, not buddy, Charlie Noble, was too besotted with Raylene Skank's breasts to notice his tendencies.

Barnes earned his police pay cheque by doing the minimum possible. If only the lunkheaded duo Yvonne and Daryl would keep their stupid noses out of his police work. He wasn't called "The Iceman" for nothing. He knew he was on a highway to receiving police awards, medals, and the coveted Inspector position. He didn't want anyone ruining his rise to detective stardom.

CHAPTER 29
VELVET NATION

DARYL WINCED as his turtle-bitten pinky finger throbbed with pain. It was a few minutes past eight, and he hurriedly logged into the Zoom conference for the mandatory book club meeting led by Chief Kennedy. Opening his laptop, he eagerly clicked on the email from Kennedy, joining the virtual get-together. Unaware of Daryl's presence, Chief Kennedy animatedly discussed Velvet, her sister Meredith, and the horse called The Piebal—the book's star. Daryl smirked mischievously before intentionally switching to audio-only mode. He knew that the meeting would be hilarious. Daryl's finger was pulsating with pain. Even though the turtle only made a shallow bite on the fleshy part of his finger, Daryl reacted as if the turtle had devoured half of his hand. He turned off the sound and placed a few Tylenol tablets in his mouth. He couldn't wait to hear Kennedy explain how and why *National Velvet* got confused with *Velvet Nation*.

Yvonne had insinuated that their boss and the mayor engaged in a risqué affair. Due to a mix-up, some provocative sections from their own R-rated book collection may have been inadvertently switched, resulting in the delivery of *Velvet Nation*.

With careful preparation, Daryl had mapped out exactly what he would say and how he would behave. He assumed Kennedy would have, with a hint of embarrassment, explained to his team the unfortunate mix-up in sending out the incorrect PDF to the entire group. Now, it was his boss' turn to explain the mix-up to Daryl in front of the rest of the team. Daryl was indignant about giving up his personal time for the meeting. He never heard of a Chief of Police or a public figure making their subordinates join a book club.

Furthermore, he had heard that Chief Kennedy recruited Barnes and Noble not for their law enforcement expertise but because their last names coincidentally matched the well-known American book publishing company. Daryl and Yvonne planned to discuss the serial killings in the forthcoming days. The three murders had gone cold, and Alfonso "Iceman" Barnes' involvement caused the investigation to stall. Chief Kennedy and Mayor Quipp hesitated to disrupt the local economy due to concerns about tourism with a serial killer on the loose.

Daryl's mind conjured up possible media headlines: "Fish cop arrests serial killer in Nova Scotia," and "Crack ex-detective solves mystery killings." Daryl's dream bubble was abruptly shattered.

"Daryl! It's good to see that you finally showed up." Kennedy's voice had a disciplined, military quality, sounding sharp and measured.

Barnes' voice cut through the background, dripping with undeniable sarcasm. "Something fishy is going on . . . I guess it's better late than never."

Kennedy spoke once again. "Turn on the camera so we can see your face!"

"Sorry, sir. I can't," he lied. "Sketchy reception. I'm in Quincy Woods working deep, deep undercover."

Barnes burst into laughter. "Are you looking into the thefts of rainbow trout, sardines and kippers from boats at Lighthouse Bay?"

Kennedy interjected, "Fisheries Officer Smith is doing important work in the rural area. By the way, in the UK in the '80s, a person named Mr. Kipper falsely claimed to be the Yorkshire Ripper."

"Can we call Daryl 'Mr. Kipper,' please?"

"Enough! We need to crack on with the book."

Daryl cleared his voice and spoke. "Sir, sorry I'm late. Can I get up to speed?"

Without waiting for an answer, he coughed and told the group he had prepared his answers. He started to spit out the references to *Velvet Nation*. Chief Kennedy tried, unsuccessfully, to interdict, his voice filled with urgency, "Daryl—"

"Sir, I'm sorry to inform you that this area's reception is quite bad. CRACKLE. CRACKLE. I can't understand what you're saying. Hopefully, you'll all hear my answers. I'll kick off by answering the two questions given to the group—"

Kennedy shouted, "DFO Smith—"

Daryl ignored his boss' desperate pleas. "The genre of the book is classified as deep and dark erotica. The sub-genre revolves around BDSM, specifically bondage and domination. Comparative titles? *Fifty Shades of Grey* or *Debbie Does Dallas?*"

"Daryl, I need to talk to you—"

"Question 2. The story unfolds in different settings. In a bed. Within a stable. Underneath a table. Inside a pool. Even while driving a Fiat Pinto. The main character is getting busy all over the place. Domination galore. On page 4, she's like, 'I love how I attach a crocodile clip to your nip—'"

"What? Stop! Daryl, I ORDER you to stop. Did you get my email regarding the error?"

Daryl smirked, *Yep, I sure did* and pretended not to hear. "That first chapter is the real hook that gets people interested. Yes, our protagonist loves kinky cavorting in the presence of horses. The clue is on page 3: 'Making my slave do my bidding is orgasmatronic. It's even better when horses are watching me tie up the thoroughbred's owner.'"

Daryl was ejected from the Zoom meeting.

The chief sent an urgent DM to Daryl.

> CHIEF: STOP! Read the previous email I sent.

> CHIEF: I forwarded the group the wrong PDF file.

Daryl chuckled and punched the air. His phone pinged with multiple messages from Kennedy, Barnes, Noble, and Yvonne.

> YVONNE: OMG, that's hilarious! He's cancelled the meeting and promised a full explanation next week.

> BARNES: Fish face, you're SOOOO dead. Enjoy early retirement.

Noble sent a glyph of SpongeBob burning some bread.

> NOBLE: You are toast. LOL

> CHIEF: It wasn't Velvet Nation . . . it was supposed to be National Velvet. My bad

> CHIEF: I was under pressure from Mayor Quipp and sent the wrong file.

> CHIEF: It was probably Russian hackers. Be sure to show up at the team meeting at 9 a.m. sharp.

> CHIEF: I may be tied up in a meeting with the mayor. I'll entrust Yvonne with the briefing.

"Tied up." Daryl chuckled, packed away his kit and checked the list of provisions he needed for future visits to the camp. He looked at his bandaged pinky finger, padlocked the mobile home door, and climbed into his truck.

He scrolled through his phone's playlist, searching for the perfect song. When he selected Depeche Mode's "Master and Servant," the band's iconic synth-pop melody instantly filled the truck cabin. He smiled, looking forward to getting in touch with Yvonne in the morning. There's no doubt about it, the so-called "Mallet Murders" were going to be solved.

CHAPTER 30
BORN TO BE WILD

WITH THE VOLUME TURNED UP, Howie Dorcas unleashed his love for music, belting out the lyrics with all his might. "Jolene," "Jesus Take The Wheel," and "Country Roads" were a few of the songs that he had listened to countless times, so he knew every lyric by heart. Otherwise, he would roll down the windows of the vehicle, singing gibberish as he replaced the lyrics of a well-known country song. As he drove from Halifax to Yeovilton on Highway 4, he couldn't resist singing his little old songs throughout the four-hour trip.

Howie's rental car was a luxury SUV, and he planned to stay on the south shore for a week or two. He believed that his bestie, Daryl, was at one of the three hotels in the town. "Can't wait to see you, buddy!" Howie loved to talk to himself, and he did so incessantly. Among his many imaginary friends, there was always someone available for him to converse with, no matter the time or place. He knew he had to escape the relentless grind of his heavy-duty mechanic work at the campsite in Northern Alberta. The constant temptation to use and sell drugs was becoming too much to bear. One of his closest imaginary friends was called Daryl Smith. "Long time no see, buddy."

"Daryl, how great to see you. Let's have a beer together and talk. I've much to tell you. I've missed you."

"Yes! Let's chat. I've been thinking about you all day and all night, my dearest and best friend. I'm so excited to hear your stories," said Daryl's imaginary voice.

"Can't wait to touch base with you, too. I knew we would be best friends forever when you started talking to me on the Air Canada flight a short time ago."

Fantasy Daryl said, "Howie, buddy, you're always welcome at my place. How long do you want to stay, buddy? I'm so happy to see you."

Howie responded, "I need to get out of this hotel life. Maybe we could find a place together and be roommates. We could rent a ranch or somewhere nice to relax and hang out. I'm bringing 'sunshine' with me, as you requested."

Howie couldn't wait to see his friend Daryl. He promised to kick the coke habit. However, he did have a few baggies left in his luggage—just in case Daryl wanted to have a little snort of a line or two in celebration.

"Born to be Wild" blared out of the speakers. "I'm heading down the Yeovilton highway, Daryl. We can look for adventures. You and me, baby, we were born to be wild!"

CHAPTER 31
THORN IN THE FLESH

Saul was eager to check in on Old Tom now that he had his new eyeball. He was proud of how he had used the pilfered veterinary surgical books and watched gory videos to perform the intraorbital implant surgery upon his best friend.

Saul winked at Boris. "*Vorsprung durch Technik*, them damned Germans sure know how to make a decent eyeball—no wonder their cars are so reliable and expensive." Saul continued to nonchalantly chat to Boris, who he assumed would understand him due to the cat's Russian pedigree, as the Russians had kicked the Germans' butt during the Second World War.

Becoming tamer and more comfortable with his new master, Boris purred when he was with Saul. Staring at Old Tom's new eyeball, Saul muttered, "It may look a bit odd, Boris, but it will make Old Tom look way better. The mollies will want him to mount them; now he has a nice new eye."

It would soon be time for him to remove the sutures and see how handsome his best friend was. He was looking forward to the unveiling of Old Tom 2.0. Gently stroking the top of Old Tom's head, he whispered, "You've just got to stay away from them damn porcupines, that's for sure!" Saul reached over to a meowing Boris and scratched his neck affectionately as the jealous cat lent into his hand.

"You are a handsome one. We'll make big bucks from your seed, young fella."

SLAM. BANG!

Saul and Boris jumped. The sound of the basement metal doors that led to the furnace startled him.

"Who's in my cellar?"

Saul moved quickly, closing the barn door behind him, instinctively picking up an axe handle that rested against the outdoor shower unit. He walked briskly, turned the corner into the rear yard, and saw several young children running away from the rear of the barn, the cellar door of which was now closed. He counted. "One, two, three, four, five, six . . ."

Saul growled. He stood by the metal doors, waving the axe handle. One of the eldest children stopped before reaching the distant tree line and turned round to face Saul.

"Hey old man . . . piss off!"

The girl was giving Saul the finger and laughing hysterically. One of the other girls joined her and also gave Saul the bird. She called out "Pervert" and "Freak."

The eldest and most sassy girl put her hands on her private parts and yelled, "You ain't getting this, you old prick!"

The two sisters laughed heartily; the remaining children continued to run into the dense woods. Saul could take no more and chased after the kids. One of the girls screamed, laughed, and ran to join her siblings in the woods. The remaining teenager was about fifteen or sixteen. She held her ground and yelled, "Dirty old man," and "You shit-eating, old fart."

Red mist had descended upon Saul. When he finally reached the tree line, the petulant girl had vanished. Saul halted. Rage bubbled up deep from within.

"Damn British kids from that dumbass family."

He asked the trees, "What do I do with them?" He knew he couldn't have these brazenly rude girls trespassing on his land. He baulked at turning up at his neighbour's home and asking the parents not to allow their children to trespass on his property. He knew that pastors' kids were simply the worst. He disliked his new neighbours—they were outsiders—buying up land with their foreign currency. These outsiders were also spewing out a weird cult vibe and had feral kids. What irked him the most were the rampant rumors circulating about his younger brother's affair with the damned woman, who was a tart yet she was telling everyone in the community she was holier-than-thou. "Prophetess, my ass."

No, he didn't want to turn up at the door and confront her. She was seldom at the house with the brats, and her flashy red Mustang wasn't often in the driveway. No, he needed to speak with the man of the house, Mr. Skank, Pastor Skank, or whatever he called himself.

Saul hated being "on the radar" for obvious reasons. However, the tribe of banshee-like daughters needed to be taught a lesson—but how?

CHAPTER 32

WHODUNIT

"Tell me about the murders."

"Have you no shame?" Yvonne giggled.

Daryl smirked. "About what?"

"Chief Kennedy. Your contribution to the book club Zoom meeting? Poor man."

Daryl jerked his head back.

"The chief was clearly struggling."

"*Velvet Nation.* Give me a break. The guy is clearly the biggest jerk—"

"*National Velvet,*" corrected Yvonne.

"The idiot sends out Triple X-rated erotica to his staff—that they *have* to read *in their own time* and—"

"*National Velvet,* a cute story about a child and a horse, and you brought attention to our boss' mistake?"

Daryl lowered his brows. "Yup."

Yvonne's scowl turned into a smile. "Well, it was hilarious. To hear him stumble, stammer, and mutter to himself through the first five minutes and hear his ridiculous excuses was golden."

Daryl rubbed his eyelids. "He told me someone hacked his account."

"Oh, his super-secure police account. Right."

The two colleagues fist-bumped each other.

Daryl frowned. "Changing subject, the murders . . . any updates?"

"Nope. Detective Sergeant Barnes said it was now a cold case."

Daryl rolled his eyes.

The detachment was empty, and the civilian employees working in the front office were separated. Yvonne winked at Daryl and walked to the front of the room to the whiteboard, picking up a marker pen. "This is how we used to do it in Quantico. So, who do we have as victims?"

A familiar voice from the canteen hatch cried, "Rub-a-dub-dub, three maids in a tub, and who do you think were there? The doctor, the banker, and the candlestick maker are not going to the fair."

"Constable Noble, can you just grab your coffee and skedaddle off to where you're supposed to be going?" Yvonne snapped, not wanting to do her profiling until only Daryl was present in the room.

"Touchy," he replied, with coffee in hand. "I hope Alfonso doesn't catch you reopening his cold case file." Yvonne pulled a fake smile and waited for him to leave the canteen.

"What's with the candlestick maker thing?" asked Daryl.

"It's an old British nursery rhyme. He was being a jerk. So, this is what we have so far, in chronological order:

Victim #1 The Banker.

Victim #2 The Doctor.

Victim #3 The Vet."

Daryl was now in his cop zone, relieved that he wasn't thinking about crustaceans. "Spill the tea for the banker."

Yvonne scribbled on the board:

- Two years ago
- Blunt force trauma to the rear of the head
- Tidy crime scene
- No prints or other DNA
- Bludgeoned in the living room
- No forced entry
- No sexual assault
- Half-opened can of Clover Leaf tuna in the kitchen
- No sign of kitty cat
- Out of towner, French.

Yvonne did the same for Dr. Hussain, adding a fact that Daryl wasn't aware of, "She had a prosthetic eyeball—very high quality, apparently—and three fingers cut off."

Daryl's head jolted backwards. "What? Where, how?"

"We talked to her husband in Jordan after breaking the news to him. His wife was a doctor and lost her eyeball in Germany, having been attacked by a crazed patient."

"Ugh. You're kidding."

"Nope. Anyway, the eyeball was missing. Sarah from SOCO 'looked' everywhere."

"They have 'an eye' for things like that."

"We kept the information from the media. Dr. Hussain was a German National."

With a puzzled expression, Daryl ran a hand through his hair, questioning, "I mean, who would even think to take someone's eyeball?"

"Maybe they like playing marbles? I don't know, Daryl."

"Funny, not funny."

Yvonne turned to the board and added, "Missing eyeball, kitty, and half-eaten can of tuna."

Daryl fidgeted, waiting for his coworker to record their observations from the vet's murder scene.

- Messy
- No forced entry
- Half-eaten can of tuna
- Blunt force trauma; back of the head
- Three fingers were cut off
- *Helter Skelter* messages, including PETA WOZ HERE, DIE CHEAT, SWIPE RITE and YOU SUCK on the vet's car—all written in blood with the vet's index finger
- Animals released
- Meds and textbooks taken.

"It was staged to look like a jilted lover or a crazed animal rights enthusiast," said Daryl.

Yvonne sighed. "Sergeant Barnes and his sidekick, Chief Kennedy, believe that it was some kind of revenge gay-slaying. The vet recently broke up with a local boyfriend, Frankie Maçon-Muise."

"So, it could have been Frankie?"

"Nope. There was more chance of it being George, the white rabbit. However, Barnes put Frankie through interview hell; his alibi was verified—he was in a bar in Halifax with a male exotic dancer. Barnes travelled north and stayed overnight to personally interview the dancer."

"Was that really necessary?"

"Barnes claims to be fastidious." Daryl's eyes widened. "I didn't say either diligent or bright. Barnes is convinced that Frankie took out a hit on his former lover. A crime of passion—without any other suspect."

"And . . . that's it?"

"Yep. Kennedy signed off on it. Death by suicide."

"What the fu—"

"Just kidding. Calm down. It's now a cold case."

"After a few weeks? Cold?"

"Yup. That's why they call Barnes *The Iceman*. The Mayor, Bronwyn Quipp, is hellbent on not involving outside sources and wants the case closed. Bad for tourism."

Daryl shook his head in disbelief, so much so that there was a danger of it leaving his neck. "Bad for tourism? So is being murdered by a nutter who likes cutting off fingers and snacking on cans of tuna." Daryl frowned and walked to the whiteboard, holding out his hand to receive the marker pen from Yvonne.

"Sit down. This is my job." Daryl quickly stepped two paces back and stood, arms folded, staring at the board.

Yvonne continued, "The coroner believes the perp for each killing is a right-handed male. Six-one to six-five. SOCO shared the vet was slain standing with his back turned to the examination table and dragged to the centre of the clinic, fingers chopped off and one of them used to write the messages in blood."

Daryl read the masses of marker pen written on the board and pointed at it. "So, commonalities. All victims were out-of-towners. No forced entry. Blunt force trauma from behind, possibly a wooden hammer or mallet. Cans of tuna. Pets missing or released. The latest two had three fingers chopped off."

"Good, we have a theme here."

"All serial killers have some kind of name attributed to them."

Yvonne returned a frown and shook her head.

"I think we go for The Kitty Cat Killer; Tuna Fish Finger Fairy; The Out-of-Town Slayer or—"

"The Mallet Murderer."

"Ooh, I like that one!"

"What is obvious is that the killings are getting gnarlier."

The colleagues discussed the lack of forced entry, assuming the victims either knew the perp or he had access to the buildings. Blaze Maçon's name was mentioned, as all three properties had recently been renovated. They disqualified him as a prime suspect, as Daryl pointed out that he would have to have used a step ladder to strike the victims going by the coroner's suggested height.

Daryl sighed. "We must leak this to the RCMP in Halifax."

"Can't. Kennedy would go batshit, and you'd be so fired."

Daryl shook his head; his neck was becoming sore with excessive movement.

"And . . . his dominatrix of a boss, Miss 'Good with the Whip' Quipp, would make sure you never worked again."

"You can't make this shit up."

"Nope. But who will be next?"

"The candlestick maker," said Constable Noble, returning to the room for his break.

CHAPTER 33

CONUNDRUM

SAUL WAS IN A PREDICAMENT. Old Tom's injured eye was healing well, and despite being slightly larger than his good eye, it gave him a sophisticated and charming appearance. Saul might need to readjust the orbit to make it more secure, requiring more medical supplies in the future. In that case, he would have to buy them from a legitimate supplier or send Dr. Sue Van Arden, the only remaining veterinarian in the area, through the unicorn gates to meet up with her pesky colleague. Despite the incompetence of the police investigators, Saul Maçon couldn't take the risk of being discovered. He had Boris as a substitute for breeding, but it was still in the early days of the process. Saul let out a prolonged breath, his cheeks deflating as he exhaled.

However, the pesky Skank family was driving him nuts. The brat children grew bolder, with the older two seemingly immune to fear. Their mother, Mrs. Skank, seemed to have an unusually close relationship with his brother, just like she did with most of the community's male members. This enchanting outsider had a way of captivating everyone with her irresistible charm and sensual energy. Her husband, the pastor of the stupid culty church, appeared to be an utter dick.

"I can't believe he dared to move into my hood, buy a multimillion-dollar home, and try to influence the community with his wackadoodle religion and love of soccer." Greeted by meows, he continued, "This parasite is drawing locals away from Acadia's traditional sports, like hockey and lacrosse." The cats meowed. "Hmm," he told his feline family. "I hear you. I did promise that I'd be taking an extended break after the vet's slaying. Sooner or later, the proper cops would get involved, and it may be difficult to stay under the radar."

What Saul did like to do was murder in his imagination. "Cats, if I were to take out a Skank, which one? Husband or wife? Or the entire family? It would be very close to home. Next door. The police would be bound to come and talk to your papa, being neighbours and all that."

Saul's rule of thumb was to eliminate if—and only if—absolutely necessary. The Skanks had no cats to rescue. However, the young 'uns made his blood boil. He looked at Old Tom and scratched his neck. Old Tom purred. "Let's hold the 'absolutely necessary' plumb line to this situation. The Skanks." He put his index finger to his mouth.

"Are they outsiders? Yes. Are their deaths useful to Gabe and my purposes? No, but murder for the common good may be a yes. Has Blaze completed any renovations at their house? Yes, and he was currently renovating the 'priestess.' Would it be risky? Yes. Would I enjoy dispatching them? Oh, yes." Winking at Old Tom, he said, "Mmmm. I need to focus on you, my old friend. Let's see if Gabe can pull off the pending molly exchange with a wealthy Florida woman."

Old Tom vibrated and rubbed up against Saul's face.

Saul had promised Gabe that he would ensure Old Tom looked as good as new with the perfect match Gabe had found for breeding. With the molly's owner paying a substantial deposit for the cat's mating, Saul devised a plan to bring Old Tom to Gabe's place and let nature take its course. As Old Tom purred beside him, his mind zeroed in on the task ahead.

"The Skanks will have to wait," he muttered, determined to prioritize his and his cat's needs. "In the worst-case scenario, I will try to talk sense into Mr. Skank. After that, if the girls trespassed, it would be at their own risk."

Saul picked up his best friend, kissed him gently on the nose, and studied his handsome face.

"Yep, I think you'll be just fine," he reassured him with a smile. Each eye was so similar that it was hard to tell them apart. "What molly could resist a handsome fellow like you?" he said, unable to hide his playful smile. Several other cats tried to leap on Saul's lap, desperate for their master's attention.

Old Tom batted them away with his large paw. "I'll reach out to my brudder, drop you off at Gabe's, and leave you for a night or two. After you've finished with 'Golly Miss Molly,' we can make a few thousand bucks and then move on to Boris for the next set of matings."

Old Tom leapt from Saul's lap and headed to the washroom's toilet bowl to slurp some water.

"Old Tom! Stop. How many times have I told you? Drink water from your bowl like your other family members." Old Tom stopped what he was doing, trained his neck to look at his owner, hissed, and headed to the water trough.

"Attitude," reminded Saul.

Old Tom caused a kerfuffle with the other cats by hissing and swiping at them to get out of his way. His siblings all fled the scene, and Old Tom slurped down the water. Happy that Old Tom had obeyed him, Saul emptied some Friskies onto a saucer and placed it next to the stroppy cat, who rubbed his neck against his master's fingers. "Good chat," he told the tomcat, happy he had decided his next steps.

CHAPTER 34
CHERNOBYL

HER DATING PROFILE looked promising to Charlie Noble:

- Fluent Acadian speaker
- Loves books
- Military parades are a turn-on
- *Call of Duty* champion
- *Dungeons & Dragons* Adventurer
- Enjoys travel
- Thin as a noodle
- Has great boobs

Sonda McAllister appeared to be the perfect match from the get-go. The first date went well even though she turned up to Taco Bell in her PJs and rubber boots. They both ordered fried food, and she glugged down two big refills and swore like a trooper. Noble didn't mind her attire, as most Nova Scotia women dressed up like this, and he wanted to connect with a real-life Acadian.

She didn't warm up to his best pal, Sergeant Barnes; she confided that there was something "of the night" about him. Moreover, she loathed the new, trendy church that attracted most of the eligible men in the town due to the Skank woman giving them all boners.

Sonda and Churr sounded a bit like a famous '60s pop duo when referred to as a couple.

"Sweetheart, I've never been keen on my own name . . . but why did your parents call you a girl's name?"

"Churr is hardly a girl's name."

"It sounds like a type of girlie salmon."

"That's why I like being called Noble."

"You haven't answered my question?"

"My father had a sense of humour."

"A sense of humour?"

"You know the answer to the question; you just want me to say it."

"I have no idea what you're talking about?" Sonda lied.

"He was fascinated by nuclear fission and reactors."

"I don't understand?"

"You do, you just want me to say it."

"No, I don't. Tell me?"

"He was obsessed with a certain nuclear power plant in the Soviet Union in the '80s."

"Hun, that's way before my time. What did he call you again?"

"Churr Noble."

Sonda spat out her coffee and belly laughed, rolled on the floor, and nearly choked on her tears.

"There it is!" Noble shook his head in mock disgust.

"The joke never gets old. BOOM! Sorry, inappropriate, 'boom,' not as in the reactor exploding." Sonda continued to laugh at her own joke.

Churr "Charlie" Noble loved it when Sonda laughed, though he would not readily admit to it. The couple loved to dress up and engage in role-play. Sonda, a heavily set woman, unlike her dating app profile and picture, would don her Daenerys Targaryen dragon-rider kit; Noble liked to dress up as an English clergyman with a dog collar, a large cross and a black robe. Each time, Noble would ask her to stand before him and read from the *Book of Reverse Moroni*, the Skank's holy book, while he grabbed her tits and stuck his finger in her heavily lipsticked mouth.

"You need to stop with the finger thing," she complained. "How can I read your favourite passages and suck your finger at the same time?"

"It's a big turn-on for me. I love the sucking feeling."

"For crying out loud, are you thinking of that Skank bitch again?"

"No, no, my love," he lied, looking shocked and hurt.

"It's a freaking cult. If you want to go there and wet your pants, then go fill your boots. But don't expect me to be here when you return."

Noble shook his head in mock disbelief.

Sonda offered a compromise. "Look, I'll grab my old shield and sword, paint my face red with fake blood, and whisper Norse swear words to you while you bonk me?"

"You know I have a soft spot for Lagertha, the shield-maiden from *Vikings*."

"Then stop dreaming about Raylene Skank, and I might fulfill your deepest fantasies."

Their joy of role-play started during an innocuous game of *Dungeons and Dragons*, where they conversed in an online chat room. However, their relationship grew deeper playing *Pokémon*, and they became inseparable after an extended *Polly Pocket* Tiny Garden game.

During one memorable date, Sonda made Noble vow not to go apeshit after she took him to the Rum Runner for his first illegal drink. He kept his word but warned her that it wasn't the kind of establishment that a police officer should be seen at. Noble moved into her home and then took out a mortgage on a property about a fifteen-minute drive from the town centre. Sonda recommended that Blaze Maçon help with some minor renovations before Charlie moved into the property.

His new place was twice the size of hers, and she already had young children from previous relationships—Arnold and Barney, two very rambunctious kids at elementary school. Aware of Noble's fixed budget, Blaze walked around the home, measuring and jotting things down in a small pocketbook. Blaze's list included two large windows, one attic and one skylight. Noble explained he wanted the large living area converted into three rooms, including two small ground-floor bedrooms for the boys. He also wanted the master bedroom modernized to include an en suite for himself and Sonda.

Noble asked the carpenter how much it would cost, as he had a minimal budget.

"I can't say," Blaze responded, "but not much. You'll be thrilled with the end product. I'll need a downpayment to buy the materials." Noble complied, wrote him a cheque for a few thousand dollars, and continued living at Sonda's place. Blaze asked him to wait until the job was finished before he saw what a fabulous reno he'd done.

"I'm a perfectionist," he said. "When it's ready, it will blow your mind."

Month after month passed, and Noble gave Blaze an ultimatum. He, Sonda, and the boys were going on a four-week trip to Florida. He asked Blaze if the house would be ready for them to move into on their return. Blaze Maçon said his word was his bond and guaranteed the home would be ready on their return to Canada. As he would have to work overtime, Noble took out a loan to pay him upfront, as he also required more materials.

It was a fantastic and well-deserved vacation for the couple and their boys. A single message from Blaze popped up on Sonda's screen a few days prior to returning home: "Surprise! Surprise!" It left her curious and excited.

After arriving back in Yeovilton, they dropped off their bags at Sonda's house, where they enjoyed a glass of chardonnay and made arrangements for a friend to watch the kids. Then, they ventured across town to see the newly renovated house and discover Blaze's "surprise."

As Noble pulled up to the driveway, he noticed the front bedroom windows were obstructed by a thick plastic sheet and the roof entirely concealed by a massive blue tarpaulin. Leaving the car behind, they made their way to the main entrance. Above the doorbell, an envelope had been pinned. Noble took the note from the envelope, unfolded it, and read it aloud to his partner: "Hi guys, I've got fantastic news that will make your day! I've been offered a full-time job with another company. I'm sure you'll both be thrilled for me. What a fabulous surprise! All the best, Blaze M."

"Good for him," remarked Sonda. "Let's go in and see how he has worked his magic."

With a heavy heart, Noble sighed, the world's weight evident in the sound. A sense of unease washed over him as if something was not right. Opening the door, the couple walked into their recently remodeled home. The first shock came when they saw a gaping, ten-foot hole in the wall that divided the living room and kitchen. The previous carpet had been removed, discarded, and left in the corner of the room, revealing only the bare floorboards underneath.

"What happened to the carpet?"

Sonda smiled. "Well, it will look better with laminate flooring,"

"The hole in the wall?"

"Kinda looks funky," chirped Sonda, who was obviously a glass half-full kind of girl.

Tentatively, they made their way up the staircase, anticipation building as they approached their new sleeping units.

The second shock *almost* caused Sonda's once half-full glass to become half-empty. They looked at a full-blown construction site. The absence of a window was evident in the exterior wall, as a massive hole was patched up with a thick layer of plastic film. A gigantic window dominated the space with its grand frame on the right side of the hole. A note on the window was carefully attached with a piece of tape. Sonda eagerly snatched the note, her hands trembling as she unfolded it to read it aloud to her partner.

"Whoops. I found this window on eBay. It was a screaming deal. Wrong size. It didn't fit, LOL. Blaze."

The window was about a foot too small for the rectangular hole in the wall.

"LOL?" Noble scowled.

Sonda took a deep breath and centered herself. "No biggy, hun. I'm sure we can find another twelve-foot window. At least he put a plastic sheet on the hole to keep out the elements."

The third shock was that all of the walls had been knocked down. Several construction poles supported the retaining wall. A large note attached to one of the poles said: "DO NOT TOUCH. BUILDING REQUIRES SAFETY INSPECTION."

"What the fu—"

"Honey. You are going a dark red colour. Blaze has left us enough space for the boys to put their foosball table here. We can tidy up the debris and all huddle together by setting up a tent. It will be fun."

"Are you saying this because you are related to that retard? It was supposed to be three bedrooms with an en suite washroom and an additional bathroom for the boys or guests. He has removed the toilet, sink and faucet, shower, and vanity cupboards and has left us with a hole in the floor."

"We can pretend we are in India, hun. I watched a TV program about a place called Latur. They don't use sit-down loos as it's healthier for you, apparently."

"How do we wash our hands after shitting everywhere, as our aim may not be that great—especially the boys. Barney always has diarrhoea in the morning before he goes to school. My knees are dodgy, remember. I can see myself squatting and not able to stand up."

"Hun, don't sweat the small stuff. Bottles of sanitizer will do the trick—and, hun, stop having a go at my fam. Blood is blood. This can all be fixed."

"I have no more money. Your 'fam' has spent it all. I gave him a whopping advance, and I still have to pay off our holiday."

"At least he found a full-time job!"

"You recommended the moron."

"Sometimes, my cousin gets a bit distracted. He's a fine workman. A blue seal builder, but he has a few issues."

"Mental retardation?"

"No, cocaine."

"Oh great. Now you tell me. I'm a police officer, and you take me to your cousin's place, the Rum Runner, which is an illegal public house, and then you tell me your cousin—"

"Second cousin," Sonda corrected, matter-of-factly.

"Your second cousin . . . is a cokehead."

Sonda walked away, and over her shoulder, she chirped, "If you love me, you love my family, warts and all."

Charlie Noble stood in the middle of the mess, his mouth hanging open. He told an imaginary Blaze Maçon, "You've got me by the short and curlies. One day, shit for brains . . . I will pay you back for this!"

CHAPTER 35

THE VISIT

R AYLENE S KANK WAS impossible to ignore with her bleach-blonde hair, mesmerizing blue-green eyes, and perfectly shaped lips. The fillers made her look even poutier, allowing her mouth to comfortably fit all her teeth. Her figure was commendable, but she wasn't the sharpest tool in the shed. Although her presence exuded an undeniable sensuality, she seemed to repel women, who would purposefully avoid eye contact with her. Men found themselves enchanted by her, entirely consumed by thoughts of her day and night. Raylene's seductive powers were unparalleled as she effortlessly identified the perfect targets and moments to captivate men with her alluring charm. Additionally, she was aware of whom to avoid flirting with. The fish cop, Daryl, who visited the church and went to Mary's rappie pie dinner, was one of those guys who appeared oblivious to her sensualities. She knew it was pointless trying to charm him. Her neighbour, Blaze's older brother, was another one she knew she couldn't beguile. Deep down, she feared the man and understood why her discerning daughters didn't like him. When she looked at the man called Saul, it was like his heartless, ice-cold eyes went right through her.

Despite her best efforts, it was getting increasingly difficult for Raylene to keep her older daughters in line. With her time consumed by the responsibilities of the church priestess—holding meetings, reading holy books, engaging in prophetic liaisons, and seeking converts—there was little time left in the day to spend with the kids. With Blanche and Alison in charge of babysitting, the sisters had the entire land at their disposal for fun and exploration. The elder sisters were fiercely independent and had grown accustomed to roaming the streets of Islington, London, while their mother worked as an escort before undergoing a life-changing transformation. The older siblings owned iPhones and walkie-talkies as a precaution. Raylene had a gut feeling that trespassing onto the grumpy neighbour's property would spell trouble—she could practically feel it in her bones.

"Stay away from him, girls—that's final!"

"Mumma, we're going to do what we wanna do."

"Yes, what are you going to do? Report us to Aphrodite, the Goddess of Bullshit?" scoffed Alison.

"If Dad hears you talk like that—"

"Mum, that guy next door is a creepy weirdo."

"The guy next door?"

Fifteen year old Blanche curled her lip and spat out, "The old fart that looks like he's starring in a zombie apocalypse movie."

"Mr. Maçon's a tosser," chimed in Alison.

Raylene continued to dry dishes that had been left by the sink.

"I bet he sits all day in his barn and jerks off to cat porn," added Blanche.

"That's not nice," said her mother in rebuttal.

"He's creepy as fuck," chimed in four-year-old Hoddle.

"Shush. If your father hears you say words like that, he will wash your mouth out with soap and water."

The twins sniggered, then both repeated, "Creepy fuck, creepy fuck," and scampered off towards the living room.

"Enough!" yelled Raylene.

Blanche cocked her head. "But Mum, he's got all kinds of weird shit in the basement of his barn. Alison and I caught him sitting in front of one of his billions of cats getting a blow job."

"Girls! What are you doing over there on his property? It's out-of-bounds. He has every right to report you to the police for trespassing. Do you not read the warning signs?"

"Trespassers will be shot?"

"Yes, those ones."

"Mum," argued Allison, "we were exploring."

"And investigating," chimed in Stevie.

"Well, you can't on someone else's property."

"Well, if the crypt keeper chases after us, he will probably drop-down dead, and we could buy his place, too," said Blanche hopefully.

"Stay away. Please. You know how some locals are around these parts of the woods. We're trying to make friends with the community, not watch them have cardiac arrests and dance on their graves."

Blanche scowled.

"Also, you know how the locals are related to each other . . . insult one, and you don't know who else in the town will be offended."

"That's 'cause of incest," said Alison.

"Inbred shits," replied Blanche.

"For heaven's sake, stop. All six of you."

"What about Patsy?"

"She's too young to speak, you numpty."

"Living here is like being in *Game of Thrones*. Everyone is having it off with their brothers and sisters."

"What?"

"The Targaryens. Jamie Lannister."

"Where have you been watching *Game of Thrones*?"

"We like the sex scenes."

"In the brothels," added Stevie.

"You are *not* allowed to watch programs like that."

Blanche nodded. "And the beheadings."

Harry Skank knew very little about the shenanigans that his daughters were up to. He was devoted to spreading the word and ensuring his church would grow exponentially. He loved it when his church members prayed for him using terms like "anointed one," "the new Pope," and "apostle." His soccer sermons were a massive hit with the men, and this was an area where the womenfolk towed the line. His beautiful wife was the hook that brought many men into the flock. His charismatic charm and handsome looks appealed to many womenfolk.

Harry was aware that Raylene was practising an old-school method of evangelism called flirty fishing. Her body was the Divine One's, and her sexual trysts were necessary for advancing the Kingdom. Harry was not a jealous man, and after reaching the divine number of daughters, his interests lay elsewhere.

The momentary silence was broken.

BANG BANG BANG. The door thudded.

Everyone froze. Raylene turned to the kitchen door. She wasn't expecting any visitors, so she approached the front door and peered through the window at the figure standing outside in the large yard. It was Saul Maçon, Blaze's brother.

"Shit. Girls, go to your rooms this minute. Now."

Raylene picked Patricia from the floor and held her with one arm, her hips supporting the child's weight. The twins were already upstairs; another sister joined them. Blanche, Stevie, and Alison stared at their mother defiantly, refusing to budge.

Raylene opened the door. "Hello," she said with a smile.

Before Saul could respond, Blanche pushed her mother aside and sneered, "Look who it is . . . the child abuser!"

"What do you want, you old wanker?" yelled Alison.

Raylene's eyes were wide open, and she could not believe what she had just heard. Saul's expressionless face was a mere foot away from her. His eyes looked maniacal. Raylene felt his stare pass through her brain. Her legs became jelly, her face still composed.

Blanche's voice yelled, "Piss off, butt face."

Allison screamed, "I wish my dad had shagged your mum; you'd be a hell of a lot cleverer."

Unable to resist joining the melee of insults thrown at the enraged neighbour, Raylene turned to Allison, chortled, and answered, "And much better looking."

CHAPTER 36
WARM SUNSHINE & SNOW

AFTER PARKING his car so that it took up three of the four guest spots, Howie Dorcas popped into the Rodney Hotel to see if his BFF was staying there. No luck. The reception guy suggested the Best Western and one or two other guest houses downtown. The Rodney staff was reluctant to share if a dude called Smith, aka. Daryl, had checked in at the hotel.

"He's tall, quite buff, with a beard and clumsy look?"

"I'm sorry, sir, we can't share any information with you."

"He's a really good listener. No, a *great* listener."

"I can't help you, sir."

"We go back a ways. He'll cream his pants when he sees me."

Just like before, the receptionist strongly suggested the Best Western, assuring him it was a good option, with its affordable rates and excellent amenities. The receptionist wanted the man from "Out West" to leave their prestigious hotel due to his brash and uncouth behavior. In addition to his constant use of expletives, he continued to talk non-stop, causing a long line to form behind him. Despite their attempts to be polite and interject with "Yes, sir," and "No, sir," the man paid no attention to them and continued to expound on his views and conspiracy theories about COVID and masks.

"Listen here, Serge," referring to the receptionist's lapel batch, "that was such a hoax! Bull crap. How many *sheepies* walked around with Bill Gates' microchip inside of them? Dumbasses."

"But sir—"

"All government bullshit, Serge, ain't nobody going to track ol' Howie down, hell no."

The lineup grew and grew, and the fact that his phone tracked his every move seemed moot. Serge smiled knowingly at Howie, leaned in to his colleague, and whispered, "Do you think this guy will ever stop talking? Look at the line forming behind him."

A guest, a man in his late sixties wearing a mask, politely tapped him on the shoulder. Howie looked behind him. "Holy shit," said Howie. "It's the Lone Ranger!" Howie stuck up his hands in mock surrender. "Stand and deliver! COVID-19 or your life!"

Serge coughed loudly, getting the tall man's attention

"Sir, here is the address of the Best Western and their phone number. I've written down information for three other *fabulous* guest house names."

Howie thanked Serge. "I better go and hunt my partner-in-crime down or," he winked and thumbed behind him, "the old dude here, the masked bandito, is going to rob the shit out of you. If so, just shout—ol' Howie will return and put the old bastard in a chokehold."

"Yes, sir."

As time passed, the lineup grew in size, with more and more people joining. Turning around, Howie Dorcas locked eyes with the man wearing a medical mask, raised his hands, and mimicked the sound of a sheep as he walked by. As he approached the entrance doors, he couldn't help but notice the line of more than a dozen and a half people patiently waiting their turn. With a firm handshake, he greeted them as Howie, proudly representing Fort McMurray, and bid them farewell before exiting the Rodney Hotel. He left his car where it was and climbed into a waiting cab.

"Take me to the most happening bar in town. I wanna get shitfaced tonight and then call a few of the numbers old Serge gave me."

The cab driver smiled, nodded, and hoped that the talkative client would share his life story with him as the cab was on the clock.

BY ALL ACCOUNTS, the Leprechaun Irish pub was a dive of a bar. Popular with fishermen and other locals, Howie noticed most patrons wore gumboots; the ladies present wore their pajamas. He approached the serving area, propped himself on a stool, and called out, "Guinness, please."

The large barman, whose face looked like it had been hit by a double-decker London bus, scowled at Howie. With a nose that appeared to have been broken numerous times, the guy had piggy blue eyes that contrasted against his shiny bald head. A ginger goatee beard completed his distinctive look.

"Guinness," barked Howie.

"No, Guinness," snarled the hit-by-a-bus-faced guy.

"I'll have a Beamish then."

"No Beamish."

"McKinney? A Harp?"

The barman sighed. "Nope," he said and continued to dry glasses with a tea towel.

"I'll have a Jamison whiskey, then."

"Good luck with that."

"This is an Irish pub, right?"

"Sure is."

"Forget the brand names. I'll have a shot of Irish or Scotch whiskey."

"Sorry, we're out of whiskey."

"Kennedys, I'll have a double Kennedys."

"Sorry, we're out of that too."

Howie frowned. "What do you have then?"

"We have coffee, tea, dandelion, and burdock pop—very Irish."

Howie's neck snapped back.

"We have some Irish stew in the freezer. If you're hungry, we can microwave some for you."

"I want a drink."

"You must either be stupid or an outsider. All booze has been outlawed. Thanks to the Blue Wave. We are a full-blown prohibition province."

Howie's disappointment knew no bounds. "Oh well, I'll have a Coke."

Bus-face pointed at a short-looking man with a bushy moustache and grubby baseball cap that had been turned back to front on his head.

"I just want a Coke," moaned Howie

Bus Face, once again, nodded in the direction of the mustached dude at the end of the bar.

Howie tutted, shook his head, got off his bar stool and approached the small guy with the moustache.

"Howdy."

The little guy nodded his head and tipped his cap at the stranger.

"All I want—"

"Is coke?"

"Yup," said Howie, "I'd rather have something alcoholic, however—"

"Are you a cop?"

"Do I look like a cop?"

"Prove you ain't no cop."

Howie sighed, pulled out his Fort McMurray camp card and shoved it in the little guy's face. "I'm Howie Dorcas."

The little guy grinned. "I got this." He threw a small baggie containing fine white powder onto the table. "It's good coke."

"I just wanted a drink. I've given up the snow."

Blaze Maçon had a puzzled look on his face. "Given up? Why?"

Howie pulled up a chair. The one thing Howie liked was being asked a question. For the next ninety minutes, he told the small guy his entire life story, from infancy to adulthood. Finally, the two men shook hands. Blaze said, "Some story, dude." At times, Blaze found himself nodding off. Howie would nudge him awake and carry on his story.

"To be honest, my brain is a bit fried, Howie. I think it's the local coke —it's not that good—but it's all we can get our hands on."

Howie reached into his large bum bag and took out three baggies, each twice the size of Blaze's. "I bought these to give to my best mate, Daryl. I wanted to do one more line with him before I stopped snorting the snow for good. But, now you're like my new best friend, I'm giving you these as a gift. This is the best stuff money can buy. It's from the Fort McMurray cartel."

Blaze's eyes widened, "They got cartel up there?"

"It's more of a cooperative. Anyway, it's the best Colombian shit available. We call it 'Warm Sunshine' as it makes you feel like you're on a trip to Acapulco or the Maldives. My gift to you."

"Warm Sunshine, huh?" Blaze examined one of the baggies.

"It is potent shit. I need some info on a local dude, my bestie who lives in these parts."

Blaze raised his eyebrows.

"He's a tall guy almost the same height as me, with a big beard and some salt-n-pepper hair. His name is Daryl; he's new to town."

"Is he a bit gormless looking?"

"Yeah."

"I know him; he's the new fish cop who works with the real Five-O." Blaze pointed into space. "I met him at a lunch held by a nice old gal from church called Mary. He puked all over me. I can't forget him in a hurry. I gave the guy a ride home afterwards. He's a bit of a strange dude."

"He's the best listener, though." Howie reached out and took Blaze's hands and placed the baggies of Warm Sunshine in his palms, covering them with his own, large calloused mitts. "That is good shit. You'll enjoy it for sure."

Blaze beamed. "Bring on the sunshine, my man!"

Howie explained that he had to leave because he needed a place to stay and showed him Serge's hotel recommendations. Blaze looked at the numbers, recognising two or three establishments. He pointed at one of the guest houses' names. Blaze whispered that if Howie wanted "a brewskie" he'd best stay at the Manor Guest house. "It ain't nothing fancy—but, for a price, they'll get you some rocket-fuel hooch. Tell them Blaze Maçon sent you."

He thanked his new friend. He placed his large hands over Blaze's, who had the cocaine covered with his own. "The snow I just gave you—it's a hundred percent pure cartel cocaine. It's potent, so make sure you only have a bit when using it. Otherwise . . ." Howie made the exploding brain emoji hand gesture. "So, remember, snort safely." Howie pulled back his chair, patted his new best friend on the shoulder, picked up his large backpack, waved at Bus Face and headed towards the door.

CHAPTER 37
BREAKING POINT

Saul was rarely emotional. He prided himself on staying calm and not displaying how he felt deep down inside. Truth be told, he didn't feel much for anything apart from his cats. The interaction with the rude British neighbours went differently than planned. He imagined a blunt, terse word spoken to the mother, the mother reacting in remorseful shock. The chastised children, with heads bowed, apologizing to the infuriated neighbour. That was what Saul had *hoped* for.

Nope! After the longest pause, the mother pulled down her skimpy crop top, exposing even more cleavage. She opened the door and greeted the visitor with a fake, toothy smile. Before Saul had managed to enter a few syllables, the two rude older daughters pushed past their mother, placing their faces a few inches away from Saul's chest. He recalled parts of the encounter.

"Mum! It's the perv!" cried out Blanche.

"He's come over to try and rape us, call the cops!" yelled Alison.

"I-I-I-I've come—"

Stevie held up her hand and backed away. "Eww. He's cum in his pants."

Raylene held her hand to her mouth to cover up her laugh. One of the children pushed past their mother, looked at the shocked middle-aged man, and said, "Don't you know who we are? My dad has the biggest church in

Canada. If we tell them you've tried to force yourself on our mum or on us they will burn you at the stake, you harryteck."

Raylene glanced at Stevie. "Heretic," she corrected.

"Piss off, you dirty Acadian inbreed!"

Raylene Skank mildly rebuked her daughter. The eldest child, Blanche, yelled in his face, "Don't touch him, Mum, he smells of mothballs, death, and rotten egg farts."

Seething with rage, all Saul could splutter was, "Your daughters—"

"Hate you because you are the zombie crypt keeper," snarled Alison.

"Yes," added Blanche. "Darwin would look at you and add another theory to his collection. You are evolution in reverse."

The barrage of insults did not cease. Saul finally turned on his heels and stormed off along the drive towards his vehicle. He stopped, turned, and saw the mother with her infant in her arms and the two brattish older daughters heartedly laughing at him. They doubled over and made inappropriate hand gestures.

Saul bared his teeth and shook his fist at the family from hell. "Don't let those animals ever come on my land again. You have been warned." Once again, Saul turned on his feet and walked briskly to his truck. He opened the door, turned on the engine key, glanced at the laughing family, and noticed two of the girls not only giving him the finger but giving him the "reverse V-for-victory" sign. Although he couldn't swear to it, he thought the infant in Raylene Skank's arms was also giving him the bird.

"That's settled. I'll take great delight in knocking her brain right out of her head. And while I'm at it, when her brats are asleep, I'll mash their stupid craniums with my trusted mallet. Maybe I'll spare the smaller ones and the idiot father so he can take them back across the Atlantic to never step on these shores again."

For Saul, this meant breaking a golden rule. There were no cats to be rescued, no financial gain from taking veterinary supplies, and he didn't want to murder someone too close to home. However, he talked to himself as he pulled into his own long driveway, stopped the truck, and exited to share his rationale with his precious, purring family. He had never been so disrespected in his life. It wasn't even close to the time the school bully picked on him and made everybody in the school call him "the creepy lurch." As he crunched along the gravel path, he yanked open the door and was greeted by a cacophony of meows and purrs.

He plonked himself down on his favourite leather rocking chair. He picked Old Tom up from the floor and placed him on his lap. He grabbed a sheet of paper and a pen with his other hand and continued the conversation. Saul jotted down the questions and answers.

- She is an outsider. Tick.
- She is a whore who is having an affair with my brudder. Tick.
- Her religion ain't our religion. Tick.
- She shamed Mary's household by throwing up the delicious rappie pie. Tick.
- She spewed all over my little brudder. Tick.
- Her brats are feral. Tick.
- She shames the Acadian flag. Tick.
- They called me a pervert. Tick.

"She is going to die!" This time, the tick turned into an angry blob of ink as he destroyed the paper in a rage.

Saul was snarling. One or two cats fled their angry owner; three cats replaced them and jumped onto his lap, as if they sensed he needed to be calmed down.

"I've got to plan this well," he said. "Leave no trace, no clues, and I'll have to spend the night at Gabe's for an alibi. It will coincide with the breeding of the molly."

For the first time in quite a while, a broad grin went from one ear to another. "Yes, my lovelies. I'll frame it on the husband. Yes, yes, perhaps having found out his wife was a slut, conducting a string of affairs, the poor man finally snapped." Saul rubbed his dry, wrinkly hands together. "When it's all done and dusted, and the wretched family have returned to the UK and the kids placed in foster care, I will find out their address and send them a postcard telling them 'I wish you were here, from Saul, the crypt keeper.'"

CHAPTER 38

MILLY MOLLY MANDI

MILLICENT MOLYBDENUM MANDI was well-known in Hollywood circles, not for acting in a couple of Netflix series, but for her glamorous wedding to superstar director Gene Cohen. Gene was twenty years older than Milly and had married her after the constant nagging by his mother to get hitched. He had little interest in becoming intimate with his beautiful, buxom wife as, amongst friends, he identified as being gynosexual—he was sexually attracted to women regardless of whether they were female at birth. Gene had travelled to Thailand and fell in love with Tan, a ladyboy who worked in a bar called "Cock-a-doodle-doo" on the Nana Plaza. Desperate to appease his Orthodox parents, he met Milly on a film set and was attracted to her high cheekbones, piercing blue eyes, perky boobs, and voluptuously filled lips. Unfortunately, Milly lacked what Tan had—a *shmuck*—and a deal was made in a Starbucks near Hollywood and Vine. Milly would marry a Cohen and share Gene's vast fortune, promising to turn a blind eye to Gene's paramour. Gene agreed that Milly could have as many lovers as she wished, provided she remained discreet. Milly insisted on keeping her maiden name, as Cohen sounded too Jewish.

"But you *are* Jewish," argued Gene.

"Hun, for like *ever*, I've been known as Milly Mandi."

"Your parents are called Molybaum. The 'Mandi' is a fake name, like your tits and lips," said Gene, with an almost flamboyant bitchiness.

Milly rolled her big, blue eyes and folded her arms against her chest. "*If we get married, I want to change my name, hashtag official, from Molybaum to Millicent Molybdenum Mandi*—aka sweet as sugar candy."

"Why Molybdenum? Why not Denise, Sandra, or Hannah? Hey, or even a simple Millicent Cohen?"

Milly touched her heart. "Because y'all know I love heavy metal." She followed up her proclamation with a deep frown. "Also, I hate anything ending with Baum, like Goldbaum, Miracle Balm, Lip Balm or Rosenbaum or—"

"That's antisemitic, and two of your examples are not spelt B-A-U-M."

Milly crossed her arms and pressed her lips into a white slash. "Whatever, Gene." She frowned and countered with, "Hold your horses. I'm not antisemitic—I love semen."

Gene sighed. "You really want to be Millicent Moly-bed-num Mandi?"

"Molybdenum. Mo-lyb-de-num. One syllable."

"Four, actually. So, you're happy with being my arm candy at The Academy, Grammys and BAFTAs, *and* you're okay sleeping in different beds when Tan visits?"

"Of course. You hankered for the boy—I ain't stopping y'all having fun."

The couple had a traditional Jewish ceremony with chair dance as their well-heeled guests sang *Hava Nagila*. Tan was present throughout and consummated the marriage while Milly snorted cocaine and played with her newly acquired Persian kitten.

Twenty or so months later, having purchased a small mansion for herself, Milly and her housemaid, aesthetician, and driver settled into their new home in Satellite Beach, Florida. Milly had an eye for adventure and thought she could bump into an astronaut, dump Gene, and live happily ever after. Meanwhile, she decided to find a hobby that interested her: cat breeding.

Milly noticed several images of the perfect specimen to impregnate her tawny and white Persian cat. Butterkins had the sweetest face and bluest eyes, and Milly thought her sweet baby was "as pretty as a peach." The tomcat, "Thomas the Tank," appeared to be a robust, fertile pure-bred

Chartreux owned by a professional breeder, a genuine Frenchie called Gabriel Maçon, who lived in some Okie from Muskogee town in Nova Scotia. "Look at his name, Butterkins, my sweets. Gabe's got a cute little squiggle under his 'c.'"

Thomas' online profile had boasted that his testicles were large from enforced celibacy and was, literally, "busting a nut," waiting for Ms. Right to be bred with. "That boy is full as a tick." She smiled, rubbing another layer of factor thirty on her already bronzed stomach.

The process would be relatively simple. Milly's driver, Miguel, would drive Milly and Butterkins to Portland, take the fast catamaran across the Atlantic, disembark at Yeovilton, and book into a hotel for the night. After breakfast, Miguel would follow Gabe's directions and deliver Butterkins to her destination. Milly would peek at the tomcat to make sure all was in order, then leave her precious with Gabe and head for the downtown shops the following day.

The overnight stay wouldn't be an inconvenience as she hoped to be shagged senseless by her hot-blooded Spanish chauffeur, who had the stamina of a thoroughbred horse. Being new to the cat-breeding scene, Milly assumed that Butterkins would be aroused by grunts, snorts and groans made by her owner and Miguel during their frantic lovemaking sessions. Concerned that Butterkins had a delicate personality, Milly could only hope and pray that Thomas the Tank would be as chivalrous as Miguel was to her. Meanwhile, Gene was vacationing with Tan in the Maldives, having earned millions of dollars making another record-breaking box office movie.

First thing in the morning, they would get up and go to Gabe's to introduce the cats.

Milly texted Gabe before their visit.

MM: Is Thomas Jewish?

GM: HE IS WHATEVER YOU WANT HIM TO BE

MM: I want Butterkins to have a spiritual experience.

MM: It shouldn't just be sex .

GM: HE'S CIRCUMCISED

MM: Awesome.

MM: Maybe play them some Jewish music?

GM: TOTALLY

GM: "I WAS MADE FOR LOVIN' YOU"

MM: ????

GM: I WILL PLAY KISS DURING MATING

MM: Kiss? WTF?

GM: THE BAND, KISS

GM: GENE SIMMONS IS JEWISH

MM: Perfect. Jewish but not too Jewish.

Milly was ecstatic. Of course, what Gabe promised the owners did not quite marry with what would actually occur. Gabe informed Milly that the copulation ritual was "top-secret." However, he would monitor and record the procedure for safety's sake. Gabe's routine was to gently place the molly into the comfortable copulation chamber, allow the in heat pussycat to spray everywhere, and then, at the appropriate moment, he'd throw the hissing and horny tomcat into the pen where the magic would occur. Old Tom usually took nanoseconds to corner the female feline, do his business, and return to the traumatized recipient for seconds. Gabe eventually rescues the molly by removing and rewarding the satisfied tomcat.

Initially, her plan went pear-shaped, as she tried to book into the only four-star venue in town, The Rodney Hotel. Miguel waited nervously in the "no parking zone" with the SUV while she checked them into the hotel. A selfish driver of a hire vehicle had parked their car so that it was impossible for other guests to park directly outside the hotel's entrance.

Having entered the double glass doors of The Rodney Hotel, Milly couldn't believe the size of the queue for check-in.

"Ya'll checking into this hotel?" she asked half a dozen people waiting before her.

She crooked her neck to see what was causing the bottleneck. It appeared that a couple of clerks were on duty and only one clerk was yapping to a man wearing a large Stetson the size of Texas. She sighed, huffed, and puffed, yet the line didn't move; it appeared to grow steadily behind her. She felt discomfort from the previous night's sexual shenanigans with Miguel. She was not enjoying the experience of waiting for what seemed like an age to book into a room.

Milly stood impatiently in line, eyed the people in the lobby, and judged them. Midwest Americans were terrible enough, but these Canadians were a hell of a lot worse. She muttered, "With y'all's damned Nazi-right wing views and 'I'm sorry' this and 'I'm sorry' that attitude, y'all couldn't organize a piss-up at a brewery . . . if y'all allowed to go into one."

She tapped the clean-shaven, well-groomed, non-mask-wearing guy standing directly in front of her, who happened to be a businessman from Charlottesville. He had been politely clearing his throat because the lady behind him wore so much perfume. Worse still, he worried that his wife would think he'd been unfaithful or engaged in some outrageous, bacchanalian orgy.

"Damned Canadians. They want to take away our right to drive our Teslas and drink booze. They're makin' kids at school recite Leviticus rather than their times tables. These turkey-brained Canadians even have a hockey team called the Oily Oilers. The dumbass up front in his Calgary Stampede Stetson with a maple leaf on the back of his hoodie sums up Canada for y'all. What a dick."

The Virginian blew out his cheeks and shook his head—he begged to differ. "Edmonton Oilers, not Oily Oilers, actually. The New Blue Wave has enforced a 'Drill until it kills' policy. They've put an 'e-tax' on all electric devices. I'm all for it!" He tried to waft away the cloud of perfume that enveloped him.

"Well, that idiot up front makes me madder than a wet hen. Y'all is full of shit, too." With a deep sigh and several loud tuts, Milly looked one more time at her Rolex, then back again towards the Stetson man, still conversing with the receptionist. Tapping her watch, she turned on her heels, returned to her gas-guzzling SUV and commanded Miguel to find them another hotel before she lost her shit.

Within minutes, Miguel pulled into the Best Western on Main Street. Her driver's English was mostly incomprehensible, but she liked it that way. Men were stupider than Jupiter and should keep their pie holes shut in her presence. Although Milly did not like speaking to riff-raff hotel workers, she took Butterkins from her travel box and marched into the musky-smelling hotel. Relieved to go directly to the reception desk, Milly booked two adjacent rooms.

"Breakfast is included, ma'am," reminded the petite receptionist wearing a "bad-hair-don't care" ball cap on her head.

"Hun, with the tips I give y'all, sweety, I'm telling you the truth—bless your heart—but y'all need to see a senior stylist *tout de suite*. Maybe take some growth hormones while you're at it." The fourteen-year-old turned scarlet, adjusted her ball cap, and said, "Yes, ma'am. Sorry, ma'am."

Finally, Milly noticed an intelligent-looking employee at his desk in the lobby. She dropped Miguel's room key into the concierge's hands. "Y'all keep wearing uniforms in front of me and I'll be jumping on your bones." Without waiting for a reaction, she made her way to her room with a smile.

CHAPTER 39
THE PLOT THICKENS

Saul made contact with his little brother. Realizing that Blaze's habit was spiralling out of control, he sat beside him, determined to discover the extent of his interactions with the Skank woman. In his intoxicated state, Blaze believed Saul was genuinely interested in listening to every scandalous aspect of his encounters with his neighbour. Blaze hinted at his recent lover's preference for passionate encounters on the expensive mahogany desk in the study at the house but refrained from disclosing any names. They would wait for him, and he would satisfy his horny lover until they screamed, under their breath, to stop, or their head would explode. To maintain his composure, Saul listened intently while an overwhelming sense of disgust washed over him. His brother's sexual showboating had an odd and desperate quality to it.

"They message me that the coast is clear, to come over immediately, let myself into the home through the side door, and make my way to the study, where my lover will be faced forward, staring out of the window and twerking with her naked, lily-white ass fully exposed, waiting for me to enter them."

"How do you communicate and find out the coast is clear?" Saul asked.

Blaze winked, "You're a smart one, bro. Yes, their partner has no idea what's going on. They have a big, big family, too. We have yet to be caught. Such fun."

According to Blaze, the couple stayed in touch through frequent text messages. Once the kids were tucked in bed, he checked in to see if it was a good time to visit and fulfill their desires. Under the cover of darkness, he'd embark on his paddle board adventure across the lake, the only light coming from the stars above.

"It adds to the thrill. When the wicked deed is done, I return home for some much-needed shut-eye."

"Be careful, little brudder. It won't be good if you get caught."

Blaze laughed. "My lover will sometimes crush sedatives in their partner's bedtime hot milk when they haven't left the house. Mostly, they are at all-night meetings and return first thing in the morning. It's all golden, bro."

Saul became hard down below and had to cover up his groin. It wasn't his brother's erotic tale that excited him; it was the realization that his ten-pound wooden mallet would crush the Skank woman's skull into smithereens. The smirking face that he saw standing at the doorstep would be "at one" with the fancy wooden floorboards or desk in the study as he'd pound her head as flat as a pancake.

Thoughts raced through his mind, presenting him with a couple of scenarios, each causing his heart to beat faster. If Harry was there and sleeping upstairs, he'd pin the blame on the scoundrel. He would sneak up the stairs, cautiously waking Skank from his slumber. He would then compel him to write a letter of confession, desperate to shield his children and their mother from the same cruel destiny. Finally, he would force him to hang from the balcony. This would be an excellent first thing in the morning graphic for the wretched kids to see—almost better than bringing his trusty mallet down upon their insolent faces while they slept.

"Pervert, am I? Crypt keeper? The smell of death and farts?" He grinned to himself. He could daub Harry's prints on Thor's hammer and ensure Raylene's blood was all over Harry's clothes. He snickered, thinking that the dumbass cops may put the incident down to "accidental death." However, if the brats woke up, he would take the greatest pleasure in dispatching them and making the crime scene look like a family affair.

If Skank was not there, he'd flatten her head and frame one of her lovers. If the cops thought the vet's bizarre murder was possible suicide, then it wouldn't be difficult to point the finger in someone else's direction. Raylene Skank had so many devotees that the entire town would be under suspicion.

He bade farewell to his brother and made his way back home. Yes, the Skank lady would have to go. Blaze may have already crossed the line by sharing too much information with her. His habit worsened with each passing hour, and he couldn't resist boasting about his conquest to Saul, fully aware of how much his brother would disapprove.

As Saul entered his home, the sound of purring and soft meows filled the air, his audience of cats waiting patiently for his attention. "Yes, my precious darlings, the arrogant Brits will soon face a new reality . . . Saul Maçon's reality!"

CHAPTER 40
HAPPY HUMP DAY

SAUL GLANCED at his rugged black Casio Illuminator wristwatch. "Big day today, Old Tom. I've seen pictures of the molly, and she's a stunner!" He cupped his hand to the cat's ears and whispered, "Butterkins. Stupid name, but that's not her fault."

Old Tom was putty in Saul's hands; they adored each other. Saul confidently stroked Old Tom's smooth, lustrous coat, which looked magnificent. The cat had impeccably trimmed claws, a pristine appearance, and teeth as white as a game show host's. Saul gently caressed his best friend's chin, a look of adoration in his eyes. It was Hump Day for Old Tom, and the universe seemed to align in his favour as if it had conspired to make this day his lucky day. While Saul groomed him, he emitted a contented purr of delight. Old Tom's face remained as handsome as always. The look of "the wicked winketh with their eyes" was no more. Old Tom's new eyeball socket had fully healed, and even though one eye appeared larger than the other, Saul believed it added a touch of sophistication to his appearance. If he were to don a monocle, he would instantly resemble the esteemed Kaiser Wilhelm and the upper-class Germans of his time. Regrettably, it was impossible for him to notice the contrasting eye colours. Fortunately, his brother Gabe had shared photos of Old Tom before the porcupine encounter with the molly's owner.

Saul gently put Old Tom into his cat carrier, gave him some Friskies, and closed the door. As Saul left the home, the sounds of meowing, wailing, and crying echoed from the rest of Old Tom's family. Perhaps, on this occasion, it was their way of wishing Old Tom good luck as they witnessed his departure. As Saul sat in his truck, he turned the ignition key and the engine whirred to life, filling the air with a low rumble.

"Given the extensive tasks for tonight and tomorrow, my utmost priority is ensuring your prompt arrival at Gabe's. Soon enough, Boris will team up with you when he's ready. If it goes well with the Butterkins molly from the USA, you and Boris can become one hell of a tag team for future breeding. You both will produce stunning litters."

GABE MAÇON WAS a digital genius and had created TomMolly, the premium "dating and mating" site for cat breeders. The brothers were making a small fortune, especially from wealthy North Americans who sought purebred litters of kittens. Yes, most of the ideas had been "borrowed" from Tinder. Swipe left for a "no" and right for a "yes." Gabe introduced sound effects with a loud MEOW for a perfect match, a PURR for a possible match, and a loud HISS for any match made in hell. When Millicent Mandi swiped right for her precious Butterkins, seeing Old Tom's images and reading his profile, she and Gabe knew that Thomas the Tank and Butterkins would not only mate but also create an expensive and much-coveted litter of kittens.

In addition to the three-day luxury stay-over fee, Gabe made it a point to include an expensive medical inspection conducted by a veterinarian as part of the package. Since his brother had eliminated their greedy, blackmailing vet, he tasked Saul with examining the molly armed with his understanding of the feline species, recently acquired textbooks, and Dr. Timothée Caniton's letterhead.

Gabe worked the front end of the enterprise. In a built-in annex connecting Gabe's home and The Rum Runner, he would introduce the cats to each other in a specially designed love nest, taking care to show "Thomas the Tank" to the molly.

Gabe was relieved that Old Tom had shed his previous monikers, Captain Jack Sparrow and Long John Silver, and no longer sported an eye patch. This would often cause fear in the molly. Unbeknownst to the owner,

Gabe took on the task of introducing the cats to each other. He would watch the mating event unfold on CCTV, amused by Old Tom trapping the hissing molly, asserting his dominance, and engaging in typical tomcat behaviour in a cramped space. Gabe knew that his brother had performed surgery on Old Tom's eye, which had been declared successful. Gabe had completely overlooked the fact that Saul was colour-blind. He assumed with Saul's attention to detail, everything was bound to go smoothly. Now Saul had another pedigree male cat from the doctor's slaying, a Russian Blue; they would indeed have cash-raining cats and dogs.

The molly's owner had paid a significant amount of money in advance for the match, ensuring the commitment from this Millicent woman. Given that Old Tom was a pure Chartreux, it seemed highly improbable that she would back out of the deal. In the worst-case scenario, if Old Tom looked a bit weird after the surgery, Gabe could make him look "mysterious" by putting a mask on him. Saul's cat was terrific as he was compliant, knowing that he would "get his oats" in due course. If the peculiar-looking tomcat did scare Butterkins shitless, no one would ever know. Ultimately, having two eyes was preferable to having just one, so Boris would be a welcome addition to the team.

CHAPTER 41
HYPNOTIC BREAKFAST

MILLY WOKE UP, energized for the day, and jumped into the shower. After drying off, she turned on Fox News, eager to catch up on the latest headlines. The news anchor reminded the viewers about the rapists, drug mules, child molesters, and terrorists that were flooding through the southern states. However, the new President had signed an Executive Order to use the latest biotechnology to spray anthrax along the entire border wall.

"That should stop the little shits, Butterkins." Her cat purred in agreement. Despite being undocumented, Miguel wasn't one of those sexual predator types or a serial killer, unlike many other asylum seekers the President talked about. His only "weapon" was his Latin libido—a clear asset to the Floridian cougar.

Getting ready, she puckered her lips and quickly kissed the vanity mirror before grabbing the luxurious cat basket and heading out the door toward the hotel's elevator. Squeezing into the claustrophobic space, Milly covered her nose to escape the unpleasant stale smell. She quickly made her way to the self-service breakfast area. She noticed a few people and turned her nose up at them as they milled around the croissant and muffin station. She quickly found her seat and waited eagerly to grab a waffle.

The sight of a middle-aged man in a uniform eating ham and eggs captivated her. He stared vacantly at the large television screen on the side wall. With the cat basket securely pressed against her chest, she approached his table and politely requested, "May I join you, young man?"

The scent of perfume greeted Daryl's nostrils even before she spoke. As Daryl looked up, he inwardly cursed the woman for intruding on his solitude during breakfast, not wanting his meal to be tainted with the scent of Hypnotic Poison and mindful of his mild cat allergy. *Only twenty tables are available, and she wants to sit next to me.*

"Sure, I'd love you to," he replied, his voice dripping with insincerity.

She thrust her neck under Daryl's nose. "Do you like my perfume, young man?"

It's awful. "Yes, what is it?"

"Hypnotic Poison."

"It's very . . . interesting," he said, wafting the scent away from him with his hand.

In a noticeable southern drawl, she made her introduction as "Mrs. Mandi," this time thrusting the basket containing Butterkins under Daryl's nose.

Ugh! The cat smells no different from its owner.

"Could Butterkins keep you company while I go grab some breakfast? She's extremely expensive, and I can't bear the thought of losing her."

Great, I'm allergic. "Of course."

Daryl dutifully stood up, grabbed the large cat basket, and placed it on an adjacent chair.

"Oh, I love a man in uniform. Thank you for your service," she said, thrusting out her well-apportioned chest. Milly made her way towards the waffle maker. Daryl followed the breakfast gatecrasher with his eyes. It was hard to determine her exact age, but the lady's graceful demeanour and mature presence suggested she was in her late forties or fifties. However, she had so much foundation and makeup on her face that it was impossible to accurately determine her age. He thought she may be anywhere between twenty and two hundred years old. The lady had her lips filled so much that Daryl considered wearing a face shield in case they burst while she ate a waffle.

My God. If she sat five feet from me, her lips would be close enough to kiss me. He shuddered at the thought. Then, feeling guilty, he muttered to the cat, staring through some mesh, "Sorry, Butterfingers or whatever . . . it's first thing in the morning. I don't mean to be judgmental." The cat meowed as if accepting his apology.

Milly returned, placing her plate of blueberry waffles on the table; she sat down and settled her silicon-filled bum on the chair. As she flicked her long, silky black hair to the back, revealing her diamond-covered earlobe, she grabbed her knife and fork and stared deeply into Daryl's eyes.

"Army?" she asked, raising an eyebrow. "Navy? Coast Guard?"

With the anticipation of the flavour of sausage and egg dancing on his taste buds, Daryl paused mid-action, not uttering a word. "No, no. Please, tell Butterkins and me that you are a hunky firefighter or a sexy policeman?" Daryl noticed when Milly spoke, her lips didn't appear to move. In fact, Botox had frozen her entire face, so when Milly spoke, she neither blinked nor smiled.

"None of those, ma'am," Daryl replied, sensing the cat lady's growing disappointment as if she had just received news of a tragic loss. Once again, her eyes sparkled with excitement. "A Marine?" she exclaimed, her eyes trying to widen in astonishment. "A Paratrooper? Are you an airline pilot or an astronaut?" Leaning across from Daryl, the cat lady carefully fixed his tie, her fingers brushing against his collar. "It's lookin' all cattywampus."

Cattywampus? WTF? "No, I'm a Federal Fisheries Officer."

Milly had difficulty putting the 2 percent Oikos Greek yoghurt in her frozen mouth. As soon as she found out about Daryl's occupation, she had a visceral reaction, coughing and spitting out a mixture of cultured goat's milk and bacteria, most of which ended up on Daryl's jacket. "A fish cop?" Thankfully, her face couldn't distort, but her voice expressed her disdain.

Daryl quickly picked up a serviette and daubed the white splatter from his jacket.

She finally uttered, "Ugh. You've disappointed us, for sure."

"No worries," Daryl responded, patting the remaining yoghurt from the tunic.

"I was referring to your occupation—not your messy eatin'. A fish cop is lower than the elevator attendant or the—"

"Nice cat." Daryl attempted a classic distraction. Initially, Daryl mistook the musky smell for his guest's perfume. However, a heavy, dank whiff wafted towards him from the cat box. The cat was in a state of heat. Tears flowed from Daryl's eyes. The odour was so overwhelming that it completely masked the litres of Hypnotic Poison the lady had doused herself in that morning.

"Thank you. Don't cry. Y'all have to make a living somehow. I didn't mean to hurt your feelings. What's your name, young man?"

Once again, Daryl failed to bite the juicy sausage perched on his fork. "Daryl."

She repeated his name without moving lips as she looked at the ceiling, "Day-ral. Day-rhul." She latched onto his arm with her long, bright red fingernails, refusing to release her grip. "Millicent Mandi," she added, "Mah lovers think I'm as sweet as sugar candy and can't resist my Southern charm."

With a spluttered laugh, Daryl regained his serious expression, giving a respectful nod while desperately trying to ignore the nauseating miasma of In Heat/Hypnotic Poison that lingered around him like a cloud of mustard gas.

"Butterkins and I are embarking on an exhilarating adventure."

"Nice, an adventure." Daryl struggled to feign interest.

"Yes, my beautiful molly is set to engage in a fiery and passionate cat-sex session with a tomcat later today. Together, they will create a litter of beautiful kittens."

Daryl frowned. *Molly? What the heck is a molly?*

Milly sighed, picking up the fish cop's blank expression. "A molly is a female cat that is ready for breeding. Don't you fish cops know anythang?"

"Oh. With your accent, you must have travelled far for . . . Butternuts to—"

"Butterkins," she corrected. "Accent, my dear man. Y'all the ones with the accents," she said indignantly. "I live near Cape Canaveral, Florida. You know, the rocket site. Man on the Moon, and all that stuff?"

Daryl nodded, a small smile playing on his lips. "Are there really no eligible bachelors for Butterball in Florida, Maine, or North Carolina?"

"Butterkins," Milly emphasised, "requires a particular pedigree to breed with. Travelling to Nova Scotia is much easier than the Alsace area in France."

"France?"

"Her suitor's breed is rare. He's a Chartreux."

Daryl nodded but didn't have a clue about cat breeds.

While incessantly wiping her mouth with a napkin, Milly explained Thomas' owner lived in Quincy, a quaint village near Yeovilton. She was eagerly anticipating her meeting with the charming Frenchman, Gabriel Maçon. A perfect match had been made for Butterkins on the new dating app, and pussycat sparks flew from the very first message. She'd paid a significant deposit for the privilege and would pay Monsieur Maçon a shit load more when her molly became pregnant. She abruptly moved her half-eaten waffle away, nodded at the Fisheries Officer, and said they would be leaving.

"Good luck to you both," said a relieved Daryl. "I could never imagine myself doing what you do."

"Cain't never could," she winked, wagged her finger at him, and walked out of the dining room with cat box in hand.

CHAPTER 42
HOWIE'S LAMENT

HOWIE LOUNGED on his queen-sized bed, flipping through various cable channels in his new home. The Manor Guesthouse wasn't exactly the Ritz, that's for sure, but the illicit moonshine was a sight for sore eyes, its golden colour shimmering in the dimly lit room. The bottle of premium grog, came with a hefty price tag of $100. Money was not a concern for Howie, so he selected the most expensive option: "Olde Smokey on the Water." Although he had quit cocaine, he expressed regret for not having snorted a few lines with his friend, Daryl. Surely Daryl found his lobster cop job monotonous, so he thought an excellent buzz might lift his spirits. Hoping for Daryl's participation, he intended to cover the costs of having a few strippers come for a private performance. Howie was determined to find Daryl and free him from the mundane reality that had probably trapped him.

"Who in their right mind would wanna be a fish cop?" he slurred, asking the host of Family Fortunes on the TV.

He didn't mind giving his remaining drugs to the guy he met at the pub, as Blaze had spoken well of him and helped him stay at the guest house, where he was provided with the much-needed liquor. Howie, being his usual uncouth self, took another slug of the illicit firewater, and let out a huge sigh and an extra loud fart. Wafting the gas to his nose, he giggled, nodded, and labelled it four stars.

The Albertan clicked the remote control once more to switch the channel. It was difficult for him to concentrate on a single program for more than half a minute. He ceased clicking and grinned in response to the advert he had witnessed. At first, he thought he had accidentally stumbled upon the forbidden Adults Only channel. With her peroxide blonde hair, ample curves and seductive pout, the model leaned forward, sensually licking her cherry red lips, "*Come . . . as you are,*" the attractive lady urged in her charming British accent. "*Come . . .* and join us this Sunday morning. Your presence would mean a lot to us."

Howie was astonished, his mouth hanging open. In a captivating display on TV, the charming British lady sent kisses his way with a subtle pout, enticing Howie to embark on a profoundly erotic yet spiritual journey. A man in an expensive suit appeared and rudely disrupted the show. "Hey, you jerk, get out the way." Howie waved at the TV as the suited guy stood in front of the red-hot lady.

"Hi, I'm Pastor Harry Skank; please join Raylene and me for our Sunday service at the White Hart Lane Fellowship in downtown Yeovilton —where we promise you a very happy ending!"

Feeling aroused, Howie exclaimed, "Man, I'm not religious or nothin', but I wouldn't mind going to that joint, especially to see that hot Raylene lady."

He clicked and changed channels again. He recognized the show *Narcos*. Howie always rooted for the DEA cops, even though he had often been a real-life dealer at camp. His mind thought of his friend Blaze once again. "Buddy, I hope you go easy on the snow I gave you. It's a hundred percent pure *screw-your-head-up,* eighty percent Colombian coke with ten percent Mexican fentanyl and the remainder ten percent Nicaraguan amphetamine. A South American special blend."

Howie pondered. Yes, he wished he'd warned his new second-best buddy more explicitly. The coke was at least one hundred times stronger than the typical street variety. He didn't have Blaze's phone number and didn't want to ask the guest house owner for personal contact information. He made the sign of the cross and took off his woollen socks to give his size-fourteen feet a chance to breathe. He held one of the socks to his face, turned his head away, scrunched his nose, and announced, "Man, you stink!"

Howie rolled off the bed and stumbled to the bathroom, undid his zipper, and peed like a horse into the sink. He stopped mid-flow, placed his dirty socks into the basin, and continued to pee.

"Yup, you's a clever one. Just like Howie Dorcas' super-strong urine can sterilize jellyfish stings, it can also disinfect my socks," he slurred as he stared at his reflection in the bathroom mirror, drunkenly expressing his awe for the wonders of science.

After a thorough sloshing and hand agitation in hot water and urine, Howie sealed the deal by adding hand soap from the dispenser to the mix. A smaller TV was in the corner of the bathroom, so he clicked back onto the *Narcos* show. Taking a few drunken strides into the bedroom, he retrieved the rest of the moonshine sitting on the bedside table, returned to the bathroom and took a big swig. With the bottle raised, he offered a toast to his friend, "Cheers, Blaze! I hope you have a great time when the snowstorm arrives." Howie burped and slumped onto the bathroom floor.

With the theme tune to *Narcos* playing in the background, he shook his head and drunkenly slurred, "I pray to the narco gods you ain't stupid enough to snort the whole lot in one go."

CHAPTER 43
THE BEST DAY OF MY LIFE

SAUL PULLED into his brother's driveway. Gabe's breeding process was slick, as they'd used Old Tom several times. The Rum Runner normally opened at six o'clock in the evening. However, on certain days, like today, it was closed. Saul carried Old Tom in his basket into the empty bar and grunted a welcome that would be reciprocated by his brother. Gabe asked if he wanted a drink, and Saul politely declined. This happened on almost every occasion that a cat exchange occurred. Once the pleasantries had been exchanged, Old Tom would be taken into the "Royal Chamber," as Gabe called it, an annex just off the bar area, sandwiched between Gabe's house and the Rum Runner.

Old Tom would have his final grooming and purr away, waiting for the introduction of the molly.

Saul was a man of few words, especially when humans were involved, but on this occasion, he decided to show off Old Tom to his brother. He wanted Gabe to admire his recent veterinary skills.

Holding Old Tom before his audience of one, he exclaimed, "Damned handsome—once again!"

Gabe edged towards Saul to get a closer look. He rubbed his chin. What's going on with his eyes?"

Saul grimaced. "What do you mean?"

"I know you fixed his Johnny Depp look—but without the pirate eye mask, he looks a bit . . . a bit odd."

"He looks fine, brudder. As discussed earlier, if the silly cow from Florida asks you about Old Tom's appearance, tell her it's a sign that he's super frisky and interested in her molly. Just say Old Tom's one eye always gets bigger than the other when he is aroused."

Gabe smirked, "Does his eyeball also change colour?" He didn't want to hurt Saul's feelings. "My dear bro, this will have to be Old Tom's last hurrah. Maybe your new cat will be ready next month?"

"Eye colour. What are you talking about?" Saul shook his head and frowned. "Do you think Old Tom needs another operation?"

"Yes."

"I don't think the American lady will notice the difference. You're being too critical."

"Saul, I can't see us pulling this one off. Half of Old Tom looks normal; the other half of his face looks like he's become a fluffy-tailed lemur. All I can do is expect the worst and hope for the best. The cat's owner is Milly Mandi, a loaded owner from The Keys, and she'll be arriving here with her chauffeur within the hour."

Saul rubbed his chin. "Brudder, you might need to book into Specsavers. Old Tom looks great. He may need a touch-up; I can figure out how to make him look perfect."

Gabe's jaw dropped as he looked at Old Tom and back at Saul several times.

"Look, that's not important right now. I'm on my way to see our drug-addicted sibling. He's wrapped up with the Skank woman, and his lips are mighty loose."

"I'm worried about him too."

"I'm due to drop off Mother's inheritance cheque to him. He's getting worse, asking for advances so he can snort it all up his nose. It has to stop."

"Surely, our little brother won't say anything to the priestess or whatever they call her?"

Saul recounted his recent talk with Blaze. Gabe couldn't help but shake his head, gesturing with both hands to mimic an exploding-head emoji. The brothers were deeply worried about the risk of him revealing family secrets to the British woman.

"He says he's one of her disciples. He also has a big mouth, and who knows what he may share with her during a confessional?" said Saul.

"True, especially if he's as high as a kite."

"Anyways, it's time for his big brudder to talk and lay down the law. It's either cheque and distance himself from the damned woman, or we shun him. Are you in favour?"

"Of course. Make it a tough talk. You have my backing." Gabe glanced at Old Tom through the cat box mesh and rubbed the back of his neck. "I have to focus on the Old Tom situation now. This ain't going to be easy, bro."

"Nonsense. Remember, if anyone asks, I was here all night with you playing cribbage."

Gabe gave a slight nod. "Yes, bro, but why—"

Saul thrust the cat box at Gabe. "Don't lose him!"

"It's hardly easy to do that when he has one eye the size of a large grapefruit," quipped Gabe.

Saul rebuked his brother for using derogatory words in Old Tom's presence.

Gabe chuckled. "He always has his wicked way, despite how he looks. Maybe you should rename him Cyclops?"

"Stop."

"Okay, big brother. I'm just jerking your chain." Gabe shook Saul's hand and held onto Old Tom with the other. Old Tom purred. He was a handsome cat, for sure, even without one eye, but Old Tom's new look caused Gabe concern, especially with the imminent arrival of the American's molly. He wished he could do the handover under the cover of darkness. The Rum Runner area was floodlit for security purposes.

Saul turned around and headed back to his truck, feeling the weight of his mission pressing on his shoulders. Blaze was expecting him. His behaviour was becoming completely unhinged. He called Saul "my boy" and urged him to try his new drug. He even interrupted their conversation to sing Clapton's "Cocaine" and Madonna's "Like a Virgin," teasing Saul about his supposed virginity.

Saul's plan, like his previous encounter with the blackmailing vet, was riddled with uncertainties that weighed heavily on his mind. Nevertheless, he realized that he had reached a pivotal moment where he had to take action. The moment had arrived to lay the Maçon family's cards on the table. Contemplating his options, he weighed the idea of brandishing his trusty wooden mallet as a gentle reminder to Blaze to stay quiet. Saul affectionately kissed his reliable, formidable weapon of mass destruction, savouring the wooden taste on his lips, and whispered, "Thor by name, the bringer of chaos."

He stashed it in a hockey bag filled with his usual crime-scene tools at the rear of his truck. Saul Maçon checked the inventory, a grin spreading across his face as he imagined Raylene Skank's head flattened against the floor. With his arsenal of tools, including duct tape, a hunting knife, hazmat suits, disposable booties and gloves, face shields, ether, a pre-typed letter, zip ties, white spirit, BBQ fluid, Clorox, and a lighter, he was confident he could commit the perfect crime once again.

As he turned on the radio, the upbeat melody of American Authors' "Best Day of My Life" filled the air. With a smile, he tapped the steering wheel and sang along to the catchy pop song.

CHAPTER 44
SWEET BUTTERKINS

Milly Mandi was lost in thought, staring at the love of her life. "I hope this Thomas the Tank perfectly matches you, sweet Butterkins. I did my utmost due diligence, beautiful lady, and this Tommy fellow has an excellent pedigree. A very handsome boy for you to meet with. We will have so many beautiful children—you and I—and Miguel, of course." Her mind briefly wandered to her Spanish lover.

"My sweet Butterkins, you know Miguel is not your real papa? However, you can think of him as your step-papa. He's far better to me than the old fart of a husband I have. I hardly see him as he's gallivanting around the world with his ladyboy friend. I really don't know what he sees in her-him, they, whatever the hell Tan is."

Butterkins, a sensitive creature, immediately shied away from her owner, sensing the change of tone. "Sorry, sweetheart, for my angry words." Butterkins appeared to accept her apology by purring. "I wouldn't mind, of course, if Gene showed me just a modicum of attention. I shouldn't pick on Tan; it's my husband—he's the problem."

Milly stood before the hotel's large vanity mirror, admiring her full lips as she puckered them and playfully winked at her reflection. "Anyway, he has his ladyboy, his golf, his Hollywood friends, and I have you, dear Butterkins . . . and Miguel," she said, her voice filled with affection. As she held the molly, she meticulously brushed Butterkins' long Persian coat, preparing her for the meeting with her handsome lover. "I love you so much," she whispered to her cat, her voice filled with affection. "Your eyes are like the vast expanse of the ocean, a mesmerizing shade of blue."

The anticipation of her litter of amber and blue-eyed kittens made her heart race with excitement. Milly kissed her cat's nose and then rummaged through her travel bag, her fingers searching for something specific. Finally, she pulled out a large black glass bottle. She sprayed the room with an overpowering dose of Hypnotic Poison, filling the air with a scent so potent it could have subdued the entire German army during the Normandy Landings. She lifted Butterkins into the air, hoping to catch a whiff of the alluring perfume she believed would captivate her cat's lover. She gave her one last tender kiss before gently placing her in the cosy lambswool-lined cat travel box.

As she left the hotel room, she joined Miguel in the car park, where he was patiently waiting with the car engine running. Milly winked at Butterkins and said, "Oh my God, when he sees you, his eyes will surely pop out of his sockets."

Little did Millicent know how accurate her words would prove to be.

CHAPTER 45
LET IT SNOW! LET IT SNOW! LET IT SNOW!

Saul was a man on a mission. He had worked out the timeframe for what he was about to do—there wasn't much room for delay. He'd made his decision; he was about to break his own killing rules and his very own code of conduct. The British bitch had to die. Today was the day that the town of Yeovilton would rejoice.

Speeding along the pothole roads, avoiding the larger ones when and where he could, he pulled into his little brother's secluded drive and parked behind Blaze's vehicle. Saul sighed and felt for the little baggie of animal sedatives in his inside jacket pocket. He had brought them with him as well as a Texas mickey of moonshine. The plan was to sit down with his little brother, offer him a conciliatory drink, and try to talk sense into him about his drug use and the reckless affair he was conducting with the pastor's wife.

Although the two brothers saw eye to eye on very little, Blaze had been helpful when he'd given Saul information about the newcomers' homes, properties, and whether there were any feline occupants. Blaze had little care in what would happen to the residents as he was always paid in advance by the customer, a term of his employment. He was one of the best carpenters in the area and was always in high demand.

As the executor of his mother's estate, Saul gave his little brother an allowance each month from their mother's riches. Wise Philomena Maçon knew her youngest child was profligate, and any monies left to him should be carefully administered by her trustworthy and sensible eldest boy.

Today was allowance day, and Saul would hand-deliver Blaze his stipend. However, this evening was different; he was to read his little brother the riot act. It was a simple choice: dollars or lust. There would be no hard feelings if he chose Mrs. Skank over his inheritance money. However, there would also be consequences.

Saul and Gabe were fully in agreement about what was about to transpire—well, most of it.

On several occasions, Blaze's truck was parked outside the pastor's home and alongside a Skank vehicle in remote locations. The little British blonde firecracker had cast her seductive spell on the locals as well as Blaze, who was now entirely under her beguilement. Saul shrugged; the sound of the door slamming shut echoing through the air.

With a bottle in hand, he approached Blaze's house's large green wooden door. Blaze had complained about being stuck with the smallest of the three properties—a cosy three-bedroom rancher with a garage that rarely saw any use. He failed to appreciate his property, which held a delightful lakefront, a jetty, and a charming boathouse tucked away in the back. The three-hundred feet of lakeside beach was a highly sought-after amenity in the surrounding area. Despite this, Blaze grumbled and raised concerns about the fairness of his mother's will.

Saul pounded on the door using his clenched hand. There was no response. He knocked once more, twisting the handle and pushing the door. The entrance was locked. The curtains were closed, blocking the view through the large front windows of the house. He tapped on the glass, but there was no response. He glanced at his watch and let out a frustrated grunt, knowing Blaze was home; however, the silence in the house suggested that his brother had probably fallen asleep.

As Saul approached the back of the house, he peered through the kitchen window. The glass was like a canvas, displaying the breathtaking hues of the sunset; his face appeared distorted, courtesy of the reflection from the sunlit lake. He grasped the doorknob, twisted it, and fortunately, it yielded.

A sense of urgency filled Saul's voice as he broke the silence. "Blaze! Blaze! I'm here. Are you there, brudder?"

There was no response. Closing the door, Saul carefully entered the dining area next to Blaze's kitchen. His heart skipped a beat as he caught sight of a pair of legs sprawled on the floor in the lounge, partially concealed by a wall separating the kitchen/diner. Despite its tidy appearance, the home had a half-eaten meal sitting on the blue laminated countertop, revealing recent activity. Blaze, who both brothers thought was pretty much useless, proved his carpentry skills by renovating his mother's home.

"Blaze! Blaze!"

With a brisk pace, he took a deep breath and entered the lounge area. As Saul's eyes opened wide, he felt a surge of adrenaline course through his veins. Blaze was sprawled on the floor, his back leaning against the sofa, his head drooping with his chin resting on his chest. A solitary ornament adorned the table—a captivating black-and-white metal figurine depicting a man and woman in a salsa pose, their bodies intertwined. With each step, Saul closed the distance between himself and Blaze, his movements deliberate and calculated. His brother's breathing was shallow. His eyes were tightly shut, and saliva was dribbling from his mouth in a steady, stringy stream. Saul clutched Blaze's arm and detected a feeble pulse. His brother's cell phone lay next to him, partially grasped in his right hand, suggesting he had been using it before losing consciousness. Saul's eyes were drawn to the glass table in front of Blaze. They rested on a stack of three baggies containing white remnants and he noticed a fine layer of white powder on the table—like freshly fallen icing sugar. Upon closer inspection, it became apparent that Blaze's moustache was sprinkled with snowy dust, giving it an almost ethereal glow.

"You idiotic clown. Well, looks like you've done me a favour tonight, haven't you?"

Once again, Saul checked his pulse, and it was undeniably weak. The cautious brother hesitated to touch the phone in Blaze's hand, mindful of the need to wear his latex gloves. He was worried about the potential contamination of the cocaine with fentanyl, knowing that even the slightest contact with the drug could be fatal. He had to return to his truck and collect his small kit bag on the passenger seat to take it back to the house.

Saul needed to be quick to take advantage of the situation. He no longer needed the hooch. Blaze was almost comatose, but he needed him to be asleep for at least another hour, maybe ninety minutes. He put on his booties, latex gloves, and hazmat suit and returned to the kitchen via the rear doors. Blaze was still stupefied, so he propped up his little brother.

"You silly little bastard, what have you done?"

Using his brother's index finger, Saul unlocked Blaze's cell phone. He noticed it still had a decent charge. The last time he used his phone, Blaze had been messaging someone. His eyes focused on the name of the contact: "Goddess."

He shook his head in disgust, muttering, "Goddess, my ass," under his breath. With each message Saul read between Goddess and Blaze, he could feel the tension and excitement building, as if he were right there amid their dialogue. He shook his head repeatedly, the movement becoming more pronounced with each shake. The messages were filled with declarations of love and promises of elopement.

The lovey-dovey messages were terrible enough, but to Saul's astonishment, the "Goddess" urged him to betray his brothers for their criminal deeds. Blaze had even written that his older brother was "a psycho freak that liked pussy—the feline kind." Goddess and Blaze sent memes to each other, showing Saul having sex with a different cat each night.

Saul's face turned scarlet. Blaze groaned but didn't open his eyes.

With a furrowed brow, he unzipped his white plastic onesie, reached into the inside pocket, and took out the brown-hued medication bottle intended for veterinary use sedation. Saul did not want his half-witted brother to wake up—he needed him to remain where he was—fully sedated. Delicately, he gently slid two small tablets under his tongue in his half-open mouth. He couldn't resist reading more messages between the two.

> GODDESS: HOTLIPS . . . I ♥ U

> BM: I Love you more, sexy chick.

> GODDESS: I WANT U 2 TAKE ME FROM
> BEHIND. AGAIN!

Saul looked at his brother with a face full of contempt.

> BM: I need you now.

> GODDESS: COME OVER

BM: My dumbass brother is visiting.

GODDESS: THE CAT FREAK?

BM: Yeppers. He's bringing me my cheque for being a good boy. Jerk.

GODDESS: HURRY UP! GET RID OF THAT INBRED, LOL. MY ASS IS BURNING UP IN ANTICIPATION

BM: I need—

GODDESS: U NEED?

GODDESS: WHAT MY ♥ ??

GODDESS: HOTLIPS R U OK???

Blaze had yet to complete his last response, due thirty minutes ago. Saul began tapping on the phone's keypad.

BM: Goddess? Are you there?

BM: I'm back. This is important.

BM: It's Urgent. OMG. Quick!

A minute went by. Saul closed his eyes and took a deep breath.

GODDESS: MY HOT LOVER. WHAT IS IT?

BM: I need to see you right now.

GODDESS: GIRLS R TUCKED UP IN BED

BM: Where is your other half?

GODDESS: ALL NITE PRAYER MEETING - BACK AT 6.30AM

BM: I'm coming over. Right now.

GODDESS: U SAUCY BOY

BM: I want to take you over the pastor's desk in the study.

> GODDESS: U NEED 2 B QUIET. COME OVER
> BY PADDLE BOARD

> BM: Will do. Get ready for me. I will message
> you when I come ashore. Be ready.

> BM: Bare your ass, look out the pastor's window
> and imagine him watching you. I will come up
> behind you and—

> GODDESS: STOP. I AM 2 HORNY

> GODDESS: HURRY UP

Saul smirked. "You won't feel so 'horny' when you meet my friend, Thor," he whispered at the phone. Saul slipped the phone into his own pocket. He deftly examined under his brother's tongue. No sign of white remains of the sedative.

Saul returned to his vehicle, removed the hazmat suit, placed it in a big bag, and swapped it with another one. He grabbed Blaze's O'Neil paddle board and paddle, along with his backpack, from the storage hooks outside the back of the rancher. Then, he switched out his booties for flexible rubber board shoes. Despite being too small, he could fit them on his feet by removing his work boots and putting them in the backpack. He descended the incline towards the lake with a small electric motor in hand.

The paddle board on his shoulder added an extra weight to his steps. Shaking his head in disbelief, he couldn't help but giggle to himself. "Saucy boy? My hot lover? Hotlips?" His face quickly contorted into a scowl, and with an irritated tone, he muttered, "So, apparently, I'm inbred, and I have sex with my cats, do I?"

Balancing himself on the jetty, he carefully placed the board and motor on the calm lakefront. He launched himself onto the water with a long paddle, using the motor to propel him across the lake on his twenty-minute journey to the Skank property.

"Finally, that damned family will get what's coming to them."

CHAPTER 46
THE CROWN JEWELS

MILLY WAS DEALING with much nervous energy; trusting another cat was a big issue for her. Once Butterkins had been handed over to be impregnated, there was no turning back. Her baby was a beautiful pedigree, so her kittens also needed to be. This would be her first litter—so she could feel the dampness forming under her armpits, despite it being April. She had paid half of the fee on the TomMolly app and would transfer the second part once setting her eyes on the tomcat. There was no guarantee her precious Butterkins would be with kittens; however, Thomas the Tank's track record spoke for itself. What a handsome boy he was: Amber eyes and blue-grey coat, stocky build, and kind temperament were no sweeter match for her precious Persian.

Miguel and Milly were only five minutes away from their destination. As dusk settled, the tall cedar trees stood like guardians of the night, obscuring much of the stars and moonlight. Amidst the shadows, the signpost for Quincy Lake emerged, revealing the beauty that awaited in the unknown.

"SAUL, WTF?" Gabe said, taking a much closer look at Old Tom. He was dumbfounded. Not only was one of his eyes twice the size of the other, but it was bright green, while the tomcat's other eye was amber-yellow.

"Shit! Shit!"

Gabe could hear the client's vehicle pulling up on the drive. He peeked from the window and saw two bright headlights, almost causing him to wince as he looked at them. The SUV door swung open, revealing a shadowy figure stepping out from the rear. Gabe wisely chose the one Thursday each month when the Rum Runner was closed for the day, allowing him to handle his errands and enjoy a well-deserved break from work.

Once Old Tom finished the bedding, his reward would include unrestricted access to the pub, a bowl filled to the brim with luscious cream, and a can of sardines in his grandiose "I am the King" bowl. Saul would receive a message informing him that his moggie had sown his seed.

Gabe took the mating ritual very seriously. Gabe monitored the cats' interactions on CCTV. He would step in if Old Tom became overly playful or irritable, just as he had done before when the female cat had been petrified by Old Tom, aka Long John Silver. The entire situation turned into a bloodbath, but luckily, it concluded when Gabe rushed into the breeding chamber and rescued the injured molly from the furious tomcat. Evidently, one-eyed cats didn't appeal to mollies. That was then, and this was now. Despite Saul's efforts to restore Old Tom's appearance, he still had a sinister demeanour, and the faux pas of the enormous green eyeball was hard to ignore.

There was a knock on the door. Gabe covered half of Tom's face with a soft woollen hood. He tentatively opened the door and welcomed Millicent Mandi. Although the porch was lit up and the house lights were on, Milly, Gabe, and the cat that Gabe held close to his chest were shadowy figures.

Through the cat box, Gabe could see Millicent's molly was a stunner. It was a Persian breed with beautiful blue eyes and a well-groomed coat. Butterkins became agitated and began trill-meowing.

"Hello, you must be Monsieur Maçon. Are you going to introduce me to—"

"Yes, I am Gabe," he said, holding out his hand. "Pleased to meet you." He looked down at Old Tom's partly covered face. "I hereby introduce you to . . . Sir Thomas the Tank," proclaimed Gabe.

Milly caught a glimpse of old Tom's handsome face. Old Tom purred in Gabe's arms.

"Can I hold him?" Milly asked. "If so, I'll let you hold my precious Butterkins, the Queen of the Florida Keys."

Gabe could smell the molly's scent, which Old Tom noticed as he began to hiss, growl, and grunt.

"I'm not sure if Sir Thomas will want to be held by a human he has never met."

Gabe also smelt an unfamiliar perfume, which hung like a cloud above both breeder and cat. Butterkins yowled, and Old Tom's purrs vibrated through Gabe's hands.

Trying to deflect Milly's question, Gabe chortled, "Your molly is surely giving off the musky scent odour; I'm almost choking on it."

Milly looked perplexed. "Odour? I can't smell anything. If there is any smell, it will surely come from your cat, not mine."

The smell of cat and perfume had become unbearable; Gabe started to cough and splutter. "I think it's time for these two to couple up."

Milly wrapped her fingers around Gabe's muscular arm. "Wait," said Milly earnestly. "I don't need to *hold* Sir Thomas. I just want to look into his beautiful amber eyes. Show me his face!"

Gabe sighed. He could see thousands of dollars going down the plug hole. He pulled back the woollen hood and—

The lights flickered and went out. The area was plunged into total darkness.

CHAPTER 47
LIGHTS OUT!

Saul's heart pounded. This was what he lived for—the feeling of thrill. The adrenaline surging through his body made him feel alive. Cocaine had nothing on the buzz of hunting down prey. A sensory explosion, with sights, sounds, smells, tastes, and textures all hitting him at once. The closed curtains in Skank's study couldn't hide the inviting glow of the light that spilt out from within. He knew she was waiting for him.

He changed his latex gloves and wore his brother's jean jacket over the onesie. It didn't fit him properly, and he really didn't care. This would be the perfect crime, and the blonde "thing" that had beguiled half of the town would soon be gone. He replayed scenes in his mind of Raylene Skank and her spawn laughing and mocking him at her front door. He'd only need his trusty mallet and a face shield to keep him free from Skank's triple-B's: her bone, brain, and blood. Saul left the backpack behind the rear window of the house, careful not to make a sound as he moved around the side of the property towards the kitchen. He had familiarized himself with the house's layout, so he knew that beyond the dining area, the study awaited him to the right.

The door would be unlocked. Upon entering the house, he noticed that it was adequately lit. Even though he'd targeted his victims under the cover of darkness, he broke his pattern and carried out the slaying of the vet with the lights fully on. Saul definitely preferred *seeing* Thor complete his mission. Creeping through the kitchen, he reached for Blaze's phone one last time.

> BM: I'm almost here. The lake was calm to cross tonight

> BM: Are you ready for me?

> GODDESS: HOTLIPS . . . COME QUICKLY. MY VAJAJAY ACHES 4 U

He whispered under his breath, "Disgusting whore, it won't be your vajajay that aches in a few minutes." Saul typed:

> BM: I'm in command. Turn away from the door. Get yourself ready. You will feel my thick, throbbing hammer.

> GODDESS: CAN'T WAIT 4 U 2 POUND ME!

> BM: Do as I say. If you want your reward.

> BM: Open your legs and say no more

> GODDESS: Yes, U horny fox

Saul heard a muffled squeal from inside a door adjacent to the kitchen.

"So, you're in there, huh?" He calmly walked to the door with a metal sign that was marked "private." He pushed it open. The first thing he saw was Raylene Skank bent over a large wooden desk. She wore a short miniskirt, fishnet stockings and red high heel boots. He could see the top of her peroxide-blonde hair. Both arms were stretched out as if they were in the crucifix position.

She whispered, "Take me."

He slowly approached his nemesis and drew within two feet of his fourth victim. Skank moved her body seductively, gyrating her hips and giving a teasing tap to her rear end, then smoothly placed her hand back on the desk.

"I know you're standing there," she said in a gruff, low-toned, sexy voice. "Hurry up and bang me." Her distinctive, overly bleached blonde hair was spread over the wooden desk. Saul took one step towards her and snapped down the face shield. He smiled, raised his hammer and—

The lights went out.

Nevertheless, he followed through with a mighty swing. THUMP! He hit her with all of his might. "Priestess, meet your maker!"

The sudden darkness was eerie. "What a time for a power outage. That damned Poskett family's Easter Bunny hydro-surge. Every frigging evening."

He retraced his steps in the pitch blackness, went back outside, lifted the bloody face shield, reached into his backpack, and grabbed his flashlight. He still had a lot of work to do to make the crime scene speak to the dumbass cops and forensic team. He felt good, looked up at the stars and muttered to the universe, "The witch is dead, the witch is dead, the Wicked Witch of the East is dead."

Saul walked back to the study room and shone the flashlight upon his bloody footsteps and the slumped over-the-desk body. "I can't wait to see the bitch's pancake-shaped head." He bent down to pick up his trusty wooden mallet in case he had to flatten her bonce some more. Saul shone his light on the end of the hammer. Something was attached to it. His heart skipped a beat.

The lights flickered and came back on.

He blinked and hid his eyes momentarily from the sudden brightness. His eyes could now see what was on the end of his hammer—a mass of blood, brains, and strands of blonde nylon hair.

"What the—"

He slowly walked up to the pastor's desk and couldn't help himself—he had to run his gloved fingers over the mahogany. "Beautiful workmanship. God, I love wood." Then he turned his eyes to the body of his victim.

"What the fu—"

Saul bent down to look at a bloody mass of hair partly covering her face. Lifeless eyes stared at him through the mop. He grabbed a tuft of hair, and it all lifted into his hand. "Holy shit!"

Raylene Skank was not Raylene Skank. It was her husband, Harry.

Saul's heart was in his mouth. He stared at the body; the upper half was prostrate on the wooden study desk. He had put his all into the death swing, but his aim hadn't been true due to the last-second darkness. The back of the head was completely caved in, the face untarnished.

"Harry Skank? My brudder, Blaze, was having an affair with . . . Pastor Harry Skank? Holy crap." Harry's mascaraed, bloodshot eyes were wide open. His black lipstick made him look like a goth. "Shit. Who'd have thought?"

Despite the heavy thud that echoed through the house, an eerie silence was still coming from the upstairs rooms. "No wonder your kids are all messed up," he muttered under his breath, his eyes filled with contempt. He reassured himself, "Everything is fine. These power outages are really getting on my nerves. If I can make it through this, Poskett's in for a rude awakening, no doubt about it."

He took another deep breath and reached into his blood-stained jean jacket pocket, took out Blaze's signature Home Hardware beanie and the cell phone, and smeared blood onto both hat and device. Saul removed sections and clusters of the blonde wig from Harry's head and carefully stored them in a Ziploc bag. After wiping his gloved fingers in the pool of sticky blood, he boldly wrote the word "CHEAT" on the smooth mahogany surface. Dipping the latex glove into more gore, he then removed it, placed it in the bag, expelled any remaining air, and securely sealed it. He put a spare mitt onto his bare hand. He conversed with Harry as if he were alive:

"This will give your girls the surprise of their lives when your body is discovered. Welcome to a world of pain, Skank Family."

He grabbed the mallet, left the study room, and caught his reflection in a mirror, noticing Blaze's blood-stained jean jacket. The murder weapon's end was still dripping with blood. He reached the door, flipped the light switch off and used the flashlight to navigate. Time was now of the essence and every second counted. He had to escape, but he also needed to find a hiding spot for the murder weapon—a place where the police would stumble upon it. The torchlight swept across the yard, revealing the frosty tips of the grass and the many patches of bare, hardened soil.

"There it is. Perfect!"

Saul approached a small, circular concrete slab a few feet from the house. He carefully placed the hammer on the ground next to him, then dropped to one knee and exerted his strength to lift the concrete slab and move it aside. His nostrils flared at the recognizable smell of the septic tank. Pulling Thor towards him, he guided it downwards into the pitch-black void. Pausing for a moment, he whispered, "Goodbye, my dear old friend.

Until we meet again." The mallet fell into the sewage with a resounding splat. Removing Blaze's blood-soaked beanie hat, Saul disposed of it by lobbing it into the tank. Mockingly, he gestured with a sign of the cross while partially replacing the tank cover, leaving no doubt to anyone searching the area that it had been disturbed. With a flashlight, he stood up and examined what he had done. With a nod, he quietly muttered, "Yes, even that incompetent detective would stumble upon this clue."

Saul jogged to the lakefront to be reunited with his paddle board, paddle, and motor. He gingerly stepped onto the board, keeping his balance by placing the paddle in the water, which touched the bottom of the shallow part of the lake. Saul started the quiet engine and set off towards his brother's house, which was directly across the lake.

He chuckled. "Gotta get back before the real Mrs. Skank returns from her prayer meeting to find her husband in a compromising position."

CHAPTER 48
HERE, KITTY KITTY

IN THE ABSENCE OF LIGHT, Old Tom and Butterkins were introduced to each other in the love chamber. Their chemistry was instant, leading to a feisty interaction. As the light returned, the CCTV captured when Old Tom was on top of the molly. Gabe couldn't believe what he was witnessing. As the camera zoomed in on Old Tom's face, he couldn't help but laugh. The cat's fake eye bugged out so much that Gabe thought Old Tom looked like a cartoon character whose eye kept popping out and was being held in situ with a spring. As a savvy entrepreneur, he figured he could make some serious cash by turning the still shot into a viral meme.

When Tom and Butterkins completed their act, amid the squawking and howling of the molly and frantic panting of the tomcat, they faced each other for the first time in the light. Butterkins hissed. Old Tom's big green eye was still bugging out of his head. He approached her again as if he were going in for seconds. Butterkins was undoubtedly shaken by her lover's distorted facial features, as evidenced by her frantic movements around the sanctuary's perimeter. Old Tom struggled to regain his balance as he searched for the elusive Persian cat, a shadow scurrying around the edge, his one good eye desperately trying to bring the creature into focus.

Gabe sensed that proud Old Tom might not have dealt with the rejection well. With claws out, the hurt tomcat made a sudden leap towards

Butterkins. Gabe caught him in mid-air. "Good boy!" he said, stroking him as he backed out of the doorway.

Old Tom was released for his deserved reward. To calm down the freaked-out molly, Gabe picked her up and placed Butterkins back into her luxurious travel box, with the flap open, in case she wanted a drink or to use the cat litter. Partially closing the door behind him, Gabe watched Old Tom scamper towards his lavish salmon, tuna fish, and kibble meal. The hungry tomcat tucked into the feast.

Old Tom finished his meal. The richness of the food and his frenetic activities in the bedding chamber must've made him thirsty. He dashed to the washroom, ignoring the bowl of water next to the kibble as was Old Tom's habit. With practised agility, the sly cat hopped onto the toilet bowl and lowered his face towards the water in the basin. After a few deep slurps, something unfortunate happened. The exertion of the mating experience with the molly had dislodged his new eyeball due to ocular pressure. It had loosened, and the muscles could no longer hold the glass prosthetic eye in place. Although Saul's ligatures and sewing skills were excellent for an amateur, the inevitable was bound to happen. When Old Tom drank from the toilet, gravity caused his prosthetic to pop out with a splash. Seeing a giant, green eyeball in the basin freaked out Old Tom. Making a sudden squawking noise, he instinctively used his front paws to push himself backwards, emerging from the toilet bowl with the flair of a character in a Bond movie being ejected from a sports car.

Gabe caught a fleeting glimpse of the thick-set grey-blue cat darting by, its paws barely making a sound on the floor as it raced towards the mating sanctuary through the slightly ajar door. Meanwhile, having seemingly calmed down from seeing the googly-eyed tomcat, Butterkins came face-to-face with a cat with a gaping hole next to his one amber eye. She hissed and patted her paw at the one-eyed feline. Old Tom backed away and ran out of the door to find a dark alcove hidden far away from the world.

Gabe spent a good hour searching for Old Tom, who emerged from his hiding spot enticed by the aroma of cat treats and soft whispers of "Here, kitty kitty." Watching the cat tuck into his munchies, he couldn't get the image of the meme out of his mind. "Haha, you looked like a total goofball, my friend."

CHAPTER 49
THE STAGE IS SET

THE FULL MOON gave Saul enough light to navigate the lake to reach Blaze's beach. Upon arriving at the shingled shoreline, Saul dragged the paddle board halfway up the thirty-degree incline that led to his brother's garden hut and the kitchen door. Abandoning the board and paddle halfway up the hill, he headed back to where, hopefully, Blaze was still unconscious. He kicked off the uncomfortable board boots by the back door.

Saul had left the house lights on when leaving his brother's home. Walking through the kitchen door, he was relieved that his brother hadn't moved an inch. Blaze's head hung down as if he was staring at the floor. His back was still propped up against the leather sofa, and his legs spread apart in a V-shape. The empty baggies of drugs were still on the glass table. Remnants of his cocaine fest were still present: fine white dust spread over the table, himself, and the surroundings, making Saul anxious. He bent down and felt for a pulse. Nothing. He put his ear to Blaze's mouth and watched the movement from his chest. His brother was still alive, barely. Saul carefully examined Blaze's arms for intravenous use. Needle marks were not present. He grabbed his backpack and carefully looked for a vial of clear liquid he had used on Old Tom for pain relief, courtesy of the murdered vet. He unscrewed the container, removed the lid, and emptied the white powdered remnants of the baggies into the vial. "I'd make a fine pharmacist," he shared with his comatose sibling. Saul had created his own concoction of fentanyl and anaesthesia. He replaced the lid and shook it furiously until the liquid was clear. Saul took out a syringe and placed it in Blaze's hand, pressing his brother's fingers against the plastic plunger. His original plan was to talk to his brother and warn him to back off the pastor's wife, but Saul had a change of heart as his brother was clearly an idiot and knew way too much about the Maçon brothers' recent antics. Having read several texts that went back-and-forth between him and "the goddess," there was a real danger he may have shared secrets, not just to Skank, but to his other lovers. No, he was too much of a liability and a total disgrace, so Saul intended to put him to sleep for good.

He felt like God, or his mother, Philomena, was looking down upon him, sanctioning him to not only slay the cult leader but also his dumbass junkie of a brother at the same time.

"Goodbye, baby brudder," he said without emotion, tying a make-do tourniquet to his upper arm and finding one of Blaze's now prominent veins with the syringe he was inadvertently holding. Blaze grunted as the needle pricked his skin and slid into the vein. Saul helped Blaze empty the cocktail of narcotics into his arm. "What a nice way to join your lover. Better than getting a whack on the head from Thor, don't you think?" Saul loosened the tourniquet. With one last sigh, Blaze Maçon slipped away.

Saul removed his syringe hand and lay it next to his body. He grabbed his backpack and retrieved the Ziploc containing the glove, hair strands, and gore. He lifted up his brother's right hand, placed the bloody latex glove over Blaze's fingers, stretched out his index digit and smeared "I'M SORRY" onto the glass surface.

Saul removed the glove, put it back into the Ziploc, then daubed Blaze's skin with remnants of blood, hair, and some of Harry Skank's brain, taking the hand and wiping it, leaving finger smears on his jeans. He took Blaze's phone from the denim pocket and opened his last dialogue with "Goddess." With Blaze's finger, he tapped out:

> BM: I am sorry. I can't live without you.
>
> BM: Meet you in heaven, my love.
>
> BM: Thank you for not telling anyone about my other killings.

BM: With a heavy heart, I say goodbye, I'm gonna get high.

BM: LOL

Saul pressed send. He left the phone on the floor next to him and dropped his brother's soiled hand back by his side. Saul stood up and surveyed his handiwork—the syringe continued to stick out of Blaze's left arm. "Just one more thing to do, my brudder." He removed the denim jacket he'd been wearing, walked into the kitchen area and placed the coat on the back of one of the chairs. Now he had to get out of the house lickety-split. Checking that he hadn't left any clues to his own presence at the house, he retraced the crime in his head.

The only spanner in the works was that he pummeled Harry Skank's head and not Raylene's. "This should cause enough stink for the dumb Brits to go back to where they belong and leave our town and our community." He grinned. "They'll have to close down the stupid church; me and Gabe will share our dead brother's estate."

As he stripped the hazmat suit from his body, placing everything in a bright yellow hazardous waste bag, he psyched himself up to tell his story to Gabe. It was as if he was talking to his mother. "Yes, I'll tell Gabe that I had found our brudder dead on arrival—it looked like some kind of murder-suicide. I'll tell Gabe that his brudder was having a sordid affair with the Skank woman, and the shit would soon hit the fan. It was awful to see my brudder. I don't think I'll ever get over him sitting there with a needle in his vein."

Gabe would give Saul the perfect alibi, and then he'd collect Old Tom and return to his home. He was delighted that he'd no longer be hassled or interrupted by the awful Skank daughters. "I only wish I could see their horrible little faces when they wake up in the morning to find out their beloved father had been brutally murdered while wearing their mother's clothes. Mother, God is surely good."

CHAPTER 50

911, WHAT'S YOUR EMERGENCY?

Central Dispatch received the 911 call in the early hours of the morning. Chief Kennedy directed Sergeant Barnes and Senior Constable Noble to Colonel Road, the home of Pastor Harry. A distraught Raylene appeared inconsolable, in shock, sobbing and yelling at her daughters to get back to their rooms. Raylene had ended the call from dispatch, and Chief Kennedy had received the message directly from the confused operator at the call centre in Halifax.

Initially, Chief Kennedy had told dispatch that he was "tied up," as he actually was—bound up in the mayor's large bondage closet at the time. Mayor Quipp held Kennedy's cell phone to his face and continued to caress his testicles with a vibrating sex toy. With much coaching from Mayor Quipp in Kennedy's ear, he said to the dispatcher, "Okay, okay. Please calm down. I'll send my crack crime unit to the scene."

"Sir, do you want help—" Bronwyn vigorously shook her head, and ran her finger across her neck from ear to ear.

Kennedy's eyes widened in surprise as he quickly shook his head. "No. I don't want help from the RCMP or other police services."

The mayor silently gestured "You've got this!" and gave Kennedy's nuts one last squeeze.

Kennedy squealed. "For heaven's sake—get me out of here."

"Sir? Get you out of where? Are you in danger?" asked the confused dispatch worker.

Mayor Quipp leaned in close to Kennedy's ear, "If you say please, I'll let you go."

Kennedy locked his eyes into his lover's. "Please, Bronwyn, please. There's been another murder. This time, it's *awful*."

"Sir, who is Bronwyn? My name is Susan Nickerson. Senior Dispatch Officer. Yes sir, it sounds really bad."

The mayor unbuckled the harness that supported the police chief's body. Kennedy sounded distressed and began to panic. "Yes, yes. Ten four. Over and out. Nickerson, get off the damned line." The call ended.

Mayor Quipp gave her submissive another squeeze of the testicles. "Mistress. You call me Mistress; you don't get to call me Bronwyn," she snarled.

Filled with desperation, Kennedy's voice trembled as he addressed the mayor. "Please, I'm begging you, let me go. This can't keep happening."

"Oh, diddums. You want to stay hanging up there?"

"No, of course not."

"No, of course not, Mistress."

"Of course, not . . . Mistress."

"Your new safe words are, *I'm a Dumbass*. So, say it."

"I'm a Dumbass."

His kinky lover released the final two wrist restraints, and Chief Kennedy was set free. He reached for his phone and immediately called Sergeant Barnes, who was wide awake playing *Candy Cane Chase* on his laptop.

"Get your ass to Colonel Road, the pastor's house. He's been malleted to death."

"Oh, no!"

"Oh, yes. Grab a SOCO set and meet—"

"A SOCO set?"

"A Scenes Of Crime Officer kit, moron. You're supposed to be a detective. This isn't your first rodeo."

Mayor Quipp whispered in Kennedy's ear, "Tell him he's a fucktard."

He shook his head furiously, ignoring her, he said, "Mrs. Skank found her dead husband, prostrate on his study desk, wearing her panties and looking like the lead singer of the Cure."

"What colour panties, sir?"

Kennedy winked at his lover, and directed the response at the cell phone. "You're a fucktard. Now, get out there—remember the twenty-two-minute rule."

"Yes, sir. Sorry for being a fucktard, sir."

"One more thing . . . the millions of daughters they have—"

"Seven. The Skanks have seven daughters, sir."

The chief pulled on his uniform pants. "Get an officer to take Mrs. Skank and her gaggle of girls somewhere safe. I want the house cleared of Skanks."

"Yes, sir."

As the mayor approached Kennedy, she playfully blew into his ear and gave him a wet lick that sent shivers down his spine. As he tried to slip his arm into his shirt, he frantically brushed away the distraction. "Get off!" he shouted; his voice filled with irritation. "Stop it!"

"Sir?"

"Stop turning me on!"

"I'm not trying to, sir. I'm just awaiting your instructions. I didn't mean to turn you—"

"Not you, you idiot." Chief Kennedy's eyes darted towards Mayor Quipp's tongue, which flicked in and out like a snake. "I'm a dumbass," he whispered the safe word, his tone laced with a mix of frustration and amusement.

"Sir?" he asked, his tone respectful yet hesitant. "You're not, sir. I have immense respect and a genuine love for you, sir."

Kennedy snarled at Mayor Quipp and then said to Barnes, "Just go, and this better be solved by the morning Sergeant. This is the fourth murder, and the RCMP will get itchy feet and stick their noses into our business. The perp's name has to be on my desk by 11 a.m."

"Yes, sir."

Barnes appeared slightly confused during the exchange with his boss. Unfortunately, the slaying of the cross-dressing pastor happened at an inopportune moment for him. He had just reached level 247 on *Candy Cane Chase* and was on the verge of surpassing his personal best score.

CHAPTER 51
DSM-5

RAYLENE COULDN'T MOVE or speak as she sat on the stairs of the house in complete and utter shock. After holding a late evening vigil at the church, her prayer warriors anxiously awaited the possible second coming of the prophet Bhagwan from Oregon, hoping to witness his visit to their town and his plans for new communities in Canada. The Canadians appeared like ripe fruit, just waiting to be plucked by the Bhagwan's message. After everyone had left the church building, she met up with a fisherman from Neck Point to engage in a special prayer and ministry session, offering insightful oral input.

Raylene had no idea of her husband's sexual peccadillos. Harry had kept his secret fascination with fetishism hidden from her. When she marched into the house, she immediately felt a sense of unease. As she walked past the side, kitchen, and open study doors, she couldn't help but notice the disturbing blood smears. An acrid metallic odour lingered in the air, causing her stomach to churn. However, nothing could have prepared her for the shocking sight of her deceased husband. He was wearing one of her beloved teddies. The sight of her exclusive pair of mid-rise thong Victoria's Secret panties hanging from his lily-white backside caught her off guard. Her husband slouched over his mahogany desk, leaving an imprint of his mashed-up head.

She let out a blood-curdling scream, instinctively covering her mouth with her hands. Blanche's familiar voice echoed from the upstairs hallway, shattering the eerie silence. "Mom, is everything okay? Are those nightmares about eating rappie pie haunting you again?"

Realizing that her husband's killer might still be in the house and overwhelmed with fear and adrenaline, Raylene rushed to the kitchen. Her eyes scanned the room, searching for any signs of the intruder. She grabbed the largest knife from the wooden block.

"Blanche, stay upstairs—"

Unfortunately, Blanche and two other girls had already raced down the stairs, their hair dishevelled, and they were wearing matching Winnie the Pooh pajamas.

Blanche yelled, "Mom, what the fuck? You've killed Dad." Her eldest daughter's eyes were wide open, taking in the full horror of the crime scene. As if choreographed, the trio turned their heads together, their gazes fixated on their mother brandishing the carving knife, her appearance reminiscent of a deranged banshee.

Raylene fumbled in her purse for her cell phone and called 911, her hands shaking so badly that she nearly dialled 191, Bangkok's ambulance service.

The girls crept forward, eager to see what had happened in their dad's study.

"Get upstairs," their mom yelled, as she spoke to someone on the end of her phone.

"Shit," said Stevie.

"Is Harry dead?" asked Alison.

Blanche was quickest to respond, "If he is, I hope I get his MacBook. My Acer sucks ass."

Stevie looked at her sisters and said, "I bet it was the creepy guy next door."

"You mean the crypt keeper?"

It was a rare occasion when any of the daughters listened to and obeyed their mother. "Get upstairs—all of you!" she yelled hysterically.

With a forced laugh, Blanche squinted her eyes and replied, "Chillax, you've already butchered Dad, and now you expect us to go upstairs and wait for our turn. Ain't happening." With arms crossed, Alison and Stevie stood in solidarity next to each other, nodding in affirmation alongside their eldest sister.

Within ten minutes, blue and white lights, accompanied by the wailing of sirens, headed towards the Skank residence. Police cars, ambulances, and even two fire trucks arrived at the scene. Detective Sergeant Barnes stepped out of his unmarked police car and shook Noble's hand, who had arrived in the Bravo Lima four-two patrol car with Officer Bear.

"Have you been inside?" asked Barnes.

"Nope. Just arrived before you, bro."

Barnes barked an order at Officer Bear, "Go take Mrs. Skank and her Skankettes somewhere safe for the night."

Turning towards Constable Noble, he snapped, "Let's secure the perimeter. Remember, the nut job might still be here."

"Are we going to call the dog unit from Halifax, Sarge?"

"Nope," he replied. "The chief wants us to handle it. He also demanded the perp's name by 11 a.m. So we've got our work cut out."

Noble scratched his head. "Eleven? This is the fourth murder—and we still have no clue as to the identity of the killer."

With a knowing smile, Barnes said, "This is bound to be a crime of passion."

"It is?"

"Yup," he replied with a nod. "I received a warning from the chief that the pastor is a cross-dresser."

"Sarge, nowadays we refer to that as a transvestic disorder."

"Whatever, Constable Noble. He's a gay. All pastors are super gay . . . and he's had his gay ass drilled for the last time."

"Actually, in the DSM-5, the transvestic disorder is described as a specific paraphilic disorder in which individuals experience sexual arousal by cross-dressing as the opposite gender. Sergeant Barnes, we both attended the Diversity and Inclusion course."

A female voice from the darkness yelled, "DSM-5, 302.3, to be precise."

Rubbing her jaw, Officer Bear looked confused. "Hang on, are you sure you're not talking about frotteuristic disorder?"

Emerging from the shadows Officer Gimble said, "Nope, that's when someone has an intense sexual arousal resulting from touching or rubbing against individuals who are nonconsenting."

"A groper, in other words," added Noble.

"I think he probably struggled with transvestism, rather than a transvestic disorder," declared Gimble, matter-of-factly.

The conversation continued for another twenty minutes. All the attending officers engaged in a heated debate as to the difference between a transgendered person and a transvestite. Meanwhile, Raylene remained in the study, on her knees, rocking back and forth in a catatonic trance, clutching the carving knife in her hand. The Skank children were contaminating the crime scene by fighting over chocolate treats from their father's candy cupboard beside his large mahogany desk.

Back outside in the Skank's driveway, Sergeant Barnes decided to have the final say, "Oh whatever, a gay is a gay. Let's go, Noble, and make sure the queen-killer—"

"Killer of a person with transvestism," corrected Officer Gimble.

Barnes glared at his coworker. "—is not hiding amongst the dresses and swimsuits in the master bedroom."

Officer Bear exchanged an exasperated glance with Officer Gimble before setting off to round up Mrs. Skank and her daughters.

CHAPTER 52
MONKEY SEE, MONKEY SAY, MONKEY DO

MARY TOMAHAWK's house was hosting the Skank family. At the same time, Officer Bear diligently gathered information from the sorrowful wife of the deceased Harry Skank. Sergeant Barnes, Constable Noble, SOCO Sarah Mills, and Chief Kennedy converged at the crime scene.

"Give me the Coles Notes right now, Sergeant Barnes."

"Coles Notes?"

"For Heaven's sake, man, we use this term monthly in our book club meeting. A summary. Bullet Points. Salient parts to or of the crime."

"Okay, sir. No casings, gunshot wounds or bullet holes."

Chief Kennedy rolled his eyes.

Constable Noble stepped in where angels feared to tread. "Pastor Skank's body was discovered in the study, his head brutally crushed and his brains splattered across the table, evoking memories of JFK's assassination and Jackie's blood-stained pink Chanel suit."

"Are you sure it was a Chanel suit?" asked Barnes.

"What kind of table was it?" asked Chief Kennedy.

"I think it was good quality mahogany," replied Sergeant Barnes. He then added, "It appeared he was waiting for someone to give him a good rogering from behind."

"Rogering?"

"Drilling. A good drilling."

"Inappropriate," muttered SOCO Sarah Mills, taking photos of the unfortunate victim.

Barnes continued, "He was wearing his wife's panties, half pulled down his hairy ass. His upper body was found prostrate on the desk, with his legs remaining on the floor in an inverted V-dash shape . . ."

Kennedy huffed in frustration. "Coles Notes, man!"

"Sorry, sir . . . his wig—"

Noble couldn't help himself from giggling. Kennedy and Sarah Mills threw death stares at the detective and his sidekick.

"Thank you, sir," continued Barnes. "He was wearing a blonde wig with skull fragments that included parts of the frontal lobe, cerebral cortex, cerebellum, corpus callosum and a squashed eyeball."

Chief Kennedy's mouth hung open momentarily.

"Sorry, sir. I was rather good at human biology in high school, sir."

Sarah Mills stopped what she was doing, winced, and said, "TMI, detective. The pastor's table also had the same kind of messaging, written in blood. It spelt out the word 'CHEAT.'"

Noble added, "Blunt force trauma, sir."

"No shit, Sherlock," muttered Sarah Mills, shaking her head.

"Detective, is there any good news to share?"

"Yes, sir. Forensics believe his ass wasn't penetrated."

Seeing the chief's furrowed brow, Noble added, "He had been holding a cell phone in his right hand."

Kennedy nodded. "Good, do we know who he had been talking to?"

"Yes, Mrs. Skank gave the password to Officer Gimble, who bagged the phone for us and gave the number to SOCO Mills."

"Then un-bag it, now! He may have been communicating with—"

"Um, sexting," corrected Noble, trying to keep a straight face.

"He may have been communicating with . . . *the killer*," said Kennedy indignantly.

The chief sighed, walked through the crime scene, grabbed a pair of latex gloves, pulled them onto his long, skinny fingers, and snatched the Ziploc bag labelled "Exhibit 3" from one of the SOCO totes. Chief Kennedy's actions left the SOCO in shock and horror at the tainting of key evidence. Noticing Mills' open mouth and wide-eyed expression, he cleared his throat and reminded his team of his mantra, "The first twenty-two." He pulled out the victim's phone and shouted at Sarah Mills, demanding the password. Reluctantly, the astonished officer surrendered the information: "SPURS1961." Kennedy eagerly opened up the text messages.

Noble asked, "Sir, what does it say?"

"The majority of the previous texts have been deleted. Nevertheless, one of the first texts was to someone called 'Hot Lips.'"

Barnes and Noble quietly sniggered.

Kennedy's eyes widened in astonishment as he exclaimed, "My God, we have a suspect!" His voice was filled with a combination of shock and urgency. He read out, "I'm almost here. The lake was calm to cross tonight."

"The lake?" Barnes queried. With a commanding presence, Kennedy announced to the room, "The murderer travelled across the lake." The chief went back to the shocking information on the phone and recited, "Open your legs and say no more," and "Yes, you horny fox."

With his shoulders beginning to jiggle, Sergeant Barnes spluttered out, "Horny fox?"

Kennedy continued, "Blah, blah, blah. What's important right now is the messages are sent by someone called . . . BM."

"BM?" questioned Barnes

"BM from across the lake," said Noble.

All three officers said in unison, "Blaze Maçon!"

Kennedy directed Barnes and Noble to Blaze Maçon's home, ensuring they were prepared for any potential confrontation. The two officers saluted in perfect synchrony, their polished boots echoing loudly on the study's wooden floor, and responded with a sharp "Yes, sir. Rest assured, sir, we will handle it!"

The officers sped away from Colonel Road, their flashing lights and wailing sirens echoing through the early morning light. They sped down Colonel Road, the tires screeching as they took a sharp left onto Lakeside Road, heading towards Blaze "Hot Lips" Maçon's house.

With a mischievous smirk, Kennedy locked eyes with Sarah Mills, giving her a knowing nod before triumphantly declaring, "Gotcha, you little shit!"

CHAPTER 53
ALIBI

WHEN SAUL ARRIVED at Gabe's house, he appeared to be in a bit of a tizzy. Putting on an Academy Award-worthy performance, he asked his brother for a glass of strong liquor and suggested that Gabe pour himself a generous one as well. With one swift gulp, he swallowed the fiery liquid and mustered up the courage to inform a stunned Gabe of their brother's passing.

Gabe's face turned pale as the blood drained from it, his mouth hanging open in shock. Saul said he had every intention of giving Blaze a stern warning about the drugs and the pastor's wife, just as they had planned. However, when Saul entered Blaze's home, he encountered a disturbing scene—Blaze lying against the sofa, his head down, and a needle protruding from his arm. Gabe shook his head in disbelief.

Saul reported finding empty baggies and a white powdery substance on the glass table. He said he'd assessed Blaze's vital signs, listened for any signs of life, and determined he had passed away. Moreover, he noticed that Blaze's jeans and iPhone were covered in gore.

"Holy shit, bro. This news is absolutely shocking," Gabe exclaimed.

"Worse news than when Mother died."

"Sometimes, the pulse can be weak. He may have had an overdose but was alive."

"And cut himself shaving?" Saul added sarcastically. Gabe glared at Saul.

"Brudder, believe me, I looked for some evidence of him being alive, a pulse, but there was nothing." Saul began staring catatonically past Gabe's face.

Gabe cleared his throat. "Did you call for an ambulance?"

"No, I didn't want the cops sniffing around me, and that would've led them to you, too. You know how stupid they are with their conspiracy theories."

Gabe nodded.

"Brudder, I need you to say I've been with you all of the time . . . or I fear that they'll set me up."

Gabe cocked his head and rubbed his chin. "Set you up, how? Why?"

"Remember our dear cousin, Frankie, who was accused of killing his ex-boyfriend, the vet? He was nowhere near Yeovilton at the time of the incident. He was dancing to Village People in Halifax. Yet, they insisted on taking a polygraph. Even then, he passed it, and the idiot detective, Barnes, informed him that he failed it because he was gay and all gay people lie."

Gabe scrunched up his face. The two sat in silence for a brief moment.

"Brudder, you know Blaze and my business dealings with him regarding the moggies and the out-of-towners—" Gabe raised his hands to cover his ears.

"Stop it, Gabe. We all know what I do to get the next breeder cat. Blaze knew, too, and he was becoming feral, almost uncontrollable. Who knows what secrets he spilt with that priestess woman?"

"Skank?"

"Yes. The word around town is that he's been seeing her for months."

"He said he had found the light hidden under a bushel."

"More like he found the bush hidden under her skirt," mocked Saul. "The further away I am from our brudder and his tragic death, the better. My crime? To find our own flesh and blood, dead in one of Mother's homes." A tear rolled down Saul's cheek.

Gabe reached over and rested his hand on Saul's shoulder. "There, there. There, there." Saul wiped his nose with his sleeve. "It's okay. I get it. There, there." Gabe suddenly pulled his hand away. "But what if he wasn't dead?"

Saul recoiled as if offended. "Brudder, I'm not an idiot. Blaze was dead as a dodo. Do you think I don't know how to take a pulse? Do you think I don't know how to perform surgery?"

"Talking about surgery, that eye job you did on Old Tom almost cost us a wealthy client."

Saul ignored his brother's comment. "Blaze was hiding something from the both of us. I don't know how to break this to you."

"Saul, be straight with me. Spit it out, bro."

"Pour me another stiff drink. Before I tell you something else. I need some Dutch courage."

Gabe obliged and filled Saul's shot glass to the brim.

Saul knew it would only be a matter of time before the body of Harry Skank would be found, and the breadcrumb clues he left the idiot cops would lead them to his dead brother's house. He was cognizant that they would try to call Saul and Gabe. Saul's personal phone had been deliberately left inside Old Tom's basket so any triangulation of cell signals would place him firmly at or near The Rum Runner. Worse still, they may turn up to inform them that Blaze was not only dead, but he was also the prime suspect in the Skank slaying, as well as for the murders of the vet, the doctor, and the bank manager. The geniuses would believe that Blaze Maçon was, indeed, the Mallet Murderer and the serial killings would be solved.

"Spill the tea, I'm feeling sick inside." Gabe shook his head. "I can't believe our little brother is dead."

Saul downed his shot, placed it on the coffee table and said, "When I arrived at the house, all the doors were open. There was blood and gore . . . everywhere, and brudder, the weirdest thing was . . . it looked like Blaze had written 'sorry' in blood with his own fingers."

"Just like the vet's slaying."

"Yes, brudder. I'm trying to unpack it all. I can't get the scene out of my mind. He had a blood-covered phone in his right hand and 'sorry' smeared on the table. You wanna know what I think?"

"Go on."

"I think he's gone and done himself in, but he's also done something foolish."

"Stupid? Like?"

"Our brudder may have killed someone."

CHAPTER 54
OPEN & SHUT

Both Daryl and Yvonne received a call from Chief Kennedy requesting their presence. They were taken aback by the news: the White Hart Fellowship's beloved pastor had been found murdered, wearing a blonde wig and in a compromising position.

"Another senseless act of violence?"

"Yes."

"Are we talking about blunt force trauma?"

"Yes."

Daryl mouthed to Yvonne, *Finally, he wants to use our expertise.* Yvonne jerked her head back. Daryl was momentarily excited. "Sir, you want us to go to the crime scene and—"

"No, you blockhead. The pointy end is handled by experienced officers."

The ex-detective shook his head. "Nonetheless, sir. I'm an experienced—"

"That's enough. Yvonne is with you, correct?"

"Yes, sir."

"You both need to go somewhere else."

"Is it okay if I ask a question?" Yvonne interrupted.

Kennedy's groan was so loud it could be heard across Yeovilton County. "If you insist. I'm swamped trying to crack this ghastly crime."

"Can you explain the motive behind the killer's slaying of the pastor?

How did a blonde wig end up being found at the scene, and what significance does it hold? What were the messages that were found on the phone?"

"Could the killing be a set-up?" added Daryl.

Kennedy highlighted Daryl's title by calling him "Fisheries Officer, Smith," dismissing the question as stupid, "start looking into fish-related offences."

Yvonne grimaced in Daryl's direction. Daryl nonchalantly shrugged his shoulders, inhaling a deep breath of air.

"No matter which road you take, they all eventually lead to Blaze Maçon. Without question, he is the killer. Mayor Quipp is planning a press conference, coordinating with the media, and preparing her speech. The residents of Yeovilton County can finally sleep soundly in their beds once more."

Yvonne's eyebrows furrowed in a deep frown. "What if the killer—"

"Blaze Maçon," added Kennedy.

"What if the killer, um, Blaze Maçon, um, targeted Raylene Skank but discovered her husband was dressed up as her and killed him anyway?"

"This isn't *Silence of the Lambs*. You need to focus on profiling."

"And making the tea for the team," Yvonne snarked under her breath.

Daryl chimed in, "Are you suggesting that Blaze, known to be a ladies' man, couldn't see the difference between a smooth-bottomed lady and a dude with a hairy ass sticking out of —"

Kennedy lied and said, "Smooth and well-groomed. Barnes noted that his ass had recently been waxed."

"And the killer couldn't distinguish between Raylene's long, platinum-blonde hair and a Dollar Store wig?"

"Enough. I was going to ask you to come to the scene and help the search party, but I've changed my mind. I need you at the blunt end of this investigation. Go to Blaze's brother's place and break the news to him, then do the same to Gabe."

"One last thing, boss," Daryl asked without waiting for a response. "Was there a half-opened can of tuna at the crime scene and a few lopped-off fingers?"

The phone went dead.

CHAPTER 55
CLASS ACT

BARNES AND NOBLE arrived at Blaze Maçon's home with their service weapons drawn. The detective sergeant slowly prized the already open door with his ungloved hand and gave a knowing glance to his comrade. Barnes pushed past him, weapon pointing forward, his heart beating out of his chest.

"Calm down, and let me know when—"

The inside lights were on, improving the light of the dawn.

"Clear."

Barnes joined Noble. The place smelled musky. Noble was the first to see a pair of legs jutting from a coffee table in the living room.

"Blaze. Armed police. Throw down your weapon."

"What? A lipstick?" scoffed Barnes.

The two officers entered the living area and immediately holstered their service pistols.

"Shit," said Barnes.

"Shit a brick—the guy's had some kind of overdose. Look at the syringe."

They walked towards the body and stood over it, noticing the phone in Blaze's pale hand. "Grab the phone," commanded Barnes.

Noble responded, "Shouldn't we wait for SOCO to arrive?"

"SOCO can kiss my ass. Kennedy wants this solved by midday. The evidence we need is on the phone."

Noble remained hesitant, so Barnes donned a pair of latex gloves and levered the bloodied phone from Blaze's rigor-mortised hand. "Take his pulse."

"No, you take his pulse."

"He's obviously dead." Using the sole of his foot, Barnes pushed the body to the floor. "See, he's dead. A stiff. Deader than the deadest person since Dead McDead's remains were found buried in his grave."

Noble tugged at his ear. "Dead McDead?"

"Just take the dead guy's pulse. That's an order."

Noble kneeled down and knocked Blaze's head with his knuckle three times. "Yep, he's dead."

Barnes pointed at the bloody writing smeared on the table: "I'M SORRY." Nodding, he said, "Yep, I bet you are, pervert." He cleared his throat and stared at the unlocked phone, and his gloved hand tapped and swiped.

"Yep. It's him. He's talking to Mrs. Doubtfire from across the lake."

Noble looked directly into Barnes' eyes. "The vet killing . . . there were smeared letters written on his pink bug."

Barnes stared back and grinned. They high-fived each other, yelling, "Solved it!" and warmly embraced. Having pulled away from his colleague, Sergeant Barnes stood over the body and surveyed the room. "We need a murder weapon. A hammer, an oar, or something."

"An oar?"

"Blunt force trauma, Charlie Boy. Think outside the box—you might make a detective one day."

Noble nodded, and his eyebrows squished together.

"Come on, give me some ideas?"

"Okay, Sarge. A baseball bat, a crowbar, a pipe—"

"A wooden dildo?" added Barnes.

"A motor vehicle?"

A smile grew on Barnes' face, "Better, Noble. What make of car?"

"A Mercedes-Benz Sprinter."

Barnes punched the air. "Good work. Everyone knows that blunt front-end vehicles create significant hazards."

"Yes, I read that vans with a hood height above forty-odd inches are fifty percent more likely to cause a fatality than one with a sloping front profile."

Barnes patted Noble on the shoulder, then asked him to call the chief to send Sarah, the SOCO, to the scene of the apparent suicide. "Tell him your theory about looking for a hidden Mercedes Spritzer in the forest—I'll let you take the credit. If the blood on Blaze matches the blood found in Dame Edna's study, we are golden and will get commendations for this."

SOCO ATTENDED Blaze Maçon's home and, in the words of Alfonso Barnes, "Did her thang." Sergeant Barnes' "thang" was to fool around with the victim's body before being taken to the county morgue.

"Selfie! Smile, serial killer!" Barnes posed next to Blaze's ashen-faced body.

"My turn," demanded Noble and used his own personal phone to snap a few shots of him smiling next to Blaze's very dead face. This was Noble's opportunity to pay Blaze back for the horrendous building work he'd done on his home.

"Pull his head up and open his eyes—he'll look even creepier," said Barnes with a laugh.

"Will you guys grow up? I can't believe they allow adolescents into the Police Academy these days," SOCO Mills snapped. "Have some respect."

"Respect? This dude was bonking the married pastor of the largest church in Nova Scotia."

"Love is love," replied Sarah. "He is someone's son, someone's brother or lover."

"Someone's lover? His lover stole his wife's lingerie and hooked up with this drug-addicted psycho freak," Noble scoffed. "And that bastard ripped me off. I'm still thousands in debt because of that clown."

"Dead clown," Sergeant Barnes pointed out, reprimanding Sarah Mills for her party-pooping, politically correct behaviour. The SOCO stuck out her tongue, refusing to take the bait. Barnes kicked Blaze's lifeless body, sneered, and pointed to the doorway.

"Mills, hurry up and take drug-boy to the morgue. Charlie and I have some serious celebrating to do!"

CHAPTER 56
WHO LET THE DOGS OUT?

CHIEF KENNEDY MADE the three-way call to Yvonne and Daryl, who had messaged each other and met at the detachment's headquarters early in the morning.

"As promised, I now have important work for you both."

Yvonne looked at Daryl and held her breath. "Thanks to Barnes and Noble's genius, we have solved the case. And get this, not only this one but three other murders."

"What? When? How?" spluttered Daryl.

"Blaze Maçon had been having a consensual physical relationship with Harry Skank. Our crack team—"

Yvonne covered her mouth, trying not to snort. Daryl mimed, "Crack team?"

"—discovered that Maçon had topped himself and was found dead with a syringe in his arm. Skank's blood was all over him, according to the initial report from Sarah, the SOCO."

Yvonne put her phone on mute and nodded at Daryl's phone, asking him to do the same. "How did SOCO find the blood type out so quickly?" Daryl ran his hands through his thick hair, opened his eyes wide, and shrugged his shoulders.

The chief continued, "Blaze had messaged Pastor Skank and the texts on his end were congruent with the messages received by the victim."

Yvonne unmuted her phone, cleared her throat and said, "The other murders, sir. It doesn't make sense—"

Ignoring Yvonne's comment, Kennedy said, "The vet slaying. Barnes believes there was a gay motive. Perhaps Blaze had mother issues, and the vet failed to follow his cross-dressing request."

Daryl's mouth gaped open. Yvonne pretended to bang her head with a clenched fist.

"The same MO. Angry messages were written in blood in the proximity of the victim. Open and shut case. All done and dusted in less than twenty-two minutes. Teamwork makes for dreamwork."

Daryl grabbed Yvonne's phone. "Sir, what about the first murder? The banker? Also, do we know why the killer slaughtered Dr. Astrid Hussain?"

Yvonne grabbed it back. "And . . . what about her prosthetic eye? Why steal an eyeball? Why the chopped-off fingers?"

Daryl continued the double act. "Then there was the catnapping issue. The disappearance of cats from the murder scene. The half-eaten can of Clover Leaf tuna—"

Kennedy gasped. "You and your obsession with fish. For once in your life, you can focus on reality. We have dead *human* bodies. For crying out loud, you two. Give Barnes and Noble some credit."

"Please, sir. Did they find Dr. Hussain's missing eye in Blaze's home? Her fake eyeball? A digit or two?"

"Maybe he used the eyeball for watching their sordid sex acts."

"Sir, the murder weapon?" an exasperated Yvonne asked. "Don't we need to find the object that crushed the victims' skulls?"

"We're looking for the murder weapon as we speak. We are, of course, looking for obvious tools like a mallet or hammer. However, we are also open to finding a dildo or a small Mercedes van."

The duo exchanged wild looks at one another, muted the phone once again and burst out in laughter. The phone remained deadly silent. Finally, Yvonne broke the silence. "Sir, sir, are you there?"

"Stop it," hissed the chief.

Yvonne blinked rapidly. "Stop what, sir?"

Unknown to Sparks, Chief Kennedy was lying on his back, partially mummified in duct tape, from his feet to thighs, then from his belly button to his pectorals. Mayor Quipp had attached a crocodile clip to his left nipple. The dominatrix did not like her subject making demands of her in any way. However, to be told to "Stop it" made her blood boil.

She attached a large spring clothes peg to the chief's nose.

"Did they find the doctor's missing eyeball?" repeated Yvonne.

Kennedy's eyes were wide open, staring at Mayor Quipp in a "what are you doing—please don't do that" kind of way.

"Sir, are you okay"?

"I am fine."

"Sir?"

"Go to Blathe's bruthar'th home and ask demb to go to thur hosthpital to I.D. their bruthar."

Daryl grimaced, and Yvonne's eyebrows squished together. She needed clarification: "Sir, we don't quite receive that. Over."

"I'm a num—I'm a numbath."

Mayor Quipp grinned, and upon hearing her submissive's safe word, she yanked the peg from Kennedy's nose, and he let out a yelp. With nose liberated, Kennedy barked out,

"Go to Saul Maçon's home. Yvonne knows how to get there—then the middle brother's house up in Quincy Woods." He took a deep breath. "Tell them Blaze was found with a needle in his arm; it looks like suicide. Open and shut case. One of them needs to identify the body at the hospital morgue. Do you understand my commands?"

"Sir, yes sir," Daryl and Yvonne said in unison. Kennedy ended the call.

The one thing Daryl dreaded was delivering the heart-wrenching news of death to grieving family members. As a uniformed officer in Vancouver, he frequently received orders from his senior officer, not due to his empathetic nature or eloquent speech, but because he tended to stumble over his words and speak nonsensically under stress. The moment he received the directive from his superior, a wave of flashbacks washed over him.

"Are you the widow Taylor?"

"No, officer. I'm happily married."

"Sorry, ma'am, you're not now."

Then there was, "Sorry to disturb you, sir. Apologies, I wouldn't have come here in the dead of night, I'd rather have come much earlier, but your wife was alive then."

Death messages were by far the worst job in the world. On one day in spring, Daryl had been tasked with breaking the news to a middle-aged woman, Mrs. Jones—her husband was dead, killed in a car accident. As per police protocol, he turned off his radio, knocked on the widow's door, and a forty-something, attractive lady in a dressing gown appeared. On seeing the uniformed officer and fearing the worst, the poor lady turned deadly grey and collapsed in the hallway. With a certificate in first aid, Daryl placed the lady in the recovery position. Her robe had loosened, and one of her breasts was threatening to pop out. Turning a deep shade of crimson, he disappeared into the kitchen and turned on the kettle so she could have a cup of tea when she recovered. He still hadn't told her that her husband was dead. After a few minutes, Mrs. Jones recovered, and Daryl helped her get into a nearby chair.

Daryl took a deep breath and released it slowly. "It's about your husband, John. I came here to inform you something happened. I'm sorry, he's dead."

"Who's died?" said a deep-voiced man walking into the room.

"Mr. John Jones has tragically passed."

Mrs. Jones sat bolt upright. "My husband is . . . dead?"

"I'm very sorry, yes." The widow slumped back in the chair, tilted sidewards, and landed on the carpeted floor with a thump. This time, her breast spilt out of her bathrobe. Daryl didn't know where to set his eyes. The stranger stood over Mrs. Jones, his nostrils flaring as he lifted his eyes towards the police officer. "Is this some kind of a joke?"

"No joke, sir. He died a few hours ago as a result of a car accident."

The man looked bewildered. "But . . . but . . . it can't be so."

"Yes, sir. Sadly, it is." He didn't know whether to cover the widow's perky boob or ignore it, pretending it wasn't jutting out like Mount Blanc, with a giant strawberry on the summit. He gathered some semblance of composure. "Sir, can I ask who you are?"

"I'm John, her dead husband."

In shock and feeling every emotion under the sun, from shame and humiliation to thankfulness and relief. Daryl shook the dead guy's hand, apologized profusely, and informed him he had to call his sergeant as there appeared to be some misunderstanding. He left the home and turned his radio back on, informing dispatch that he had given the death message—to the wrong person. John was very much alive.

"April Fools!" a crowded dispatch room cried, with howls of laughter. Daryl's commanding officer ordered him to return to the house and let the couple know that he had caught wind of the couple's April Fools prank.

Daryl seethed. Reluctantly, he returned, opened the front door, and saw Mrs. Jones tightly embracing Mr. Jones. As soon as they laid eyes on the uniformed officer, their expressions shifted to one of surprise. Pointing at her bathrobe, Daryl said, "Woof, woof. Glad to see you've put your puppies back in the kennel." He was met with scowls from the Joneses. Making his way across the room, he reached into his pocket and withdrew his handcuffs. In one swift motion, he clicked them onto the couple, connecting them to each other. "I'm placing you under arrest for potentially filing a fraudulent report, engaging in indecent exposure, and for needlessly occupying a police officer's time."

Mrs. Jones passed out once again. Dragged down to the floor, Mr. Jones had a bewildered expression on his face. Once again, one of her breasts popped out. Daryl stood over the couple and sang, "Who let the dogs out." He laughed heartily as it looked like the couple were playing a game of Twister. Little did the greenhorn cop know that the sudden jerking motion would lead to Mr. Jones herniating a disc.

"Haha, April Fools, you guys," mocked Daryl. "How does it make you feel to be pranked?"

Daryl promised to never deliver a death message again when he realized the couple were not in on his squad's joke—his team had double April Fooled him. After facing a disciplinary panel, he was fined a month's wages.

He struggled to maintain composure as he spoke to Chief Kennedy. "S-s-s-sir, couldn't someone else deliver the bad tidings? I have PTSD from—"

"No. Do it, that's an order!"

Bronwyn Quipp leaned in close to the chief and whispered, "Make sure that shit delivers the message and stays focused on his job—cracking down on fish crime," as she rammed her wet tongue into Kennedy's ear.

Daryl and Yvonne clearly heard the mayor's hushed voice on the phone. Yvonne coughed and took control of the phone. "Yes, Chief Kennedy. We will break the news to the Maçon brothers for you. Ms. Mayor, DFO Smith will also do his best to reduce the number of illegal lobster catches and lock up as many poachers as possible," she said and promptly ended the call.

Daryl's fists clenched. "I hate this damned job," he hissed.

"Grab your things, and let's head out to Saul's and the Rum Runner before Mayor Quipp decides to put you, rather than our boss, in some bondage straps."

CHAPTER 57

THE HOUSE OF SAUL

As they pulled up to a long driveway on Colonel Road, Yvonne glanced at her passenger and grinned. "Get ready for some fun," she said mischievously. "Being awakened at dawn to the news of your brother's death. BTW a heads up, he was also a killer. Have a great day!"

"*Serial* killer, according to the testimonies of Officer Dumb and Sergeant Dumber. What's this Saul guy like anyway?" asked Daryl.

"He's weird. Odd. Alone. He gives off a creepy, harmless kinda vibe."

"Creepy enough to be his brother's killer?"

"I'm familiar with Saul, but only from afar. I can't imagine him as someone who would be a serial killer. It's also hard for me to imagine short-assed Blaze climbing a step-ladder and brutally assaulting four people with a blunt object."

The two colleagues jumped out of the fisheries truck. Daryl had tried to persuade Yvonne to break the news to Saul. They flipped a coin—Daryl lost, and it was he who had to tell Saul the bad news; Yvonne would give the death message to Gabe Maçon.

They cautiously neared the front door of Saul's home, their footsteps barely audible. Darkness filled the space. There were few lights besides a faint glow from a nearby window. Just as Daryl was about to ring the doorbell, he spotted a red light from a small CCTV camera on the vinyl siding panel. Daryl stared straight at the camera. Usually, he would pull a silly face but now wasn't the time. Daryl pressed the doorbell. The visitors were startled by the sudden, overwhelming chorus of meows and purrs that erupted inside the house. No reply. He slowly moved across the porch to look inside the window. To get a clearer view, he pressed his face against the glass. He let out a fearful cry, "ARRGHH," as he made direct eye contact with a black cat with pale eyes. The startled feline on the inside window ledge let out a loud, drawn-out yowl. Yvonne moved to the window to find out what the brouhaha was about.

"OMG. How many cats are there in his house?"

In Daryl's mind, at least twenty or so cats had to be in the kitchen. His mouth twisted grimly. "Interesting that Maçon's house is swarming with felines. Cats. We have had victims' cats disappearing and half-tin tuna left at some crime scenes. I really feel like poking around, but I'm mindful of the task Kennedy has given to us."

Yvonne winked. "And the CCTV camera."

"He's clearly not answering the door, or he may be at his brother's home or—"

They decided to bite the bullet and visit Gabe Maçon's place. Yvonne suggested rock, paper, and scissors to break the news to Gabe. Daryl declined. The cat experience left him unnerved, and the prospect of going to Quincy Lake filled him with dread. He instinctively reached for his old revolver in its holster without realising it. Despite its primitive nature, having the Webley was still better than having no weapon. Yvonne's intuitive nature was evident as she reached out and touched his shoulder, locking eyes with him.

"No need to fret," she assured him, a hint of amusement in her voice. "You've got your gill net." Their laughter filled the air as they approached the truck. "Oh, and let's not forget," she said playfully, "you also have a speargun."

CHAPTER 58
TWITCHY

Saul paced anxiously back and forth, his footsteps echoing in the room. Gabe urged him to relax and find his composure before the authorities came. "Stick to your story, bro. Truth remains truth. We need to support each other despite the bad news."

"Can you believe it? The cops sent the fisheries guy and the tea lady to spill the beans about our brudder. Don't trust them."

"They're here to break bad news, not play detective. Bro, I don't get why you didn't stay there. Why didn't you wait for an ambulance? Blaze was known for his love of snow."

"Brudder, again, there was blood everywhere. Words were smeared on the table by his own finger. It was horrible. It didn't feel right—I needed to leave."

The Maçons had indulged in a generous amount of moonshine together, and they had spread out playing cards on the kitchen table to imitate a game of cribbage, with piles of dollar bills placed next to the board. As they waited, they drank increasing amounts of hooch.

Saul's phone buzzed multiple times, alerting him to new messages and notifications. The two officials had visited his residence and were probably on the way to Gabe's. Similarly, Gabe's own CCTV and sensors positioned along the driveway alerted him multiple times. He illegally possessed various countermeasure systems, such as an unlawfully acquired Stinger Spike

System capable of penetrating any type of tire. He had two camouflaged gun nests controlled from his headquarters—his ultimate weapon. There was a lot of money on the line, and he was ready to take on any cartel or government agency that tried to get in his way. He received a heads-up about a Tacoma truck carrying two individuals en route to the Rum Runner. Without hesitation, Saul got up from his chair and rushed into Gabe's dim office to take a look out of the darkened window.

"They're here!"

"Calm down," yelled Gabe. "You're acting all twitchy, like a cat on a hot tin roof, excuse the pun."

Saul scampered back to his chair, breathed deeply, and took a sip of water to hydrate his dry mouth.

Gabe studied the surveillance screens. "You're right, it looks like the fish cop and the black lady."

"Yvonne Sparks. She's a smart one. An FBI-trained profiler, I believe. The cops use her as a glorified tea lady, thank God."

"The fish cop may be a gormless-looking creature, but was a detective sergeant out west. Don't underestimate him."

Saul nodded.

"Stick to the story, bro, and we'll be golden."

CHAPTER 59

AN EYE FOR AN EYE

Yvonne and Daryl arrived at Gabe's home: an attractive, large blue rancher adjacent to a smaller property joined to the Rum Runner Bar. What looked like a neon display was turned off, but the Rum Runner sign hung over the pub's double doors. The three structures were surrounded by a wall of conifers and other tall trees. It was noticeable that CCTV cameras were scattered around the property.

"What's with the heavy surveillance?" asked Daryl. "There are cameras everywhere."

"They're prepared for a federal bust or are concerned about rival organizations. Gabriel Maçon has made a shitload of cash since prohibition."

"It just seems weird, but whatever."

Yvonne led the way, and Daryl followed closely behind. Gabe met them both at the rancher's door.

"What brings you to these here parts? The sea is about twenty-five clicks away, due south. If you've come for a refreshment, we're closed."

Yvonne cleared her throat. "We would like to come in and talk to you about something."

He extended his hand, welcoming the couple into his home as he moved aside from the door. Yvonne nodded an acknowledgement and continued along a short hallway, which opened into a large living room adjacent to a modern kitchen area. Gabe quipped, "We do have a boots-off rule here. I guess I can give exceptions to a couple of government workers."

He followed closely behind Daryl, closing the door behind him. "You enforcement types would probably quote the Health and Safety Act and keep them on anyway," he muttered.

Daryl's heart pounded in his chest, relieved that Yvonne was taking the bullet for the delivery of the death message. As all three entered the living area, Gabe said, "Meet my big brother, Saul."

Okay. Thank heavens. This will be a BOGO—buy one, get one free kind of deal. Go for it, Evie.

Yvonne and Daryl stood in the front room, shook Gabe's hand, and extended theirs to Saul. Saul responded with a grunt, leaving his hand on his knee.

Oops, Awkward.

Yvonne broke the silence. With a grave expression, she focused on Gabe, whose face was slightly more expressive than Saul's deadpan look.

"I have some unfortunate news."

"One of my cats is dead?" spluttered Saul. "I saw you both at my house."

Yvonne looked like she had been thrown off guard. Her practised "someone is dead" pitch went out of the window. She stuttered, "No, no." A flush crept across her brown cheeks. Like a worm twisting in Daryl's mind, he tried to make himself less awkward by thinking dark thoughts.

Do you want the good news or the bad news?

Give us the good news.

Two older brothers are still alive.

The bad news?

Your younger brother is not.

"Blaze has passed away. It looks like he took his own life. We are so sorry. Our deepest condolences," said Daryl, looking down at the floor.

"How, why, what, where?" spluttered Gabe. "Surely not. There must be some kind of mistake."

Dark thoughts flooded Daryl's mind. *April Fools!* He shook his head, trying to remove them and not say anything wrong.

"Oh my God."

Yvonne recovered and nodded. "It's believed he had an overdose. A syringe was found in his arm."

Saul looked catatonic. Gabe put his hands to his mouth and muttered, "Holy shit. Blaze. We all knew that he had a habit . . . but he loved life."

And Pastor Skank, apparently.

"There was also blood found in his home. He may have been involved in another person's death."

Both brothers looked up in unison, with eyebrows raised.

"Yes, he may have been having an affair with, with—" Saul's brow furrowed. "Mrs. Skank, or someone fitting Mrs. Skank's description."

"That's impossible. How did Mrs. Skank die?"

Yvonne grimaced. "The victim suffered catastrophic head injuries. Blunt force trauma. That's what we've been told. The details have yet to be fully released."

Daryl interjected, "I know this is difficult news. We do need you to identify your brother's body."

Gabe looked crestfallen. He asked Saul, "Why would he want to kill her if she was his lover?" Then, turning to Daryl, he said, "What if it wasn't him? How can you be sure?"

"We can't be totally sure that the body found at your brother's home was Blaze Maçon. Not officially . . . that's why we need one or both of you to go to the morgue."

Saul nodded at Daryl. Gabe looked daggers at Saul.

"We will get to the bottom of this," reassured Daryl.

"Just like the three other killings that had occurred recently. Despite our nephew being nowhere near the scene of the crime, you all accused him of being involved in the Frenchie vet's murder. That clueless detective couldn't find his own reflection in a mirror."

Daryl cleared his throat. *That is the truest thing I've heard in years.*

"Do you want to meet us down at the morgue?" asked Yvonne. "I can't even begin to understand how you must be feeling right now. It's a lot to process."

Saul glared at Daryl. "Give us an hour or so, and we will be there."

Yvonne bowed her head and looked towards the front door. She tapped Daryl on the arm. Daryl began to turn to walk away, then stopped and looked at Gabe. "I'm really sorry to ask you this. Where were you both last evening?"

Saul frowned and gave Daryl a death stare. Gabe turned his head towards the kitchen and nodded at the countertop, where the cribbage board, cards, and money sat. "We were both here playing crib."

"Oh, you played cribbage? All evening and night?"

"Yup," said Saul.

Gabe confirmed that they had played all night and were about to go to bed when Saul saw images of the two at his front door. Daryl's eyes felt irritated. He wasn't super allergic to cats but sensitive to dander. However, there was a faint, but familiar smell he couldn't put his finger on. Before leaving the home, Daryl had a favour to ask Gabe. "My bladder is so full. Can I use your washroom? I'd relieve myself outside so as not to bother you both, but I'm with—" He nodded towards Yvonne, who rolled her eyes.

"Fish cops. They don't make 'em like they used to do," grunted Saul.

Gabe faked a smile. "Go ahead. Choice of two. Small one in the hallway or a larger one to the left of the kitchen as you walk into the annex."

"Remember to wash your hands," said Yvonne as Daryl made his way to the larger toilet. Daryl grimaced. *Oh, Yvonne, I'm not sure this is the time or place to tease me.*

He felt an itch in his eyes. Upon entering the washroom and closing the door, he realized someone had left the toilet lid open. He smirked and muttered, "Typical guys—Yvonne wouldn't approve."

Hurriedly, he undid his zipper. The stress of death messages on Daryl was profound. He felt terrible, even for a couple of odd bods like the Maçons. He didn't think he could survive the bumpy thirty-minute trip without peeing his pants. Just as he started to urinate into the toilet, he noticed it, or rather, it noticed him.

A geyser of urine erupted, gushing out wildly like a blowout from an uncapped oil well, splattering the walls, floor, and ceiling, completely missing the bowl.

All Daryl could mutter was, "What the feck?"

CHAPTER 60
A GREEN EYE FOR THE FISH COP GUY

Yvonne put the pedal to the metal and broke the awkward silence.

"What the heck, Daryl. Why? Just why? You knew the victim was Harry Skank, not his wife Raylene—so why did you tell them otherwise?"

"Just a hunch," he said.

Yvonne shook her head. "It makes no sense."

Daryl held out his closed left fist so that it was virtually at Yvonne's eye level. It was getting lighter, and the dawn was upon them, and the road remained clear of traffic.

"Calm down, compadre. There's always a method to my madness."

Yvonne chortled. "Can you get your hand away from my snout? You men never wash your hands after touching your John Henrys." She wrinkled her nose. "I don't know where that's been."

"I always wash my hands after doing the business. However, on this occasion, I not only had to wash my hands, but I also had to wipe down the walls and the washroom floor."

"I wondered why you were taking such a long time. Did you shit yourself?"

"Nope." Daryl slowly opened his hand to reveal his prized possession.

Yvonne hit the brakes and uttered several profanities, bringing the Tacoma to a sharp halt. Thankfully, Daryl was wearing a seatbelt, which held him firmly in position. Yvonne's eyes bugged out and blinked rapidly. A green-coloured eyeball stared back at her.

"It's a fecking eyeball!"

"No shit, Sherlock, as Bobby Bobbitt would say."

Yvonne shook her head like she was about to have a seizure. She looked back and forth between the eyeball and the guy holding the prosthesis in his hand.

"It was in the toilet basin. I was just about to have a slash, started to pee and noticed something was watching me from down below."

"In the toilet bowl?"

"Yup! It took me by surprise, and I ended up peeing over the back wall, floor, and sidewall—such was the shock. It took me ages to clean up after myself."

"It's . . . It's—"

"My bet, and this is just a hunch, that this here green glass eyeball is very similar to Dr. Hussain's missing fake eyeball—the same one that went AWOL when she was bonked on the back of her head."

Yvonne grimaced. "In the toilet?"

"I've no idea how it ended up being there, but I wasn't going to ask the happy-looking brothers without either backup or a working firearm."

Yvonne gasped. Daryl continued, "And . . . I left my gill net in the truck. Anyway, I took a few pictures with my phone, with the eyeball in situ, then scooped it out of the toilet with my hand—"

Yvonne recoiled. "Eww."

"No worries," he reassured his colleague. "All of my pee went everywhere but the toilet basin. I shoved the eyeball in my pocket, as this fish cop didn't think of bringing evidence bags to the scene of a death message."

"So, Gabe is the killer?"

Daryl shrugged and shook his head. "Gabe or Saul, or Gabe *and* Saul or any combo you want to make, including Blaze, the cross-dresser-slayer."

"It's now making sense."

"The other weird thing," continued Daryl, "was that I felt allergies coming on as soon as I approached the washroom. This happens to me with certain pins, dust, dust mites, and . . ."

"Cats."

Daryl nodded. "There was also another smell. It was bugging me, as I couldn't quite place it. Then—"

"I didn't see any cats," said Yvonne.

"Well, we didn't *see* any, but I had a chat with some nutbar of a lady during breakfast in my hotel. She happened to be taking her cat, Butterfish or Butternuts or something, to Quincy Lake for her cat to get impregnated. The smell was a combo of her in heat cat and her revolting perfume."

"Saul's place was cat-central. He's obviously into cats."

Daryl sighed. He knew in his heart that something wasn't right. The four murders, five including Blaze if he was also linked . . . and the missing puzzle piece had to have something to do with the green monster eyeball that was resting snugly in the palm of his hand. The pair sat in the truck and stared out the window, deep in thought. Daryl recalled the whiteboard he and Yvonne had been working on: cats, cans of tuna, renovations, blunt force trauma, missing eyeballs, severed fingers, and out-of-towners.

"Renovations!" he cried out. "Blaze was Mr. Reno. What if—"

Yvonne interrupted, "Blaze was eliminated because he knew too much, and his predilection for substances and urge to make sexual connections put him in the other brothers' cross-hairs."

"We need a murder weapon and a stroke of luck," said Daryl.

They continued the journey in silence, only their thoughts whirring away in the higher centres of their minds. As Yvonne pulled into the detachment car park, she stopped the truck and turned off the ignition. "You know what?"

Daryl nodded. He knew what.

"Our team won't want to hear from us. Our discoveries will be a thorn for the likes of Barnes and Noble, Chief Kennedy, and Mayor Quipp-the-Whip."

Daryl agreed. He knew their minds were already made up. The Fantastic Four had "heroically" solved the four murders—with Blaze the scapegoat, who conveniently killed himself—leaving clue upon clue like breadcrumbs from the Skank property to his own.

"Yep, they're already patting themselves on the backs for a job well done. A press conference has been arranged for this morning. Kennedy et al are ready to announce the good news."

"Shit! What on earth do we do?"

CHAPTER 61
MEDIA MAYHEM

THE TOWN HALL conference room was filled with national and local media representatives. The entire community was eagerly anticipating the news and updates on the latest murder in the municipality. Chief Kennedy and Mayor Quipp had kept the three other slayings shrouded in secrecy, with little information reaching the media. However, this was not only a high-profile murder; it was a crime that sent tremors through the entire community. The reign of terror caused by the brutal serial killings would cease, as the perpetrator responsible for the murders had met his own demise. The only task remaining was to present medals and exchange congratulatory pats on the back.

Bronwyn Quipp tapped the microphone, the sound echoing through the room, and welcomed the journalists, TV crew, and the Yeovilton Community with a warm smile.

Mayor Quipp introduced the Chief of Police, Michael Kennedy, who stood confidently in his immaculate ceremonial uniform, adorned with a collection of medals hanging gracefully from his lapel. On his left, Sergeant Barnes sat, his stern expression matched by the focused gaze of Senior Constable Noble.

Yvonne and Daryl joined a couple of officers in the detachment recreation room to watch the broadcast. "This is going to be awkward," said Daryl, his voice filled with discomfort.

The mayor announced she had good and bad news. Pastor Harry Skank, a prominent figure in the community, had been brutally murdered at his home. Gasps echoed through the room.

The mayor hushed the spectators. "Thanks to outstanding police work, we tracked down and apprehended the perpetrator." Cheers and clapping broke out; the sense of relief was palpable. The mayor nodded, held up her hand, and gestured for the audience to quiet down. "This man, a familiar face in our community, was trusted and admired for his remarkable home renovation skills."

Yvonne and Daryl watched in awe, their mouths hanging open.

"The man guilty of brutally murdering four innocent citizens was none other than—" The room was so hushed that the faintest sound, like a pin hitting the floor, could be heard with crystal clarity. "Blaze Maçon."

A shockwave went through the room. Blaze's name was repeated as people shook their heads in disbelief. Multiple clicking sounds were heard from the cameras, interrupting the cacophony of murmurings.

"Order, order," the mayor's voice boomed like Judge Ito's in the OJ Simpson trial. It was time for Chief Kennedy to get to his feet; his authoritative presence filled the room.

"Thank you for your incredible leadership, Mayor Quipp." Kennedy started to clap; almost everyone rose to their feet and followed suit. When the applause died down, the chief continued to address the media. "Sergeant Alfonso Barnes skillfully extracted a deathbed confession before Maçon died and sank into the depths of hell."

Daryl looked at Yvonne. "Death bed confession. Depths of hell? Is he serious?"

Kennedy continued, "With the assistance of DNA evidence, we were able to crack the cases of the three previous murders that had happened in the past year or so. In a tragic turn of events, Mr. Maçon not only took the life of beloved pastor Harry Skank but also ended his own miserable life, leaving a trail of sadness and unanswered questions. The coroner pronounced Maçon's passing as, 'death by syringe.' Clearly burdened by remorse for his crimes and deviances, he confessed everything to the detective."

Yvonne repeated back to the screen, "Deviances? How can a dead person confess to anything?" Daryl shrugged his shoulders. The audience murmured loudly once again.

"Blaze Maçon chose to end his life by injecting himself with a lethal mixture of cocaine, fentanyl, and other potent substances. The analysis of the drug concoction and residues found at the crime scene provided confirmation that these drugs were obtained from an external source, potentially originating from the Fort McMurray cartel. The Canadian Drug Enforcement Agency confirmed that the illicit substance was known on the streets as 'Warm Sunshine.'"

"How did they find this out within a few hours of Blaze's death? Also, DNA results take at least two to three days to return from Halifax," said Yvonne.

The audience looked at each other blankly, as Warm Sunshine was not well-known in these parts.

Chief Kennedy sat down, Sergeant Barnes took his place, and he held the microphone, resembling a hopeful auditioning for *Canada's Got Talent*.

"The cocaine, known as Warm Sunshine, used by Blaze Maçon contained a powerful blend of narcotics. These substances might be to blame for the serial killer's actions." Cameras clicked; flashes filled the auditorium. "Diligent and extensive research by myself and other eminent scientists on—"

"He's probably talking about Melony Gagnon, the canteen lady," added an increasingly frustrated Yvonne.

"—Facebook showed snorting or injecting Warm Sunshine can lead to heightened aggression, mania, and excessive yearnings to do weird things."

Daryl burst out laughing. "Weird things? What is the guy talking about?"

Yvonne looked away from the TV screen, closed her eyes, and shook her head. Barnes continued, "Unless we find the source of these drugs, all those close to us—friends, family, and work colleagues—could be in danger. One snort of this substance could turn you, or anyone in the community, into a psychopathic killer like Maçon."

The reporters and photographers clicked away at Barnes as what he was about to share appeared to be big news. "Before Blaze Maçon came into contact with Warm Sunshine cocaine, he was just a regular guy who liked the ladies. We now know that this type of cocaine scrambled up his brain, and he became super-angry and fetish-orientated."

Sergeant Barnes went on to say that Blaze's drug addiction probably drove him to commit the four gruesome murders because of his altered mental state. He looked into, and pointed at the camera. "I'm talking to YOU out there. YOU, the supplier of the Warm Sunshine cocaine that ended five people's lives. YOUR actions as a drug trafficker have caused untold suffering and anguish in our tight-knit, peaceful, and caring community. Prepare yourself, Mr. Drug Dealer, as the full force of the law is about to descend upon you! Get ready for someone to knock on your door. We are on our way!" The auditorium erupted in applause and shouts of "Kill the dealers" and "Bring back the death penalty."

Daryl felt inside his tunic and touched the hard, round object that he'd found in the bottom of Gabe Maçon's toilet. He knew he had to talk to Chief Kennedy before the Warm Sunshine Express gathered more momentum.

IN THE COMFORT of his guest house, Howard Dorcas, a former heavy machine operator from Fort McMurray, treated himself to a hearty breakfast and a long, hot shower before turning on the TV and drying himself off with a plush, complimentary towel. This morning, he was determined to track down his BFF, Daryl Smith, and let him know he was eager to hang out. He wrapped the towel around his waist and posed in front of the TV, showing off his muscles. Howie grabbed the TV remote, cranked up the volume, and tuned into what appeared to be a press conference involving the police and media in Yeovilton County.

"Woah! That's here," he said to himself. An image of the dead serial killer flashed on the screen. Howie pointed at the photo and declared, "No way, that's my pal, Blaze." In a large font, underneath the image was written, "MANHUNT for Fort McMurray dealer of death." A stern-looking police officer spoke to the viewers watching the media conference from their homes:

"I'm talking to YOU out there. YOU, the supplier of the Warm Sunshine cocaine that ended five people's lives. YOUR actions as a drug trafficker have caused untold suffering . . . be prepared for a knock on your door. We are coming for you!"

Howie's hands instinctively flew to his mouth, his face paling as he felt the blood drain from it. Convulsing with shock and fear, he fought the urge to vomit, feeling the heaviness of the breakfast he had recently consumed: eggs, beans, sausages, bacon, hash browns, tomatoes, liver and kidneys, fried bread, black pudding, toast, and four mugs of coffee.

"Howie, you dumbass. What on earth have you gone and done this time?"

He could only do one thing before the cops knocked on Howie Dorcas' guest room door—find Daryl and explain what had happened. After all, it was Daryl who'd asked Howie to bring the Warm Sunshine with him.

"Are they really conducting a manhunt for poor old Howie? Oh, my goodness. This really sucks ass."

CHAPTER 62

THE TRUTH DOESN'T ALWAYS SET YOU FREE

Daryl rolled the glass eye along the bench table, having turned off the TV at the detachment. The eyeball didn't roll like a marble; it went with a wobble; Daryl had to grab it before it fell off the bench. "I really don't know what to say. Yvonne, are those two idiots for real?"

"Just two idiots?"

"Kennedy and Barnes."

"What about Mayor Bondage and Domination and Senior Constable Chernobyl?"

Daryl laughed. "What's with the deathbed confession? Are we not privy to that kind of information?"

Yvonne said, "It's bullshit. Let's write up our report; print out your pictures of the eyeball staring at you in the toilet, share our trip to The Brothers Grimm's place, and submit it to our illustrious leader. We believe the serial killer is still at large. He faked the suicide of the little carpenter. We request permission to bring Gabe and Saul in for questioning and seek a search warrant for both of their homes. We'll also take SOCO Sarah, who will know what evidence to look for."

"Right, our boss will sign off on your brilliant plan? It will, of course, make him look beyond stupid."

"If the cap fits?"

"Nevertheless, you're right. Let's write it up to cover our own backs. All we can do is present him with solid evidence and probable cause. We still haven't found the murder weapon. It will either be in Saul or Gabe's tool shed, or the killer has planted it somewhere for us to find."

"Like a Mercedes van dealer," snarked Yvonne.

"Okay, but he won't buy it. Steam will come out of his flappy, elf-like ears."

YVONNE WAS RIGHT. Later that day, steam did shoot from Chief Kennedy's ears when the two colleagues submitted their findings in a no-frills report. Daryl swore he saw his curly hair straighten. They made an appointment to see the chief, who had been celebrating with Barnes and Noble. He was due to attend a meeting with Bronwyn Quipp at 5 p.m. sharp.

Yvonne and Daryl stood before their leader and waited for his reaction as he read the five-page document, which included photographic images in an appendix.

Chief Kennedy shook his head and looked up at his two subordinates. "What a load of bollocks! Are you both out of your minds? You find an eyeball in the toilet of Gabe Maçon's home, and you want me to sign off on a search and arrest warrant for the two grieving men?"

"Not just any old eyeball—Dr. Astrid Hussain's eyeball," said Daryl, matter-of-factly.

Chief Kennedy's eyes narrowed. "There could be thousand reasons that the eyeball was in the toilet bowl of Gabe's home."

"Like?" asked Yvonne.

"Blaze planted evidence in his brother's home or it dropped out of his pocket as he used the restroom."

Daryl drummed his lips with his fingers. "Mmmm. Maybe the doctor lent it to him?"

"To keep a close *eye* on the house?" suggested Yvonne.

"Don't be flippant, Sparks!"

Yvonne mimicked Daryl and tapped her chin. "Okay, sir. Let's think outside the box. Blaze borrowed the doctor's eyeball when they shared a romantic meal, placed it on the plate, and forgot it was there. While looking lovingly into her empty orbit, he accidentally ate it—thinking it was a pickled egg. While at Gabe's house, he pooped it out a few weeks later."

Chief Kennedy's lips pulled back. He no longer looked like Buddy the Elf; he morphed into Little Red Riding Hood's Big Bad Wolf. "ENOUGH! You are both clearly mentally retarded. The case is CLOSED. Everyone is happy with the outcome."

Yvonne took a step backwards, moving closer to the door. "Sir, why would Blaze bludgeon his lover to death?"

"The drugs scrambled his brain; didn't you listen to the press conference?"

Daryl gave it one last hurrah. "One of the brothers went to the pastor's home to kill the wife, but a power outage occurred due to Mel's Easter Bunny light extravaganza . . . saw a blonde woman bending over the desk and . . . whack! A case of mistaken identity."

Chief Kennedy stared blankly at his two staff members.

Daryl continued, "The Maçons were fed up that their drug-addicted brother was shagging Mrs. Skank, neutralized him, took his phone, sent messages to his so-called lover, then killed Harry Skank by mistake and carried out their plan, regardless. They laid a breadcrumb trail back to Blaze's home."

Kennedy's jaw dropped open. "You two have watched too many episodes of *The Lincoln Lawyer* on Netflix."

"Sir, the eyeball, the missing fingers, and the half-eaten can of tuna—"

"For the love of God, STOP! Listen to yourselves. Eyeballs, fingers, cats, planting evidence, cans of tuna . . . I never took you both as flat-earthers. What you're saying is *Looney Tunes*. Sergeant Barnes, our best detective is—"

"Not right in the head," said Yvonne.

Ignoring the jibe, Kennedy finished his sentence, "—going to be decorated for solving these crimes." He looked at his watch. "Crap, I'm going to be late for my meeting with the mayor."

"Tell her you've been tied up, sir," Daryl said unhelpfully.

A giggle left Yvonne's mouth; she quickly covered it up.

Kennedy's nostrils flared. He smashed a closed fist on his desk and yelled, "Get out of here right now. You are both on one week's paid leave. If

I hear any more of these insane conspiracy theories, I will terminate your contracts!"

Kennedy picked up the report and rushed out the door, leaving his employees dumbfounded and standing like statues in his office. Yvonne's eyes were tightly closed, her hands clenched, and her knuckles were white—she was about to explode.

CHAPTER 63

TAKE A CHANCE ON ME

IF BLAZE HAD spilt the beans about Howie being the supplier of his super-strong cocaine, there was a chance he would've told them where his "dealer" was staying in Yeovilton. As usual, Howie's audience of one was not lost for words: "Why did I need to share my entire life story with him? Why does every person I meet want to hear my every detail about my life?" Howie's anger boiled over, leading him to deliver several forceful punches to the side of his own head. "Stupid man. Stupid man. Old Howie was just trying to bless another dude."

Howie felt queasy, not due to the barrage of head-punches, but knowing that his mugshot would soon be spread across the media and featured on *Canada's Most-Wanted* TV show because of the deaths of five people. Howie found it surprising that the cops hadn't come to the guesthouse. His dead buddy probably just gave the cops his name and description, and that was all they've got.

Howie had been keeping up with the news. Blaze Maçon totally bashed the head of some religious dude. At the Irish pub, the carpenter told him he was currently seeing a blonde beauty but didn't mention that she wore a wig and went by the name Harry. "My buddy didn't seem like the type to be into cross-dressers, but what does Howie know?" After all, Howie Dorcas had met lots of kinky types at his camp in Fort McMurray, and he was all about live and let live.

Like a dark cloud, remorse enveloped Howie. It saddened him to know that his baggies of cocaine were associated with death. The only person who would believe him was his best buddy, Daryl—so he had to find him. The three-and-a-half-hour plane ride from YVR to Toronto totally confirmed it. He spilt his guts to his friend from the West Coast and was so glad they connected on such a deep level.

He remembered Daryl saying, "Catch you later, sometime," which was like an open invitation for Howie. As Daryl walked away to catch his connecting flight to Halifax, Howie shouted, "Can't wait to grab a couple of beers with you!" Daryl kept walking and raised his right hand in the air as if to say, "I can't wait, buddy!" He recalled shouting at him down the passageway, "I'll bring snow when I come!" Daryl shouted back to him something about there being an abundance of snow in Nova Scotia. To seal the deal, the fish cop marched away, and signalled his approval for a cocaine-fest with a thumbs up. "I'd prefer you to bring warm sunshine," he'd yelled over his shoulder. What a fun dude! Now, well out of hearing range, Howie had bellowed, "You want Warm Sunshine—Howie Dorcas will bring it to you!" He didn't care that Daryl was choosy and preferred the expensive cocaine variety over regular stuff—buddies are buddies.

To finally connect with Daryl, he'd have to turn up and ask for him at the police detachment or the fisheries office, which would be super risky. Nevertheless, with Abba's "Take A Chance" playing in the background on MTV, he knew it was a sign from the heavens—he had to risk it. Howie was notorious for his gambling skills. He would drive his car and park it near the Department of Fisheries office, waiting for his friend to arrive or leave.

CHAPTER 64
BREAKFAST OF CHAMPIONS

DARYL FELT an overwhelming reluctance to turn on the TV, as the media was in a frenzy over the serial killings and the supposed heroism of the Yeovilton crime squad. He scoured the internet to find a media outlet reporting on more lighthearted journalism. He felt as if he had lockjaw reading headlines from the popular *Daily Goss*:

CARTEL COKE HORROR. CRAZED CARPENTER KILLS FOUR IN NOVA SCOTIA HORROR SHOW. VALIANT COP TO BE AWARDED CITIZEN OF THE YEAR ACCOLADE FROM CITY MAYOR.

The worst, by far, was from the popular gutter press courtesy of Australia's *The Morning Yarn*:

TRANNY CULT LEADER SLAIN BY PERVERTED COKE HEAD CHIPPY!

Daryl tossed and turned in his sleep, not knowing how he'd spend the rest of his week on suspension from work. He decided to get up early, have a hearty breakfast with many cups of coffee and call Yvonne. She might have ideas on how to shift the chief from a position of stupidity to open-mindedness. Having showered to clear his foggy head, he got dressed. He felt on the outside of his trouser pocket for the hard, glass eye. He couldn't make the connection between the eye found in the toilet bowl at Gabe's and Dr. Hussain losing her eye at the murder scene. A newspaper had been delivered, pushed under his door. He bent over, rolled it up, placed it under his armpit and headed downstairs towards the hotel's dining area.

The breakfast room was virtually empty, and Daryl breathed a sigh of relief that he could pick and choose the table where he could have his breakfast in peace. He went to the furthest table in the room, closest to the window. He unfolded the newspaper and placed it on the tablecloth. Resting his cell phone between the knife, fork, and spoon settings, he removed his jacket and left it on the back of his chair. He strategically moved the newspaper to take up more room, hopefully as a deterrent for someone joining him at the table. He stood up to walk to the buffet when his heart skipped a beat—the crazy cat lady sat near the entry point where the servers brought in fresh food. At first, she appeared to be talking to herself, but as Daryl approached the buffet table, he noticed a cat basket on a chair next to her.

The nut job is having an in-depth tête-à-tête with Butternuts. Daryl, avoid eye contact at all costs. He smelt the faint aroma of her or her cat. *Oh, thank the Lord . . . she's nowhere near me. No, I just can't stomach her at the moment.*

Convinced she hadn't seen him, he took a tray, placed a plate upon it and walked along the buffet, serving himself sausages and scrambled eggs. His heart rate doubled, as did his desire to get away from the buffet area and head back to the sanctuary of his window seat. Grabbing a couple of croissants and a small carton of jam, he briskly returned to his table. A server came to him with a pot of coffee. He cheekily asked for a mug rather than a small cup, and the server obliged with a smile.

I'll start my diet tomorrow. Daryl took a deep breath, unfolded the newspaper, shook his head, and noticed the front page was chockablock with stories about the killings. He turned to the back page and looked at the crossword puzzle. Yes, that's better. He reached for a pen in the inside pocket of his bodywarmer, clicked the top several times and looked at the "one across" clue.

Which animal family relies on their facial hair for perfect navigation? Seven letters.

He cut one of his sausages, pushed it toward a clump of egg, and placed it into a very welcoming mouth. "OMG, that tastes divine," he said, briefly looking at the crossword again.

Which animal family . . . relies on their facial hair . . . for perfect navigation? He looked up towards the ceiling. Another mouthful of breakfast entered his mouth. He reached out to wash it down with a sip of coffee.

Seven letters.

A voice from behind said, "F-E-L-I-D-A-E. The pussy cat family. One across solved—you're welcome." The smell of dense, musky perfume made the sausage and eggs taste like Hypnotic Poison.

"Butterkins and I have decided to join you."

Daryl, with a mouthful of sausage and egg, muttered, "No, no. I'm happy to be on my own." However, what came out of his mouth was unintelligible and probably sounded to Millicent Mandi more like, "Yes, you sexy cougar. Happy for you both to join me."

"Perfect. Say hello to Butterkins. She wants to sit next to you. Don't worry, I also have my eye on you," she chortled. Milly plonked herself down next to him. Daryl was still masticating and trying to gulp down his food.

"I see you're *not* in uniform today. I like you far more in uniform; I'm just being candid. I would've jumped on you if you'd been wearing it."

Daryl started to choke. Clearing his throat, he spluttered the lie, "I'm married."

Milly stared at his left hand and chuckled. "Where's your wedding ring? Oh, I see. You're a bit of a naughty boy. When the wife's away, the husband does play."

Daryl cleared his throat. "I take it off for work."

"By the way, in case you get any ideas, I'm married too, but my husband's a bit of a dick. He's having an affair with a ladyboy called Tan," Milly said.

Daryl slurped down his coffee. "It's Milly Something, isn't it?"

"Millicent Molybdenum Mandi. My friends and lovers," she cackled, "call me Milly." Daryl's crazy cat lady nodded at her purring feline and with wide, inquisitive eyes asked, "And who is my sweet Persian companion, young man?"

"That is Butternuts," Daryl replied, a hopeful smile spreading across his face.

"Tsk, tsk. Butter-KINS. May I make a suggestion?"

No, for goodness sake, go away. Daryl smiled. "Please do."

"If you go back into your room, put on your uniform, I'll let you drag me back there by the hair and bonk me like there's no tomorrow."

Daryl choked and spat out a mouthful of coffee over the table. He had flashbacks of the rappie pie incident. The regurgitated coffee soaked the two sausages and scrambled eggs on his plate. Clearing his throat, he croaked, "Mrs. Mandy—"

"Milly," corrected the brash woman, who was staring into his kind, blue eyes.

Daryl's neck was a deep puce colour.

"I'm just kidding. My chauffeur gave me a damn good shagging this morning, and my legs are still a bit wobbly."

Daryl's eyes stared at his plate of coffee-infused sausage and egg.

"Age is a bugger. My pelvis isn't quite what it used to be."

Daryl desperately wanted to get away. Milly reached out and held his hand. "Y'all a funny bunch down here!"

Daryl's eyes went from his submerged breakfast to his arm, then met Milly's coral blue peepers. "Why's that?"

"I guess I expected Nova Scotia to be more, well . . . more friendly."

Daryl shrugged his shoulders. "I'm from British Columbia." He tried to dry off one of the croissants on the tray with a napkin. Like a boa constrictor, Milly moved from arm to wrist without releasing the pressure. She reached for his limp hand and told him she traveled from Florida to get her cat inseminated. Milly travelled to a place reminiscent of where the *Texas Chainsaw Massacre* movie was shot and met an Acadian tomcat owner. She'd paid a considerable deposit and insisted on seeing his cat before the mating occurred. Daryl's eyebrows raised. Milly continued.

"He shows me his cat, and before everything goes dark, all I briefly see is a cat that looks like he's been rescued from the epicentre of an atomic blast."

Daryl frowned. "Atomic blast? Why?"

"He had a freakish eye."

"A weird eye?" echoed Daryl.

"Yes. One of them appeared quite normal, a pretty amber-yellow colour. The other was emerald green and looked like the size of the planet Jupiter."

Daryl wanted to ask questions, but Milly was in full flow. Milly couldn't bail; she'd invested too much money and time. The image of the tomcat on the cat dating app was very different. Milly mentioned to Mr. Maçon that his cat's eyes were odd. Maçon's excuse was that when his tomcat gets horny, the spermatozoa pressure affects his eyeball, and his eyeball grows three times the normal size. Milly said the cat's eyeball changed colour. "A dog-gawn, big, green eyeball—but when lights went out, everything was in pitch darkness."

"Excuse me?" Daryl interrupted. "A big, green eyeball? You mentioned a large green eyeball?"

Milly nodded. Daryl reached down into his trouser pocket to find the prosthesis.

"Mr. Smith, am I making you frisky with all this mating talk?" She held her hand to her mouth and giggled. "Maybe later, you old horndog. For now, please stop playing with your thang." Daryl shook his head and kept feeling in his pocket. "Mr. Smith. Really, sir. You're making a Southern gal blush."

"When you said a green eye—"

Milly's interest was piqued as she raised her tattooed brows.

"Was this, perchance, one of them?" Daryl placed the beautifully crafted eyeball on the breakfast table, and to add a sense of drama to the occasion, he flicked it with his finger. The eyeball wobbled as it rolled. Milly's scream could be heard throughout the dining room. Butterkins wailed, hissed, and squawked. Staff and patrons froze momentarily, all heads turning towards Daryl and Milly's table.

"Y'all get that thang away from me—you wretched man," she bawled.

Daryl turned red, reached across the table, and picked up Dr. Hussain's eyeball in his right hand. He placed his other hand on Milly's shoulder in an attempt to calm her down. She couldn't take her eyes off the hand he'd made into a fist. Encouraging her to take deep breaths, he shared the story of how he and Yvonne visited Gabe's home and discovered the eye in the toilet.

"That thang you have in your hand was in Mr. Maçon's cat's eye socket. I swear to God."

Daryl was tempted to open up his hand once again, hoping to terrify the crazy cat lady so that she wouldn't bother him again. However, her revelation was golden.

"The cat that mated with my Butterkins had your eyeball in his eye socket."

"Dr. Hussain's eyeball," corrected Daryl. "The lady was murdered by a serial killer."

Milly Molybdenum Mandi fainted, her head landing smack into the middle of her bowl of fruit salad.

CHAPTER 65
HEARTBEAT

Howie's heart was pounding so hard that his Apple Watch was like, whoa! "High Heart Rate" was displayed on the red warning sign, indicating tachycardia. "Your heart rate rose above 180 beats a minute while inactive for ten minutes." Taking long, deep breaths, he drummed his fingers on the steering wheel, feeling the tension dissipate. Mumbling to himself, "I could really use some Ativan." He regretted not having his Warm Sunshine blend to give him courage. "Dumbass watch. Haven't you realized that I'm under a lot of stress? Why doesn't Apple send messages like, 'You look great!' and 'Hello, handsome!'"

From his rental car across the joint task force building on Main Street, Howie constantly looked left and right every ten seconds.

"Please, Daryl, you're my last chance."

Howie was struggling to accept his status as a fugitive. He wasn't even a blip on Yeovilton's police radar; they had no record of him. Sergeant Barnes hadn't received a dying confession from Blaze Maçon; he had made the whole thing up to make himself look good. Despite that, Howie was certain he was not only at fault for the death of his second-best friend but he was now one of the most wanted individuals in North America. He had no place to escape to. Daryl Smith was sure to be his saviour because that was what best friends are for.

Out of the corner of his eye, a miracle occurred. "Eureka! Daryl, my saviour—"

Howie's joy was short-lived. Daryl appeared out of the detachment's front door, followed by a black lady in a swanky suit. He muttered, "She must be a detective—serious crime squad, by the look of it." He pounded the front of his head with both hands. Another alert popped up on the watch face, with a noticeable thumping vibration: "It looks like you've taken a fall. SOS Emergency detection." Raising his heartbeat to another concerning level, he tapped the "I'm OK" button before emergency services were dispatched to his location—a stone's throw away from the cop shop. The two figures walked by an old-looking fisheries truck and climbed into a dark blue Santa Fe.

Howie spoke to Siri, the one person he could always talk to in the morning, noon, or night. "She must be his subordinate as she's chauffeuring him around."

Siri answered, "If you think it could be serious, ask me to call Emergency Services or someone you trust."

Howie shook his head. "Dang Siri, now even you're against me."

The Santa Fe pulled onto Main Street and headed towards the highway.

Howie was stumped as to what to do next. He could follow the Santa Fe or walk into the detachment and proclaim, "I'm here, cuff me—but I'll only confess to DFO Daryl Smith."

"Hey Siri, it really sucks being on the run."

"That's not nice," she responded in an empathetic voice. "Try reaching out to a friend."

CHAPTER 66
SLEDGEHAMMER

Daryl and Yvonne hid in the tree line on Saul Maçon's property. A light appeared from the skylights on the barn's roof, and after the longest couple of minutes of their lives, the barn became dark again. Lights flicked on in the house. They waited, not knowing what their next step would be. The ground-floor lights switched off, and the upstairs ones came on. A silhouette moved back and forth.

"The bugger is going to bed," whispered Yvonne. Daryl drew a deep breath.

With much stealth, the duo headed towards the rear of the barn and followed the contours of the wooded area; breaking into a trot, they reached the rear of the building, their backs hugging its siding. Daryl wore his DFO-issued, small, lightweight backpack. He held the harpoon gun with one hand and gill net in the other. Raising her eyebrows, Yvonne stared at the harpoon gun, the net, and then back at the gun. "What the feck?" she mouthed.

Daryl smirked and wanted to bat her comment away with his hand, but the gill net prohibited him from doing so. "It's all I got. I have a hunch they may come in handy," he whispered back at her.

She muttered, "If you capture a serial killer with those items, I'll be the first to recommend you for a medal."

Daryl looked unfazed by Yvonne's scepticism.

"If you don't—a Darwin Award."

Yvonne peered around the corner to a covered corridor that joined the main house with the barn. Daryl's head appeared above hers. In the dim light, he could see the door to the house where they'd visited Saul a couple of nights before. A small red pulsating light from a white box was problematic. He reached into his small backpack and grabbed some of his toxic camo spray. He showed it to Yvonne and whispered, "It comes out a phlegmy colour, a bit like Mary's rappie pie."

Yvonne shook her head and ushered her partner to take the lead. Daryl gently placed the awkward-to-carry harpoon gun by the corner of the rear of the barn but held onto the gill net. Checking the way was clear, Daryl noticed the outside shower area, which seemed odd. With his back to Saul's place, he shuffled along until the camera was within range of his all-purpose bug repellent. His eyes widened as he made a pointing gesture towards the camera, a look of determination on his face. With his lips moving silently, he signalled, "Once the camera is covered in this spray, head straight to the barn." In fear of awakening the cat army lurking inside, Daryl resisted the temptation to peer through the house windows. Yvonne nodded and dangled a set of skeleton keys in front of Daryl's surprised eyes. With the press of a button, the can released a forceful mist of droplets, coating the lens and camera case. He stood before the brown-green mess and tossed a handkerchief over the box, thankful he was tall.

The barn door was locked. Yvonne pushed past Daryl and made quick work of opening the door. She turned her head towards Daryl and deliberately stared at his left hand. She mouthed, "Why are you holding that stupid gill net thing?" She smirked. "Remember, you have a revolver."

Reluctantly, Daryl let the gill net fall onto the bottom step at the barn entrance before taking a step to venture further into the dimly lit barn. Exchanging the camo spray for the flashlight in his pack, he turned it on and shone the powerful beam before him. Yvonne joined him, her flashlight doubling up the light.

He and Yvonne explored the room with each step on the worn-out wooden floorboards. Knowing Saul was a few yards away, hopefully tucked up in bed, his heart pounded and felt super-anxious. Daryl sniffled; he couldn't help but notice the pungent combination of musk and dampness, but the cat dander made him wrinkle his nose. The beam from Daryl's torch exposed what appeared to be a sizable animal pen. His words were barely audible as he whispered, "A cage?"

"No, you donkey. It's a grocery store," Yvonne muttered sarcastically.

Daryl frowned and turned his neck around to look at Yvonne. "Yes," she said, "it's some kind of—" Her torchlight revealed two staring eyes.

"Cat, a pretty cat at that. Look at its cute, silky coat."

Daryl continued to shine the beam of light around the barn. "They all look the same to me." Daryl didn't realise it, but he was looking at Boris, Saul Maçon's latest acquisition.

Suddenly, an angry hiss echoed through the space, causing his heart to race. "What was that?"

A second sound, more like a deep, guttural growl, filled the air. Their combined flashlights pierced through the darkness, reminiscent of Second World War airborne searchlights scanning the skies for bombers during London's Blitz.

Another sharp hiss surprised Yvonne. Their eyes darted around in the gloom. One of the lights caught a glimpse of a face. Yvonne shrieked. Daryl squinted. A one-eyed cat stared back at the couple, looking like a product of a zombie apocalypse movie. The freaky-looking creature continued to hiss at them.

"I think he likes me," said Daryl nervously.

"Why'd you say that?"

"He's winking."

"He's the one-eyed cat who needs to be reunited with the object you roll around at every opportunity."

Daryl reached into his trouser pocket and pulled out Dr. Hussain's eye. "Are you missing this, chum?" Old Tom hissed. Daryl backed away. "I guess you are."

The tomcat moved quickly and aggressively, leaping upon Daryl's chest, and burying his claws deep into his bodywarmer. The large cat clung onto Daryl's chest for dear life, his one-eyed face a few inches from his own. Daryl panicked, dropped the light, and tried to grab the cat. The room darkened with only Yvonne's flashlight shining on the cat and her partner. She screeched, "What the—"

"Don't you dare move," a menacing voice growled, the sound of a gun cocking echoing in the barn.

Daryl instinctively reached for his sidearm, his eyes darting back and forth into the darkness.

"Don't even think about it, stupid balls."

"Stupid balls?"

"You, Sparks, drop the flashlight to the floor, or I'll blow your annoying face into a thousand pieces."

Yvonne complied; her big brown eyes bugged out of her head.

"You move, fish-boy, and she dies."

"Okay. Go easy," Daryl said as calmly as he could, with a sizable Chartreux cat attached to his chest. The revolver was pulled from Daryl's holster.

"Umm. A 1917 Webley. An officer's weapon. Nice. The fisheries look after their staff well." The sarcastic voice was vaguely familiar to Daryl.

The voice gruffly commanded, "Get down, cat!" Like a well-trained dog, Old Tom heeded his master's orders, retracted his claws from Daryl's tunic and dropped to the floor with one last hiss.

"Now, hands up." Daryl and Yvonne complied. "Turn ninety degrees and face the cage you were nosing around." They both looked perplexed, especially Daryl, who had issues with geometry since elementary school. A bright flashlight shone against their backs, the cage, and the rear barn wall, helping him get his bearings.

Saul was preparing for the perfect swing to Daryl's head with a sledgehammer, its handle resting on his hip. The fisheries cop, sensing his possible death by a round to the head or blunt-force trauma, bellowed out, "Wait. I may have something of interest for you."

Saul scoffed. "You had to come snooping around, didn't you? Not happy with your idiot boss announcing to the world that he and his dumbass sergeant—"

"Barnes."

"Yes, dumbass Barnes had solved the crime of the century—with his bullshit 'deathbed confession.' You are all corrupt pieces of garbage."

"We aren't," shouted Yvonne, praying the impossible, for an intervention by God.

"Oh, no? Maybe you two are the most honest people in Yeovilton County," he said mockingly. "Where's your search warrant? When I report I killed two armed intruders who intentionally disabled my security system . . .

your boss, who has the IQ of a yucca plant, will write it off, like he did for the other killings."

"More like the IQ of a pebble," Daryl mouthed to the wall. "Hey, Saul, are you pissed that Yvonne and I figured out that you and your brother killed four innocent people and staged the death of your little brother?"

"Gabe didn't have anything to do with the killings. He helped with the breeding, that's all. We had a good gig going on, then my stupid-assed brother starting having an affair with—"

"Pastor Skank."

"Why Vet Timothée?" asked Yvonne. "And why the doctor?" Daryl added, blinking to relieve his increasingly sore eyes.

"The vet tried to blackmail my brudder and me; I needed surgical supplies for Old Tom." Yvonne feigned surprise. "The doctor," Saul continued, "I went there to rescue her cat—Blaze told me the bitch was going to have him declawed to save her precious furniture."

"No other reason?"

"I enjoyed it and wanted her Russian Blue."

Daryl shuddered.

"The banker?" asked Yvonne, trying to keep him talking for as long as possible.

"For Old Tom, of course." Saul tucked his gun in the back of his dungarees and replaced it with a sledgehammer. "Now, make peace with Neptune or Poseidon, fish face."

"Wait. One last thing." Daryl slowly lowered his hands into a crucifix position, opening up his left palm.

"No trickery," barked Saul.

"She's looking at you," Daryl revealed Astrid Hussain's glass eyeball. Old Tom purred like he was looking at an old friend.

"Where'd you find that?"

"Before I tell you, what's with the angry cat and his missing orbit?"

"Damned porcupine quills blinded him; he had them removed by the vet, who knew I had taken the banker's expensive Chartreux. He was dirty, that's for sure."

"No one likes a dirty vet," said Daryl, running out of things to say.

"Made Old Tom look too fierce. None of the female cats, or mollies, wanted to mate with him."

Daryl remembered his encounters with the crazy cat lady and swore he had imagined smelling Hypnotic Poison perfume. *Dear God, please don't let the smell of this barn and Milly's acrid pong be my last.* "So, the eyeball?" he said, rolling it with his fingers.

"After I bashed her, the eyeball shot out onto the floor. It was a stroke of luck. I put the eyeball into Old Tom's empty socket—to make him look handsome again."

Yvonne coughed to hide her nervous laughter. Daryl said, "But Millicent, the crazy cat lady, told me his eyes were different sizes and colours?"

Saul smirked. "They looked the same colour to me. I'm colour-blind. See, you don't know everything." Saul raised the sledgehammer above his head.

"Wait," cried out Yvonne, fearing the worst. "One more question before we die?"

"What?" said Saul out of pure frustration.

"How did Blaze meet his maker? Are you using the same murder weapon, or did you dispose of it somewhere?"

Saul lowered the hammer and sighed. "That's two questions. I went to Blaze's place to tell him to stop seeing the Skank woman and quit the cocaine, as his big mouth was beginning to flap."

"He was the contractor for all the murder victims?"

"Three questions. Yes, he'd give me floor plans, take pictures, and I'd pay him handsomely. The Skank brats insulted me one too many times, and I was all set to bash the mother's head in. The detective was right for once—the stuff Blaze snorted wasn't from around these parts. When I arrived, he was out for the count. I took his phone and arranged to meet his lover across the lake, and as I was about to swing my mallet, a power outage occurred—Mel's stupid bunny lights."

"Drains the grid every year," muttered Yvonne in agreement.

"When the lights came back on, I realised that—"

"Your brother was involved with Mr. and not Mrs. Skank."

"I have standards. No Maçon is going to be messing around with a tranny—"

"The term is cross-dresser," added Daryl, matter-of-factly.

"Transvestic Disorder or tendencies, according to the DSM-5," added Yvonne.

Maçon looked bewildered.

"You said you used a mallet?"

"Yes, Thor. I dropped it down the septic tank with a few of my brudder's personal items. I left the lid ajar for you fools to find it."

Yvonne: "What about Skank's blood at Blaze's?"

Daryl: "The *Helter Skelter*-type writing on the glass table?"

Yvonne: "The profanities daubed in blood on the VW bug?"

Daryl: "The three fingers hacked off their hands?"

Yvonne: "The half-eaten cans of tuna?"

Daryl: "Why Clover Leaf rather than Fancy Feast Tuna Feast for cats?"

The duo had become lost in the narrative as if they were piecing together a Hercule Poirot mystery from an Agatha Christie book.

"Shut the hell up! You're doing my head in . . . so much so that I want to hit my own head with this sledgehammer to free myself from your never-ending questions." The large hammer was raised above Saul's head and pulled back to brush the rear of his dungarees. "Bye-bye, fish-head."

CHAPTER 67
YOU GIVE LOVE A BAD NAME

"No! Don't do this, Saul," Yvonne shouted.

"Think of the mess and the cleanup," said Daryl, who was seconds away from having his head smashed to smithereens. "The detachment knows we're here. You may kill us, but you won't get away with it this time."

Saul hesitated; the hammer poised to strike.

"Both you and Gabe will go down for this. We've written everything in a report, and our boss will be acting upon it as I speak."

Daryl decided to give one more Hail Mary, cupped his hand around the eyeball so that Dr. Hussain's bright green eye stared directly at his would-be killer. In a Humphrey Bogart voice he said, "Here's looking at you, kid."

Yvonne started to say a whispered prayer.

Daryl was panicking and often what came out of his mouth, when stressed, didn't appear to make sense to anyone. He thought of his favourite Rocky Balboa movie and began to hum Survivor's "Eye of the Tiger."

Saul grimaced. Yvonne laughed. "You think this is funny?" said Saul indignantly.

Daryl made air-guitar riff sounds, "Duh. Duh, duh, duh. Duh, duh, durr," and closed his eyes, imagining he was on stage.

With his feet shoulder width apart, Saul held the twenty-pound concrete-breaker with both hands. Daryl turned around to face the crazed man. Daryl's eyes widened.

Saul sneered, "Well, fish cop, I prefer '80s music, to your '70s shit. So long—" and used his hips and core muscles to deliver the final blow. The hammer was about to come down when—

The sound of a loud "THWANG" and a swift "WHOOSH" filled the air. Yvonne's lips twisted into a grimace, and then her mouth fell open in sheer surprise.

Saul froze, his breath caught in his chest. There was a loud thump. The heavy hammer hit the floorboards. In astonishment, he stared downward, chin dropping and eyes locked in shock. All eyes were fixated on the blood-soaked arrowhead protruding from Saul's chest.

Saul let out a loud groan, grabbed the sharp object that jutted out of his chest, glared at Daryl's blood splattered face, and dropped like a felled tree at Daryl's feet. The duo's eyes didn't leave Saul or the embedded shaft of the spear that protruded from his back, or from the attached line that disappeared into the darkness of the barn.

"Dang," said a voice in the darkness behind the dazzling light. "It wasn't meant to go off. You're gonna think old Howie is crazy . . . but I saw a one-eyed beast and nearly shit myself."

"Trigger finger. All good," said Daryl, not knowing what to do next.

Yvonne stood rooted to the spot.

"You think he's dead?" the unfamiliar Albertan voice asked.

"Uh. Not sure. Maybe. Probably," Daryl said in shock.

The voice came forward from the darkness into the light, and stood in front of Daryl. "Your face looks familiar."

Howie bent down and grabbed the end of the spear. "No, wait," said Yvonne. Ignoring her, he yanked it out with his large right hand while still holding the handle of the empty barrel with his left. Howie proudly held the offending steel missile up for all to see, the barbed arrowhead covered with blood, muscle, fat and possibly parts of Saul's liver and lungs. "When I saw the dude about to bosh you, I intended to put the tip of the spear against the fella's neck. But I see this monster staring at me and it—" Howie waved the flesh covered tip in front of Daryl's nose, "and it kinda went off. Dang, they'll be framing ol' Howie for yet another crime."

The trio stood in silence—an impossible task for Howie. Yvonne broke the ice, "You saved our lives, Mr.?"

"Howie Dorcas, Daryl's best buddy. We sat next to each other on the plane to Toronto." He turned to face Daryl. "I came all the way over here to hang with you." Looking at Yvonne, he smiled. "He's one of the best friends I've ever had. I brought the Warm Sunshine across with me at Daryl's request. We were going to get high together."

Daryl rubbed his chin.

"It's me, Howie. Air Canada. Remember?"

"You're the guy from the Fort McMurray camp?" *With the foul-smelling feet.*

"Yep, I told you I was coming to see you. Remember, you gave me the thumbs up.

Yes, I remember. The guy who put his stinky socks on my arms. The guy that sat next to me and wouldn't stop talking. The guy that laughed when the child behind us threw up on my head. "What . . . what are you doing here?"

Yvonne looked at Daryl with a scrunched-up face. "Mister, Whoever You Are, you saved our lives."

Howie continued to talk to Daryl. "I've been trailing you since you two left the cop shop, I wanted some alone time with my buddy."

"Alone time? Howie, I hardly know you."

"Oh shucks, Daryl. You're like my best friend ever! I saw the news and heard about the cops finding my pal Blaze's body, saying he confessed to a load of shit before he died."

"That was all BS," said Yvonne.

"The cop on the TV said I was to blame for all the killings because I gave Daryl's baggies of cocaine to Blaze."

Daryl looked stunned. "It was *you* who gave him the killer-cocaine?"

"Buddy, I gave my habit up for you. I brought one last hit over here, just for you. Remember, at the airport when I said I'll bring you some snow? You shouted back, 'No, I'd prefer you bring Warm Sunshine.' So, I bought you the last remnants of *my* Warm Sunshine stash from the Fort McMurray cartel."

Yvonne stared at her colleague, and spat out, "You asked him for what?"

"I followed you two and saw my buddy put the spear gun down by the wall and head to the barn. The next thing I see this lanky guy holding a gun, then the sledgehammer with you guys facing the wall. I watched and listened in the darkness. When he was about to bonk you on your bone dome, I—"

Daryl rubbed his head. "Well, you appeared in the nick of time. Otherwise, my brain would be splattered all over the barn."

"I saw something that looked like a one-eyed monster."

"That was this guy's cat, Old Tom." Daryl stepped to the side to avoid Saul, who he presumed was dead. Yvonne called for backup and an ambulance.

A familiar angry hiss echoed through the barn. Old Tom, claws first, jumped onto Daryl's torn bodywarmer once again.

Yvonne smirked. "You're right, he likes you."

Daryl tried to shake off the cat, who was hanging on for dear life.

"Looks like he's got a new owner," said Yvonne

"No way! I'm not a cat person."

"Ugly looking critter," said Howie. "Look at him, he's winking at you."

With a police escort, the paramedics arrived and quickly took Saul to the hospital. His grip on life was tenuous. Even though he was a serial killer, Howie still felt sorry for hurting the guy. On the way to the hospital, he insisted on sitting with the victim and shared some of his is life story with the paramedics and Saul during the twenty-minute ride.

"The spear just missed his heart. When Howie pulled it out of him, I thought he was a goner. But no, he's like the Gloria Gaynor song, 'I Will Survive.'"

Yvonne chuckled. "When you started to sing that damned *Rocky* song, I nearly peed myself."

"It's the song I want played at my funeral. I thought—"

"Well, you ain't ready to meet your maker just yet, DFO Smith."

"I should have chosen an '80s power ballad, maybe sung him a bit of Bon Jovi."

Yvonne cocked her head to one side, closed her eyes as if trying to recall the song.

Daryl saw her confused look and added, "It would have been prophetic: 'Saul's SHOT THROUGH THE HEART . . . and Howie's to blame—'" They both broke into, "Saul gives love a bad name."

CHAPTER 68
CRAPPY EVIDENCE

Bobby Bobbitt had been asked to recover evidence found from the Skank's septic tank. Yvonne, Daryl, Barnes, Noble, and Chief Kennedy stood nearby. SOCO was still at the barn, doing their forensic thing, following Saul's harpooning. The SPCA was trying to collect the twenty or thirty cats at Saul's home. Having pried Old Tom from Daryl's bodywarmer, he couldn't break free from the damned cat, who followed him everywhere he went, meowing furiously until Daryl picked him up.

"Looks like you have a new buddy." Yvonne smirked.

"I really don't like cats. I'm a dog kinda guy, but the damned thing won't leave me alone. What can I do?"

"Let the SPCA take it," suggested Yvonne.

"A one-eyed cat? It's not likely to be adopted by anyone."

"What about the crazy cat lady?"

"I already called her. She said both Butternuts and her have been traumatised by the fake eyeball."

"Butterkins."

"Whatever. She didn't want old Cyclops anywhere near her. I feel bad for the cat, so I've decided he's coming with me."

The voice of Chief Kennedy cut through their chat. "Enough chitter chatter, you two. It looks like Bobbitt has found something. He says it feels large and heavy."

"Let's hope it's not a huge turd," said Yvonne.

Bobby Bobbitt had his arm submerged deep into the septic tank opening. He huffed and puffed, frustrated that his sturdy rod and net failed to pull a large item from the reservoir of septic waste. Having sunk both arms into the foot-wide hole, he cried out, "Eureka," and took hold of what felt like a large object covered in filth. All eyes were on Bobbitt as he used his free hand to grab the net, pulled the heavy object from the dark abyss, and placed it next to him while he continued fishing for evidence.

"Smith, go grab the item he's retrieved," commanded Kennedy.

"No way, sir."

"Don't ask me to do it, either," said Yvonne.

Bobbitt retrieved more items.

"We need the fingerprints," exclaimed Kennedy.

"I can't deal with him," muttered Yvonne, rolling her eyes. "Like the poop wouldn't have washed them away?"

"Okay. Sergeant Barnes, you retrieve the evidence."

"Why me, sir?"

"Because you are full of shit, officer. Your deathbed confession was bullshit."

"Sir, that's what I thought he told me. It was an honest mistake."

Daryl and Yvonne both splattered out coughs.

"I have to hold another press conference. And you, Barnes, will come clean, or you'll lose your job and place in the book club hierarchy."

"I understand, sir. I've been writing my speech. It will all come out," he replied.

Kennedy walked away, nodded at Bobbitt, Daryl, and Yvonne, and headed to his vehicle, looking at his watch several times.

Daryl shook his head. "He didn't even say 'well done, you guys. I'm sorry I was wrong.'"

Bobbitt approached Daryl and patted him on the shoulder, leaving a slight mark on his jacket. "Well done, son. You did well." He turned his head towards Yvonne and praised her, too. The septic tank operator handed Daryl a partly-washed wooden mallet, a filthy beanie hat, and a few condoms. Daryl reluctantly took the items with a gloved hand. He deposited them into large baggies and handed them to a grimacing Sergeant Barnes. "That's the last favour I do for you, I look forward to your press conference."

As Bobbitt placed the lid back onto the tank's opening, he said, "Remember to send me some pictures, Yvonne. I'll use them for my next advertising campaign: No Shit, Sherlock solves another crime!"

"What's happening to the rest of the Skanks?"

"They're going back to England, I hear. Raylene has started an OnlyFans page on social media. Apparently, she's getting thousands of hits already."

Yvonne shared that Raylene was selling the family home and wanted a fresh start in the UK. "It will take her a while to sell. I mean, who would be interested in buying a place with a study room that still has pieces of bone and brain embedded in the walls and desk . . . with a mortally wounded serial killer as the neighbour?"

"Don't say a word, but I've already talked to Raylene. I made her an offer for a quick sale. The house with all its contents, including the mahogany desk with her husband's face print embossed into the grain. She accepted, and we exchanged contracts."

Yvonne's jaw dropped, and her eyes blinked rapidly like a semi-automatic rifle. "Shut up! There's no flies on you, Daryl Smith."

"It's time for me to put down some roots. Maybe Mrs. Smith will come down and see me."

"You're still flying that flag?" Daryl's smile amplified his rosy cheeks. He looked at Constable Noble. "I hear that Gabe is renting out Blaze's home?"

"Yep," said Noble. "Me, Sonda, and the kids are his new tenants—with an option to buy after a year."

"Let's keep it in the family," said Yvonne sarcastically.

"He's Sonda's second cousin. We got a friend and family rate. Blaze messed up my home, and it will take a year or so to make it livable. When I told Gabe about it, he felt bad and suggested we stay at the lakefront property. When our house is ready to move back in, we can flip our Blaze-renovated one."

There were no charges for Gabe, despite possibly being an accessory to several murders. Unless Saul implicated him in them, which was unlikely, he would continue serving the community with moonshine and kittens.

Daryl said, "I think the hardest property to get rid of will definitely be

Saul's place. I mean, how do you sell a serial killer's home that's hosted billions of cats who have lived there, peeing, and spraying everywhere?"

Yvonne clarified, "There's around twenty-seven cats, and many of them are spayed or neutered." The smell wasn't that bad. A good spring clean, and you'd hardly notice."

"Anyway," said Daryl, "it's going to be a hard sell."

"Point of fact," she answered, "the market in Yeovilton County appears to be thriving. I believe Gabe, having the power of attorney, has already accepted an offer."

"No way? The only person who would be interested in the home would be someone who is fascinated by serial killers and cats or is a complete weirdo."

"Yes way! The buyer is just a regular dude."

Daryl's nose wrinkled, "Who in their right mind—"

Yvonne laughed. "Your mate, Howie, your saviour and BFF neighbour."

CHAPTER 69

THE TRUTH SETS HIM FREE

AFTER THE CAPTURE of Saul Maçon, Kennedy had mentioned to Daryl that if he didn't create waves, he would do his best to have him restored to a Detective Sergeant status once Barnes had taken the heat for the current debacle. Also, he would overlook Howie's involvement in Blaze's death. Kennedy would, of course, link the baggies of drugs to Daryl, as Howie had claimed that he had brought them to Nova Scotia at the request of the Fisheries Officer.

The town hall was overflowing with media hacks, reporters, TV cameras, and members of the community, creating a chaotic and bustling atmosphere. Everyone had taken their seats. In their quest for the perfect shot, photographers knelt at the front of the room. Senior Constable Noble, Yvonne Sparks, Daryl Smith, Sergeant Alfonso Barnes, Chief Michael Kennedy, and Mayor Bronwyn Quipp were seated at the front of the chamber on a very long table.

The mayor tapped the mic and warmly welcomed everyone present. The air was filled with the cacophony of clicking cameras as reporters jostled to hold their portable mics skywards.

Bronwyn Quipp held up her hand to silence the clicks and murmurs. "All in good time. Patience."

Chief Kennedy looked particularly uncomfortable, to say the least. Yes, this would be a humbling experience for him. Admitting that his department messed up does not look good. Furthermore, the serial killings had been solved by a DFO Fisheries Officer and a civilian profiler rather than his "elite" investigation team. However, his principal source of discomfort was that Mayor Quipp had made him wear a stiff leather chastity belt with a built-in pouch attached to his testicles that contained a 10-amp vibrating cup. Bronwyn warned him that any mention of her, other than her genius, would be met with agonizing vibrations in front of the world's media.

Mayor Quipp introduced Chief Kennedy, turned to him with a smirk and sat down, taking the vibrator control device from her jacket pocket. To remind him of the consequences of saying anything negative about her or her town, she gave the control knob a slight tweak from the off position to on and then off once again.

Chief Kennedy, at first, stood wide-eyed as he felt the vibration shoot from his groin to his brain. After a few seconds of awkward silence, he welcomed the audience.

"Thanks to the genius of Mayor Quipp, with her brilliance and due diligence, a serial killer has not only been stopped but eliminated by members of our joint task force."

Reporters stood up in droves, shouting questions and yelling inaudible responses, mostly to do with the previous press conference the chief had held.

Kennedy held up his hands to quash the noise. "Settle down, please," he said in a commanding voice. "All will be explained in due course. Sergeant Barnes, who presented the last meeting with extreme disinformation—"

The press stood up en masse, yelling questions at the chief. The mayor tweaked the dial again, turning it from zero to three on a scale of one to ten.

"Argh! Argh! Oh my God!" yelled the chief.

The outburst silenced the town hall, many of whom may have believed he was about to have a cardiac arrest. "Th-th-th-thanks to the m-m-mayor, with the help of two of our fabulous task force officers, the case was . . . reimagined. However, here is Sergeant Alfonso Barnes to give a full statement, explaining everything to you." The chief glared at the mayor and took his seat.

Media hacks and reporters filled every inch of the town hall, their presence overwhelming. The words "reimagined" and "confession" reverberated through the assembly, capturing everyone's attention. Standing up abruptly, Sergeant Barnes steadied himself. He tapped the microphone nervously, the repetitive sound filling the room, and cleared his throat, trying to steady his voice. It was clear this would be difficult for him. Beads of sweat appeared on his forehead, and large stains began to form under both arms of his blue dress shirt. Daryl felt a pang of sympathy for the guy for the first time since joining the task force. Yes, he was clearly an idiot. The mayor and the chief were eager to close the case, putting no thought into it. Daryl and Yvonne's alternative hypothesis led to them being placed on administrative leave and threatened with termination. Sergeant Barnes cleared his voice for the last time, shuffled papers before him, and blew into the microphone.

"Thank you, Mayor Quipp and Chief Inspector Kennedy, for allowing me to speak before all of you. Yes, I lied."

The audience erupted into gasps and excited chatter. The air was filled with the clacking of cameras and murmurs of excitement.

"There was no deathbed confession. I made it up because—"

More gasps echoed in the room.

"My entire life has been a lie. Yes, Blaze Maçon was indeed found deceased. The evidence pointed to him as the culprit behind the murder of Pastor Harry Skank. I was blinded. I acted foolishly. I deeply regret my actions."

Daryl looked dissatisfied. The media seemed to be growing impatient. There was an abundance of grumbling and murmuring. A community member yelled, "Charlatan!"

"Yes, I was—but not anymore. Fisheries Officer Smith and Profiler Yvonne Sparks diligently conducted their investigation, working closely with Mayor Quipp, whose intelligence and cunning proved invaluable once again."

"We love you, Mayor Quipp," shouted her campaign manager from the crowd.

As Bronwyn pulled the microphone to her lips, the crowd fell silent, hanging on her every word. "Remember, I only do this for the people," she declared. "My heart belongs to you, and yours to me. This November, vote Quipp and let your voice be heard."

Daryl turned and looked at Yvonne, his eyes widening in disbelief as he silently mouthed, "What the heck?"

She added, "And many thanks to our hero from Fort McMurray, Howie Dorcas, whose courageous actions prevented Saul Maçon from claiming more lives." The audience applauded and cheered. Sergeant Barnes enthusiastically clapped his hands, igniting a lively "Howie, Howie" chant.

Sergeant Barnes remained standing. "Please, please, I have something important to say."

The spectators fell into a hushed silence, the only sound being the continuous snapping of cameras.

"I, Sergeant Alfonso Barnes, want to confess in front of the world's media and clear my conscience. I am—"

"An idiot," Daryl muttered under his breath, his voice dripping with disdain.

"—gay."

"What?" said Chief Kennedy.

"Yes, sir. For years, I concealed my true self as a gay male behind a facade of tough, unwavering, hunky, macho, toxic masculinity . . ."

Daryl scoffed. "Yeah, right."

"It's time for me to face the truth about myself. I have longed to follow my heart and not continue my career as a detective. My lifelong dream, spanning not just years but decades, has been to become . . . a wedding planner. Oh, how I've longed to wear vibrant tangerine and refreshing lime green instead of being confined to this dull, dark blue uniform."

Sitting next to Barnes, Kennedy glanced at him, gave him a little nudge, and said, "That's enough."

However, this was *his* moment and *his* time to shine. Despite the increasingly painful digs in his thigh from Kennedy's elbow, he forcefully tore off the buttons on his blue police shirt. In a daring move, he hopped onto the media desk, quickly removing his service pants and boots. The crowd's astonishment grew as he revealed a striking orange onesie with whimsical pink flamingo patterns.

Punching the sky, he exclaimed, "I have come out, hashtag 'pride,' hashtag 'loveislove,' hashtag 'nationalcomingoutday.' I'm SOOO glad to be gay!"

"No shit, Sherlock." Yvonne chuckled.

Constable Noble stood up with Chief Kennedy and tried to pull Sergeant Barnes from the table as he started to sing Frank Sinatra's

"Chicago." Mayor Quipp took charge of the situation. "Clearly, Sergeant Barnes, or EX-Sergeant Barnes, has bravely come out before you today. Back to business, thanks to the courage of the remaining members of the task force *and* Howie Dorcas, Daryl's best friend from Alberta, the streets of Yeovilton are now safe, once again."

Cheers and applause from the crowd.

"I'd also like to announce that Daryl Smith has accepted the position of detective sergeant, and Yvonne Sparks has been promoted to our criminology consultant and profiler—both come with an increase of pay."

The crowd celebrated.

Meanwhile, Chief Kennedy and Constable Noble continued to wrestle with Alfonso Barnes, desperately trying to force him out of the side door. His voice filled the room as he belted out Tom Robinson's "Glad To Be Gay" anthem. Bronwyn Quipp's eyes were fixed on Chief Kennedy, who was wrestling with the exuberant Barnes. With a mischievous smirk, she cranked her dial from zero to ten.

CHAPTER 70
CAT'S EYES

Yvonne opened the first button of her shirt and loosened the collar, giving her neck some air. Her breathing was quick and shallow like she had just finished running a marathon. As usual, Daryl was late. Unlike the one she was accustomed to at the detachment, the interview room had a distinct odour that she despised.

She experienced a vivid flashback. The impact of her time at Millhaven left her deeply shaken. Hardened convicts referred to the high-security J-Unit as a "gladiator school." The tension was palpable upon entering. A riot suddenly erupted in the building next door as she communicated with Saul through the barrier of thick plexiglass. His gaunt appearance and premature ageing were evident after months of confinement in Millhaven. Gunshots rang out, alarms blared, and she found herself trapped in the room, facing a serial killer.

"It's alright," he said, trying to reassure her. "The screws have put everyone in lockdown. This room is one of the safest places to be."

"I'd rather not be here at all," she whispered, her voice strained as she fought to conceal her terror.

Her eyes, a rich shade of brown, betrayed her anxiety as Saul gazed into them. "A deal is a deal? Yes?"

"If the higher-ups agree. It's a yes, from my end."

With a pleading look in his petrified eyes, a guard pressed his bloody face against the small observation window. He left a smudge of red on the glass of the steel door separating rioters from visitors.

Startled by the loud crash, Yvonne jumped when the door swung open. "Daryl, you idiot," she muttered, her heart thumping against her chest. "I was having a moment."

"Are you thinking about Millhaven?"

"Yes. That damned place is impossible to forget."

"Ugh, Kennedy and the Crown Prosecutor took forever to sign the paperwork. The chief was pumped to get it done, but the CP wasn't."

"Good to go?"

"I'm as ready as I'll ever be."

Daryl pounded on the observation room door and parked himself on one of the metal chairs. The door flew open. Saul Maçon entered the room accompanied by a prison officer and his lawyer. Daryl nodded and received one in return. Saul took a seat and directed his gaze towards Yvonne.

"You got it done then?"

Yvonne inhaled deeply and said, "Yes."

Saul gathered and carefully examined Daryl's documents. Addressing the lawyer, he questioned, "Is this all good in your eyes?"

The lawyer acknowledged with a thoughtful nod.

"I can't wait to see him," Saul said with a smile, excitement gleaming in his eyes.

"Later," Daryl said. "First things first." His fingers were poised over his phone, ready to hit record.

"Everything's recorded, anyway." Saul pointed at the walls. "You know, there are bugs everywhere, like in Millhaven."

Yvonne's spine shivered.

"Whatever." Daryl waved his iPhone at Saul. "This will be for our notes when we play it to the chief." Saul nodded, folded his arms, and smiled. Daryl pressed the red record button.

There had been an unexpected turn of events. With his life hanging in the balance, Saul astonishingly survived the spear that had been driven into his chest by Howie. Miraculously, it narrowly missed Saul's vital organs and heart by a mere fraction of an inch. Grave and serious charges were brought against him by the authorities, including four counts of first-degree murder.

Despite their efforts, The Crown was unable to gather sufficient evidence to prove his involvement in Blaze's death. The trial was scheduled in less than a month. Saul's remand would occur at the maximum-security prison in Millhaven, located in Ontario. He wanted to talk to both Daryl and the chief. Daryl preferred going to Millhaven with Howie instead of Michael Kennedy, who couldn't stop talking about Amazon's top-selling books and his plans for an autobiography ghostwritten by Bronwyn Quipp.

In order to fully acknowledge his crimes, the three men met and agreed upon certain conditions. Maçon would not mention the incompetence of Chief Kennedy, Leading Constable Noble, and ex-sergeant Barnes, who was currently training to be a cosmetologist. If a plea deal wasn't agreed upon, Mayor Quipp would also face intense scrutiny and public criticism—not good in an election year. Her threat to Kennedy was chillingly detailed, including being flayed alive and the exposure of every intimate detail of his sexual preferences in a book she intended to author. The only ones smelling of roses would be Daryl, Yvonne, and Sarah Mills, the sassy SOCO. Saul's agreement to be the subject of Yvonne's PhD thesis, "Inside the mind of a feline-loving serial killer," left her both excited and grateful.

Throughout her visit to Millhaven, she was amazed by his willingness to participate as her subject. During the riot, Saul's attitude towards her revealed a tender side to his character that both impressed and disturbed her. In return for Saul's cooperation, admissions and silence, The Crown had agreed that he be moved to lower security Burnside prison near Halifax, and into a sizable solitary cell with a TV and a sofa—he could even wear civilian clothes every Sunday. However, the most important part of the deal was allowing him to have Old Tom, as a "forever" cellmate. He knew that Daryl had reluctantly adopted the tomcat yet continued to struggle with allergies. Gabe agreed to keep Boris and take in a couple of Saul's other cats. Saul would talk to Sparks for three hours, with a break for snacks. Yvonne committed to visiting him regularly and updating her supervisors with details from the interviews.

Daryl was sad but thankful to give the one-eyed Chartreux back to Saul. The Yeovilton community formed a pressure group to urge the municipality to fund a Make Old Tom Great Again (MOTGA) campaign, with support from individual contributions and the Nova Scotia Cat Association. The remaining vet in the area, Dr. Sue Van Arden, volunteered to restore Old Tom to his former glory and re-operated on his sad-looking, inflamed eye socket. Hearing about this, Saul, vicariously through Yvonne, requested the vet insert the missing glass eyeball, as it was no longer needed for evidence. She agreed. This time, she employed her surgical expertise to increase the size and enhance the airflow of the socket. The vet sewed a black polymer gasket around the inside orbit to prevent the eyeball from popping out.

Saul thanked his adversaries for reuniting him with a healed-up Old Tom. In a return act of goodwill, the convicted felon also encouraged the newly promoted sergeant to buy a Russian Blue, like Boris. These cats produced way less Fel d1—the allergen protein cats secreted from their skin. Ignoring Saul's advice but still yearning for company to reduce his loneliness and anxiety, Daryl obtained an emotional support dog from the SPCA. He called the cute-looking labradoodle "Henry." Unfortunately, Henry was neither calm nor well-behaved, as Daryl had to step in and offer Henry the necessary emotional support. Little did Daryl know that Henry had witnessed the crime scene where the veterinarian was killed, which explained why the dog kept biting his new master's fingers. To make matters worse, Henry, with his curly coat, bore an eerie resemblance to Chief Michael Kennedy.

SAUL SETTLED into Burnside and secured a trustee's position in the kitchen. He discovered a new talent, and epigenetics had a part to play. It was as if psycho-social factors had switched on certain methyl groups in his genomes, and he could tap into his mother's extraordinary ability to make the most delicious soups and stews. He was soon the talk of the (correctional) town, and his reputation grew as he made the best darn beef and barley soup in the province. He named it "Philomena's Finest" in honour of his mother.

Within a few weeks, Saul's life took an unexpected turn when bags of letters from admirers, including men, women, and non-binary individuals, arrived. While sitting with Old Tom, he relished examining the mail, smiling at marriage proposals and Polaroids that had been censored by the prison.

One lady caught his attention and started communicating through phone calls and visits. The middle-aged beauty from abroad spoke with a cute accent, regularly using "y'all," and cuss words that belonged in a locker room. Her short, simple vowels turned into diphthongs, rising and falling melodically. They had much in common; if possible, they would talk to each other for days.

As Saul's attitude and behaviours towards the prison staff and other inmates became impeccable, he was no longer seen as a threat. *Au contraire*, he became the most popular inmate in the facility. He loved on his cat, and the staff enjoyed petting the cute tomcat. It wasn't too long before his prison fiancée visited in person, and he was allowed conjugal stays. She walked through the institution's corridors, her heavily perfumed scent lingering in the air. The fragrance's notes of jasmine, bitter almond, and sensual vanilla essence drove the guards and inmates nuts.

The staff finally allowed her to bring her pet to the visits. With each trip, the guards' examination of the luxury basket became increasingly relaxed, allowing for easier passage.

"I think she's pregnant again," Millicent Molybdenum Mandi whispered in Saul's ear.

"More cute kittens from Tom and Butterkins." Saul grinned proudly.

"Pure, pretty as a peach Persian and Russian Blue mix. They'll be jaw-openers."

Saul nodded in agreement.

"Our first batch of kitties were gorgeous. They made us both a lot of Benjamin's; I kept a couple *just for us*."

"I can't wait to see them all—" then mouthed the words, "when I'm free."

"Soon, baby," she whispered back, slipping Saul yet another bone from Butterkins' uneaten fish to add to his lock-picking kit. Saul winked, picked up Old Tom and placed him upon his lap, facing Milly.

"I love you, sweetheart," he said, for the benefit of listening devices. Saul placed his fingers under Old Tom's left eye and applied gentle pressure. Dr. Astrid Schmidt's glass eyeball plopped into his hand. As Saul stroked his fur, the moggie responded with a loud and contented purr. Tossing it between hands, he displayed the eye with its striking green iris.

Millicent leaned across to stroke Old Tom's well-groomed, silky grey-blue coat. As she moved her hands to Saul's trouser legs, her striking, red-painted fingernails left deep imprints on his skin. Inch by inch, her hands crept towards Saul's groin as she gasped and complimented, "Great stash!"

Saul gulped and breathed heavily. "You think?"

"I sure do, baby." Her grip intensified, her cheeks hot and flushed. She continued to pant and stare—not at Saul's bulging genitals—but inside Old Tom's eye socket. Milly licked her lips when she saw the blister packs of cyanide, midazolam, and pancuronium bromide. She returned her gaze to her lover's face, swept back her long, raven-coloured hair and chuckled. "Do let me know when the institution is holding their food competition—your momma's beef and barley recipe is going to *rock the block*!"

"It'll be in three Sundays' time, at noon."

"*Mon cheri, votre soupe au bœuf et à l'orge sera une tuerie, j'en suis sûr!*"

Saul's eyes mischievously sparkled. "Yes, my dear, my beef and barley soup will surely be a killer."

ACKNOWLEDGMENTS

I want to express my heartfelt gratitude to the people of Nova Scotia who have touched my family and me. I never had the chance to thank many of you personally, as our family moved from the East Coast to start a new life in British Columbia. Although I can't name everyone, I hope you know who you are. To Wayne and Jo, thank you for being incredibly kind, generous, and loving to my family and me. To Anne, my former boss, you are one of the most inspirational people I have ever worked with. To April, you are an adorable, beautiful, funny person, and I cherish having met you. To Susan, my friend and a wizard with numbers, thank you for your support. To Troy, even though we drifted in and out of each other's lives, you were a passionate and lovely soul who helped me settle in a foreign land as a Brit. Lastly, to the late Sheila, a kind-hearted person with a wonderful sense of humor, and to her incredibly talented daughters, I extend a big thank you.

I want to thank my partner in crime, Shelley. You have shown me such kindness, love, patience and understanding. I thank God for Him bringing you into my life. You are the most beautiful hearted person (apart from my kiddo's) that I have ever known.

Thank you, Gina, Anja, Nadia and Natashja for your love and support over the years. I love you all so much.

Thank you Kerryn for you fabulous editing, encouragement and support. You are a rockstar!

Finally, thank you, the reader, for buying my books and helping me with my writing journey. I am genuinely grateful that you have taken the time and invested your hard-earned money to read my writing, whether as Denny Darke or Gary Trew.

Drop by and say hello on my website/s: www.darkematter.ca (for Denny Darke) & www.garytrew.net (for Gary Trew)

ABOUT THE AUTHOR

Denny Darke was born in the UK, raised in Brighton & Hove, and now lives on boujee Vancouver Island in Western Canada. His love of dark humour helped him successfully survive careers as a police officer and a child protection social worker. His long-suffering and gorgeous wife describes him as "silly," as he forever practices his terrible impersonations and embarrasses her whenever they are out in public.

Denny has four children who have not yet disowned him, and his three grandchildren are among the few individuals who truly understand him. Denny said, "I love them—Jack, Micah, and James—because they accept me for who I am. Interestingly, even though they are just four, one and a half, and six months old, respectively, I have the deepest conversations with them."

Denny also writes under his super-secret undercover name, Gary Trew, who has one of the funniest middle names given to a human. Thanks to his lovely mother, Gwendoline, he was named after the 50s heartthrob actor Gary Cooper, famous for his role in the Academy Award-winning movie *High Noon*.

ALSO BY DENNY DARKE & GARY TREW

Denny Darke

The Man with the Pink Sombrero

Gary Trew

The Hate Game: Screaming in the Silence